Red Earth - Red Blood

Acknowledgements

Why in old age dabble with fiction when previously my endeavour had been in
"fact"?

My interest in local history meant I sensed a story. I set out to tell a fictional
story carrying the shadow of many "true" scenarios. The Far North Coast of
NSW, and particularly the "Big Scrub" plateau does carry a unique universe
fire brand of its own.

Alas, mine is an old-fashioned story, that probably lacks the hot spice of the
modern novelist. Yet I have a hope it may cause some modern reader to raise
an eyebrow and take another look at the picturesque, rolling red soil hills now
mostly covered in ordered macadamia plantations.

The Bundjalung nation people wandered its vine clad rain forest paths. In
season they harvested the fruits it provided. This happened for millennia prior
to European seafarers cruising the Great South Land's eastern shore. The dark
Bundjalung man or woman's footprint was almost imperceptible, melding
with deep leaf litter through the many toned green rain forest.

It was a different timeframe when commercial enterprise entered the shaded
scene. The speed with which tough cedar cutters and then land hungry settlers
removed what looked immovable, was breathtaking.

Red Earth Red Blood is a factual fiction of ordinary people. It happened.

I give thanks to many persons for help in a long process of this story.

My late wife, Marie who tolerated the many hours that I spent sorting words.

My large family who are more computer literate than I, were prepared to offer
help. My son, Christopher and grandson, William read and advised.

My thanks to a literate, good friend, Margaret Ireland, who read the early story and thought it worth nurturing.

The only professional I have employed in writing this, my twelfth book, was Samantha Elley who, I am sure, has improved the final result.

Lismore Printers kept afloat after the 2022 flood and their expertise means this book is an entirely local product.

My intention was that Red Earth Red Blood be a large two-part, time broken tome: Samantha's prevailing decision is that the first half stand alone.

Should the reader wish to follow this story into the 20th century, its net is thrown with a much broader geographic cast. I hope there are still readers who find enjoyment in a simple story: written by a North Coast of NSW person with some work gained knowledge of his subject.

GS 13/9/2024

Introduction - Prologue.

In its beginning, the Far North Coast of New South Wales was, from the perspective of the European colonists, something of a no man's land. It was a long way from the population areas of Sydney, Newcastle and Port Macquarie. Probably, it was better fitted geographically to tack on to the rough desperado settlement at Moreton Bay, that later became Brisbane, and the southern end of Queensland.

From the 1840s onward, and with the depletion of red cedar stands on the South and Central Coastal regions, tales of vast rain forests north of the Clarence, drifted back to Sydney. Escaped convicts and intrepid adventurers told stories of heavily timbered pockets between northern coastal ranges and the sea. It was claimed that huge red cedar stands blotted out the sun and that the butter soft, money making *Toona ciliata*, awaited in plenty for those prepared to travel north.

Of course, there were small problems. The difficult river entrances to the Richmond, Brunswick and Tweed rivers left much to be desired. These rivers had treacherous ever-changing outlets over ill-defined shoaling bars. The Clarence had a good deep-water entrance, but most of the cedar was further north and therefore had to be shipped out from Ballina or Tweed Heads. There were persons a plenty prepared to tackle the problems of transport, provided the cash incentive was attractive.

It became a fait accompli in a surprisingly short period of time. The ever-green blanket of the Big Scrub disappeared and farmers drifted in to work the rich, red earth that had once nurtured a significant world scale coastal rain forest.

The axe swingers, sawyers and timber agents were soon replaced by occupations needed to birth this coastal top of NSW. Adventurous, versatile settlers soon turned the "no man's land" into a desirable farming area.

My story is fiction. I am confident my characters had counterparts, real people who were prepared to toil in the difficult new area, who would have lived similar personas with different names. The mix of endeavour: Education, Transport, Recreation, Religion, Politics, these were common and constant building blocks, that enabled communities to function. This story touches most themes of what made the area come to life, though my characters are mainly committed to Transport, Education and Sport.

On The Track

The morning was sticky hot. Already, flying ants and hard-working, rampant bush flies were out on the wing testing the heavy moist warm air, that with the developing day squeezed out the astringent cool of a previous evening's thunderstorm. It was the sort of November morning with conditions remaining favourable, another afternoon storm would brew and bubble out of the sou' west.

Some of the deeper wheel ruts in the dirt road contained miniature, moist stormwater gullies, soon to evaporate or soak into the hard baked earth. Gumtree leaves and forest grasses gulped life from past gifted evening freshness. The scent in the air of breathing earth and eucalypt leaves with the backdrop of a symphony of birds and insects; these lent their pleasant harmonics upon the well-used Grafton to Casino bush track.

A lone horseman, aiming north from Grafton, had swung into the saddle at dawn. Some five hours later, the rolling river flats lay behind. His plan was to cover as much distance as possible in the cool of the morning, rest his horse in the hottest part of the day, and push on hoping to reach Casino by nightfall. The distance on a good mount was attainable in one day.

However, things could go wrong. Several miles back, the leggy bay slipped his off fore foot down a slippery narrow cartwheel rut and loosened a shoe. The rider, clad in a dark serge suit, with leather leggings to protect the trousers from sweat, did not look the customary bush horseman. He was experienced enough to know that the loose shoe should be replaced, or at least removed. He carried no blacksmithing tools so there was little he could do except press on slowly.

Several miles further, and the bay was favouring that forefoot; only a matter of time before real lameness set in. The rider dismounted and led the horse. It was a short period of time, when under the heavy serge suit, biting sweat rivered down back, chest and legs of the now pedestrian horseman. Shiny, black boots, made for paved streets, were far from comfortable on the rough track. Soon the shine was gone. The boots became scarred and scuffed, as roots hidden under the leaf mulch grabbed cramped unsuspecting toes.

Around a bend in the forest track heading south, lurched a heavy dray, pulled by a solid grey draught horse. It plodded steadfastly on, while behind, tethered to the dray on a long rein, a nimble stepping brown hack was obviously bored by their slow progress. He would dance a few steps, then realising there was nothing for it but to shorten his stride, would settle down again to the slow rolling pace of the dray.

As the travellers came together, the driver on the dray said a soft, 'Whoa boy.' The dray stopped rolling. The driver jumped to the ground, easing the stiffness from his legs, and advanced on foot to meet this fellow traveller.

'Good mornin' to you, a great day it is after the rain. My name is Pat O'Reilly.'

He thrust out a bronzed, firm hand, which the Reverend Martin Baillie accepted with softer clerical fingers, but fingers that contained surprising strength.

'Looks like that lad of yours may need a little help. What say we have a look,' said the red headed Irishman.

He lifted the front foot of the bay, wriggled the loose shoe around and noted the involuntary wince when he applied pressure to the inside sole of the foot. These were easy calm movements of a man whose fingers could read signs from an animal, that eyes had no hope of seeing. He whistled a tune from his native land in between a soft running commentary to the horse.

'Just hold him while I fetch the tools.'

Pat whistled his way to the dray and returned with a neat bag roll of farrier's gear. He unclenched the loose nails, removed the shoe, and used his large pincers to gently apply pressure to the sole of the hoof. There was always a revealing wince when he reached the sore spot where the inner quick of the foot was damaged.

'This lad would not carry weight for far before he was really lame,' was the diagnosis. 'Let's boil the billy, have a bite to eat, and see what we can do.'

'It is kind of you to bother,' said the suit clad cleric horseman.

Martin Baillie was 28 years of age. Above medium height, he was a thickset young man, with strong, solid features, and dark wavy hair. Although disguised under the black, serge, clerical suit, his outdoor upbringing on a lowland Scottish farm, gave him a muscle and substance in appearance that theology studies at an Edinburgh Presbyterian College had not completely destroyed. Two years in New South Wales, and his duties as curate in two developing Sydney parishes gave him an inkling of what the colony was about. He had jumped at the opportunity of leaving the city with an appointment to the developing area of the Far North Coast of New South Wales and had arrived only three days previously by boat to the main Clarence River township of Grafton. The first task given him by his mentor, the Reverend Thom, was to shift himself to the little township of Casino. From there he would go to the coast and make a census of Presbyterian families. Ballina was a growing seaport with a treacherous river entrance and a growing trade of cedar.

He set out with a sense of adventure and an inherent keenness to tackle this allotted new duty.

Already, Martin had decided if his horse couldn't make the journey with him in the saddle, well, he would lead the bay and eventually they would reach Casino.

Pat O'Reilly was 36 years of age. He had been 20 years in New South Wales, and some 10 years on the Clarence. With an elder brother, Michael O'Reilly, he had left Ireland during the potato famine and settled in Sydney. Patrick and Michael soon headed for the Far North Coast, lured by talk of big money in the timber trade. While the cedar lasted, they, at times, made good money, but Michael was a thirsty Irishman. He had a capacity to quickly blow the proceeds of a cedar stand when they managed to fall and float the logs to a buying agent. It had not been the road to riches that they expected. Pat was now operating on his own, and was the proud, recent selector of a 60 acre "big scrub" block on Duck Creek Mountain over in the developing Richmond River hinterland.

Patrick had married Bridget O'Brien, daughter of a coastal shipping captain. They had a family of two daughters, aged four and two. He was in the process of shifting their few worldly possessions by dray to the modest slab home, recently constructed with his own sweat and skill. Sometimes on the homeward trips to Grafton, he was able to act as a carrier and make a few shillings. This trip, no luck, and he was travelling with an empty dray.

The horses were tethered in the straggly shade of a bloodwood tree, with a few tufts of stringy native kangaroo grass to nibble upon. Pat applied himself to a twig fire and the task of boiling a blackened billy. A handful of tea leaves to the boiling water and a couple of empty boxes from the dray, early lunch was ready. Martin had been well supplied by Mrs Thom with a variety of sandwiches for his journey. Pat had nothing left, other than a doughy damper of his own cooking, to see him through to Grafton. The two men of vastly different backgrounds and circumstance sat on their box seats, shared their food, drank their black tea, and were at peace with the drowsy hush of noon in a dozing bush.

Each told a little of their immediate endeavours and found a rapport that would have been unlikely had they met in their differing normal social environs.

'Seems to me Reverend there's no problem at all,' said Pat. 'You are not dressed for walking, and there could easily be another storm late in the afternoon. You take Shamrock, he will have you in Casino by night. I will take your bay, look after and drain that stone bruise should it develop into an abscess, and bring him over on my trip next week.'

The Reverend Martin Baillie had been brought up to mistrust Irishmen. Brawling, boozing, fornicating Papists, that was how his theology professors had described them. However, instinct told him this red headed Irishman was to be trusted, and if God wanted him in Casino tonight, he had best accept this generous offer. He thanked Pat and guaranteed good care of his horse.

They changed gear on the two hacks. The lively brown Shamrock sniffed his new rider suspiciously but was pleased to be released from his slow march behind the dray. The bay would be only too happy to slowly tramp the trip back to Grafton at the pace of the grey Clydesdale between the shafts. The men shook hands, Pat promising to let the Reverend Thom know of their arrangement.

They waved to each other, went their ways, and were soon swallowed up by the eucalypt forest. Such was the lack of traffic of the time that neither man was likely to see another traveller until they were close to their destinations.

Home Base

Bridget O'Reilly walked to the cottage door and looked down the road. It was the third time in an hour she had followed this pattern of behaviour.

Probably it was too early for Pat, but she carried an expectancy that would not deny the occasional hopeful glance. The girls had been asking all day, 'When will daddy be home?'

She had kept replying, 'Not till tonight,' but that did not stop those quick glances. Now it was four o'clock, and she knew he would be trying to make it home before the threatening storms broke again.

She was a pretty girl. Auburn-haired, fair-complexioned, tall, not looking 23 years old. She had spent much time on boats as a child and teenager. This had developed a crop of freckles that may have been frowned upon by the seekers of peaches and cream complexions. Pat laughingly called them her beauty spots. The small cottage overlooking the busy Clarence River had been home since their marriage five years ago. Her father had paid six months' rent as a wedding present, and with the constant work of her hands, it was now a comfortable, though unpretentious home for the family. She knew there would be sadness when the day came to load their final comforts and bid farewell to this dwelling. It should mean more togetherness, and they would be working their own block of land.

Bridget had been 10 years of age when her mother died, and education had been at the hands of a city convent. When she was 15, her father had become a captain on the Sydney to Grafton coastal "cedar run". Although he claimed it was against better judgement, she spent a considerable time with him aboard ship. This was a strange mix of sheltered refinement and raw life that made Bridget a different young lady to most of her time. A capable pianist, scholar and artist, she was also capable of climbing a heaving mast and wrestling with, and setting, a heavy canvas sail. She claimed an unusual list of skills.

The first meeting with Pat had been on board ship. He had come to talk with her father about a consignment of logs, supposed to have left for Sydney, and which his brother Michael claimed had not been paid for by the Sydney agent. There was good reason for the non- payment story. It turned out Michael had sold the logs for cash to a speculator, spent the money on grog and women, while blaming the lack of funds on a dishonest agent. The captain knew something of the reputation of Michael O'Reilly and was sorry for the younger brother. He had offered advice that Pat would probably be better off working on his own. It was when Captain O'Brien insisted Pat stay on board for supper that the young man and Bridget first met. Less than two years later they were married.

Once more she looked down the road, and this time was rewarded by the sight of a familiar grey horse, and a well-oiled dray, approaching against the cloud draped western sun.

'Mary, Janey,' she called, 'here comes Daddy.'

The three went down the road as fast as two-year-old legs could travel. Pat left the grey to follow and ran to meet his family, picking the three up in turn and tousling the girls' already unruly red hair. He put his arm around his wife and waited for the horses and dray to arrive. The girls were thrown aboard the dray while he and Bridget led the cavalcade to the rough stables behind the house.

'Where's Shamrock?' Mary demanded, noticing the strange bay hack.

'He's all right, but I lent him to a traveller,' said her dad. 'That one has a sore foot, but we'll fix him up.'

By the time the horses were fed and bedded down, it was close to dark. The storm clouds in the sou' west rumbled and grumbled in the sky's churning belly. Lightning flashes spat grotesque splintered strands of liquid blue, white wire, from the approaching cloud front. Inside the cottage, a kerosene light glowed and a friendly fire silhouetted the simple familiar contents of the meagre, but adequate, kitchen. Pat O'Reilly would not have swapped the scene for any luxuries dreamt of, unfound, and untried in his lifestyle.

Dinner was a joyous meal, much of it grown in the cottage garden, supplementing fresh fish that came from the well-stocked Clarence River. Bridget knew, and was on friendly terms with the fishermen, so she bought her fish at a small cost. It was not long before Janey was asleep and Mary demanded her father's attentions to put her to bed, careful saying of prayers and reading of a story. Soon she was asleep. Pat looking down at the handsome child, felt at peace and realised he was a lucky man.

Siren Song of Cedar

He had come a long way from a rough cedar cutter's bark hut to this peaceful family scene.
The cedar cutters were tough men. Some were time expired convicts, some were men with a past to forget, some were men in search of money that would allow the chance of a better lifestyle could they strike it rich. With axe and saw, they pursued the cedar trees. There was an insatiable market in the growing Australian cities for *Toonis Australis.* The soft red, heavily grained timber was used almost exclusively for high class joinery and furniture. Its habitat along the eastern coastal belt of Australia was roughly bounded by the Great Dividing Range in the west, from the south coast of New South Wales to the north coast of Queensland. Anywhere along the 3,000 miles where true rain forest abounded, often in sheltered pockets, the trees were to be found.

Sometimes they grew in groves of close proximity, but often the big trees were loners amongst the other inhabitants of the rain forest. Beech, Coachwood, Teak, Fig, Rosewood, Booyung, to name but a few of the forest dwellers. These were more numerous than the cedars, but in those early days, they were only considered an obstruction to the habitat of the sought after red giants.

To find the cedar and fell it was a difficult task, but to make the tree a marketable commodity was even more difficult. It had to brought to a waterway and floated to a shipping point. Many trees were felled that never reached market. The felled log was fire branded with the mark of its owner, and whilst there was a code of honour amongst these tough, rough men, it was possible to cut off a brand and insert another. Until such time as tracks and bullock haulage appeared in the timber industry, the only form of transport for the felled tree was to wait for a stream rise, then herd the logs together into crude rafts, and float those log rafts to the shipping centre.

The living conditions of the cedar getter were tough in the extreme. A simple bark hut, usually damp, sometimes with the refinement of a canvas lean to, an open fire to cook upon, and a menu of salted meat or scrub birds. Usually, men worked in pairs and kept information about locality of worthwhile trees a guarded secret. At times, when other cutters came into an area, or when they met at the bush shanties, there would be drunken binges that continued until the grog ran out or a fight developed to break up the fraternisation.

As the cedar was worked from the banks of the streams, the cutter was forced to push on exploring new country, finding new stands, and leading a nomadic type of existence. Pat O'Reilly had headed for the little known Richmond River valley after telling his brother Mick that the time had come for each to go his own way. There was a limit to the tolerance of lies and a brother's drunken habits. The money that had come his way from five years of hard work was little enough, but sufficient to buy his horses and a few tools. There was, he felt, opportunity as the country away from the rivers developed, for a man to cart goods for the settlers. He had made a few pence as a stable boy back in Ireland and had learned all he could about horses. He had an eye and feel for a horse, inherent and common to many Irishmen.

Pat O'Reilly was at peace with the world. Ten years flashed through his mind, almost as quickly as the lightning flashes of the outside storm. A final look at his sleeping daughters, and he was back to dry the dishes for his wife.

'You took your time,' she teased him. 'You know how to wait for the dishes to be finished.'

He slipped an arm around her waist, took the plate and wiping towel, and placed them on the table. He twisted her body towards him.

'You talk too much,' he said and proceeded to kiss her, gently at first, and then with passion as her arms tightened around his neck.

The soft intoxicating warmth of her body pressed into him. They seemed of one skin that merged, defying the clothes that kept them apart. He blew out the kerosene light and allowed the lightning flashes to illuminate the way to their bedroom.

'I had my best nightgown to wear tonight,' she whispered when they were both naked, 'but maybe you like me better as I am.'

The joy of their love flashed as bright as the lightning of that summer storm.

Carrying The Word

Martin Baillie made good time. He followed carefully the instructions delivered by Pat, if he was in doubt at any of the intersecting tracks, give the horse his head. Shamrock would certainly follow the road he was used to travelling. He was pleased to leave the forest behind. The country opened out to brown waving grasslands. He knew the town of Casino could not be far away. Through the eucalypt forest, wallabies and paddymelons had occasionally shot across his path. Now it was a treat to see the big grey 'roos' grazing the open grassland. They would hop away from the track to what they considered a safe distance, stand erect on powerful hind legs, sniff the air, and eye the traveller as he went by. It was a strange and thrilling sight to the Scottish minister. He said a prayer of thanks to his Lord, whistled a mixture of hymns and reels - part theological training, part the crofter background of his childhood. How far away that training, and further still his childhood, and family left behind. He was happy with the peace of a man doing what he desired.

This land was so different from his homeland, that it was almost incomprehensible. He felt sure there was a place for him in the struggles of people striving to establish new lives for a myriad of reasons.

His thoughts were interrupted by a first glimpse of the town. It was growing dark in the sou' west and the sun had slipped away. He reined in Shamrock, patted the horse on a strong firm neck, and was amazed at just how little the town appeared to offer. His contemplation was interrupted by a snort and toss of the head from Shamrock who could see no good reason for not completing the last half mile, and then he would be fed. Martin patted the horse again.

'You've done well, laddie.' He gave the horse his head and trotted towards the ford of the river with the town on the other side.

The township of Casino in the early 1860s was little more than a public house, a blacksmith's shop, a general store, a police station and a straggle of shanty dwellings. In Martin Baillie's coat pocket was a letter from Reverend Thom addressed to David Cameron, proprietor of the general store. It asked that Martin be given lodging, information and advice of known Presbyterian families. If David Cameron, a man in his late fifties, was surprised by the appearance from the approaching gloom of a suit clad clergyman, he did not show it. Having deposited the two well filled saddle bags, Martin's only luggage, on the floor of the shop, he escorted his young guest to a holding paddock behind the attached dwelling. Here his own cart horse and hack were held in a small yard, with access to a rough shed should it rain. As one of Martin's immediate requests was feed and shelter for his borrowed mount, the Cameron horses were shut out of the shed for the night.

Martin declined an offer of help with the horse, rubbed Shamrock down, let him cool off and led him to the water trough for a limited drink. He found chaff in the feed room and tipped a couple of measures to the wooden feed manger.

It was then almost completely dark and time to become

acquainted with his hosts.

Mrs Cameron was clearly more nonplussed than her husband by the arrival of her clerical visitor. Life in the bush was tough enough, she thought, without the extra burden of a visitor probably used to city comforts. However, when the three were seated at the dinner table, the Reverend Martin gave thanks for their meal, and asked a special blessing on his hosts for welcoming to their family a wandering servant of the Lord. She was appeased and started to relax. The meal of roast beef, potatoes, beans and gravy, followed by dessert of custard, was a more than adequate meal. It probably explained why the Camerons could best be described as bordering on plump.

After dinner, Martin plied his host with a series of questions aimed at gleaning a working knowledge of the people and places that would be the orbit of his new lifestyle. It seemed there was an increasing population and the settlers were already trying to find ways of eking a living from the forest as timber was still by far the most important product, but since the new Robertson Land Act, some of the large pastoral holdings were being split, and persons with a desire to farm land now had opportunity to try their hand.

Around Casino and west to the ranges, there was sufficient native grass land for cattle to graze successfully in most seasons. However, a paddock full of fat cattle did not necessarily mean wealth for the grazier. A small number could be sold for the local meat trade, but there was no way of supplying, and little demand in the city markets. The only practical way of utilising prime cattle was to slaughter and boil away the flesh and offal, so the fat or tallow was collected into large wooden casks. These casks could be shipped out of Grafton or Ballina and, according to the whims of a fluctuating market, supplied a grazier with some income. This "boiling down" industry required labour in the form of stockmen, some European and some Aboriginal, and persons to supply the wood and tend the fires. East of Casino, at Tomki station, was a large boiling down operation, situated close to the extremity of navigable water on the south arm of the Richmond River. David Cameron described the tallow industry as a poor way of utilising cattle; its wasteful approach contrary to the frugality of a Scotsman.

The men talked long into the night. Outside the summer storms rumbled and some rain fell, but not the downpour threatened by the heavy afternoon cloud. Their kerosene light flickered when the occasional remnant of a wind gust filtered into the living room. The flickering flame attracted insects. Small moths lured to its fatal attraction, ended as a blackened corpse and a pungent puff of black smoke.

Martin Baillie was able to take on a clear word picture of the temporal state of the settlers. Who better than a storekeeper to know how things were faring with persons who depended on him for supplies? In general, it could be stated that for most settlers their lives were tough. They were there for myriad reasons. The most common being, they were leaving a lifestyle of little opportunity to search one they perceived as giving better chances. Their spiritual state was something David Cameron did not dwell upon, but the Reverend Martin knew a little of the snares of the Devil in lonely communities.

It was midnight when they went to bed. The day had been a long one for Martin, his feet were planted on a one-way track. A track that began in a small stone church in a lowland Scottish kirk. Where would that track lead in this harsh land of his adoption? His last philosophical conscious thought of the night was that only his God could know.

O'Reillys to Duck Creek

The years since leaving Grafton had been kind to Bridget and Pat. A healthy charming little boy, Thomas, had joined the family. The hours in a day were never enough to meet their tasks but they were content in their self-contained lifestyle. Some of their block was cleared and the simple house was comfortable with the skill of Bridget's hands adding refinements to make the simple slab cottage a home.

A couple of cows grazed in a paddock and supplied the family's milk and butter. There was a home garden where vegies grew in the rich humus red scrub soil. A paddock of maize supplied corn on the cob for the O'Reillys and ripe grain protein for the horses, also a free food bonanza for the much maligned parrots and cockatoos.

Pat was always threatening war on the cockatoos, parrots, pigeons, doves, and crows that feasted on the ripening crop, but other than a shot or two interrupting the feast, the birds were unmolested in their newfound, easy diet.

The part-time carrying business had grown to a full-time operation. Pat now had three horses and a large wagon, as well as the cart. When boats crossed the treacherous Ballina bar, he was usually waiting at the wharf, and had earned a reputation for reliability in delivering goods from Ballina to as far west as Casino. It was a job determined by the capriciousness of the sea, so he had little chance of regulating a schedule, but the storekeepers, hoteliers and farmers knew that once goods were in Pat O'Reilly's hands, they would be delivered. There were other carriers likely to be sidetracked on the way, especially if delivering grog to some of the shanty hotels. It was hot, thirsty work and one muscle helping nip of alcohol often lead to another - and another.

Bridget and the girls knew his lifestyle meant long hours of rough, tough travelling and that they had to be capable of fending for themselves. They also knew he would always be home as soon as possible. It was not unusual for him to arrive late at night or even early in the morning. No matter how wet, cold, or tired, there was always another hour of work drying the sweaty horses, feeding them and their bedding down. Captain the grey, had been joined by Sailor, a handsome baldy faced black, and Tar, a young roan Clydesdale, still learning his craft from Pat and the two older horses. Pat O'Reilly took a pride in his horses and knew that for him they would go wherever horse and wagon could go.

March days had been hot. A monsoonal depression had ambled down the Queensland coast with little pattern to its ramblings. The rain that lashed the Big Scrub plateau and tributaries of the Richmond had turned the river to a fat, swollen, brown serpent. It was by no means a major flood, but sufficient to give the river a strong flow. I It scratched a temporary greater depth at the entrance where it crawled to the sea through the shoaling treacherous surf near the Ballina Lighthouse. For some days two close hauled coastal schooners had wandered up and down the coast from Byron Bay to the Clarence hoping for a chance to cross into Ballina. The rough weather made it uncomfortable for the sailors, but once the sea abated, a safe depth of water would be available.

The evening of Tuesday, 23 March, 1867 saw the sun win a battle with the scudding cloud and sink in a clear western sky. The seas calmed overnight and the pilot was able to lower his black ball of danger from the headland trapeze. He was up at dawn to hoist a new signal declaring the bar open to shipping. It was noon before the *Andrea* made a run for the bar. A nor' easterly enabled her to carry enough sail to keep momentum against the strong run of the river. Any river bar was dangerous and Ballina was the most villainous from Sydney to Brisbane. Captain "Scot" McGregor knew the danger of any crossing into Ballina, and breathed a silent prayer as they made the calm, free-flowing, comparative safety of the river. He sent a couple of men aloft to reef in some sail and handed over the ship to his first mate. The fingers that struck a match to the old black pipe were rock steady, but the first gulp of nicotine loaded smoke calmed taut jangling nerve ends. A good Scottish friend of his had lost his ship and his life on that bar some twelve months ago, before the help now offered by the new temporary lighthouse and its keeper. A coastal sailor could never forget the danger of his calling.

Patrick O'Reilly Hauler and Settler

From the western veranda of Killarney, named for his home county in faraway Ireland, Pat O'Reilly had watched the sun sink in a clear sky. The cottage on Killarney was almost completed, four rooms and a veranda front and back. Built with the toil of his hands, from timber felled and pit sawn from the bounteous big scrub. He knew tomorrow would probably mean freight to be shifted from the Ballina wharf. Already the harness, that he kept soft and supple with mutton fat or lard, was laid out ready for an early start. For now, it was time to relax and enjoy a quiet pipe of tobacco, before dinner. The sounds of Bridget and the kids drifted through to where he sat. He was at peace with the world and metaphorically counted his blessings. A Catholic upbringing in a poverty wracked Ireland, prompted him at times to give thanks for the comparative plenty of their new land.

It was some eight miles from the O'Reilly farm to Ballina, about two hours trip with an empty wagon in good conditions. The red soil track that ran down from Duck Creek Mountain to the coastal swamps was difficult, sometimes impassable in wet weather. It was chiselled through the overhanging timber with a steep gradient, and sharp bends. The overhanging timber slowed the drying process. At times Pat had to restrict the wagon loads to small weights or face the blister raising task of digging out the wagon. To reach the village of Duck Creek (later known as Alstonville) from Ballina or from Blackwall (later Wardell) meant a steep climb from the river. It was little wonder that most settlements favoured the riverbanks where supplies could be picked up from a good selection of wharves.

Clearing of the Big Scrub meant people were living and farming further from the riverbanks. In addition to established Ballina there was a wharf and primitive saw milling village at Blackwall. A steep climb lifted out of the swampy heath land of the low flood plain country to the red soil plateau. The track up through Meerschaum Vale was a shocker, steep, and greasy, very slippery white clay that became a bog when a shower of rain fell. It was almost impassable when a wet period arrived. All supplies had to come in from the water terminals, and Pat's hunch that a carrying business could have a sound future was proving correct.

It was seven a.m. when Pat arrived at Ballina wharf. He had decided on the big wagon, as opposed to the quicker cart. He reckoned there was a fair chance of major supplies for the inner areas, as the shipping of late had arrived very irregularly.

'Morning Paddy boy, you be late. It must have been too cosy in next to that pretty wife of yours, for a young bloke like you.'

This greeting came from Tom Ronan, a cart carrier, already taking on a load for the locals of Ballina.

'Good morning, Tom, maybe there's a little left for me. I'll check it out with Captain McGregor. We don't want to knock you up, do we?'

Both Irishmen, they had a good rapport and sometimes were able to give each other work. They shared a common dislike of their main rival Bob Beames, a bullying northern Englishman, strong as a bull, and about as dangerous when he had a skin full of grog.

Pat tethered Captain, his lead horse, to a hitching post and whistled his way across the wharf to the side of the *Andrea*. Here there was plenty of activity and goods were being derricked onto the wharf. Enquiry brought an invitation to Captain McGregor's cabin. These two greeted each other as friends as they had done business many times and the captain knew Pat was capable of most jobs.

'How are the wee girls Pat, they must now be real young ladies? We could have a cup of tea or coffee.' Scot McGregor ordered tea and the two men chatted. Refreshments arrived and it was down to business.

'Well now, it seems we have a large saw and engine on board for a mill near Lismore. It weighs about a ton and a half and the owners reckon it will take a strong wagon to get it to their mill. It could be that you are the man. Are you interested?'

Pat whistled softly through his teeth, raised his eyebrows, and looked at the captain.

'If I can fit it in, anchor it, and the weight is no more than you say, we should be able to handle it. The owners would have to realise, that rain could mean delay with a weight like that. How would they lift it out of the wagon?'

'They say there is a good lifting jib at the mill to pick it up from your wagon.'

'Alright, let's have a look and maybe we'll talk price.'

The deck was a scene of activity, easily carried articles were going down the gangplanks onto the wharf. Large items requiring use of jib and crane, sat waiting on the clean scrubbed planks of the *Andrea*. The largest piece of the miscellaneous collection was the mill saw and engine. Pat walked around the hessian draped monster, made careful measurements of length, breadth and height. It would fit in the tray of his wagon, just, but the weight and height were something of a worry. He knew this was a chance to show he could handle jobs a little out of the ordinary, and he knew that the word would quickly get around.

'Yes, I'll take them. Three pounds the price, you place them in the wagon and the mill takes them out.'

He would take nothing else, make sure the load was securely tied, and pray the rain kept away until at least the next afternoon. He knew the cutting was still greasy from the recent fall, but it should be okay if no more rain fell. The morning was fine and clear, but a heavy bank of woolpacks sat wide on the sea to the south. He had marvelled earlier on his way down the mountain at the gold fringes to the clouds as the sun came up over the ocean. It was a great morning to be alive and at peace with a challenging world.

To bring the wagon in against the *Andrea* meant walking the horses along the edge of the wharf. He decided to leave Tar on solid ground; at times the give of planks under their weight could spook a young horse. There would be better times to educate the youngster, and he knew the two tried horses would have little trouble moving the wagon off the heavy, smooth tallowwood planks. The young horse would be called to throw his great strength into the collar when the climb up the cutting commenced. There that strength would be necessary.

Pat watched as the bosun and a couple of deckhands arranged the slings and attached the winch through the derrick pulley. They took the weight and determined all was well. Now it was time for Pat to go into action and bring the wagon into position.

He took the horses around in a big loop and up onto the wharf. Walking beside Captain, he talked softly to the grey, bringing him and Sailor in so the wagon wheels were rubbing the massive 12-inch by 12-inch binding stringer of eucalypt that framed the wharf.

Always, when a ship made it in over the bar, there were a few hangers-on to watch proceedings with various motives. Some wanted to work for drinking silver, some wanted just to watch, some wanted to air their knowledge to anyone prepared to listen. This morning was no different, and the sight of a large piece of machinery going into a wagon, fired more than the usual enthusiasm.

Slowly the engine and saw swung clear of the deck. Cog by cog the wire rope lifted to the strong muscles on either side of the winch and up went the load. When high enough to clear the ship's side the load was swung out and poised above the wagon. It was at this stage that Bob Beames decided to try his humour.

'Well, I suppose we can throw the scraps over the edge and clear the wharf. I've a busy morning and don't want to be held up by O'Reilly's busted wagon. That thing will collapse for sure when that weight goes in.'

Pat glared quickly at his tormentor, but all his attention was on the lowering load. Again, cog by cog, the weight descended until it was sitting squarely over, and then in the wagon. All seemed well. There were those who did appear somewhat robbed of entertainment through the smooth operation. Pat securely tied the load from every angle. Gently he talked to Captain and the grey leant into the collar, felt the weight, swayed ever so slightly side to side, and then moved forward. The wheels creaked and turned, and Pat worked a very slow turn, heading for the plank ramp off the wharf, the big shod feet of a horse could slip on the timber. Fortunately, the timbers were dry. Once off the wharf, he re-harnessed Tar to his following role behind the old experienced and trusted Captain, with Sailor following. He knew that there was a long and possibly difficult trip ahead.

Bridget and Mary, Jane and Thomas

Bridget's day always started early. This was particularly so when Pat had taken to the road before daylight. He always told her to stay in bed, but she was happier to be up and to double check that his lunch was packed, and he had spare food available. This was the wet time of the year; the roads could be treacherous and she knew delays often happened. So, after the wagon wheels had rumbled off into the first hint of daylight, she checked on the children, and sat for a minute at the scrubbed kitchen table.

Her convent time and a responsive nature that recognised her God as deserving of praise, meant Bridget used some of her precious free time to thank her maker for the good things in her life. Her children had been baptised by visiting priests who made rare one-off trips to an area devoid of any regular attention by clergy. Now they lived on the Alstonville plateau, visits by priests were indeed few. The last visit by a clergyman had been Martin Baillie, who had kept in touch with the family and dropped in to see how things were going on his infrequent trips to Ballina. They talked farming, they talked music, they talked family, but somehow the Presbyterian minister and the Catholic couple stayed well clear of religion.

After her minute at the table Bridget swung into action. The kindling was set for the fire in the big black cast iron stove. There was another quick check on the children who still slept soundly. Then it was time to pull on boots and go looking for Clara, the fawn jersey cow who supplied the milk and butter, that never seemed quite enough. Clara knew when she was on a good thing and the sound of a tin with some cracked corn shaking against the sides, was enough to bring her at a trot. There was a little open bail that kept her anchored, should the eating end before the milking. In time the paddocks would grow grasses and there would be more cows for more milk, but for now Clara was the queen of the dairy.

Bridget and Clara had a good working relationship. Clara knew there was always more cracked corn in the bucket when Bridget, and not Pat, was the claimant on her milk supply. Pat worked on the theory that she was entitled to a fixed ration of his precious grain and enough was enough, also his strong fingers were far quicker at milking. With Bridget there was a certain amount of graft in the extra corn, she needed extra time, before Clara began fidgeting. On this bright, clear morning all went well. Bridget's supple fingers worked on the well-formed spongy teats and the metallic tinkling of the first squirts of milk on the bottom of the bucket became a steady swoosh, swoosh as the creamy milk, topped with half an inch of froth, climbed the bucket.

On the way back to the house, Bridget walked close to the ripening corn paddock and shooed the birds. Parrots, doves, and crows took off in a display of agitation, knowing only a short flight was required before they flopped back into another part of the field. However, the crows knew when Pat was home their vigilance was required, otherwise a blast of shot could deplete their numbers. Their sentry system made any unexpected approach difficult for a would-be hunter.

It was now fully light, but the tall scrub on the eastern side of the cleared area kept the early sunlight from falling on the dew-covered ground. Where the morning's first golden fingers touched the moist native grasses there was a fleeting display of spectrum colour. Away to the west, those climbing golden fingers clawed through the thick early mist, stroking the tops of tall trees.

The O'Reilly's sixty acres was a gently undulating plateau with its own little creek wandering through a valley, leading away to the northeast. Pat had chosen well; the deep red soil was fertile and grew all sorts of crops. The basaltic base rock formed by the primeval lava flow of Mount Warning, was topped by a self- mulching breakdown of leaves from the heavy rain forest and vines over aeons of time. The deep soil, bright red and friable, was the resulting agricultural gift to those clearing the scrub. Fire to destroy the fallen timber added a rich bonus of ash to the topsoil. After a good hot burn, it was possible with just a hoe to chip maize seed straight to the surface and expect a good crop. The birds were part and parcel of the standing scrub. Parrots, pigeons, the beautiful yellow and black Regent bower bird, whip birds, lyre birds, this was their home. Early morning carried a mixed cacophony and symphony of song.

Back at the house, Bridget sat the bucket on the kitchen table, placed a muslin cover over the milk, and checked on the children. Janey and Thomas slept soundly, but Mary was awake and keen to be up and doing things with her mother. Mary knew this was a time of the day when she could have her mother to herself. The little tasks around the kitchen were a welcome part of being family. She was a pretty child, of serious nature and keen to learn. It was a constant worry to Bridget and Pat that no school was available, and although Bridget put aside part of every day to teaching some of the fundaments of the three "Rs", the parents knew it would soon become very tough to instil adequate knowledge to their family. There were now other settlers on the plateau facing that same problem of education. Talk of a school for the growing number of children was a constant topic of conversation whenever women came together.

The kitchen fire crackled merrily and chimney smoke climbed a straight grey spire to fan out and merge with the morning mist. An odd wisp of tangy scrub wood odour roamed back through the closed cast iron door, to give an almost incense touch to the cooking rolled oats, the basis of their porridge. In a pan, eggs poached, each in its cocoon of protective albumen that turned to shiny white around the quickly hardening golden yolks. Soon the fire would burn down and it would be time to open the door and toast the thick slices of home- made bread. Breakfast was a happy time of the day. Food was simple but plentiful, and much of it came from the resources of Killarney.

Mary drew up a chair close to the stove and waited for her mother to open the door of the firebox, declaring the toasting time to begin. A long two-pronged fork, made from strong fencing wire, speared each piece of bread and Mary expertly assessed the toasting time according to the fire. It was a job requiring concentration and the right angle of the fork to make sure the bread did not fall in and become a charred disaster. This happened occasionally and Mary considered it a blot on her professional skill; it must be avoided at all cost. Her mother insisted on being present at the toasting job to make sure all went as planned, but Mary was the sort of child to give any task full attention. Her sister Janey, on the other hand, was a will o' the wisp whose attention flew as quickly as her seldom still arms and legs. Already, at the age of five, she knew how to use an inherited Irish charm to smooth away scoldings, often well deserved. Thomas was a sturdy toddler, born after the move from Grafton to Killarney. He was dark headed, brown-eyed, and favoured Pat's side of the family.

They were healthy, handsome children. If they lacked some of the privileges of town kids, they were certainly not aware. To them the scrub block was a source of delight. A trip into the dank interior was to plunge into a world of surprises. Exploring on their own was forbidden, but Pat or Bridget often made trips to some of the semi cleared areas, and it was a real family adventure when they were part of the expedition.

The Brewsters

Breakfast was over and the washing up done. Bridget knew Pat would not be home until late, if at all, so the day was hers to plan. This was not difficult. There was housework, sewing, cooking, lessons for Mary, gardening, and maybe a trip to their next-door neighbours, the Brewsters. They lived half a mile away down a surveyed but unimproved dirt lane. It was good to have neighbours that close. The Brewsters were English folk, skilled in farming, but somewhat lacking in the general knowledge that Australian settlers needed. They had selected a block on the Big Scrub plateau and hoped to, in time, develop a dairy farm.

Jim Brewster had raised many blisters with axe and saw but still had not managed to clear more than a few acres. Fortunately, they had brought capital from England, and they now employed a skilled scrub faller. The percussion bite of axe and the rasp of saw, followed by the crash of trees, was a familiar sound. Scars of brown appeared at an increasing rate in the green blanket of trees that clothed the rich, red soil plateau.

The morning chores over, Bridget marshalled the family and they tramped down the track to the Brewsters. Bearers of gifts, they carried a glass jar of the morning's milk, and a muslin- wrapped large block of butter. Cherry, the roan Durham breed Brewster cow, would soon have a calf and the dairy supplies would no longer be needed. Neighbours helped each other, that was an accepted code.

The Brewsters had selected their block and employed a carpenter to build the house before moving to the district. The house was a grand affair, with a brass nameplate "Surreyville". Surreyville was certainly impressive by scrub standards of rough functional bush dwellings. It boasted an attic, a large veranda as a colonial concession, and what Norah Brewster called the drawing room. This housed a high-class German Lipp piano. It was the piano that first brought the families together. Jim Brewster had sought a reliable carrier to shift the carefully packed canvas wrapped crate from the wharf at Ballina. Pat O'Reilly had won the job, delivered the piano without bump or scratch to its pride of place, a carefully chosen niche in the drawing room, and family friendship had grown.

Norah Brewster saw the cavalcade coming and hastened down the tramped track to welcome them. She was a tall, impressive woman in her late forties. Childless, musical, cultured but certainly not a snob. From a background where English gentlewomen told others what to do, the north coast scrub was a shock and a challenge. Norah Brewster was determined to support her husband and the huge decision they had made to come to Australia. She greeted them,

'Good morning, Bridget, Mary, Janey, Thomas. Thank you kindly for the milk and butter. That Cherry of ours should soon have her calf. We will sit on the veranda Bridget and have tea. I will bring lemonade for the children?'

The kettle soon boiled on the big cast iron stove. Wood was a plentiful free commodity. The scrub timbers were easily dried and cut but burned away quickly. The tough forest hardwoods gave more heat and burned slowly, but many of the Big Scrub selections contained few hardwood trees. Jim Brewster had an order in with Pat for a cart load of hardwood blocks for the winter.

The children welcomed the lemonade and kept an eye on Thomas; he was known to drop the odd mug; that was not considered acceptable manners on the Brewster veranda. This morning all went well.

After the ritual morning tea ceremony, the children played hopscotch on the swept path. Bridget and Norah sat on the veranda and talked. Education was the subject this morning, so often discussed by bush women. Although Norah Brewster had no family in need of schools, she was keenly aware that children such as Mary would be at great disadvantage if schools did not come to the area.

'I think we will have to call a meeting of settlers with families and see what can be done about a school,' said Norah, 'Jim and I would be happy to host the meeting here and give people a chance to air their views.'

Bridget made a grateful reply. She knew the Brewster home was probably the best site for a settler meeting.

'That would be wonderful. Pat and I know the children will have to go away and board if something can't be done.'

The women talked a while of this and that, and then the O'Reillys headed home.

Carrying The Load

The big, strong wheels of the heavy wagon turned slowly. Pat had harnessed the three horses in line after leaving Ballina. There was little strain needed on the chains to keep the well-oiled wooden hub boxes turning on the heavy iron axles. The flat country heading west out of Ballina was low, swampy land with the main haulage track following Emigrant Creek. Some of the lower spots were "corduroyed" with swamp ti-tree, a system where durable logs were laid cross ways to give a very rough, but at least bog proof surface for wheeled traffic. Pat knew his big test would come as they started the climb up Duck Creek Mountain.

Pat smiled to himself; they had grabbed quite an audience in their trip through Ballina with the big engine. He was aiming to climb the cutting that day and leave another part of a day to make the trip to the sawmill near Lismore. So far, all was going well. He walked beside the wagon and whistled an Irish tune to an accompaniment of the watching magpies.

A couple of horsemen caught him up and dropped in beside for a chat.

'Hope it stays fine for you Pat, with that load on.' Tom Logan lived further on beyond Duck Mountain and was on friendly terms with the O'Reillys. 'Those horses of yours will earn their chaff draggin' that monster up the hill.'

'We'll hope we make it Tom. The horses will do their best. If it stays fine till dark, we should be over the worst.'

Tom and his companion rider held with the wagon and chatted on for a few minutes, then they left him alone with the creak of harness and the slow sucking scrunch of ironclad wheels chewing through the sticky peat earth.

The wagon clanked over the wooden corduroy pavements and they stopped for a late lunch at the foot of the mountain. The day was fine with a warm sun beaming down, but little drying breeze to form a crust on the soft earth road. Pat attached nosebags to the three horses, built a twig fire to brew a cup of tea and munched on one of Bridget's sandwiches. He was keen to start the climb. The steepest part of this ascent was a first long curving stretch of several bends. That climb lifted them from sea level to halfway up the cutting.

Lunch over, he checked that all harnesses were correct. He checked each iron shod foot of the three horses, cleaned out all the dirt to give them their maximum grip. He left the reins loosely attached to the wagon and walked beside Captain. The old grey knew all about the climb; he felt the collar come back into his powerful shoulders, set a slow, rhythmic pace that gave them smooth forward momentum and started the ascent.

Captain knew his job; he was the leader and had climbed this cutting many times. It was essential to hold the weight firmly and make a secure footing each step. Tar, the young Clydesdale was inclined to rush, but with an experienced horse front and back, he was well anchored. Halfway up the slope, Tar strode out too far, slipped for an instant and the wagon gave a lurch. Captain and Sailor took all the weight until the young horse was firmly back on four feet. Slowly they climbed, Pat talking softly all the time to the horses, praying they would not hit a deep unseen hole in the soft tracks.

After they had climbed for about 20 minutes, they came to a more even spot on the cutting. Pat called a halt, placed two wooden wedge chocks behind the back wheels and eased the horses back into their harness for a spell. They were breathing hard from their exertion, and a white scum of drying sweat edged the contact of each collar. He let them stand for five minutes, regain their wind, and then take up the strain again leaning into their collars. He placed the chocks back on the wagon, then forward and upward the climb continued.

Steadily they climbed, several times a slipping of feet caused the wagon to lurch. Each time Captain remained rock solid; the wagon maintained its balance and rolled on. It was 4 p.m. when they passed the turnoff to Killarney. Pat was tempted to pull in and stay the night but fear of what a shower of rain could do, even between here and the village, caused him to tramp ever upwards. They should make the hotel and stables by dark and the worst of the climbing would be over. So, they tramped on, stopping for a spell every half hour on the level spots.

The sun was dipping down to the western horizon when the village of Duck Creek came in view around the last bend. Pat sang a tune to his horses, promised them a big bucket of chaff, whispered a, 'Thank you, God,' and strode out the last half mile. The job was by no means over, but the worst of the climb was now behind them.

The pub hangers-on trooped out on the plank veranda to watch the wagon roll up the street. It was an unusual sight to see a large steam engine and saw. Most milling was still done by the messy pit sawing method. These men watching from the hotel veranda, many were timber workers past or present. They were an able extension to a razor-sharp axe or crosscut. It was their trade. While they knew about milling, this size of equipment on Pat's wagon was foreign to their expectation.

One of those on the veranda was Tom Logan.

'Good work! Pat, you did well. Let me buy you a drink.'

'Thanks Tom, but no. I want to get a stable for the horses. Would you just keep an eye on things for a minute, while I go and talk to Barney?'

A dozen onlookers churned around the mill gear while Pat went looking for Barney Shaw. The livery stable, out the back of the pub, was a separate business. Pat found Barney bedding down a hack for a traveller staying the night at the pub.

'Hello Barney, I'm not often a paying customer. I've a load out the front I'd like to pull around here, and I need a place for the horses. I have my own feed, but I'd like to clean them down now, and be off early in the morning.'

'Sure Pat, I've only a couple of horses. You can doss down in an empty stable yourself if you like.'

'Obliged to you Barney, we'll come around.'

Pat went, turned the wagon out of the street and along to the stables.

Barney whistled through his teeth when he saw the load.

'You are getting into the big time, my boy-o,' he said with hands on hips. 'There are not many teams of three or any number would get that monster up the cutting when it's damp. You know your horses. Get it unhitched and I'll give you a hand to look after those good neddies.'

Each horse was rubbed down with a hessian bag, his hooves cleaned of dirt and rubbed with mutton fat. Each of them was taken to the water trough and allowed a copious drink, but not an unrestricted amount. Their feeds were mixed from the supply of chaff, cracked maize and bran that Pat carried in the wagon.

'How are you off for lucerne Barney? Could we throw half a bale in the manger for them to have a munch on through the night?'

'Sure, they've earned it.'

Barney came back with the lucerne and the two men teased it out into the deep manger.

They chatted on until the nosebags were sniffed clean. They removed the bags, cast a final knowing eye over the horses and walked out of the big open stable reserved for the draft and coach horses that needed overnight shelter.

Outside the building a wooden trough and hand pump allowed a quick wash of face and hands.

'How about a quick nip at the pub, and then Maggie will be delighted to give you a bite for tea?'

'Alright, just one drink and it's my shout.'

Pat followed Barney in through the back entrance of the hotel, under a big rambling passionfruit vine. They took up a place at the end of the long cedar bar made from a massive plank that could well have made much expensive joinery in cedar hungry Sydney.

'What's it to be boys?'

Laura James, the co-licensee with her husband Rupert, bustled up, a smile on her heavily made-up face, hair just a little too red to be real, piled on top and framing a still handsome face. She held a reputation for running a strict establishment.

'We'll have two rums and some water please, Laura.'

Barney gave their order and Pat insisted on paying when the tots of rum and a small glass jug of water arrived.

They mixed their drinks, just a little water into the hot, biting spirit, and sipped the diluted fire water. The talk around the bar had the usual themes, clearing blocks, making tracks, growing crops in the rich new earth.

'Hello Pat, I hear you made it up the cutting with the new engine for Brown's Mill,' Rupert James said, hands nimbly polishing a sparkling beer glass on a rough linen glass cloth, a spotless calico apron tied around a spreading girth and heavy rimless glasses perched on a ruddy nose. 'The way the weather's been lad, you're lucky to have made it.'

Rupert and Laura were ex-Londoners and ex-Sydneysiders, who drifted to the North Coast and saw a chance for a hotel on the growing red soil plateau. They ran a strict no nonsense public house and fitted in well with the settlers.

'Yes, we still don't want any rain until after tomorrow, it's a way to go, but the worst of the trip may be over. I hope to be home tomorrow night.' Pat was not all that keen to talk about his job, but he knew it would be a good advertisement for him if this delivery went well.

They finished their rum. Barney wanted to return the shout, but Pat was firm. Not for him. They went out the back way and tramped across the open blocks to the slab cottage that was up the hill from the stables. Pat was warmly received by Maggie and their three children. Maggie and Bridget were friends, with a common interest in how they were going to educate their children. The meal was a happy occasion. Pat returned early to the stable and unrolled his blankets to make a bed in the stall adjoining his horses.

The slow coming morning was grey. A few light showers through the night disturbed Pat's sleep. He made sure he was up and about with the waking birds. The horses were fed, harnessed and prepared for the day. He declined the offer of breakfast with the Shaw family, wanting to be on the way while the weather was fine. There were still steep grades to be climbed. He reckoned on boiling the billy and giving the horses a break a couple of hours into the trip.

They rolled off into the morning. A barking dog or two, a wave here and there from an early stirring resident, but the well- oiled wagon was soon swallowed into the morning mist. It was still too early to tell whether the sun would climb in the east and burn away the dankness of night showers and the rising moisture from the deep friable red earth. Pat hoped the day would prove fine, if not, the sooner they reached the potential trouble spots the better chance he would have of getting through.

A couple of hours later, they arrived at Maguire's Creek. This was a common stopping spot for travellers and hauliers. A fireplace with a couple of wire hooks made it a good place to boil the billy. There was even a block or two of hardwood that could be split to fuel a good fire. Pat gave his horses their nosebags and prepared breakfast for himself; the morning was cloudy but still fine.

Breakfast over, Pat checked the crossing. It meant wet feet, but he wanted to be sure of the below water surface. Assured that no large rocks were lurking to cause unexpected lurches, he eased Captain into the water, the old grey horse calmly picked his footing. Tar snorted in objection to this cold dip, but given a nudge on his ample rump by Sailor, he flopped in. Sailor came in behind and the wagon eased down into the water.

This was one of the touchy parts of the trip. Pat talked calmly to Captain and, step by step, they eased across the water way. To climb the western bank meant a concentrated pull. Here, Pat clicked up his steeds and they snapped tight the chains. For an instant their momentum stopped but then the front wheels lurched up; the three big horses pressed hard into their collars and up came the wagon, water draining from the heavy hardwood wheels. Pat did not let the horses ease their effort until well clear of the crossing.

'Whoa fellas, you are beauties to be sure. It'll be easy going home.' He gave the horses a minute to get their breath back and then onward with the last leg of the trip.

The mill came into sight just before midday. It was now drizzling rain and the track was becoming more slippery with the fine film of misty moisture.

'There it is fellas. Down that slope and we are there.'

The big mill sat on a large clearing, surrounded by log piles of drying timber. Mostly eucalypt hardwood, but there was the occasional big log of hoop pine. They eased down the slope and Pat called a halt in an open area.

Duncan Brown the mill owner bustled out. The little Scotsman had a reputation for cutting good timber and being a keen, careful businessman.

'Well Mr O'Reilly, I didna expect you so soon, laddie,' he smiled. 'I received Captain McDougall's telegram to advise his arrangement with you, but we thought the cutting may have been too wet with that load. How about a bite of lunch and then we'll unload?'

Pat unhitched the horses, gave them their nosebags, and then followed a hospitable Mr Brown to his office. Over a cup of tea and sandwich they chatted.

'Yu ken laddie, those horses of yours must be good,' he said, after swallowing a bite of sandwich. 'I was going to unload with the jib in the yard but maybe we could get in near the engine bed and use pulleys from the roof. If you think it could be done, I'd offer ye a bonus.'

'Sure, Mr Brown. We'll have a look, but I had hoped to get home tonight, so I do not want to spend much time.'

After a quick lunch, they went and inspected the new prepared concrete mill bed and the access to get there. Pat kicked the heavily saw dusted floor; at least the footing was good. The space between other machinery was tight but possible; it would necessitate backing out. If he used only Captain and Sailor, he felt it could be done.

'Well, if you can set up your winches and pulleys within an hour, I reckon we could do it,' said Pat. 'I'd take two horses in and back out with one. It's going to mean I may not get home tonight, are you prepared to pay an extra pound?'

'Ye drive a hard bargain laddie,' Mr Brown responded with a handshake. 'I thought ten shillings, but if the engine sits where it's going to work, yes - a pound it is. I'll have Morton my engineer, and a couple of men on the job right now.'

An hour later, with Tar removed, Pat was ready to roll the wagon in under the big roof. Captain flicked his ears back and forth at his blinkered vision of the mill machinery but resolutely followed Pat. Slowly, they found their track, measuring with a stick and Pat talking calmly to the big horses. Eventually, the wagon was beside the mill bed. Captain was hard against a saw bench with no room for forward movement but that did not matter. Slings were attached around the big steam engine; all hands were placed to work the winches and steady the machinery over the edge of the wagon and down.

Morton checked the connections and gave the hand signal to haul on the ropes. Inch by inch the lift began, over the top of the wagon sides and then carefully down to the prepared concrete bed. With an empty wagon, Pat unhitched Sailor and worked the big black horse out sideways. He led him out to join Tar hitched to an outside log. Then he went to shorten up the chains for Captain, ease him back into the heavy breeching and ever so slowly work the big wagon back through the mill machinery. A couple of times the wagon was levered over an inch or so in its backward progress to clear an obstruction. Eventually, there was open space behind and the wagon emerged. The biggest job of Pat's career was successfully completed.

'Well done laddie,' Duncan Brown beamed his approval. 'Over to the office for your cheque, and you be on your way home. I like the way you do a job.'

To Build a School

The sun was sinking low again, this time behind him, as Pat approached Duck Creek Mountain. He knew it would be past dark when they made it home but that was no worry; he had completed a difficult job. He waved to the hangers-on, watching at the pub veranda but didn't stop. Already the thought of Bridget, the children and the warmth of home caused him to click up the horses. He knew that once through the village they would smell home and would stride out even more willingly. The weather had cleared and a cool sou'wester breeze was starting to form a drying crust on the red soil road.

An hour later and the lights of the big Brewster home were a welcome sight. Further on he knew Bridget and the girls would be watching, it was no surprise to see four figures emerge out of the gloom. He stopped the horses, jumped down, embraced them all and lifted them into the wagon. They rumbled home the last two hundred yards, the horses led by Captain made the turn into the gateway on their own and headed for the stables. Mary wanted to help with the horses, and it was agreed that she could stay and lend a hand. Like all things she did, Mary went about a task with one track dedication.

Almost an hour later, they arrived hand in hand at the house. Bridget had the copper boiling with water for Pat's bath and the tea was well underway. The kitchen was aglow with soft light and the wonderful aroma of cooking roast meat and vegies crept out the back door. Home was a great place, the very best. The evening meal was a happy affair. Pat told of the interesting parts of his trip and how he felt lucky with the rain holding off. Bridget had her news of a meeting about the proposed school.

'Norah Brewster has sent out written invitations to all the families around to attend a meeting at Surreyville,' she said as she started cleaning up dinner. 'It is to be in four weeks' time, on a Sunday afternoon. We will do some cooking; you and Jim will make tea and hopefully most people will get home before dark.'

'It seems a good idea. I reckon Barney and Maggie will come, we talked about it last night. Their eldest certainly needs a school.' Pat helped pack up the dishes and carried a nodding Thomas off to bed.

Sometime later, the kerosene lights blown out, the O'Reillys talked late into the night. There were so many things happening.

Shipwreck and Funerals

Martin Baillie had spent three days in Ballina visiting the listed Presbyterians of the area. The little coastal shipping port was fast growing. Temporal life there focused very much on the shipping in and out of the Richmond River. There was always the situation of ships trying to make it in or out of the changing, shoaling, ever treacherous bar. Already the small cemetery on the northern junction of the river and North Creek contained the remains of many sailors washed ashore or dragged ashore from the all too frequent wrecks.

This visit to Ballina brought him in contact with one more of those tragic happenings. The sailing schooner *Fortune* had hovered around the bar entrance all day. The skipper, late in the day, decided to make a run with the gusty sou'easter for the shelter of Shaws Bay. Everything went wrong. The wind dropped, the little ship with almost full sail broached on a large wave, and it caught on an outside sandbar. It all happened so quickly. Over went the *Fortune*. Of the crew only six made it to shore alive. Of the other ten, some bodies were recovered from the surf, some remained permanent guests of the ever-hungry sea.

Word came to Martin at his lodging house of the tragedy. He dressed, saddled his horse at the nearby livery and rode quickly to the mouth of North Creek. The survivors had already been rowed across to the Ballina side. He gave what spiritual consolation he could. The little crowd gathered there, hoped for more survivors. By morning, some bodies had been recovered, indicating there would be no more coming ashore alive. To these men Martin gave the rites of his church. He left what consolation he could for the sad but well organised following scene that happened with monotonous regularity. The community would pay the cost of simple coffins; at least timber was plentiful. He returned to his lodging and would come back to the little cemetery when all was in readiness for the burials.

The next day, a funeral service for the sailors attracted a crowd of residents from Ballina. All too often, businesses closed for these tragic happenings. Usually, it was possible to identify the bodies, as was the case with the *Fortune*, the surviving seamen being able to name their comrades. The religious affiliation of the dead sailors was sometimes known, often not known. Clergy were scarce to the area but when available these cooperated to provide the rites of their church to persons believed to be of their persuasion. When it was a case of no clergy, or only one available, the burial service was of standard dedication to God, and then tracking down the next of kin with the tragic news. It was a common scenario that Martin Baillie faced in his ministering to the bodies from the *Fortune*. He was the only clergyman in Ballina on this occasion, so it was his sad responsibility.

He offered consolation to the survivors, prepared to commend the bodies of the dead to the earth and their souls to God. It was draining work that left him with a feeling of mental isolation.

Before the funeral, one of the survivors, a young Irish seaman named Daniel Riordan, had approached him in sorrow about his friend Sean Sheehan. The two had lived in the same village back in Wicklow. They had worked a passage to Australia and continued on as sailors on any coastal vessel wanting hands. Daniel had made it ashore after the wreck, but Sean's lifeless body came ashore with the tide. Daniel had been one of the finding search party and took the loss of his friend and other shipmates hard.

That night he had called on Martin Baillie at his lodging to discuss the funeral next day.

'I'm sorry to worry you Reverend, but I owe it to Sean and his family back home to do all I can as a Catholic friend,' he said, visibly upset. 'You have been kindness itself, and I know there is no priest closer than Grafton, so I am grateful you will do Sean's burial.'   Daniel paused, and Martin interrupted gently,

'Daniel I will do all that is possible. What would you like of me?'

'Well, I have Rosary beads I'd like to bury with him. Mrs Flaherty, where I'm staying, has offered to pray the Rosary with me at the grave. Would you mind that Reverend?'

'That is up to you Daniel. The service will be the common Christian burial, for all eight, regardless of their faith. We know Sean's faith through you, but for many of the others it is not known. I wish there was more that I could do; be assured God will give them rest.'

The two men parted until the funeral.

It was a glorious late autumn afternoon. A gentle nor' wester rippled the waters of North Creek and the Richmond River, the low tide exposed the spits of white sand in contrast to the water shades, blue through to brown, according to depth of channels and shallows. Here and there darker shades showed where the sea grasses grew.

'Ashes to ashes, dust to dust.'

The burial was over, soil pounded in on the plain wooden coffins. The substantial crowd prepared to make the trip back to Ballina. They knew it was not a one-off occasion, all too often the sea and the river bar were adding to the numbers in this little peninsular cemetery. It was rapidly filling.

At the graveside of Sean Sheehan, four people knelt to offer a Rosary for the young sailor. Carmel Flaherty sounded out the decades and Daniel and the other two responded to the Hail Marys. Tom O'Rourke and Nell Flaherty knelt on each side of Daniel. They did not notice until the end of their Rosary that Martin Baillie had quietly stood behind where his shadow could not fall in their vision. At the conclusion he came up and asked Dan whether there was any assistance he could offer in contacting Sean's family. It could not always be assumed that sailors could read or write. Carmel Flaherty thanked him for the care.

'Ah, Reverend, Daniel writes real neat and we set out the sad news for Sean's family last night. It be good of you to offer help. Daniel will stay on for a day or two while he decides his next move. My room be empty at the moment.' She was known and liked in the community as a young struggling widow; her husband had been victim of an accident several years before.

There was often a traveller on one of the coastal ships looking for lodging, and Carmel made a few shillings through rental of a room.

Martin Baillie turned to Daniel. 'What will you do now? Is it back to sea?'

Daniel looked at the clergyman, and spoke slowly, 'I'm afraid I do not know. Perhaps if I find a job ashore, it could be I'd try it for a while. The loss of Sean and the other lads is a bit too much at the moment. Thank you for your care, I'll get by.'

The funeral crowd headed back to the town of Ballina.

The small cemetery was left to the closing day. North Creek was a liquid golden cradle nursing the last remnant of the day's sun sinking in a clear western sky. To the east, the surf rolled benignly into a calm river. Overhead, the gulls wheeled and dived, voicing a raucous dirge for those lain to rest. Life on the river flowed on, a ship under plenty of sail with the following westerly, ran for the river opening. On the outgoing ship those sailors were probably far too busy to spare a thought for the crew of the *Fortune*.

Nell and Daniel

Tea that night at the Flaherty house was not an unhappy meal. Death and accident were part of a tough life; those who came to a pioneer area such as the north coast of NSW knew the risks. The group that sat around the lodging house table were Irish emigrants. They had known it tough in Ireland, they knew it would probably be tough in NSW. After the meal of local fish and home-grown potatoes, there was a pot of black coffee. Tom O'Rourke produced a small flask of rum and laced Carmel's and Daniel's cups and his own coffee with a dash.

The town of Ballina speculated about the relationship of Tom and Carmel. Tom had drifted into town some five years before. He started an old wares business and occupied a room at Carmel's little lodging house. It was speculated by some that they probably shared the same bed some of the time, but it would have been a game person to drop that insinuation in Carmel's hearing. Tom spoke nothing of his past life but was a man of many abilities. He could repair a watch or clock, could fix a gun or rifle mechanism, and could play a good tune on his old fiddle. His age was probably fiftyish, with the fresh sandy colouring of many Irish. Many persons in Ballina had reason to be grateful to Tom, but Irish Catholics were a minority and not popular with the predominantly Protestant settlers. This seemed to have no effect on Tom, he helped those who asked for help, and kept to himself. Carmel's children called him Uncle Tom and often used him to ease their mother's strict decisions.

After tea, out came the fiddle. A couple of sedate melancholy Irish airs and then Tom broke into a toe tapping jig. Carmel took Daniel's hand

and demanded he dance; this they did with some skill. At the break in the music, she handed him over to Nell claiming she was out of condition and too old. Nell shyly reckoned she was not a dancer, but soon entered into the vibrant pulse of the rhythm, her young body supple and attractive, answering the pulse of primitive dancing genes from her strong Celtic background.

The couple were flushed, hot with foreheads on which damp sweat glistened, when the dancing came to a halt. They escaped to the tank at the kitchen for a glass of water.

'Would you take a stroll down to the river with me?' Daniel looked at the girl and liked what he saw. She was only eighteen but had grown up fast in the environs of this tough river port. Her mother had protectively seen that she had little opportunity to pair off with the town boys.

'If Ma says yes, I'll come.'

They went back into the living room and Daniel approached Carmel.

'Mrs Flaherty, could Nell and I have your permission to take a walk down to the river?'

'To be sure Daniel, I do not encourage Nell to be taking night strolls with my boarders or the lads around here, but it's her decision. Be back by ten.'

The other children went to bed, leaving Tom and Carmel to the living room.

'That one seems a decent enough lad to me,' mused Tom, 'but being a sailor is a bit of a worry. It's a way to get a few quid together if you don't drown first. I think he'd take a shore job if one offered.'

Carmel looked at Tom and shrugged.

'She's grown up and I can't keep her away from men. Just because they go for a stroll it's no reason to panic. I agree he seems all right and he is of our faith. Anyway, he no doubt only wants to take his mind off the last few days.'

Life Ticks On

Daniel and Nell walked silently across to the river. Upstream a couple of boats moored to the wharf creaked on their taut hemp ropes with mast lights gently swaying to the pull of a strong ebb tide. The sound of voices drifted down occasionally on the night breeze, otherwise there was only the sighing sound of running water and crabs scuttling down the bank. The strong smell of mangrove mud flats hung in the air; a scent not noticed by any permanent river dweller.

At the riverbank they turned downstream and followed the rough walking track. Daniel extended a questioning hand and took Nell's rough work toiled fingers. They came to the sand spits, uncovered with the falling tide.

'Is it all right to walk out on the sand?' Dan's question broke the silence.

'Yes, the sand is dry after half tide. We can walk out to the water edge and back.'

Nell had walked over and fished off these sand spits many times over most of her life.

There was a two-foot drop from riverbank to the exposed sand. Dan jumped down and held up his hands for Nell; she landed lightly in front of him and withdrew her hands from his strong clasp. His arms now free went gently around the slim shoulders and eased her body against his. She stood still, gently but firmly held; her chin rested on his left shoulder. Feelings emerged in her stronger, deeper than the few times that she had been briefly waylaid by one of the town lads. Her mother had warned her of strong feelings.

'We are here to walk,' she said softly.

Dan ran his fingers gently through her dark hair, let his right arm slide around her shoulders and they walked toward the darkness.

'A pretty colleen like you must have many boyfriends, is there anyone special?'

'No, I don't have many boyfriends and there is no one special. My mother keeps an eye on boys,' she said it with a hint of humour.

'And very right she is, too.'

Dan picked up the thread of humour. His feelings for this girl were different to those kindled by most of the girls he met up with ashore. She was young and he sensed her innocence of men, but she also gave an air of being mature and wise.

They walked on following the sand. He placed her left arm around his waist. She left it there. Reluctantly, they turned around at the bustling river's edge, where the fast-falling tide played a soft swishing tune. All too soon they headed back towards the town. He stopped and with his free arm pointed out some of the star formations. She knew only the Southern Cross; the other common constellations were a mystery to her.

'A sailor on watch only has the stars for company. I've taught myself to read and the stars are my friends. Perhaps now when you see old Mercury there, you will think of me.'

He felt the increased pressure of her slim, strong arm around his waist and the turmoil of the past few days seemed an insignificant part of

God's plan.

When they reached the big step from the sandspit to the walking track, he jumped up and held his hands down for her. Unhesitating, she willingly took those hands and he lifted her effortlessly to his level. He slid a hand under her chin and lifted it, so their faces were close in the dim starlight. They merged together and their lips met in a long, lingering kiss that opened all the promise of their warm humanity. Eventually, she took her arms from around his neck and gently eased back from the pounding awareness of their longing. Close together and arms around each other they walked home.

When close to the door, they stopped and looked long at each other.

'We'll talk tomorrow.' He kissed her gently on the forehead.

There was still a light in the living room and they knocked on the front door. Carmel was up waiting their return. She let them in, commanded they sit and announced that she would get them a cup of cocoa. They were back on time, but she sensed signs that caused a quizzical lift of the eyebrows as she warmed the milk. She realised Nell was an attractive girl, but there was an added warm glow to her in the dull light of the kerosene lamp that she hadn't seen before. Was it a good thing or a bad thing for her to fall for this young man? She guessed he was mid- twenties in age, so obviously he knew something of women- all sailors did. She didn't know any that led monastic lives while ashore. What were her prospects here in this tough river town? There were plenty of men looking for pretty girls, some were the marrying kind, most liked to have their sexual fun and resort to holy matrimony only if forced into it through the girl's pregnancy. Some of those marriages turned out well, some didn't, it was a lucky dip. Her own marriage had been that way. She had been three months pregnant with Nell when she and Bob had found a visiting priest to solemnise their vows. She wished something different for her daughter.

'Here we are, nothing like a cup of cocoa to make you sleep. Was it nice out by the river.?'

She knew the answer to that question, but they probably thought their attraction to each other wasn't so obvious.

'Mum, Daniel showed me how to find some of the stars and told me how their position changes in different parts of the world.'

'Well Daniel, she is a good learner. There was never much chance for her to have regular schooling, but she picked up reading and writing and sums real easy,' said Carmel to the young man. 'After her dad was killed, she has been my helper in making a living from this boarding house. I wish she'd had the chances the other two have been given to go to school.'

'Mrs Flaherty, will it be alright for me to stay a couple more days. I can pay. The money I had with me went down on the Firefly, but I have a little put by in a bank in Sydney.'

'That's no worry, Daniel. It's been too big a day, let's all go to bed. God bless you both.'

Carmel waited for them to go to their rooms and blew out the light. She retired to her room, which was a small annexe near the kitchen. Space was money and the four rooms had to be used to the best purpose for the paying guests. She knelt and prayed for the soul of Sean and the other drowned sailors, also for Nell that this man who had come into her young life, was for her daughter's eternal good.

Morning brought early rising to the Flaherty establishment. The fuel stove in the kitchen gobbled large quantities of split wood. This, Carmel bought from the carriers by the cart load. To get good quality slow burning hardwood it had to come from the forest hills back from the coast. As Carmel surveyed the few blocks left, she hoped that Pat O'Reilly would arrive with an ordered load very soon. It was the task of

Jim, her son, to make sure there was kindling always ready to light the big firebox. This was softwood collected in a barrow from the local sawmill and split into thin pieces to dry. It caught fire easily but made little heat. This pile also was low. Carmel resolved to prod Jim to action, and make sure he obeyed. His schooling over, although bright, he was most interested in fishing. He went out often with the net haulers; they rowed upriver and set nets. It was cold hard work, but he made a few shillings from it. They always had fish, and Jim reckoned he'd soon have enough money to buy nets and a pulling punt. That was the extent of his ambition.

Soon the fire crackled in the kitchen, a pot of oat porridge simmered on the stove top. The big black frying pan spat fat from the cooking bacon and half a dozen eggs sat on the table ready to be fried in the pan. It was the normal morning scene for the Flaherty kitchen. No paying guests complained of their meals.

Breakfast over, Tom had gone to his shop, Jim was hunted off to the sawmill with the barrow, and Nell sent off to buy fresh meat. Carmel busied herself preparing the dough for the bread baking which was a twice weekly chore. She liked baking bread and her skill was well known. Daniel sought her out in the kitchen.

'Mrs Flaherty, could I have a word with you please?'

'Sure Daniel, sure, but I must keep working this dough.'

'Perhaps you guess that I like Nell, and I think she likes me.'

'Yes Daniel, I'm not blind and I'm not that old you know, that I've forgotten being young.'

'If I could find a way of making a living for us, how would you think of me as a son?'

'Well Daniel, what I've seen of you I like, but we don't know much of you. I'm not going to say Nell is too young, but as far as I know she has had little to do with men. I appreciate your talking to me first, but I guess it's between you, Nell and I hope, God.'

'I think we would be happy together. I have a little money saved up and I'd like to try a farming block after a while if she says "yes".'

He continued, 'Sean and I had planned that's what we'd do together when our bank was big enough. We had a joint account where we put any spare money, I'll send half our money back to his mother. We came from tenant farming families back home. Thanks Mrs Flaherty, I'll talk to Nell and see how she feels about me.'

Their conversation went no further as outside there was a call of 'Wood-o'. Pat O'Reilly had arrived opportunely with a cart load of well dried blocks of tough, dry bloodwood. He backed the cart down the side of the house, close to the almost non- existent wood heap.

'I'm pleased to see you Patrick,' smiled Carmel as she went out to meet him. 'You made it in the nick of time. You can see the boarders would have gone hungry soon.'

'I hadn't forgotten Carmel, but I was trying to work it with some loading back home. There's some seed and flour to go up the mountain today, so it's a good trip for my young horse in the cart.'

'When you unload Pat, there'll be a cup of tea and I'll pay you for the load. This is Dan, he's staying a day or two. He was on the *Fortune*.'

'Yes, we were right sorry to hear the news, someday that bar will have to be made safer. I am pleased to know you Dan.'

The two men spoke briefly.

'I'll give you a hand to throw the blocks off,' offered Dan.

Dan and Pat worked through the open back of the cart and neatly stacked the load. It took little time with two fit men muscling off the heavy blocks.

They went inside where the kitchen was full of the scent of cooking bread. Carmel produced tea and fresh scones with honey.

'You know the boarders don't leave here Dan, once they get a taste of Carmel's cooking they won't go.'

'That's enough of the blarney Patrick, I'll be telling Bridget you can't be trusted out on the road with your sweet-talking tongue.'

Carmel liked the compliment; she was a little older than Patrick and not beyond feeling her pulse quicken in his presence.

'What are the chances of work for a bloke like me? I'm thinking of giving the sea a miss, if I could find something.'

Pat took a careful look at the young sailor.

'How handy are you, Dan? What did you have in mind?'

'I did all sorts of farm work back home until I was eighteen and took to the sea. I can plough and dig and milk, and I'm game to try anything.'

Pat raised his eyebrows.

'That's not a bad background, there's plenty of work but not much money around here. What are you like at fencing? I have a neighbour who is looking for someone to build fences. Usually fencing is paid by the number of posts and panels, so you have to work hard and have the knack to make it pay well.'

Daniel gave it due thought.

'Fences, as you know, back home in Ireland are mostly hedges and stone walls. I think I could learn to make fences with wood and wire but I'd be slow for a while.'

The answer showed Patrick that this young man had a slant of realism in his make-up.

'If you want, I'll put you in touch with Jim Brewster, my neighbour. He's English but a good man. We get along fine. He wouldn't rob you, but he expects a job done well. At least he has the money to pay and that's a rarity around here.'

'How would I get up there to see him. Could I walk it in a day?'

'Yes, you could. The easier way would be to hire a horse from Brownie down at the livery stable. That way it's easy and you have time to talk and look. What you like on a horse?'

'I rode back home, from when I could toddle, so I guess I haven't forgotten how, but until I get back to Sydney, no money. It went down with the *Fortune*.'

There came with Pat's quick appraisal of the lad, a desire to help.

'That's not a huge problem. I'll lend you ten shillings, that'll get you a horse with a few shillings to spare. You deserve a bit of a lift along after the past few days.'

Carmel handed over ten shillings for her load of wood, and Pat handed it across to Daniel for his hire of the horse. Pat gave him instructions and undertook to talk to Jim Brewster that night. Daniel was grateful for the assistance,

'The least I can do is come and help you load up the cart. It may save you a little time.'

Pat and Dan took leave from Carmel and headed up to the wharf with the empty cart. Pat walked Tar out onto the wooden planks; the young horse was a bit touchy to the feel of the planks and the unaccustomed noises of the wharf but did nothing wrong. They pulled up at the office and Daniel was left talking to the horse while Pat went and checked out his load. Quickly back, he moved the horse and cart further along to where bags of flour, sugar, and maize seed were stacked in a heap for transport up to Duck Creek. They loaded the twelve bags, and Pat was ready to start the trip home.

'That was a big help, I wondered how Tar would be when I had to leave him on his own, you saved that problem. I'll probably be home tomorrow when you come up. Good luck.'

They shook hands and went their separate ways.

From Ship to Stirrup

Dan followed directions around to the Ballina livery stable. There he met up with Brownie. Dugald Brown was a wizened old Scotsman. He had, in his young days back home, been a groom and knockabout jockey, who had followed the racing circuit. He'd let it slip, once when in his cups, that he'd found it necessary to "travel" before the police caught up with him. He took a job on a ship leaving Liverpool for Australia, worked his passage to Sydney, made a couple of trips on coastal boats, and settled in the growing port of Ballina. It seemed a natural progression for him to set up a modest livery stable.

He listened to Dan's need for a horse and cast a speculative eye over the young Irishman.

'Well laddie, you made it ashore from the Fortune, you should get up the mountain and back. Some of the Micks can sit a horse a bit, what about you?'

'I haven't been on a horse for years, but I rode plenty of moor ponies back home.'

'I've only three nags, and one of those has a crook back from a big heavy pommy that rode it like a sack of turnips.' He pointed to a horse tied up to his left. 'That bay is a handy mount, but he's spoke for tomorrow. That leaves Chief, he's all right for a rider, but not for a mug. Come and have a look.'

They went through the tumble-down ex boatshed and came to a small yard out the back. There, a neat fifteen hand, baldy faced chestnut, munched on his ration of hay. Mostly thoroughbred with a hint of Arabian in his background, he was a classy horse.

'He's got a mouth but knows how to grab the bit. He can buck a bit too if he gets his head down. Get him going and he's a real good horse. Unfortunately, he's a smart bugger, he can smell a mug at twenty paces. If you like we'll saddle him up, I'll put you on and see how you go.'

Dan got in with the horse, slid his left arm up under his neck, rubbed him down and talked soft Gaelic to him.

'Alright,' he said, 'we'll see how I go.'

Brownie slipped on the bridle, left Dan to place on the saddle blanket and saddle. He girthed the horse up gently and led him around. He stopped, leant in against the horse and from the front lifted and pulled out his front legs, then tightened the girth and surcingle to a safe tension. Then he adjusted the stirrup leathers.

'Right, we'll put you on in here, so he gets the feel of you, then out into the big yard,' said Brownie.

The Scotsman kept a light hold on the horse's head; Dan slipped the toe of Tom O'Rourke's unsuitable shoe into the iron, let the horse feel his weight and then lightly lifted up into the saddle. Chief snorted softly but remained firm.

'Right, just ease him around, do na let his mouth go, but do na drag on him.'

Dan eased the horse around on the nearside rein and he moved off okay. He walked around in a tight circle and seemed to accept the rider without protest.

'I'll open the gate into the big yard,' said Brownie as he headed for the aforementioned gate. 'Just do the same, walk him around a couple of times, then trot him off nice and slow.'

They went out into the working yard. The horse responded, taut and tight, then started to relax into his work as he felt his rider's weight moving with him in rhythm. Dan's hands were low on his neck, firm and smooth on the bit.

Brownie watched and felt it was safe to extend the trial to the open street.

'This will tell. Right, trot him down the street when I open the gate. Keep him in a nice firm hold, turn him around, then bring him back.'

This Daniel did without problem even though a mongrel town dog rushed out barking.

'You should handle him, just do na think he's too easy, and don't let him grab the bit. For a sailor you do na look too bad. What time will you be here in the morning.' Brownie was impressed.

'Would eight o'clock be all right? You haven't told me yet how much money for the day.'

'Well, my charge is ten shillings a day. You would na have any money after being wrecked. That horse needs work, you bring him back going well and I'll charge you five shillings. I'll lend you an old pair of riding boots, you can na ride properly in those things.'

Daniel headed back to Flaherty's feeling pleased with himself. His thoughts were constantly on Nell. Was he being fair to her? What had he to offer? Was he just reacting to the pressures of the past hectic days? No. He thought of the girl and felt God had saved him for a purpose; he wanted to believe that Nell was part of the purpose.

Romance - Nell and Daniel

After tea that night, Daniel and Nell went strolling along the track by the river. Daniel had told of his day in the conversation at the table. The idea from Pat about fencing, the ride on Brownie's horse Chief, and the plan for tomorrow's trip up to the Brewster's farm.

They walked along, hand in hand, perhaps a little shy from the previous evening happenings, but at peace with each other. The night was cooler with scudding cloud at times blotting out their friendly stars. They walked further down toward the junction of the river and North Creek.

Dan broke the silence.

'It is less than a week since Sean and I were coming up the coast on the *Fortune*. Now he's dead, buried over there. Yet I'm so lucky to be alive, and to have found you. Do you believe in destiny, Nell? Why have things gone right for me, but wrong for Sean?'

It triggered a chain of thought.

'We were friends from when we had to leave school and try to help feed our families. We were going to become rich Australian squatters when we found our farm. I keep thinking how sad his mother will be when she receives my letter. I'm going to have to get to a branch of the bank and get them to send half of our account home to Ireland. God knows they need the bit of money, but it won't replace a loved son.'

Nell's fingers tightened their grip.

'Daniel, I don't have a wise reply. Too many sailors get drowned. Too many people, like my father have accidents. Too many people go hungry. I believe in God, my mother has taught me a little, to love and fear God and not to be afraid to live life, but I don't have the answers. Sean should be in that Heaven where sailors go.' Nell left it at that and they kept walking until they came to the junction of North Creek.

They halted in the heavy solitude of night. The audible tune of the half tide was a soft, almost mournful sighing breath as the waters sped to the sea. Across the creek, far out on the emerging mangrove mudflats, a lone curlew paced the expanding area left by the falling tide. His plaintiff call for a mate was an eerie drawn out two note tune that ebbed and flowed on the soft westerly breeze.

'Nell, I want to ask you something. I don't know whether it's too soon, I don't know whether it's a fair question, but I have to ask. Will you marry me?'

They stood side by side, neither moving, both aware of the other's breathing. Another banshee wail of the curlew drifted across. It seemed to frame Nell's reply. She turned her body to meet him, lifted her arms around his neck, their mouths met in a long, hungry kiss. When the fire that raced through their bodies seemed too great, she drew back from him, but looked full into his face in the dim light.

'You have an answer. If you want me as your wife, I'll do my best to be that wife for you. What do you think my mother will say?'

'Well, I had a little chat with her this morning. It won't be a big surprise.'

'That's nice, isn't it? You take me for granted already. The next thing I know you'll have me digging postholes. We'd better walk, it's a long way home, and I don't know that I trust myself alone with you Mr Riordan.'

The walk home was a slow affair, the cloud scuds cleared. The star constellations shone ever so clear.

'You know, Nell Flaherty, I think old Neptune approves. I could think he winked his approval at me.'

They kissed again until Nell pushed them apart.

'Daniel, I've not been with a man and that's how I'd like it to be until we are married.'

They made it home and knocked for Carmel to open the door. Once more she made them cocoa. When the three were seated at the table, Nell and Dan hand in hand, unable to disguise the happy glow that oozed from their auras, Dan made the announcement.

'God bless you both and may you be happy.' Carmel planted a kiss on Dan's forehead and hugged Nell.

'You've been a great daughter, and you deserve a good man. I think you've found one. May the luck of the Irish be with you both. We'll tell Tom and the others in the morning.'

Martin Baillie and O'Reillys

Martin Baillie made the decision when he reached the top of the mountain. It wasn't far off his way to call in at Killarney and see how the O'Reilly family was progressing. His last visit was probably about twelve months ago. He had been an intermittent caller since they came to the plateau. The events of Ballina and the *Fortune* seemed to have left him with a lingering melancholy that maybe friends could ease.

His time in the North Coast area seemed to have flown. He spent much time on a horse and tried to bring a sense of God to the area's many persons of Scottish Presbyterian faith; they were spread out over a very large area. He was well known from Casino to Ballina, along the river through Coraki and Woodburn, even inland to Lismore and Bangalow. There were many households that welcomed him for a night, and many homely women who wanted to cook him a delicious meal. Some of those women had comely daughters whose praises they weren't backward in describing to a bachelor clergyman. So far, he had not been over smitten by the charms of the daughters. He felt he had more chance of reaching people while alone to wander the area as God chose to use him. Need of a wife was not a pressing priority.

He swung the bay hack into the lane that led to the O'Reillys and smiled to himself about the remarks some of his flock no doubt made about his visiting Irish Catholic friends. He was not worried about contamination by Catholics, he felt secure in his strict Protestant faith. He looked upon the O'Reilly family as special friends. He wondered whether there was anything in his saddlebags for the children.

It was Mary who saw the horseman at the gate and ran to open it for him. She recognised him straightway. In the solemn friendly way of Mary, she smiled up at him.

'Hello Reverend Martin. You have not called to see us for a long time.'

'No Mary. I never seem to have time when riding down to Ballina. Forgive me, I'm here now.'

'Yes, that's all right. Mum says you are busy doing God's work.'

Mary favoured him with her special, slow, knowledgeable smile that was so like Bridget. Martin was amazed at the likeness of the young child to her mother. He liked all children and recognised this one as special. He dismounted and started the walk up to the house with Mary.

Halfway there, they were spotted by Janey and Thomas who started down the track at speed. Their mother arrived at the front door to see what event caused her family to disappear. She recognised the solid suit clad figure of Martin, and the bay horse that he usually rode. Reckoning that there was sufficient reception already, she went to quickly wash her hands and push back the still unruly red hair. Bridget was an attractive woman by any standard, more attractive even with the maturity of her late twenties.

By the time Martin and the children reached the house she was out at the little front garden to welcome him.

'Martin, welcome, its lovely to see you. Pat was only saying the other day he'd heard nothing of you lately.'

'Ah Bridget, I've been well. God's kept me busy. It's lovely to see you, and these children, how they've grown.'

'Well, put Dundee around in the yard. Come wash your hands and we'll have a cup of tea. Patrick took a load of firewood down to Ballina and he was bringing back seed and flour for Duck Creek, he said he'd be home by dark.'

Martin and the children took the horse around, unsaddled him and let him loose in the horse yard. When they arrived at the kitchen, the tea was made and a fresh batch of scones were on the table.

'It is a fact I eat too much. Look at me, far too fat, I need work and less food. Still the Lord has provided with your hospitality so thank you. I'll push on soon and stay the night at the hotel,' said Martin as he helped himself to a scone.

'No, Pat wouldn't forgive me if I let you go. You've slept on our couch before and we'd love to have you.'

'If you stay, I'll read to you,' Mary confidentially told Martin.

'Read? Why you must be a clever girl if you can read.' Martin feigned surprise.

'I'll show you how I can skip,' volunteered Janey.

'I'll thow you Thilver,' lisped Thomas.

'Silver is Pat's new Wyandotte rooster.' Bridget supplied that vital information. 'So that's settled, Pat should be home for dinner, if not we'll look after you. Anyway, I want to talk to you about our efforts to get a school for the children around Duck Creek Mountain.'

It was close to dark when the cart rumbled down the track. The children went to open the gate and bring their father home. After the gate was closed behind them, they all climbed up into the cart and sat on a bag of seed maize as a seat. They quickly told of their visitor. Janey and Thomas hopped out at the house; Mary continued around to the stable with her father.

While Pat was unharnessing Tar, Martin arrived over at the stable. He had left behind the coat and clerical collar and was wearing an old pair of Pat's overalls over the rest of his clothing. The men shook hands and Martin picked up the rubbing cloth and went to work on the big frame of Tar. He rubbed him hard, standing the damp, thick roan coat, so that it would dry with good air circulation to his skin.

'You should have been a farmer Martin,' laughed Pat. 'I have noted before that you have a good touch with horses.'

'Ah, it's just as well, I ride plenty of hours. Old Dundee and I have travelled many miles since that day you rescued the raw city minister on the track to Casino.'

'Well, it's great to see you. Feel like a walk after tea? I'll take you up to meet the Brewsters. I have to talk to Jim about a survivor off the *Fortune* who's looking for a job. He wants some fencing done and I think the lad could probably do it well. Anyway, let's get back to the house and cleaned up for tea or Bridget will refuse to feed us.'

The three walked back, Mary in the middle, quietly listening to the men's conversation. It was a happy meal.

After the dessert of grammar pie and cream, Mary produced her reading book and handled half a page with no errors.

'You really are clever Mary. I couldn't read that well.' Martin went to one of his saddle bags that contained his belongings and produced a small book of Bible stories.

'I am sure that you will be able to read these, if your mother and father approve it is all right for me to give you this book.'

He turned to Bridget.

'The little stories are all about Jesus and not at all sectarian; I've given them to many children. Do you approve?'

'Yes Martin, we trust your judgement, you know we are Catholic and that is the way we will train our children, but we rarely have a priest through here. A book of bible stories will be fine. Mary, thank Reverend Martin and we will learn a story before he comes the next time.'

Mary gave Martin her slow, serious smile and placed her face up to be kissed.

The men walked the half mile up to Brewsters. Long before arriving, they heard the excellent piano playing of Norah Brewster, drifting on the still night air. It stopped with their ringing of the front doorbell. Jim Brewster greeted them warmly and they were ushered in to the tastefully furnished drawing room. Norah insisted on making coffee while the men talked.

Pat told Jim about Daniel Riordan and the fact he was coming to see him about the fencing job. Daniel gained another reference. Martin said that Dan seemed a good type of young man who deserved a break.

They sipped their coffee, and the Brewsters told Martin a little of the plan to petition for a school. He assured them of any help that he could give in his clerical capacity to influence the Sydney based government. The Brewsters complained of the brevity of their visit, but Pat assured them next time the visit would be longer. Tonight, they must get home to Bridget.

The trio talked late into the night and when it was finally time for bed, they bowed their heads in joining the prayer of thanks offered by Martin for the family. Martin told a little of the trauma from the Fortune sinking and thanked them for listening. He also told a little of the days back in Scotland and his family. He was in a talking mood and the company of friends eased the tensions from his mind. It was a happy night. A strange alliance for a time when religion caused Protestant and Catholic to have suspicions of each other, although in the Australian bush, a neighbour in trouble was helped regardless of creed.

Daniel – Horses and Fencing

Events of the week seemed unreal to Dan Riordan. His muscular reactions fully tuned to the lively horse he rode, his mind had freedom to wander to recent happenings. He was like a ship running before the wind, powerless to change course. His destiny seemed to be surfing a wave. Would that wave drop him gently in its wake, or broach him once more into some out-of-control situation? How could he have met a girl, proposed and been accepted in the course of a few days. He was 25 years of age. His seven years at sea seemed another life now past. It would probably soon become as different and unreal as the green poverty of Ireland. He had seen little of this land other than Sydney, and the coastal ports. Could he make a life in this untouched coastal land for Nell and himself? There was no turning back, he was committed.

He was shaken back to reality as Chief snorted and shied, grabbing at the bit when a big black and gold goanna scuttled across under his nose into the undergrowth. The horse settled again to his voice and calm hands. Chief maintained a good rhythmic mile-eating walk. They had travelled the low swampy road and now the track started the climb up the mountain. Dan felt this was a good chance to let Chief work off some of his pent-up energy. He eased the horse into a trot, and then into a brisk canter. Each time he had been allowed to canter on the flat road, Chief had fought for his head and Dan had eased him back to a controlled trot or walk. Now with this steep long slope, he was able to settle the horse into a good steady canter without risk of Chief taking control. It was great to feel the strength and easy action of the horse and Dan's confidence grew that he was now well in charge.

The road wound up the mountain, around many bends, allowing a steep but reasonable gradient. On either side, the scrub frowned in on the red soil dirt road. Some of the steeper slopes, a constant problem to hauliers, had already been lightly coated with creek bed gravel. This gravel, however, soon pressed down into the soft soil. The road remained a problem for the settlers who were clearing the Big Scrub; any worthwhile farming activity was dependent on taking produce to the river. Much of the land was surveyed, and all types of people were applying to establish a freehold title over blocks of their choice. Tracks branched off the road into clearings, some temporary shacks were visible and here and there a cottage was built as a permanent home. Crops of ripening maize dotted most of the clearings.

It was mid- morning when Dan, from Pat O'Reilly's directions, recognised the lane leading to Killarney. There was still much standing scrub, but this was an attractive plateau area. It appeared early settlers had chosen well in taking possession of this humus rich tract of deep basaltic red soil. There seemed a breath of strong pulsing life in that waiting earth.

The O'Reillys had a field of ripe corn near the lane and Pat was pulling the cobs from the stalks and throwing them into a cart. He left the task and walked out to the lane to meet Dan.

'Good to see you found us Dan. I see Brownie fitted you out with a mount. That bloke you are on has a bit of a reputation. You seem to have him going well, so you haven't forgotten your Irish horse training.'

'He kept me busy for a while, but that climb up the mountain got him going well. We're good friends now. All he wants is a bit of constant work.'

'It's nearly lunch time, so come over to the house and meet the family. I'll take you around to meet Jim later and leave you two alone.'

'I don't want to be a nuisance, and I have sandwiches Nell made for me. I wasn't sure of the time.'

'Bridget wouldn't forgive me if I didn't bring you over. She knows about you and she's been a sailor herself. So, I'll take Tar and the cart to the barn and then we'll go over to the house.'

They put Chief in the horse yard and Pat gave him a bundle of hay to munch. The children, who had run out to meet them, escorted them to the house. Bridget had a dish of water, soap and a clean towel laid out on the bench waiting for them.

'I'm pleased to meet you Dan, you are welcome to Killarney. How do you like our mountain?' Bridget smiled at the young man.

'I think this is God's country Mrs O' Reilly, it's already treated me with so much kindness, it seems unreal.'

'Ah well, Dan these are sometimes rough people but they help those in trouble. We are glad to have an Irishman with us. Come and have lunch, and my name is Bridget. Pat has probably let slip that I've spent some time on coastal ships, maybe I'd be slow climbing a mast these days but I think I could still set a sail.'

It was a pleasant meal, salad from the garden and cold corned meat. At a break in the conversation, Dan told his big news.

'I hope I can find some work, because I've asked Nell Flaherty to marry me.'

Bridget recovered first.

'Well Dan, I've met Carmel and Nell and I think she'll make you a great wife. May God bless you both. Men need a wife to steady them down, don't they Patrick?'

'Yes, I have no complaints and it took me little time to recognise the one right for me. I'm sure it will be a good marriage. Nell has worked hard since her father's death and she is a great girl. Good luck to you both and it will work out just fine.'

They chatted for a time and Dan asked questions.

'How difficult is it to get a block of land up here? How much money does it need to get started? And what sort of farming has a chance of making a living?'

It was a series of questions to which there could be many answers. Pat gave him a measured reply.

'There are still blocks of land, some a bit steep. It doesn't take lots of money but it takes lots of work if you have to do it yourself. Sometimes a settler gets tired of it and wants to get out. That can be a better way if you have a little money and some of the work is done. You'd be wise to get work and take some time to look around.'

After lunch the two men walked up to the Brewsters. Jim came out to greet them, Pat having made the introduction, left Dan and Jim to discussions of the proposed fencing. Jim had plans for developing, in time, his dairy farm. With clearing of the block proceeding well, the Brewsters now wanted the cleared land fenced into four-acre fields. Amongst the fallen timber were many big straight grained teak trees. These would be cut to suitable lengths and split into posts and rails. Each post would be morticed to carry two wide, nine feet long rails. It would be the task of the scrub fallers to split the posts and rails and the fencer to stand the posts, make the mortices, and fit the rails.

They walked across the gently sloping land to where a batch of posts and rails had already been prepared.

'I have the necessary chisels, boring bits and fencing tools,' said Jim. 'I'm looking for someone who can build a neat fence and will work on the task until the first five paddocks are completed. I'd pay one shilling per post and two shillings for each corner or gate post.'

'Mr Brewster, I don't know how long it would take me to pick up the skills,' replied Dan. 'I've used a shovel back home, but I've had little to do with wood tools. I'd like to try on the basis that you give me a week to see how I'm going. You should know then if you think I'd be good, and I should know if the job suits me.'

Dan's reply seemed to satisfy Jim. He nodded agreement.

'You could camp in the barn. We have a stretcher and some old blankets you could use. So let us see how you go.'

They walked back to the house and Daniel was introduced to Norah. She was told of the arrangement and offered sympathy for the shipwreck he had been through.

'I hope you are happy here Daniel,' she smiled.

He walked back to the O'Reilly farm and told them of his start as a fencer. Pat offered to come across and give some hints on morticing when he arrived to start the job. Declining afternoon tea, Dan said he'd stop on the way back and eat his sandwiches.

'Mrs Flaherty and Nell won't forgive me if I arrive home with my lunch still not eaten.'

He saddled Chief, swung into the saddle, trotted down to the gate, already opened by Mary, and waved back to the family on the veranda. Pat remarked to his wife,

'What do you know, we'll see how that one turns out. He's certainly a better horseman than most around here. I hope he and Nell know what they are doing.'

Bridget smiled at him.

'Ah, if he's going to live in this wild country, he will need a wife to keep him under control. From what I know of Carmel, she'll see he behaves himself as a son-in-law. You'd better keep an eye out for a block that may suit them. We need some young neighbours.'

Plans and Work

Daniel rode into Ballina at sundown. He'd let Chief trot and canter along at a good pace on the way home. The horse had only tried a couple of times to grab the bit and had settled well each time when restrained. Brownie was rubbing down the bay, when Dan arrived at the stable.

'So, you did na fall off?' he grinned as Danial dismounted. 'Looks like you raised a sweat on him a few times.'

'He went all right when he settled down,' Daniel nodded, patting Chief's neck. 'You are right though Mr Brown, he's not a horse for mugs.'

Dan pulled the saddle off, dried the horse down and gave him a brief drink.

'Tom tells me you're staying on with us and marrying young Nell,' said Brownie. 'Good luck. Perhaps lad, if you be staying around, you need a horse. I'd sell you Chief for two pounds. He's no good to me if the travellers who want a horse can't ride him. I'm offered another, not much good but a quiet old plug.'

'I've no money, Mr Brown,' replied Dan, 'other than ten shillings borrowed from Pat O'Reilly, and I owe that to you. If you take that as deposit and wait until I can get at some money in a bank account, I'll take him if you throw in some gear.'

'Listen laddie, it's me that's the miserable Scotsman,' said old Brownie with a smile. 'You Irish with the blarney, think you can sweet talk everyone. I suppose ye can't ride him bareback. Let's have a look in the tack room.'

Brownie pulled an old pigskin exercise saddle off a peg and snaffle bit bridle, with rawhide plaited reins.

'Do ya reckon ya can sit on him with that light saddle?' Brownie asked. 'It's all I can spare. Ya can keep the old boots. Now do ya want to squeeze any more out of me?'

'Thanks Mr Brown, when I can afford to buy a saddle, I'll bring the gear back.'

'Ah lad, do na worry, that little saddle was thrown on a few horses that could scamper. My riding days are over; the legs are seized up. That horse you just bought is bred to go a bit from what I was told, and watching him move, it could be that he can sprint a bit. A traveller he took off with reckoned he's never covered ground so quick. If any of the squatters challenge you to a run for cash, give him a try and you may be surprised.'

'Well, I'm going up on the mountain to try a job at fencing. I'll take him off your hands in the morning. Thanks for helping and trusting me.'

They shook hands and Dan walked down to the Flaherty cottage.

There was much to tell that night at the Flaherty dinner table. He now had a job and had part paid for a horse. He seemed on a roller coaster of change. Tom offered to find him some more clothes out of the shop, and Carmel said she would find him cooking utensils.

When he and Nell were alone after the others had retired, they talked of their future and the idea of finding a farming block. Life seemed a great adventure.

Dan squinted along the fence into the setting sun and felt satisfaction from his work. The ten chain post and rail line was straight and the tops followed the contour of the ground at a nice even height. The many blisters on his hands were healing, and the knack of morticing was coming to him.

It was almost two weeks since he started the job and his number of posts per day was steadily rising. Pat had told him that ten panels a day was an acceptable level for that type of fence, from a competent fencer. The first week his best day was six panels and at times he had found it necessary to redo a panel. His lack of ability made him despondent and he wondered whether he would find the required speed and skill.

He found there were unseen problems; large hidden roots in the ground from the cleared trees meant much grubbing to put a posthole in the correct place. Also, trimming the irregular thickness rails to fit the standard size mortice meant trial and error to produce a good, neat fit. He was learning to keep the tools nice and sharp; it was a good way of spending the evenings until bedtime. The first few days he had only managed three panels per day. Now this, his eleventh working day, he had started at sunrise and now at sunset he had finished the days eleventh panel Only the round corner post was to go in to finish one side of the first paddock. He felt a sense of achievement. Jim was still to pass the last of his work, but Dan was confident the work standard was good.

As Dan packed up tools for the day, Jim arrived. He walked along the line, counted the panels, and looked down the post tops. He noticed the roots that had been removed to allow the correct positioning of posts.

'You have achieved a good day Dan,' he said. 'It looks fine. I suppose tomorrow being Sunday you will be going down to Ballina. If you come up to the house, I'll pay you for what's done.'

'It's up to you, Mr Brewster. If you be happy, it will let me pay some of my debts.'

'Yes, Norah and I think you have done well. We wondered at first whether you could pick up the speed, but in no time you were going well and working neatly. I am sorry about the number of roots still in the ground. There are more than I expected.'

'Some of those roots take much time to grub out, but I'm getting better. The ground is easy to dig when I find all soil, so it's good, and you are allowing me use of your barn and bedding, and a yard for Chief, I'm not complaining.'

After Dan had fed Chief, cleaned up and made a quick meal of leftover stew, he headed up to the big house. He knocked at the back door, interrupting Norah's piano rendition of Chopin.

'Come in Daniel,' she said as she opened the door. 'Jim tells me you are going very well. I hope you are comfortable in the barn. If you haven't enough blankets let us know.'

'Thank you, Mrs Brewster, I've been far less comfortable. On many ships I was wet, cold and scared. Your barn doesn't roll at all, it's just fine.'

Jim came in with the cash box.

'My count was 70 split posts and three rounds to date. That comes to 70 shillings plus six shillings. Is that how you see it?'

'Yes, that's correct by me, and thank you. I'll have to take a couple of days off soon and ride over to Grafton to the bank there, so they can fix up some business for me.'

'It's just as well you have your horse,' nodded Jim. 'It's a long ride to Grafton. Take the time off you want, just let us know when you are going. Now please join us for a cup of coffee.'

Norah made the coffee.

'Let's go into the drawing room.' She carried the cups, coffee pot and a fresh baked cake on a silver tray. Dan wondered about his dress and his manners for the Brewster drawing room, but hoped he could stay out of trouble.

Norah poured the coffee to his order. He sat very much on the edge of the deep chintz covered chair and prayed not to spill any crumbs on the carpet. The cottages back home in Ireland certainly were not this grand.

'We are having a meeting here soon to try and arrange for a school, so that the children around here, like the O'Reillys, will have a chance of education,' Norah said as she handed out coffee and cake. 'Seeing as you are getting married and hopefully will have children, you would be welcome at the meeting. The more that gather together and express interest, the better chance we may have of convincing the far away government that we deserve help.'

'Well thank you, Mrs Brewster, I don't know where we will live, but should I be around at the meeting time I will come.'

'We could probably get the timber for a simple school building, milled locally, and do much of the building ourselves,' added Jim. 'Pat O'Reilly thinks some of those teak trees we are using for fencing would be fine for cutting into boards. Most of this house is teak and beech as there is plenty of each around.'

He went on.

'We would have to find a teacher but that should be possible. Anyway, sooner or later there must be schools for this country to go forward.'

They chatted on for a time and then Daniel excused himself and went back to the barn and his bed. He wanted to be up on the road early the next morning.

The first rectangular four acre fenced paddock was complete. Dan now considered it a poor day if the fence did not grow by ten panels. The only true variable was the location of below ground roots that could really slow his progress.

He had slowly constructed a letter to the bank in Sydney telling of the death of Sean, and asking for details as to how the joint account could be divided with Sean's half to be sent home to Ireland. The account in his own name he requested transferred to the closest branch to Ballina, which was Grafton. Reply had arrived stating he would need to attend the Grafton branch and sign the necessary papers as well as a statutory declaration.

He planned to set off for Grafton on the Sunday, hopefully

complete his banking business on the Monday and arrive back on Tuesday or Wednesday. With Pat's help, a new set of shoes had been fitted to Chief, and instructions given as to his best track to Grafton. It would mean a big day for the horse and rider. Pat and Shamrock had achieved it many times, but the stamina of Chief was unknown, and Dan, while a capable rider, had no experience of travelling long distances. Pat gave him a note of introduction to a settler on the Grafton side of halfway from Casino, should the trip prove too long for the day.

'It could be that a letter of introduction may be useful for you,' Jim thoughtfully volunteered, when he heard of Dan's visit to the bank. He also threw in a suggestion.

'I have heard there is a block in toward Duck Creek that's taken up by Dick Hilardt and he wants to head back to the city. He was a clerk and had decided to try clearing a scrub block. He says he does not feel country life is for him. It has a small shack and some clearing is done, it may be of interest to you. When you have your business done in Grafton, I'd suggest you take someone along and have a look.'

'Thank you, Mr Brewster, depending on how much money he's asking, I'd be interested in looking.'

There was plenty to discuss on the Saturday night at Flaherty's dinner table. Dan told of the pending trip to Grafton. When he and Nell were alone, he told her of the suggested block that Brewsters felt could have potential to be their home.

'I don't know if we would have enough money,' Dan said, 'say we did, what do you think?'

'If it's what you want, well I wouldn't try to change your mind. Do you think I'd make a farmer's wife?'

'It could be hard work for a while, maybe a long while, but it would be ours. People like the O'Reillys and the Brewsters feel the land up on the mountain will grow anything once the scrub is cleared. Another thing I like about the idea is that we could be married much sooner if we have a shack.'

'Have a look at it,' Nell replied. 'It may not happen but maybe it will. Mum has made me start preparing a trousseau. I'm not much of a sewer but I'm fast improving and she's enjoying teaching me, although she says she doesn't know how she will manage when we are married. I think she would like me to stay here for a while.'

They sat close on the old sofa, the warm communion of proximity, inevitably fused their lips together. It was hard to break apart. Both knew their kisses were but a teasing prelude to the grabbing, growing need of their love. It was always a tough break when time to head to their individual beds.

Banking - To Grafton

Dan rode out of Ballina early Sunday morning. He and his horse were a familiar sight on the road up to Duck Creek Mountain. This early morning, they went on to the crossing near Lismore, then west toward Casino. Pat's instructions were to maintain a steady speed of about eight miles per hour. He had supplied a rough map, with main points of reference, and when he should reach them. Tom had lent him an old silver pocket watch that recorded time accurately enough for his purposes. The horse settled well to his task, at times on good stretches of the track Dan cantered him along, but mainly held him to a steady trot. They reached Casino almost on his given schedule. Dan sought out the hotel livery stable, purchased chaff for Chief and a quick lunch for himself. He only stayed long enough to give his horse a reasonable break and then was back to the track.

The sun was gone for the day by the time Dan and Chief left the forest behind and hit the well-used and defined road that swung along the river flats and open country into Grafton. It was still about fifteen miles to go. Had there been any doubt of Chief's ability to travel a hard day's work, the horse had answered it well. He was still able to trot at good speed and at no part of the long trip had he required pushing along. Darkness caught them an hour out of Grafton. Dan let the horse follow the road, sometimes at a careful trot but mostly at the good swinging walk with which Chief could lay behind five or six miles in an hour. The flickering lights of Grafton appeared in the distance and soon he was in the outskirts of a rapidly growing town. Dan found the Riverside Hotel, booked a room for himself and a box in the stable for Chief. He spent half an hour rubbing the horse dry, fed and watered him, then affectionately stroked the bold white blaze.

'Good lad, you did a great job for me. I'll come and check you out after I've had a bite.'

There was still plenty of activity in the bar of the Riverview but Dan headed to the kitchen area, where the cook, without complaint, knocked him up a meal of leftover vegies and cold mutton. After this meal was washed down with strong sweet tea, some of the stiffness and tiredness eased in his muscles.

'Was that all right?' the cook enquired. 'Most travellers aren't out so late. Where did you come from?'

'Ballina, through Casino, it's been a long day.'

'You must have a good nag, not many do it in a day.'

'Yes, we're both a bit new, but we made it. I'll check him out and then turn in for the night.'

The horse had finished most of his feed and seemed bright, so Dan gave him a pat, took his saddle bag with a change of clothes and went to his room.

It was one of a line of rooms facing the upstairs hallway. The single bed, dressing table and washstand stood on a pink flower-based linoleum, the latest in floor coverings. A burning candle and box of wax matches stood beside the big, flowered wash dish on the stand. He filled the dish with water from a matching jug, washed his face and hands, stripped and carried on with the job. He awoke next morning in the dull light of dawn wondering where he was. The stiffness in his joints soon supplied a clue as to activity of the previous day.

He dressed and made his way to the stables to check on Chief. The horse whinnied softly in greeting and in anticipation of his morning feed. Dan slipped the bridle on, led him out and around the yard and over to the water trough. His action was free and the horse seemed in perfect health, so he could now concentrate on the day ahead.

The hotel breakfast was oatmeal porridge, bacon and eggs, with plenty of toast. There were several travellers in the dining room: one a small, round, middle-aged Irishman with florid complexion. He quickly claimed Dan as a fellow countryman.

'And where would ye be from, me boyo?'

Dan acknowledged his roots in county Wicklow and conversation developed. Dan found it unnecessary to say much. Toby Flanagan, the well fleshed Irishman, had a gift for the gab. He was a spirits traveller, specialising in whiskey. His appearance indicated a warm liking for the good malt product. He visited the coastal ports on whatever ships supplied safe transport. Wherever there was a harbour on the east coast, Toby knew the publicans, and from his well fitted out sample case, took many orders. With increased numbers of permanent settlers, the hotels were starting to cater to a beer market rather than the more potent firewater of rum and whisky.

Toby could see a falling off of trade and was keeping his eye out for a good place to enter the hotel business. He lost no time in quizzing Dan on the prospects of Ballina, Lismore and Casino. He had stayed out of Ballina as a place of potential business; the bad reputation it had earned for its river bar caused Toby to give it a miss. Word of disaster always travelled fast and the Ballina river bar featured far too often with sad tales of shipwreck and loss of life.

At 10 a.m. exactly, Dan walked up the steps of the impressive Bank of NSW. He was determined to be the first customer of the morning. He gave his name and the nature of his business to the clerk behind the reception counter. A few minutes later, he was ushered in to the office of the manager, Mr Giles.

'Ah, Mr Riordan I'm pleased you could make the trip from Ballina. We may soon have a branch further up the coast, but for now we will look after your interests. I have the details of your accounts. Your own account is available once we verify your signature. The combined account with the deceased Mr Sheehan, requires a statutory declaration and a copy of Mr Sheehan's death certificate.'

Dan brought out his letter from Jim Brewster as proof of identity and provided a specimen signature, which Mr Giles accepted, the same as the one forwarded from Sydney. A statutory declaration was signed and Dan supplied the bank with an address for Sean's mother back in County Wicklow. The account contained a little over 200 pounds and, in his own account, 67 pounds.

He was given a cheque book but told he could not operate off his share of the joint account until the bank had authority to split the amount. It may take a couple of months. Dan explained he was interested in purchasing a farming block, that he was getting married, and asked the manager whether the bank would consider making a loan against his joint account should he find a property that suited.

'We would need to know what you proposed Mr Riordan, but I would feel that a loan of up to 110 pounds would be possible.'

With true managerial caution, Mr Giles warned that many who attempted farming ventures had failed but he expected with better communications, the outlook for the North Coast would be better for careful farmers.

By 11 o'clock, their business complete, Dan walked back to the Riverview Hotel. The cook knocked him up a few sandwiches. He paid his account, changed back to his soiled riding gear, saddled Chief and started the long trip home. Buttocks and thigh muscles protested, at first, to the feel of the saddle but after a while the saddle soreness numbed out and he settled into the rhythm of the horse. It was a bit like being a sailor and acquiring that balance called "sea legs". It was close to dark when they reached Casino.

Once there, Dan booked a room for the night. A stable and feed for Chief, then after use of the hotel facilities he decided to check whether Reverend Martin Baillie was in town. The barman looked a trifle surprised to have a fit young traveller looking for a clergyman. Travellers were far more likely to have a different list of wants when they hit town, unrelated to the spiritual.

'He's not one of my customers,' the barman said, 'but I saw him ride up the street today. A fair chance he's in. He's the little corner house two blocks down, old demon Dorah his housekeeper will know his whereabouts, if he's away.'

'I'm obliged to you. Thanks.'

Dan set off before darkness really set in. The house was a small shabby cottage but was distinctive from the other shanties through the neat front garden. A rose bush grew there and it carried a sweet-scented red flower. There were also a couple of white and pink geraniums, and some healthy flowering purple petunias. Flower gardens were not high on the priority list of Casino residents. Most had little time for flowers. Vegetables were a more acceptable use of gardening energy; these could be eaten.

There was a light inside. The front door had a heavy brass

knocker. Dan gave a few taps on its metal plate and waited. The door was opened by a tall, dark-haired lady who fixed him with a stern stare. Daniel addressed her with his most polite voice.

'Good evening, would Reverend Baillie be at home?'

'Yes, he is having dinner. Who will I say wishes to see him?'

'Daniel Riordan, but I do not want to interrupt his dinner. Please say I will wait until he is free. I am not in any hurry.'

The housekeeper went with the message. A few seconds later, Martin came to the door.

'Come inside Daniel, I eat in the kitchen, you are welcome to join me. Mrs Phipps will set a place for you if you haven't eaten.'

'Thank you, Reverend Baillie. I am staying overnight at the hotel and I had a bite to eat before looking for you.'

Dan occupied a chair at the end of the table. He told Martin some of the Ballina happenings. That he had a fencing job for the Brewsters, that he was on the way back from his business trip to Grafton, and then the big news that he and Nell would marry sometime in the near future.

'Congratulations Daniel, I am sure Nell will make you an excellent wife,' Martin beamed.

'Well, we would like to find a block of ground. Jim Brewster has suggested I look at one with a shack and some clearing. If that works out, we will probably marry, soon as practical. If there is no Catholic priest available, I wondered whether you would marry us?'

A clergyman learns to be non-committal and answer carefully.

'As you are both Catholics and seem to practise your faith, I would like to see a priest marry you. If you can't arrange a time with a visiting priest, yes, I would be happy to marry you, if Nell and her mother approve. You could always renew vows later with a Catholic wedding ceremony. I perform weddings for all faiths if asked. It is better for a couple to be married for their children.'

'Thank you, Reverend Martin. I 'll be in touch and let you know our intentions.'

They chatted a while, shook hands, and Daniel walked back to the hotel. He declined the offer of a drink at the bar. He was tired and welcomed the idea of an early night in bed. He planned to be on the road early the next morning and back to Brewsters in time to do some fencing. He found his way to the small dingy room and turned in for the night. It had been another big day; he hoped it turned out to be a successful one. The access to a little money gave some chance of securing a block of land. It all helped bring Nell and marriage attainably close.

Land Inspection

The next couple of weeks saw good progress on the fencing. Even Pat O'Reilly was impressed at the way Dan was now fitting the rails to the mortices and the very neat job that was transforming the Brewster place to a potential farm. They had talked about the Hilardt block and Pat agreed to go with him to look it over when he had a free day from carrying. That was not often, for the carrying business was rapidly expanding. The job with the mill engine had brought other big jobs and Pat had mentioned to Bridget that it probably would pay for them to have someone driving the cart, while he did heavy jobs with the wagon.

Persistent rain for a couple of days made the opportunity to go farm sightseeing. The roads to Wardell and Ballina were a mess: Pat reckoned he would let things dry before a trip to either place. He arrived at the Brewsters after breakfast and suggested he was willing to ride in the rain if Dan thought it a chance to look at the Hilardt block.

'Yes, thanks it's almost too wet for fencing. I'll tell Mr Brewster. Give me half an hour, I'll saddle Chief and come up to your place.'

Chief was wet and cold. He hadn't been saddled for a few days and snorted his disapproval as the girth pulled in on his wet hide. Dan led him around the small yard, until he moved more freely. He held him in firmly on the nearside rein, toe into the stirrup and up onto the small saddle, as softly as possible. Chief made a grab for the bit and hunched forward in an attempt to buck. Fortunately for Dan his tight hold on the nearside rein kept the horse coming in under him. He was able to keep control, and after a couple of circuits of the yard, Chief decided to walk away. It was fact that since his big trip to Grafton, Dan had been throwing a little more corn into Chief's ration. He made a mental note to cut back on the grain.

Pat met him at the gate of Killarney. Shamrock too was a bit skittish with the cool wet morning. Both horses danced along a while and then decided to settle down.

'That bloke will try you out on that pad if he gets his head down,' Pat nodded at Chief. 'You've got him in good condition. The trip to Grafton certainly tightened him up.'

'Yes, a bit less grain from now on,' replied Dan, 'I reckoned he was under control but now I'm not so sure.'

'He's a good mover, and a good horse. but watch him, he knows how to buck and they never forget.'

They covered the couple of miles fairly quickly. The Hilardt block was 60 acres with much of it on a favourable nor' east slope. A creek ran through a deep, stony gully and another slope climbed away to the west. The slopes had a few clear areas, probably no more than ten acres in all had been felled on the block and even that was in urgent need of more work on the regrowth.

A bridle track led in from the surveyed lane, over a gentle rise and down to the slab one room shack. Smoke rose from the tin fireplace attached to the back of the shack; it appeared Dick Hilardt was home. A nondescript black dog on a long chain, barked loudly to announce their approach. The front of the dwelling boasted a door opening onto a rough slab ground level veranda. Two small glass-paned windows appeared like a pair of beady eyes trying to grab a little light, for what had to be a dark room. The little shack had in its favour the fact it looked to the northeast; it stood a chance of bargaining for the morning sunlight. Today there was no sunlight. Water trickled down and along the slab veranda. Not an inspiring house, but better than some that settlers had built to supply their basic needs.

By the time Pat and Dan reined up at the door, Blackie, the barking hound had alerted his master to the unusual reality of visitors.

'Aw, shut up Blackie. Pat's all right.'

'Good mornin' Dick. Not much of a day, too wet to work. We reckoned we might find you and we rode across on the chance. This is Dan Riordan, he's fencing at Brewsters. He heard you were interested in selling and he's looking for a block.'

'Pleased to know you Dan.'

They shook hands.

'Come in, it's a bit smoky but the fire keeps it warm and dry.'

They tethered the horses away from Blackie, threw their oilskins over the saddles, and followed Dick inside. The room boasted a bed, a chair, a table and a small chest of drawers. The floor was split teak planks and a few used corn bags supplied a track between the most used sections.

Half a bottle of rum, a bottle of water and a cup sat on the table.

'It's not a palace. Sit on the bed. I'll get you a drink.'

'Well only one Dick, to be sociable. Thanks.'

Dick went to the chest of drawers and came back with a couple of chipped cups. He poured generous measures of rum, took the cups and the bottle of water over to his visitors.

'Break it down how you want,' he said to his visitors.

They tipped in about the same amount of water. Dick poured a dose of the potent amber liquid in his cup.

'Here's luck. May we all be rich.'

'Here's luck.'

They downed their drinks. The rum exploded out from their stomach veins and burned out the chill of the morning. Dick Hilardt addressed his visitors. He was almost apologetic for his lack of clearing action on the block.

'The appeal of being a squatter seemed good, but I've gone a bit sour on the idea,' he said leaning forward in his chair. 'When I took up this block four years ago, I reckoned I'd soon have it cleared and make heaps of money. Well to date, I've made heaps of blisters, but no money. The farming types tell me it's a good block, but I'm better at pen pushing than scrub falling. I've chipped in a couple of maize crops, the birds and pademelons did well. Those greedy blighters refused to leave me even a share.'

Dan smiled at him.

'How much money do you want to get out Dick? There's no use me wasting our time if the price is too much for me.'

'Alright Dan, my price is 180 pounds,' said Dick, 'I'd throw in the tools and furniture.'

Dan was interested. It could be within his limited means.

'We have come, Pat is my advisor, so we would like to have a look around.'

The rain had eased to a misty drizzle. Both the earth and the trees were loaded with water. They put on the oilskins and set off on foot.

'The best idea for you is probably to see the four boundary pegs,' said Dick. 'We'll go to about the middle and slog out to the southern corner. I have blazed a track around the edges, but it's a while since I've been around. It could be an idea if we take a brush hook each. Do you still want to have a look?'

'Yes, I'm game. What about it Pat?' asked Dan. 'Seems a bit tough on you.'

'We came to have a look, let's go. Don't forget I tramped a lot of scrub when I was chasing cedar.'

They set off down a track past a couple of clearings. Some maize stubble remained as forlorn brown sentinels in the part burnt timber. Pat used the brush hook to dig down into the damp red soil. It came up rich and friable. A couple of Wonga pigeons foraging for a grain or two remaining from the picked crop, took off with a whirr of wings back to the shelter of their dense scrub home. Dick remarked,

'They are good eating, those fellers. They know not to hang around when I've got the old twelve gauge.'

They crossed the creek, by walking over a beech log fallen across the narrow rocky waterway. The thirty or forty yards of creek bank where it had been cleared was a dense green wall of wild tobacco and lantana. A southern gardener some years before had brought in the lantana as a hedge plant. The birds spread the seed and it had grown on cleared scrub ground with gay abandon.

In a few short years, this prickly pink flowering invader raced up the coast, keeping pace with the clearing of land. So rapidly did it grow in the rich scrub soil, that Dick Hilardt's track up from the creek was almost swallowed from sight. They brushed their way through, entered the dank shelter of the scrub and headed south.

Their progress was slow, but the track was not completely swallowed and, in most places, was still findable. When in doubt, blaze marks on the trees guided them through the lawyer vine and ground cover. Where only subdued light filtered through the thick overhead canopy, little grew at ground level except ferns, lichens and mosses. The 15 chain walk through to the corner took about half an hour. Their brush hooks were ever handy to clear gaps in the prickly "wait awhile" vine. Blood seeped from their scratches. They despatched the leeches that fed on their legs and these attachment points also continued to seep blood. Half an hour of walking through genuine scrub and any walker was sure to be a bloodied casualty.

'How about it, Dan, do you reckon you should go back to sea?' Pat's question was asked with a laugh, but he knew the first venture into the reality of the rain forest could be a sobering experience.

'Well, we came to look. I'm not sure what I should be looking for, but it's different to County Wicklow.' Turning to Dick, Dan asked, 'What's the track like from here on?

'That's the worst of it done. We can go across into Johnson's. That has been cleared, and we follow the long boundary back to the north. You can see how the land looks when it's cleared and my block is much the same.'

Dick found the survey peg and pointed out a double blazed tree nearby as a marker for the peg. They walked out onto the Johnson block and followed the approximate line of cleared land. On their right, the high climbing green canopy of Big Scrub rain forest gave a dramatic picture of difference.

The walk was mainly along a ridge, across the stony creek and up another ridge to the northern corner. Much of the Johnson block was felled with large patches of burnt timber. Some areas of maize were still standing awaiting picking, and a constant traffic of birds arose from their feast on the ripening crop. It was easy to see why settlers were constantly looking for crops less prone to attack than the golden maize. The birds of the rain forest now had a new culinary delight. White and black cockatoos, the parrots, many varieties of pigeons, the black crows, all joined in the onslaught. The farmer could build "scarecrows", shoot the odd victim, curse in Irish, Scots, English or Hindi. The result was the same, half the crop went for bird food. Dick remarked,

'Old Johnno is a good farmer; he is talking about sugar cane to anyone who will listen. He reckons that this country will be great for that crop. At least the bloody birds wouldn't eat it. How you make sugar I have no idea, but he's been talking to a planter from the West Indies. Maybe it is a real hope.'

From the north peg they headed back along another scrub track to the east. The going was better with some forest vegetation, a patch of eucalypt hardwood and open patches of native "kangaroo" grass. Pademelons and wallabies hopped away out of the showery morning to what they considered a safe distance before staring at the intruders.

It was 3 p.m. when they arrived back at the shack. They accepted Dick's offer of a cup of tea but said a firm "no" to another slug of the potent rum. The fire was kindled, catching quickly from the warm embers. A black billy soon boiled, and hot strong, straight tea was washed down with some rock-hard damper and honey. Certainly not afternoon tea of the Brewster's quality, but welcome after their long tough tramp.

Dick Hilardt was no high-pressure salesman.

'Well, what do you think Daniel? It's hard work. I surely would not try and talk you into it. I'm afraid I was a bit of a disappointment as a farmer. Maybe if the lass you are going to marry has a liking for the life, you could do all right.'

Daniel looked at the block owner.

'Yes, I'm interested. But I'd want Nell to see what she was in for if we took it on as our home. I've also got to be sure that we are able to pay you out. How long before you need an answer?'

'I would like to head back to the city within a month. Once you make up your mind, I don't mind waiting a little while for the money.'

They left the situation there, mounted and headed for home. The horses were glad to be untethered and on the track. Even the well-mannered Shamrock was keen to match strides with the more fiery Chief. After a brisk half mile canter the horses settled to a good striding walk.

The inevitable question was asked: Pat fired it with a smile.

'What do you think Dan? Reckon you could handle it?'

'I'm not sure, Pat. It looked all right to me. I'd like Nell to see the problems. It would be tough for quite a while. What do you think, would we be silly to try it?'

'I think the land is good,' Pat replied. 'The creek looks permanent and would give you water. Clearing is a big task. I still have the hardest pockets left at Killarney, hopefully I'll finish someday. If you and Nell decide to try, the people around here would welcome you; we want young people. You seem pretty capable to me and I know Nell knows how to work.'

They parted at the gate to Killarney and Dan cantered down the track to Brewsters. He hoped to be back at his fencing on the morrow.

School Plans

The meeting to discuss the need for a school and how to make it happen came to order at 2.30 p.m. on that momentous Sunday afternoon. It was a clear winter's day. A westerly breeze gave a nip in the air and shunted the odd scudding feathery cloud towards the coast. Norah Brewster and Bridget O'Reilly went into action after early Sunday lunch, making finishing touches to the preparation. They hoped there was seating for all, chairs, stools, anything to serve as a seat was placed in position on the big north facing veranda. The afternoon tea to follow the meeting was in readiness. It remained to see how many, and who would arrive to swell the forum.

From 1.30 p.m. onwards they arrived. Couples mainly in sulkies; the only buggy, a flash affair recently arrived from Sydney, brought Laura and Rupert James. The hotel was left for the afternoon in the hands of Kate, their capable barmaid to look after any travellers.

There were some women mounted side saddle who accompanied their husbands. There was the entire Cooper family: mum, dad and six children in the farm cart. They lived down on top of the Meerschaum cutting and at the steady pace of Ned their draught horse they were about two and a half hours away.

Pat O'Reilly and Dan Riordan were kept busy finding safe tethering for the horses. By meeting start time, 25 adults and almost as many children had arrived. It was a rewarding gathering of interested people. Any concerns that the settlers were too busy to worry about education for their children, could be cast aside.

Jim Brewster called the gathering to order. He was the popular choice for chairman of the meeting. Dick Hilardt, although leaving soon, was urged to the job of minute secretary for the occasion. He was known as a neat legible writer who often helped with letters for those around who had trouble reading or writing.

Jim grabbed the attention of those who had come with their desire to see education for their children. It was an immediate need. He launched into his task.

'It is very pleasing for Norah and myself to welcome so many interested people,' he started. 'We know that schools must come to this fast-developing location, but how long will it take? There are many children here today who must have the opportunity to learn without further delay. Our idea is that we supply timber and build a school and then we would be in a stronger position to approach the government for a subsidised teacher. This meeting is to hear ideas and take the names of those prepared to help. We could make a list of children who should be going to school now, to confirm that numbers are truly available. This meeting is to hear your thoughts.'

Those thoughts from the gathering came slowly at first; many shy to stand and speak at a public meeting. Then it gained momentum with the common bond of these people and their children. It was decided to form a building committee and a finance committee. Pat O'Reilly was to be chairman of the building committee and Rupert James, boss of the finance committee. These were to report back at another meeting in a month's time.

In an hour, the official meeting was over and the big veranda hosted the afternoon tea. Here the talk and the food flowed freely. Those reluctant to speak to a meeting showed little worry in airing their ideas over a cup of tea. Some of those ideas promised a chance of raising money from a community with little spare cash once the food bills were paid. They could hold a concert here at the Brewsters, they could grow a crop for the school funds, they could hold a sports day, with foot running, jumping, horse racing if a two- or three-furlong track of reasonably level ground was found. The ideas bubbled forth and the group had a common cause. People of very different abilities and backgrounds were happy to work for the hope of educating their children. The gathering broke up with insufficient daylight left for most of the far travellers. Many would not reach home until long after dark, but at least they would be helped by a growing moon and a clear night.

The Brewsters, the O'Reillys, the James, Dick Hilardt, Rev. Martin Baillie and Dan Riordan lingered on the Brewster veranda. Shafts of sunlight still fingered through the western tree lined hills. They declared the day a great success. A start had been made, it was up to the community to pitch in and make it work. It seemed there was strong hope, they were confident a school would rise to give basic opportunity to the children of settlers who had decided to tame this Big Scrub plateau. Most of those settlers came with differing agendas but cherished a common hope for their children.

Riordans for Tara

Nell and Dan had talked long and deeply about purchasing the Hilardt block. Dan's savings from his sailing days would almost purchase the land, but to improve it and build a house, the money would have to come from what could be earned, or a bank loan against the land.

The only way for Nell to look at the proposition was by horse. Dan had booked Brownie's quiet hack for a weekend. Bridget O'Reilly had welcomed the idea of a bed overnight for Nell and a chance to have a chat with the lass who seemed destined to be their future neighbour.

Early on the Saturday morning they arrived at the stable. Nell fitted out in her brother's old corduroy trousers and boots along with a change of clothes packed in Dan's saddle bag. Brownie surveyed the slim girl under the straw hat and grinned at her.

'Well, old Snowy will think it's Christmas carrying you,' he laughed. 'His last job was a fat commercial traveller. He must have weighed as much as a couple of bags of spuds. I do have an old side saddle but I reckon the way you be togged up lass, you would be better on him astride.'

'I'm not much of a rider Mr Brown. I'd be better astride and Dan says I'll be fine.'

'Sure lass, you and Snowy will be fine.' Brownie turned to Dan. 'You keep that fidgety show off of yours to a walk and don't forget it be a long ride for the lass who do na ken a lot about riding. Put her down to walk occasionally and take your time.'

So, Nell was legged up on Snowy and they rode out of Ballina. It was a morning with plenty of cloud out over the sea, but the offshore westerly breeze could keep it fine with a bit of luck.

They made reasonable time as the old grey Snowy made a good effort to keep up with Chief. The chestnut resented being held to a walk, and insisted on a shuffling dance every so often, which made the task of keeping up easier for Snowy. Nell settled to the rhythm of riding, enjoying the adventure.

Dan encouraged her. 'You're doing fine.'

Dick Hilardt and Darkie weren't home but the Riordans peered inside his humble dwelling. They walked hand in hand around some of the tracks and took their shoes off to test the clear running stream.

'If it's what you want, I'll work with you, and we'll make it. Why back in Ireland we'd be toffs with all this land.' Nell was excited.

'Maybe Nell, maybe. I reckon a lot of the lads from back home would take a look at the vines, leeches, jumper ants, snakes, and they wouldn't wait for a boat. They'd start swimming for home.' Dan put his arm around Nell. 'If you be game, I am, at least I've learned to build fences. I guess I'll learn to fall scrub and in time we may make a farm out of it.'

'Right, we can tidy up the shack and wait a while before we try and build something better. That way we do not need as much money. Our farm has to have a name, so what will you call it?' Nell fired the question at Dan.

'That can be your task. Most of the blocks seem to have impressive names.'

'Well, what say we call it Tara?'

And Tara it became.

Clearing Land

The decision made, they rode back to the O'Reilly home. Bridget and the children took Nell in charge. Pat and Dan strolled off to look at Pat's latest clearing efforts, and Pat described how at times in heavy belts of trees, you could make nature and sloping land work for you.

The idea was to work to the side of the prevailing wind on a downhill slope. The outside trees were cut through to the point of balance but not fallen. Then the same was done with all the large trees down the slope. It was a case of waiting until a strong wind blew and the partly cut outside trees fell and hopefully started a rolling, falling momentum aided by the slope. This could end with a crazy, crashing tangled mess of fallen giants.

They dragged down in their death throes a maze of vine and orchids, part of the living canopy. On the floor, fern, lichen and moss turned quickly brown in death from a flood of new light. Then it was a case of waiting for some drying out of fallen timber. When heat and wind were right, during a dry period, a wall of fire would clear much of the dead material from the land. It was a wasteful method aimed at rapid clearing of the land so that pasture or crops could be grown.

Pat had a slope prepared and was waiting for the strong autumn southerlies. Yet he had a doubt about the method,

'You know Dan, I don't like murdering trees but what else can we do? Back in the days I chased cedar. That was bad enough, but block clearing is worse. We wipe out a beauty that will never return. Our farming instincts want to see clear paddocks of crops or green grass and we stop at nothing to achieve that end. We don't even use a fraction of the timber other than to turn it into ash. I wonder as I plod along the tracks between the scrub stands, how long before it is all gone? Most of the settlers think it will take forever. I've seen enough change in a few years to know it won't be long.'

The two men talked, smoked, looked at the browning, dying stand of timber, then they made a leisurely stroll back to Killarney cottage.

Marriage - Plans Awry

A date for the wedding was set several months in the future. Nell worked toward collecting necessities for the shack and Dan took fencing jobs up on the plateau. Of a weekend Dan made the trip to Ballina and their plans for a future life were made. It was a busy, but happy time.

Nell continued her evening strolls along the river sand flats. She knew these tidal flats as people brought up in towns knew the paved streets. It was her safety valve at the end of a busy day. Always there was the soft swish of the tide swelling or ebbing, lending a soft sound accompaniment to the muted prattle of birds still working the spits. Gulls, snipe, oyster catchers distinctive with their signature chatter. At times when the tide was low, colonies of soldier crabs made their own whispered, grating, grinding song as countless busy nippers augured down into the hard sandy flats. Each temporary residence left a minute raised pattern mound that would be planed smooth by the returning tide.

Carmel was usually still up when Nell returned to the cottage. Several times she brought up the subject of a girl alone out walking the lonely river flats at night.

'I'm not happy about it,' said Carmel.

'Ah Mum, I'm fine. I've been on the banks and flats forever. I never see anybody and no one knows I am there, except maybe some of the net fishermen on the river.'

'Well, me girl, I'm not so sure. Anyway, you'll soon be making a home for yourself with Dan. Just you be careful.'

It was a black, moonless night with a strong breeze gusting across the river from the south when things went so terribly wrong. Nell was clambering up the shelf from the spit to the grassy bank after her walk when a strong, unseen arm grabbed her from behind. Another form emerged from the shelter offered by the low natural ledge. The first arm produced a rough hand that went over her mouth, while the other attacker grabbed her around the waist, seized her free arm, twisting it cruelly up behind her back.

Nell kicked back strongly with a free foot, making contact with a soft part of the attacker behind. It brought a strange, muffled foreign oath from the unseen tormentor, his grip tightened over her mouth. She bit in terror and defence. The attacker behind cruelly jerked her arm. The other masked assailant pressed the point of a knife to her throat.

'Shut up. We'll have what we want, give it quietly, or you're dead,' he hissed at her.

Her hands were bound behind her back with thin rope and she was thrown roughly to the ground. A gag was thrust in her mouth to stop her screams. Her dress thrown upwards over her head, still kicking she felt undergarments ripped from her legs.

The attack that followed was a continuing nightmare of pain and terror. Mercifully, she blacked out at times, prayed that they would kill her quickly and then it would all be over.

Then they were gone. The sounds of the night filtered back. With her consciousness, came over-powering pain, shame and terror. Cold shock set in and a fierce shivering gripped her body. There was a mental and physical numbness that preceded the waves of real pain and anguish that tore her apart. These were her immediate companions. The hastily applied gag had come loose and she was able to spit out the rough cloth. Her arms still firmly tied behind her back made the immediate task of standing a difficult assignment. In the haste of their brutality, they had ripped off and thrown away her undergarments, but her skirt gave her cover and some protection. Eventually, she was able to stand and shuffle homewards in an unbelieving nightmare daze.

Only the pain in her body created reality to the situation. It was in a stupor of deep shock that she reached the cottage and kicked against the front door.

'Mother of God!' was all Carmel said as she folded the tortured waif in her arms and brought her inside. She led her to a bed, brought a sharp knife and severed the thin hemp cord that bit into thin blue, white wrists, now totally devoid of feeling. Those wrists would soon burst into new pain as blood flowed through the restricted veins. Gently, Carmel laid her on the clean sheets and piled on blankets trying to bring warmth as a first balm of healing to a battered, shock-drained body.

Carmel filled whiskey bottles with hot water from the big black kettle on the stove. These she placed around the whimpering girl.

'Don't be in a hurry to talk. You are all right now. We'll talk when the shock wears off a little. For now, get warm. I've sent Jim to see whether Doc Mason is home.'

Doc Mason arrived in half an hour, not pleased to leave a warm bed. He had spent the previous night on a difficult birth and felt he deserved a night without disturbance. He knew from experience a bush doctor was never sure of sleep. Any thought of annoyance immediately left the doctor on viewing his young patient. He had watched Nell grow from childhood to a pretty, young woman and this ashen-faced woman child was not the Nell he knew.

'We had best have a look at you lass,' was all he said.

Some hours later he had given her a strong sedative that was taking affect. He had gently bathed and examined her bleeding body. After a while, she had dragged out a rough, broken story outline of the attack. She knew little, other than they were two in number. Initial shock was replaced by healthy weeping and indignation.

The doctor motioned Carmel to the kitchen and sat across the table from her on a chair with the fire at his back.

'Carmel, it's a sad happening,' he said in a serious tone. 'She's a sensible girl and will be all right in time. However, it will leave her mentally scarred, long after her body has recovered, but I am confident she has your toughness. She will recover. The villains that did this could quite easily have killed her. I'll see Constable Quinlan and I suppose he will need to ask her questions. There is little chance he will find the attackers - my bet is sailors off one of the ships here at present.'

'I should have been firmer that she not go wandering at night,' said Carmel.

'What's done is done. Just give her all your support. In some ways it is probably best for her that it doesn't become a widely known three-day wonder. I'll wake up Quinlan when I leave here. He may as well lose some sleep too, but it will be hard to find the attackers.'

Doc Mason went his way. Carmel sat through the long night at the bedside changing hot water bottles while the drugged girl slept in a nightmare-plagued, disturbed, shuddering sleep.

Constable Quinlan arrived before lunch the next day. He kept his questions to the minimum and took away the thin tying rope. His enquiries revealed two ships had made use of the full dawn tide to work out through the bar. Like the doc, he felt this was the most likely source of attack. He promised to send a report to Sydney where both traders were headed. The dock police would make enquiries at that end and he hoped something may give a lead when he had a word with the local net fishermen. He knew it would be a long shot. Like Doc Mason he was relieved that Nell was alive to tell of the attack.

Carmel decided that Dan must be told.

Tom O'Rourke hired a horse from Brownie and headed for the plateau. His task was to find Dan and deliver a brief note from Carmel. A note that asked Dan to make the trip to Ballina- she gave him no reasons.

Tom knew the sorry story; he and Carmel had talked long on the likely outcomes. Their decision was for him to deliver the note and leave the talking for when Dan reached Ballina. Dan read the note and tried to prise the problem from Tom, anxious but not offensively demanding as to why. He accepted the answer would only be his when Ballina was reached. Daniel accepted he must wait until then.

'You head for home; I'll clean up quickly and catch you up on the way.'

He rode back to his camp. Sluiced a bucket of creek water over his sweaty body, changed clothes, dropped a brief note in the Killarney box as he passed, and gave the chestnut free rein for Ballina.

It was past sundown when well down from the cutting he caught up with Tom. The hired horse was heading out well for home, knowing a full feed bin would be waiting.

'Don't wait for me,' said Tom, 'this old bloke couldn't pace it with that dynamo. We'll take our time and I should get him back to Brownie soon after dark. See you soon.'

Dan continued on at a long, sweeping, mile-eating canter.

There was still light in the west when he reigned up at the Flaherty cottage fence. Carmel greeted him at the gate.

'Hello Dan, it's real sorry I am to call you. It's best you talk with Nell, then we'll all talk. Young Jim will look after your horse. He'll cool him down and feed him. He knows what to do.'

Dan was shocked to see Nell's pale, listless face. Her usually bright eyes were sunken and red from too many tears. He put an arm around her and felt the pent-up spring steel tension that seemed in control of her normally warm, relaxed body. The ever-practical Carmel aimed them to the bedroom door.

'Go and talk in your bedroom. We'll have supper later.'

It took time for the story to emerge. Dan just sat and held her weeping body and let the tears wash out some of the tension. He passed no comments, asked no questions and eventually took the clean towel from the back of the iron bed to gently restore a little order to the fear wracked face.

'Nell, I love you,' he assured her. 'We will marry straight away and look after each other. Your fears don't matter, it will be fine. You're alive lass. Many I've known, no older than me, are dead. Together, in time we will drive that nightmare away.'

When they returned to the kitchen, Carmel's food smelt good. Tom and

Jim had dined and tactfully left the room. The stew that bubbled in the big, black pot on the stove was a mixture of beef suet, praties, pumpkin and some garden grown spinach greens thrown in. A scent to lift the nostrils of any Irish born who had lived through long years of famine.

Carmel stole a glance at the pair. She felt easier with what she saw. Nell still looked like a wrung-out dish rag but she obviously took comfort from the strong arm around her shoulders. Dan, sombre and grim, but calm with wisdom taught by many an unexpected crisis. There looked a unified strength in the pair that made Carmel breathe a silent prayer of thanks.

'Sit you down, and I expect you both to eat,' she said in her practical way. 'Nell has had nothing for 24 hours and you, Dan, have ridden long after a hard day's work. First you both eat and then we'll talk if you like.'

Carmel ladled out the stew, onto big strong plates. There was bread of Carmel's baking, in hewed slices, giving that yeasty invitation, common to home cooked bread in any situation.

Nell only spooned the food to start with, but the comfort of Dan sitting against her, and hunger, won the battle over shock. The warmth of the familiar old black stove flickered across the room and spoke normality. Eventually she relaxed and ate well.

Dan broke the silence.

'I've told Nell, we'll marry soon as we can find a priest. We'll be fine. That hurt and fear will take some wiping away, but we'll make it. It's best we get started with our lives, and let the past be just a bad memory.'

Carmel looked carefully at the young man across the table.

'You be sure Daniel that this is a pill you can swallow. It's not something you should have to wear; marriage can have problems enough without this one.'

Dan answered Carmel's steady gaze with his calm, blue eyes and a slow nod of the head. He put an arm around Nell and gently held her.

'Nell you be a lucky girl,' said Carmel. 'Can you rise above this and be the wife to Daniel, that he deserves?'

Nell, when she spoke, was calm.

'If he still wants me for a wife, then I'll do all I can to make him happy.'

The trauma shock was beginning to fade and maturity inherited from generations of trial by violence, emerged as a moth from its tight cocoon. Nell was prepared to look to the future.

They talked late into the night.

Early the next morning Dan returned to the mountain and his fencing job. Once that job was complete, he would spend time on the block and make the shack more liveable. It would require timber from Brown's mill. He knew Pat would cart it as a back load, and maybe throw in some practical building advice.

The prospect of a Catholic priest paying a visit to Ballina, or the Duck Creek Mountain area, was not good. Armidale, up on the high country, separated by the Great Dividing Range and several hundred miles, was the closest home base of a priest in NSW. Across the border, Ipswich in Queensland was a closer source, and the more likely chance of a priest dropping in on the Northern Rivers of NSW. The frequency of access to clergy was a worry to practising Roman Catholics. People died, were born, wanted to marry and often made the most expedient arrangement possible. Death and burial waited for no one. Any clergy person was better than none, and many were given Christian burial, by the most appropriate person available. Burial prayers were common to all.

Then babies requiring baptism, arrived without permission. It was not unusual for the parents' marriage to take place in conjunction with baptism of a child or two. This was often performed in bush huts. Settlers and clergy had to be spiritually resourceful. Life went on, with or without church buildings or trappings of clergy.

Weeks went by. Nell worked toward collecting linen for the house. She was now a very capable sewer, with Carmel's help the basic needs came together. By throwing herself into the wedding preparation she was able to cast aside some of her nightmares caused by the assault. Doc Mason had kept in touch and pronounced her to be physically healed; he assured her of no lasting damage. He warned there could be hidden mental scars.

Constable Quinlan had no success in picking up information about the attack. His report forwarded to the Sydney Harbour police had drawn no result. Crews of two departing boats out of Ballina, denied any knowledge or involvement. He assured Carmel and Nell that he was still listening on the local scene but had no worthwhile lead. He felt sure the assailants were not local.

Nell and Daniel

There was no predicted early visit by a Catholic priest for the area, nor any rumour of a pending visit.

When Martin Baillie arrived in Ballina for a couple of weddings, he intended to drop in on Carmel and check how things were going with Dan. He knew of the betrothal through Dan's Casino visit and felt confidence the couple would make a good life together. Dan had not mentioned to Carmel his sounding out of Martin as to whether he would marry them if no priest arrived.

The thought stirred in Carmel's active mind, that maybe Martin could be the one to marry them. Who knew when a Catholic priest would drift in on a visit? The preparations were at a stage that there was no practical reason for delaying the wedding.

Upon hearing that Reverend Baillie was in Ballina, a round table conference decided to track him down. Dan and Nell found where he was staying and put the proposition to him. He was willing to perform a ceremony but it required their being prepared to marry within the next two days, as that was the extent of his stay in Ballina. It meant feverish preparations.

A time was set for Saturday at 4 p.m. Only close friends would be invited, and with lack of time for invitations, it would probably be just family. The ceremony would be in Carmel's parlour come dining room with supper to follow. Dan decided to ride back to the plateau and see whether Pat and Bridget would drop everything and come. They knew the couple were planning to marry when a priest was available. The change of plan to make use of Martin would not perturb them.

It was nearly tea time when Dan reined up at Killarney. He gave Pat and Bridget the news. They hid their surprise and asked no questions. Bridget placed a hand on Dan's arm.

'You've ridden up here when you are very short of time to ask us. Provided the Brewsters will take care of the children we will be delighted to come. It will be great to have Nell living close by as a neighbour.'

Pat smiled at Dan.

'You have a wash and talk to Bridget. I'll trot that chestnut of yours up to Brewsters and see whether they can help us out, then we'll know for sure.'

Norah Brewster was always offering to look after the children, but Pat and Bridget had no need of babysitters as they seldom left Killarney together. This sudden request delighted the well organised Nora, who was confident the children knew her well enough to be happy in her care.

'Of course, of course we will look after them.' She gave her assurances to Pat.

'Our guest room never has guests, so it will be wonderful to have the children. Mary knows me well enough to be at ease here and will help keep Thomas happy if he becomes lonely. Why it's wonderful news, go and enjoy the wedding. We will find a present for them and welcome them as part of our community.'

Pat was back at Killarney in half an hour. He took Chief around to the stable and fed him hay and chaff before heading inside for his own tea.

'It's all arranged,' he announced.

'Norah will have a great time spoiling Thomas,' said Bridget. 'Mary, you see he behaves himself.'

The evening meal was a happy occasion. The children knew and liked Dan and told of the many adventures that only children enjoy. Bridget and Pat sensed there was something out of the ordinary in the hasty wedding, but they were happy for the chance to welcome their new young neighbours. Pat already had a plan brewing in his head to offer Dan part-time work in the expanding carrying business. Reliable horsemen were not readily available.

Dan headed back to Ballina in the moonlight. Many nights at sea on watch gave him a capacity for being part of any environment. The Duck Creek Mountain track, stroked by moonbeam fingers reaching through the tall trees, reminded him of ship trails on lonely oceans. Those vigil nights on watch his only companion, the whispering feathered wake that murmured a tune of ocean space. Here on the timber shrouded track dwelt a similar quality of being part of suspended time. Then a nocturnal pademelon thumped a tune in the bush and the spell was broken. Once down the cutting and out in the clear moonlight, he gave Chief rein and the chestnut, keen to be home, settled into his mile-eating canter that eased over the ground.

Saturday, 4 p.m. saw the wedding guests assembled. Tom O'Rourke gave away the bride, Pat and Bridget were her attendants. These, plus a few of Carmel's friends, squeezed into the scrubbed flower-decked parlour. The Reverend Martin Baillie commenced the ceremony. It was a simple service that committed two young people to face life as man and wife. The tough experience of hurt and trauma that Nell carried was known to few. They prayed that she and Dan would overcome this worrying start to a marriage that already would be difficult.

Martin Baillie stayed only briefly at the wedding supper. He was committed to another engagement and avoided parties that dispensed strong drink. He knew that whiskey and rum would be the tipple of the toasts and he thought it better to be gone than to toast the couple with tea or lemonade. So, he accepted the envelope containing a two-pound note from Dan, said a special goodbye to Pat and Bridget, and was on his way.

The guests settled in around Carmel's big parlour table and the festivities began. Brownie, in addition to running his livery stable, was often in demand for his melodic ability to squeeze a tune from a battered button accordion. He was made Master of Ceremonies. A Scotsman among the predominately Irish guests, he made sure the whiskey flowed and the toasts came frequently. His music, predominantly Irish, accompanied by Tom's sighing fiddle, soon had the singers singing as only Irish can when the spirit flows and a celebration beckons. Now and then he threw in a Scots tune and applauded them for their rendition of Loch Lomond.

'Do ya ken, for Irish Spalpeens, ya sing a bonny Scots song.'

It was a happy night.

About midnight, the newlyweds said farewell and headed off to their hired accommodation at Ballina's public house. Dan had a key to their room and carried a small suitcase for their night needs. Arm in arm they walked the deserted moonlit rough street footpath to the now dark small hotel. Their room was around the back of the building. Quietly they found and unlocked the door. Dan put down the suitcase, lifted Nell and squeezed in through the narrow opening, put her down and gently kissed her. He brought in the suitcase, closed the door, and lit the candle. It sputtered feebly on the marble topped washstand. Mr and Mrs Riordan had arrived with no great fanfare.

'Nell are you happy to be here with me?' Dan asked softly.

She only nodded but squeezed his hand. They sat on the bed, there was nowhere else to sit.

'I want you to know, I'll wait until you are ready to really be my wife. I know what you suffered and I want to be sure that I do nothing to bring back that suffering. Tonight, we go to bed and sleep, there is much for us to do tomorrow in moving to the block.'

Nell took his hand and looked at him squarely.

'Dan, you know that I wanted you, every part of you. I still do, but now I am unsure how I will react to lovemaking, though Doc Mason says those parts of me are now well healed and I am physically quite well. I'm your wife and you may be sure whenever you need me, I am yours. Perhaps tonight it is best if we sleep, but there are no restrictions.'

They blew the candle out, changed into their smart night wear and went to bed.

The unfamiliar situation of sharing a bed was enough to drive sleep far away. Eventually, physical tiredness of past hectic days took over. Dan's rhythmic breathing, a lullaby to his young bride. They both slept.

Much later, pre-dawn, Nell awoke. She sensed the unfamiliar but comforting firm warmth of Dan's back and drew a little closer. She had much to thank him for, his unquestioning kindness, his desire to make her "wife", even after the rape that would continue to cause them nightmares. He was different to the limited number of young men of her acquaintance. She was determined to help as a bush wife should. Work was something she understood, she would work with him.

This clean, warm closeness was pleasant. She turned inward on her side facing the nearness of his back. Her breasts through the cotton nightdress made faint contact with the heavy muscles below his shoulders, and the front of her thighs touched his firm buttocks. She went no closer. No longer was his breathing veiled in deep sleep. The touch of their bodies remained an unspoken language of awareness. Time was suspended, unmoving, unspeaking.
Nell broke the impasse of silence.

'Thank you, Daniel, for marrying me.'

She let her lips brush the back of his neck. When Dan answered, his voice was soft, in the Irish brogue of his childhood.

'And to be sure Mrs Riordan, were you not the one going to sleep the night away? It's a bold attractive hussy that you are. Even against my back, the feel of you is a magic poteen. What's a poor weak man to do?'

Nell matched the lightness of his tone.

'Why Mr Riordan you can just be patient. A girl may in time well get a taste for that poteen you mention. Just stay as you are and let's see what happens.'

But Nell's body moved in even closer, it seemed of its own accord. Pressing close to her man's back, moulding firmly against him. With her pelvic region pressed against the lower shape of his buttocks, she felt a message to her nipples stirring against that strong back. Her arm slid across his chest, fingers upwards, caressing the curly black hair on his head. Those capable fingers traced downward the outline of his face. That hand relished the freedom granted by this wonderful, exciting proximity. Gently she undid the buttons of his pyjama coat exploring the breadth of his strong chest. His tremor of feeling flowed to her fingers as they gently roamed across his male nipples.

'Ah Daniel, maybe I'm finding that 'poteen' you spoke of. Perhaps I am a bold hussy after all. Just let's stay this way a little longer. A little longer, is that all right?' He kissed her hand in answer.

She sensed the building pressure of waiting she was placing on this man. Yet she wanted to chase fear completely with her rising urges. And fear receded, giving place to awareness, waiting to welcome her husband in their mutual need. She wanted him to find pleasure with what she could offer.

Those trauma demons of hurt in her mind could go hang. It was her decision. She brought him over to face her.

'You sure it be right?' Dan huskily sought her assurance.

'Just undress me and love me,' was her determined answer.

There was some fleeting early nervous hurt. She willed it away. Discomfort ended long before completion and she welcomed their satisfied oneness. The bedcovers reclaimed, snugly warm from the early morning chill, they kissed unspeaking. His hands gently stroked her hair, her face, her breasts, her warm abdomen, her firm buttocks and lovingly welcomed her entirety.

'I like being married,' she whispered.

They slept into the approaching morning, moulded together as one.

Funding a School

Framework of the little bush schoolroom took shape. Several weekend working bees had made good progress on the block of land donated by the Brewsters. The half-acre site was fenced with teak post and rails, and the building framework was tallowood and box scantling timber carted by Pat to the site from Duncan Brown's mill. They had sought and received a basic plan from the government education authority and Pat was elected to be the builder in charge. Despite protests that his knowledge was only self-acquired, the community felt he was the man for the job. All work had to be achieved as time allowed; when people were available to supply labour.

Enthusiasm grew rapidly as the start of a building appeared. No longer a dream it was reality once a school framework appeared. Norah Brewster, as competent organising secretary, wrote letters and kept potential school parents informed of the progress. She had approached the political representative and the Sydney-based education department to find what subsidy, if any, could be found for a teacher. It was necessary to collect signed affidavits from parents requesting the school and the ages of children whom they would enrol. As an outline of the building appeared, they knew they were on the way.

Many ideas for making money were canvassed and discussed. The first big effort was to be a sports day. Foot racing, jumping, novelty events, horse events, the committee went to work first to find the ground- it must have a couple of furlongs that could be called flat and a surface suitable for racing. There were suggestions of venues, most discarded for lack of a safe racetrack. Eventually a big, sweeping, cleared plateau on the Johnson block was their choice. This was about halfway between the village of Duck Creek and the school site. It could be reached fairly easily from all directions and contained a potential track and a public meeting area of well cleared land. Three furlongs with sufficient pulling up space was available. It would start slightly downhill and finish uphill with a steeper slope behind. A foot running track, and some tree shelter for the crowd that they hoped to bring, this could all be supplied. It would require several working bees but there was a chance of making money for material and equipment that the school required. Plans went ahead.

Duncan Brown agreed to cut eight-inch chamfer boards for the school from a couple of Pat's teak logs. He would also supply the chamfer and softwood mouldings on the basis that residue of the logs was his. Timber was plentiful and milling worth far more than the raw material, the miller's offer was a generous one. Problems were met and overcome and confidence grew that their dream of education for their children would become reality. The contribution of the Brewsters and the O'Reillys was laying a foundation for others keen to help in some material way. It seemed a theme of awareness that having little education themselves, most local parents wanted more for their children. It gave common ground for often very different persons to come together in the mutual interest of the next generation.

Preparations for the big sports day went ahead. Posters were prepared by Margaret and Bridget, and they enlisted aid from the newly arrived Nell. Nell's time was scarce as the Riordans struggled to make Dick Hilardt's slab hut a liveable proposition. Yet Bridget felt it was good to include the girl in their plans; she was bright and keen to be part of the community.

Sports Day

The big important Saturday arrived. Despite an early morning ground fog, early signs were for a perfect sunny day. All roads and tracks carried signs leading to Johnson's field. From an early hour the clearing fog showed travellers closing in on their destination. They came in buggies, sulkies, carts, people on horseback, people walking, all were looking forward to a day of fun, real food, and chewing the verbal fat with neighbours. They approached with many agendas of the way to use a rare day of entertainment. And entertainment on the plateau was almost as scarce as money.

Brownie had the task of sorting and running the horse races. His reputation at the livery stable and his remarks passed on to friends from infrequent shared bouts with a whiskey bottle, meant his early days as a jockey were known to more than a few. It was reckoned he should know how to keep the sport honest. The prize money wasn't enough to pull in the big fish of the racing scene from down on the Clarence, but there was an open three-furlong flutter with a first prize of 20 pounds for horses hard fed and classed as racehorses. The other events were for horses and ponies used as hacks and cow horses. These were all two-furlong scampers, catch weights. All races had a walk in start.

The horses or ponies had to be nominated and graded by Brownie into what he considered their suitable class. The one exception was the open three furlong. This had a nomination fee of a pound and only those thinking they had a chance were likely to throw away a hard come by quid entry fee. There were three well fed, good looking likely nags that were definitely useful looking customers. Their owners and handlers eyed each other off with professional disdain, each spreading the story that their "old moke" had seen better days, but they would go around and make up the number. Then there were a couple of speedy looking part thoroughbreds who would probably go quick for a while; their proud owners willing to tell any listener that their horse was a sure winner.

Dan led Chief up for nomination. Brownie ran his calloused hands along the hard neck muscles and over the lower rump muscles.

'Where do ya want to place him laddie? Do you wanna have a go at the smarties, or if you're looking for something easier, I could throw you in one that you'd win.' Brownie recognised the responsibility of his job, but he felt an interest in the chestnut and wanted to see Dan do well.

'Well, you be the boss. I've never had reason to let him gallop,' Dan replied. 'Frightened I might fall off. I guess I've found it hard enough to keep him under control without encouraging him to have his own way. Anyway, that big grey with the mud rubbed over his brands looks pretty good to me.'

Dan eyed Brownie off, wondering, would the old ex pro feed him a clue?

'What d'ya swing the scales at?' Brownie's attention now settled on the potential rider not the horse.

'About ten an' a half when I was aboard ship. I've been working hard so maybe not so much now.'

'The smarties will all have light riders, you'd be giving them up to a couple of stone, but weight does'na mean all that much over a short distance. I like the feel of old Chief, it seems you have him fit to me. Have you a spare pound? He could be a chance if you can stay on.'

Dan handed over his pound and nominated himself as rider. Brownie gave him a word of advice.

'Trot him over the course while there are no horses around, and don't stir him up. That first furlong will sort them out, try to be on the inside when you get to the straight. I'll word Jim Skimmings the starter to see you get a fair start. Those jocks will try to get a fly, don't give 'em a break and I reckon you're a real chance.'

A couple of owners with their ponies arrived and Brownie swung his attention to them. One he passed as pony class, the other failed to walk under the "fourteen two" hand stick and was graded into the cow horse class. All nominations had to be in by 10 o'clock with the first race due at 10.30 and the main three furlong open was listed last race at 3 p.m. A restriction of six starters per race was decided on as it all the narrow bush track could safely hold. The stump holes had been filled and straight six-foot-high poles driven each three chain to define the track. It was up to the riders to stay on the course. The finish line boasted two sighting poles for the judges to sight across, that would help them declare the first, second and third.

The track was to be used for foot racing in between the horse events, 100 yards for the men and 50 yards for the women. Here the grading was simple, either married or single. What effect matrimony was supposed to have on speed seemed hard to define.

A popular spectacle was to be an open tug-o-war with much jostling for strong, heavy anchor people. There was a massive ship's hawser for the men and a lighter sail rope for the women. The team competition was strong with timber cutters, carriers, sailors, blacksmiths, butchers –all with followers who fancied their team.

There was a publican's booth under a big marquee, where Rupert and Laura James as well as Jane and Kate, two experienced bar maids, would handle the kegs of beer, sunk down into the soft cool earth. It seemed a fair bet that this facility would prove popular as the day evolved. Pat had hauled the beer kegs to the sight the day before, together with a couple of crates of rum and whiskey and a tank of water.

The women of the school building committee had a stall for bottled home- made ginger beer and lemonade with a copper continuously boiling to supply tea or coffee. Norah and Bridget had made scones for days, churned large quantities of butter and bottled jams of several varieties. Nell was to be a worker on the stall and had been helping for many days. It was all tiring work to make sure they would be ready. The serving glasses for the soft drinks and the cups and saucers for hot drinks would be washed as they went. A supply of hot water would come from an adjacent copper. It was Nell's task to see a supply of drinking containers was ever present. They depended upon the weather being fine and plenty of people coming to support the day, to make money.

So, the months of preparation were behind and the day began well. Now at 8am the dew was fast drying and those in charge of the many operations were marshalling their resources. Food and competition seemed to be the theme of the day with an invitation to entertainers that they bring any musical or special skills. It was hard to say what the day would produce, but it was hoped that the school would benefit with money. Most who would attend came because they wanted the school to succeed. They were prepared to make an effort. Contributions of a community looking to the future of its children could not be frowned upon, no matter how small each individual contribution. Money was a scarce commodity among the settlers but a little from many would make it worthwhile.

By ten o'clock the crowd was impressive, the organising committee was smiling. At least a couple of hundred adults and children surged around the open venue. The refreshment tent was already doing a great trade with scones and tea the most popular seller and bare footed children counting their pennies to see how many glasses of lemonade were available at 1d per glass.

The children's foot races were run off in age groups over the 50-yard course. Most of the field were only three or four contestants.

Pat O'Reilly decided to give Shamrock a run in the hack class. The old horse was probably past his best for racing, but Pat knew that even at 12 years of age he was fit and would be keen to run. It was Pat's task for the day to supervise the spit roasting of a donated Hereford steer. He had prepared the fire the day before and taken the light cart into Duck Creek early that morning to pick up the dressed carcass.

The spit had been made with the help of Ernest Jones, Duck Creek's blacksmith and part time emergency funeral director. An ex-pommy soldier who had drifted in several years before, he had become a valued citizen of the community. His romance with Kate, the no nonsense bar maid at the hotel, at times caused a few ribald comments. These comments were well away from Ernest's hearing, as his nickname of "Bopper" had followed him from the army. He was a big man with the strong arms of his trade. He had volunteered to help Pat with cooking and serving the steer on the spit. It had already been cooking for several hours and it was reckoned come about 1 o'clock all should be in readiness for serving. They had prepared a large deep trench under the spit and fired it with solid blocks of red gum and ironbark that burnt down to solid very hot coals. It was necessary to keep the heat constant and the steer turning to make sure it was cooked right through.

The hack race with six starters was due about 11am. Pat borrowed Dan's old racing pad that had been acquired from Brownie with Chief. He reckoned that his weight was well over 11-stone, so he wanted to lighten the load on Shamrock as much as was possible. The old English pig skin pad would help a little from his normal solid poley saddle. He left the leathers at Dan's riding length. Seeing he was several inches taller than the younger Irishman; this brought him up off the horse's back. He had knocked around the stables back in Ireland, and although the crouch seat up on the withers was not then being used, trainers knew it helped to get the weight up and forward.

A pony race and a cow horse race had been run and the results had been fairly predictable. The hack race was bringing out a more even class of horse. A couple of amateur bookies graced the day with notebooks and pencils. They were prepared to give odds, making very sure they kept the likely winner at a price they could afford. Roley Cavendish was a large, round man, with a check suit that had seen better days, as had his battered black bowler hat. He wandered the perimeter of the parading horses and offered the odds.

'I'll take six to four on Fireball, and good odds they are.'

Fireball was a classy looking young black horse, very much on the toe. He had a prominent white blaze and Brownie had deliberated long before allowing him in the hack class. His owner was a cattleman from out past Casino and he assured Brownie the horse was unraced. He had a Chinese rider, Jimmie Ah Fong, who, small of stature, would only tilt the scales at about eight and a half stone. Jimmie had ridden the previous winner in the cow horse race and looked good on a horse, with nice steady hands.

Pat knew Shamrock could hold his own against most bush horses, but he knew the old horse was probably lacking the training of the smart blaze-faced black. He entered because horses were in his blood and any Irishman was prepared to try his luck. The six starters came out of the sapling marshalling yard and Pat trotted past Roley Cavendish.

'What odds are we, Roley?' Pat quietly asked.

'Three to one Shamrock, and plenty are having their two bob on you. Tell you what, just to you, four to one, and it would be a good result for me if you topple that flash Fireball. He'll cost me heaps.'

'Ok you've got a pound of mine in your book for me, I'll pay when I get back.'

The field trotted down to the starter. Pat kept Shamrock nice and relaxed, well behind the other starters. Fireball and a grey mare named Busy Bee were keen to grab the bit and be off.

Jim Flannagan had a three-foot-high old cedar stump as his starter's platform and a pole at right angles about one and a half chains away on which to line up his charges.

'Right boys,' he started, 'I'm starting this race. There won't be any "flys", anyone lets his nag go before I drop the hanky and it will be a non-start. You walk 'em in nice and steady and I'll see you get a fair start.'

The first attempt was a failure as Fireball and Busy Bee had each other well stirred up and wouldn't walk toward the start line. Jimmie and Jack Neville, the lad on Busy Bee, were busy controlling their dancing, plunging steeds. On the second go, Pat eased up on the inside of Busy Bee and kept his eyes glued on Jim. A few strides from the imaginary start they came into a rough line and down went the white handkerchief.

Pat felt Shamrock grab the bit and jump cleanly into stride. Busy Bee had missed the start a little which gave him the inside running. He was in front as he glanced across, but he could see the white blaze of Fireball at his shoulder. Two furlongs on a galloping horse doesn't take long, certainly not much over 24 seconds. There was a slight bend into the last half furlong, Pat hugged the bend and kicked Shamrock hard for home. The white blaze was beside him and he could hear the rhythmic smack of Jimmie's whip as he tried to push the black Fireball past. Shamrock hung on with all the courage of a good horse. The crowd was a noisy blur. Pat gave the old horse a lift with his knees and the line was past. They sped up the hill and the field slowed down. Jimmie Ah Fong was beside Pat as they brought their mounts to a trot and turned back toward the finish line and the cheering crowd a furlong back.

'Who won boss?' Jimmy asked Pat.

Pat shrugged his shoulders.

'Leave it to the judges Jimmy. I don't know. It was too close.'

They trotted back and looked for the number board. Number 2 was up, over 4, and then 1. Pat had won by a whisker. Jimmie gave a fatalistic shake of the head and offered Pat his slim, small hand.

'He's a good old horse boss. We thought this bloke would be a certainty. He was too good for the others but not your horse. The rest were miles behind.'

'Thanks Jim it was a great race. The old bloke can move a bit but he's getting too old for this caper. I won't race him again.'

There were plenty of cheers for Pat and Shamrock. Mary, in

control of her excitement let it be known that she always knew her dad and Shamrock would win. She competently led the horse back to his tethering place, while Pat had to be back to work at the cooking and returned to the final stages of preparing the steer.

The 100 yards Men's Sprint was one of the attractions. There were eight entrants ready to try and lift the five pounds prize money. A popular pick was John Gordon, a young man well known around Ballina for his strength and good humour. He worked mainly at the wharf, lumping bags of corn onto the boats when the autumn maize crop was being sent to Sydney. He was always available for odd jobs where muscle was required. "Splinter" Carr was a lean, tough young blacksmith from Tunstall and was another expected to go well. He was Roley Cavendish's favourite at even money. A not so young Aboriginal stockman from Dyraaba Station was another to have his supporters. Some dark lads had ridden or walked over from Casino and were ready to have a good day out. They were used to white people ways and only spoke when addressed by someone. Another unknown quantity in the field were a couple of sailors at Ballina for the weekend. Their ship was waiting for an offshore wind and a heavy southerly break on the bar to flatten out. They heard of the sports on the mountain and headed up for a day out.

The smart punters reckoned 100 yards would be too short for old Jacky Two Bob, and Roley quoted him at four to one. It was well known that some of the Aboriginals could run, but Jacky looked a bit old and certainly he looked outclassed by a few of the well- muscled fit singlet clad young contenders. The race was scheduled for 12 noon and then there was to be a short break for lunch. The bar tent was doing a good trade and already some of the punters were gaining courage from a drop of liquor. Roley's book for the sprint was holding plenty of bets.

Jim Flannagan was also trusted as a starter for the footrace. At least he could tell the human runners the rules as against the nerve-racking task of controlling toey horses to an imaginary line. The runners were allowed to crouch or push start provided their fingers were behind the line. One of the sailors seemed to know how to push start off his toes and knees; most adopted a crouch, and Jacky just stood relaxed, waiting for the gun blank to fire.

At the first attempt, the line was broken early by John Gordon. He was warned, do it again and you are out. Bang, a second time, and they were away. Jacky was clearly last into stride, with the crouch starting sailor in front at the halfway. John Gordon and Splinter grabbed him with 25 to go and then a dark flash right on the line left the judges blinking to sort out the places. Two of the three went for Jacky, one thought Splinter had lasted to win. The majority decision ruled, and Jacky Two Bob was declared the last stride winner.

There was a roar of approval from the Dyraaba station boys; they had lost heavily on Fireball but Jacky had been their pick at good odds for the foot race. Now they had their money back. They headed for the bar with strict orders for Jacky to collect the prize money and meet them outside the big, lifted tent flap. It was unlikely they would make it back to the station that night, but the weather was fine. They would borrow a yard somewhere for the horses and sleep off the expected hangover on the softest earth they could find. They knew how to use a poley saddle as a pillow and a good big saddle blanket unfolded would keep off some of the outside chill. The more the saddle blanket was impregnated with sweat the better. It added to the weight and insulation. A few slugs of rum late in the day would mean plenty of inner warmth. Their day was planned.

Pat and Bopper pushed long, thin, steel skewers into the deep rump muscle of the now brown sizzling steer meat. It felt well cooked and the escaping juices had but a hint of pink. They reckoned the time had come to start carving, in preparation for those solid bread sandwiches the girls were lined up to sell with plenty of onions and Worcestershire sauce. This feast would cost sixpence, and a cup of tea brewed from the water boiling in the large copper would cost a penny. Soon the eager queue wound back from the serving tent and Bridget, Norah, Carmel and Nell were run off their feet. They had a perspiring liaison person supplying carved meat from the spit. The sandwiches were piled on huge crockery serving platters, and the customers took their sandwich from the constantly heaped plate.

The aroma of well-cooked fresh beef advertised itself, with its inviting smell stirring the gastric juices of all present. It meant there were plenty of customers waiting. It was a treat from the normal settler's diet of salted cuts usually weeks old. A clean, polished kerosene tin with the lid cut on three sides and angled back was the till. Jim Brewster was the cashier, kept busy changing and collecting money. The steady chatter of coins made a welcome tune to the organisers.

If there was a busier place than the food tent it was the publican's booth. The James' staff had set up well with kegs and bottled spirits. By lunch time there were already customers in the happy stage of inebriation, the testing time would be later when the arguments started. The sergeant of police from Ballina had agreed to look in during the afternoon to act as a brake on some of those who may become a problem. The beer flowed, accompanied by a loud chatter of voices. Some patrons preferred a bottle of rum, a canvas waterbag, a couple of mugs and one of the shade trees away from the tent.

The sailor named Seamus, who had led the footrace, retired to the bar with his mates to drown his sorrow. He struck up a quick bar relationship with Kate. His desire to impress and make conversation probably meant the beer was going down too fast for his own good. After each beer, Kate appeared more and more desirable, and she probably reckoned there was little risk in seductively fluttering her heavily eye-shadowed eyelids in encouragement. Kate was a natural flirt, when free of the jealous eye of Bopper, and it helped liven the very busy work hours to throw Seamus an occasional twitch of her ample bottom, bosom or bare shoulders.

'I reckon you and I would get along fine,' slurred Seamus. 'When you knock off, I'll walk you home. My ship won't sail till Monday, there's all tomorrow.'

Seamus was a well-built, handsome, dark Irishman, with an obvious touch of the Blarney stone. He had courted plenty of girls in plenty of ports and usually his charm had the desired effect on his many conquests.

'No Seamus, I'm busy all day, and my boyfriend is here anyway. Thanks, but it's not on,' Kate whispered her message with a demure glance of her liquid green eyes.

Seamus had heard "no" in many foreign languages but usually ended up enjoying what "yes" meant at the hot appropriate moment of his conquest. This may be a tricky one, but he reckoned she was interested.

Splinter Carr had shared a beer with Seamus and the sailors after the race. He thought it his duty to tell Seamus the facts.

'Be careful,' he said to the young sailor, 'her boyfriend's jealous and dangerous. He packs a wallop like my blacksmith's 10-pound hammer. There are already a few blokes without any front teeth after Bopper caught up with them, because they were eyeing off Kate.'

Splinter felt he had done his duty. Rumour had it, the charms of Kate in bed were worth some risk, but there was little chance of stealth in the present situation. He headed for the food tent with a need for at least one of the steak sandwiches he'd seen in the hands of customers at the bar.

Horses, Running, Pulling, Music

No gathering of settlers was likely to pass without a splash of music. An accordion, mouth organ or fiddle would usually appear and a performer could be sure of pulling an audience just by striking up a simple tune. Billy Montez was lean of build, medium height, a wizened, cockney gypsy. He had drifted to Sydney long ago as a cabin boy, knocked around The Rocks area for years, making existence as a tinker, sharpening scissors, knives and saws. He could tune a piano, patch or play a fiddle, fashion a finger key for a flute. These music and luthier skills picked up or inherited from his background, opened many doors. In time, he left the surrounds of Sydney, took to the tracks of NSW and wandered from place to place, station to station, wherever the fancy beckoned, he went. He heard tales of the Big Scrub and followed the ranges down the line and bridle tracks from Tenterfield, so that his visit coincided with the Sports Day.

From his gypsy Spanish father, he had inherited the natural rhythm and ear of the Romany people. He could fashion a tune from any instrument and his old Italian fiddle lived in a wool-lined waterproof metal case. It was far better housed than Billy, who lived out in the elements of whatever district he was wandering. His files and tools of trade were either pushed or pulled in a small two-wheeled cart. His music-making was well known and an over-riding passport to many places where a Gypsy was otherwise suspect. Even in wild places where the Aboriginal tribes held sway, he had wandered and camped unmolested.

He had awoken one moonlit night with a feeling he was not alone. Letting his eyes wander the clearing in which he lay, he realised some of the stumps were not there when he went to sleep. Those black shadows could have speared him long before this, if that was their intent. He felt inside his coat and eased a small mouth organ to his lips. The soft wailing folk tune of his Gypsy forbears drifted from his swag. The black shadows stopped, then drifted back to the perimeter of the trees. He kept playing. His soft rhythmic tunes stroked the night shadows. These tunes for nomadic people, played to an even older nomadic people and proved successful. The harmony of the night was kept intact.

The sports day seemed to Billy Montez a chance for a day out. Just maybe, he could drum up a little business. He set himself up during lunch time on one of the many stumps still not grubbed from the rich, red soil. The huge eight-foot-wide butt of the teak was a natural working stage. His violin seemed the best choice of his instruments to pull an audience. He tuned the four gut strings to perfect fifths from G to E. It was a hard life for a violin, but the old Cremona instrument remained crack free in its tin-covered, wool-insulated home. Billy stood on the stump and set the horsehairs of the bow galloping a rousing Scottish reel. He switched to Irish Donegal, then the folk tunes of England. His repertoire was nonstop and unlimited.

They came. First the children, and then some parents gathered around his circular sawn teak stump stage. When twenty or so gathered Billy dropped the instrument from his chin and held up the bow.

'Right folks if you want a tune just ask, maybe I know it, if not we'll find something to set the feet a tapping.'

Mary O'Reilly, released from food tent duties, gravitated to the sound of music. Spellbound, she watched the flying fingers. Her lessons on the Brewster piano seemed very dull compared to this small instrument that had a huge voice from the flying bow and the dark nimble fingers. To her it was magic. She watched the thin gypsy hand stroking up and down the strings, at times quivering on the note to give its haunting tremolo effect. It was for Mary, an introduction to a sound that touched her soul.

'Well, what's it to be folks?' Billy looked around his audience. 'Perhaps you've had enough for now, and I'll start up again later.'

Mary had worked her way to the front of the small group.

'No Mister, please keep playing. You just play we'll listen.'

Mary spoke shyly but insistently. Now that she was at the front of the group, she would be able to see better.

'Ah, there's a young lady that makes it easy for me.' Billy jumped down off his stump and sat on his solid stage. 'Probably needs a tweak on this old ringa ding.'

He proceeded to turn the black ebony tuning key, plucked the four strings in turn, pulled the bow across each string until satisfied the harmonics were right. He stepped back up on the stump.

'Now this is a happy day so why not a happy tune?'

He lifted the fiddle, flexed his fingers and plunged into an incredibly fast Romany bolero, the notes flowed, changing tempo, changing pitch, always a tune seeking the swirl of skirts and a muffled earth pounding of flying feet. His eyes closed and he gave himself over to the music of his Romany father. Billy had never seen the plains of Hungary and Romania, but the pulsing rhythm of dark-eyed forbears spoke in his veins and fingers. He stopped abruptly, as he had started. For a moment his spellbound audience were silent, then as one they clapped with joy that lingered from the music.

Tom O'Rourke had joined the group; the sound of a fiddle caused him to seek a leave pass from his job as courier for transferring meat from the spit.

'Well to be sure, you are a mighty fine fiddler, sir. That tune was something most people would not hear in a lifetime. Thank you, we will always be in your debt.'

Billy jumped down from his stump once more. Held out his arms out, embracing this mixed audience.

'Folks that will do for now, if you think my tune was worth a coin for the school building, just throw it in the old black cat.'

He sat an old black silk-covered top hat on the stump. Most of his audience delved in pocket or purse, a collection of copper and some silver coins fell into the topper. Mary waited shyly until last. She carefully

untied her threepence spending money, that had to last the day, from the corner of her handkerchief and went to drop her whole wealth into the hat.
Billy Montez spoke gently to the child.

'Now Missy, how will you buy some sweets or a drink if you give so much? Why not let me change it for you and a penny for the school.'

Mary looked unsure but dropped it in the hat. She had made her big decision and was still spellbound by this wonderful blood tingling music, so different from the simple melodic Mozart sonatas to which she had progressed on the piano.

'Will you play again later? I want my mother and Mrs Brewster to come and hear you play, but they are too busy now.'

'Of course I will, even if it's just for you and your mother.' He fished in his pocket and drew out some pennies. 'Now young lady about that gift of yours, your silver threepence, was worth three of these.'

He held up three coppers resplendent with Queen Victoria's crowned head.

'What say you put in one of these for now, and maybe another later if you haven't found a good way of spending it.'

Mary slowly nodded her head. He gave back her threepence from the hat. The three coins sat on Billy's hand; she placed one in the hat. He did not move his hand from in front of her, but closed fingers over the coins.

'Now what's in my hand is your change, right?'

'Yes,' said Mary, looking at him with large serious eyes.

'Then here it is, your change.' He opened the hand that had not moved from her view, on it sat three pennies.

'How did you do that? I should only have two pennies.'

'We agreed it was your change.' Billy smiled at the child's puzzled expression. He knew she was convinced her eyes would have seen him add another penny, but she also knew 3-1 equals 2.

'Later you may want to put the spare penny in the hat. Now go and have a good time.'

Billy Montez was a master at sleight of hand and card tricks. He had been well taught. His gypsy father had shown him many things before the wanderlust and lure of faraway scenes had caused that father to walk away from a wife and 14-year-old Billy and the cold foggy East End of London.

At three o'clock, those not prevented by their jobs, turned their attention to the racetrack. This was the big money race of the day and the six runners all had supporters. It was obvious three of the runners were ex racehorses and the other three were classy thoroughbred or part thoroughbred animals. This race would start well down the valley out of sight. The first furlong wound to the right, then rose a gradual slope until it picked up with the two furlongs already well used. Roley had set up his board and chalked up the names and prices.

'Board odds, board odds, I'll bet board odds. Two to one the field bar one.'

The Ghost, a big 16 and a half hand grey, was the "bar one". No one seemed to know his origin. Jimmie Ah Fong was his rider, and he'd drawn the number one marble. The Ghost looked a horse who had seen real racetracks, with what result, no one knew. His handler, a middle-aged wizened "horsey" looking gent, gave his name as Sam Smith. He had said very little to anyone who tried to be chatty. The gear on the horse was first class, and he paraded with an air of calm assurance.

'I'll take six to four, The Ghost.' Roley warily watched Sam Smith. He reckoned this horse wasn't here for the benefit of the school fund.

The runners trotted off toward the start and Sam sidled up to Roley.

'That's a miserable price on my old bloke. How about even money, there's some good 'uns there you know.'

'That's the price. How much you trying to lay?'

Sam pulled a small chamois bag from his pocket.

'There's 50 sovs here, but you only get them if you make it five to four on.'

Roley inwardly gulped but didn't blink an eyelid. So far, he reckoned he was over 50 pound up. There was a lot of small bets on the other runners, nothing on The Ghost. Brownie had placed five pounds on Chief. A nice bay mare named Lively Lady had also received several five-pound bets.

'Alright, you are on. I'll count your money before the race is run.' He took the little chamois bag. 'If it counts right, there'll be ninety in the bag if you win.'

Dan was having a lively time with Chief; the chestnut was right on the toe and trying to grab the bit. A false start would have him in real trouble. It would probably take most of the track to get him back under control. The six runners arrived behind the start point. Jim Flannagan went through his spiel; Dan was the only rider not to have had a previous ride. Jim could see Dan was hard put to control the chestnut.

'Keep him well back lad and bring him up slow. I'll get you away alright if you watch me and are prepared to be back a little on the line. Don't let him go until I drop the flag.'

They eased up. Dan was in the middle between Flying Lady and The Ace. He made sure Chief was tight between them and half a length back as they approached the line. With a couple of yards to the line they were in some sort of order and the flag dropped. The chestnut fireball dwelt a fraction of a second, used to being hauled back on the bit. He couldn't believe the fact he was free to run. Run, he surely did. In twenty strides he was in front. As they approached the bend onto the two-furlong mark, Dan moved over to the inside running and reckoned he had a break; he wasn't sure how far. From here home all he could do was let Chief fly and hope the momentum was there to cross the finish line in front. The horse's speed was exhilarating. Dan had galloped horses at home in Ireland but not when a race was to be won.

One hundred yards to go and Dan felt the speed of his mount slacken a fraction. He risked a glance with his left eye. Certainly, there was still no challenger up with his seat on the horse. The crowd and the line rushed to meet him. He felt, rather than saw, the grey shadow that loomed beside him. The whack of the whip, the roar of the crowd, the vibration of the earth, it was all a split-second symphony of action. As they crossed the judge's line, Jimmie Ah Fong's pumping arms and right thigh brushed Dan. He hoped they had lasted but he felt their effort was undone. The big grey with his extra size and long neck had to be in front. They sped up the rise away from the line, the riders bringing their mounts back under control. Chief slowly came back on the bit. Dan could feel the thumping of his generous mount's heart in tune with his own.

'I think we get you, right on line?'

Jimmie's greeting was a question as much as a statement. He and Dan pulled up and turned to trot back down the hill.

'Yes, I think we knocked up at the end.' Dan held out a hand to the little Chinese rider. 'I'm happy, he hasn't been trained and I'm no jock. We gave you a run.'

The riders judged it right. The verdict a head win to number one from number three; number four was six lengths back third.

Brownie and Pat were there to help him unsaddle and rub the chestnut down.

'You cost me money laddie, but you sure gave me a thrill,' laughed Brownie. 'I thought you were home when you came round the bend on the inside and two in front. You rode him a treat, nothing more you could do. That big grey was too good when he really got going, but one stride less and it was yours.'

Brownie looked years younger with the thrill in his veins of galloping horses head-to-head in that final mad surge. Pat shook his hand and towelled Chief briskly. There was no water to wash him down.

'Yes Dan, you did the Irish proud. At level weights he got home for sure. The word is that the grey has won good races in the city, but he and his original owners got sent out for pulling him up and backing another runner.'

Dan made sure that Chief was cooled, gave him a drink, and then went to find Nell. She gave him a big hug.

'Don't be disappointed. You both did great. I thought you won but then I'm on your side.'

'Ah well, Mrs Riordan, for being a loyal barracker you get the five pounds prize for running second. Use it in the house.'

Another big event of the afternoon was the tug-o-war. Once the open horse race was run, an arena was pegged on the track and the big hemp rope brought out. There were five nominated teams. Each met the other once, and the two teams with most wins pulled off for the final. It soon became obvious that the teams, called the Butchers and the Blacksmiths, had the weight and muscle advantage over Sailors, Timber Cutters and a scratch crew, made up on the spot and appropriately called the Drinkers.

Sergeant Kelly from Ballina arrived after lunch to check the day. He agreed to be chief judge of the pull. It took little time to sort out the finalists. This was to be a best of three contest, with a draw for ends and a change around after the first result. The teams were six a side and the finalists really looked able to stretch the heavy hawser rope provided for the pull. The name did not mean all the team was of that occupation. The Butchers had a couple of butchers, and the Blacksmiths had a couple of blacksmiths, the rest eyed off and recruited for weight and strength.

The Blacksmiths had big Bopper Jones as anchor, with a couple of iron benders from Ballina, Splinter Carr, comparatively small but strong, and their trump card, a huge Turkish wrestler who it was claimed could right a heavy-laden capsized cart.

The Butchers had Bob Beames, with the loop of rope around his girth. The carrier was an almost immovable object. Ted Smith, a butcher from down at Blackwall, said to be able to wrestle down a two-year-old steer. A couple of strong knock-about labourers and Luigi Peretti, an Italian who had jumped ship in Ballina and worked anywhere his strong arms were required.

Most locals knew why Luigi's flashing Latin smile was now short a couple of teeth, because he had dared to sweet talk Kate.

Sergeant Kelly occupied the same teak stump used earlier as the judge's stand. He explained the best of three format to the finalists.

'You will take an even strain on the rope. Don't pull or jerk until I say 'Pull' or you'll be out and that one lost.'

They took position with their supporters from the beer tent urging from the sideline. In their prelim clash it had been an even contest. Butchers came out on top but there was a thought the Blacksmiths were not disclosing what they might do when the pressure was really on.

There were three knots in the rope. One in the middle, and a knot ten feet either side of the middle. The rule said, once either of the outside knots passed the centre line that pull was declared over.

The sergeant was happy there was an even strain by each team on the rope.

'Pull!' he bellowed and pull, they did.

Butchers took the early advantage. Soon Blacksmiths' knot was within three feet of the centre line. Then the bulk of Bopper, his huge arms and legs, straight as stay posts, stemmed the tide. Ali, the Turkish wrestler let out a spine-chilling whoop that seemed to lift the team. They regained their ground and kept the pressure on. The Butchers lost the initial charge and were now heading relentlessly towards the line.

As the knot hit the centre line, Sergeant Kelly blew a piercing blast on his police whistle. The Blacksmiths were one up.

The second pull was a change of ends. Once more the Butchers held an early advantage, but the bulk of Bopper and the ability of Ali to throw in a surge of power made it a repeat of the first effort. In less time, the whistle blew and Blacksmiths were undisputed champs. Both teams headed for the beer tent to join the earlier contestants. Bopper and Luigi shook hands.

The day started to wind down. Some of the far travellers had to set out for home. There was no doubt the amount of monies raised would really help set up the little school. It was also apparent some of the revellers, expelled by Rupert from the liquor tent, would probably spend the night under the stars and the most friendly tree they could find, sleeping off the effects.

Mary O'Reilly told her mother and Norah about Billy Montez, his violin and the collection hat.

'If I know gypsies, we are unlikely to see the money.' Norah had waited until Mary was absent before making this aside judgement to Bridget.

'Ah well, we can't lose by his being here.' Bridget had some faith in her daughter's judgement.

It was an hour or so later that Billy arrived at the refreshment tent. He approached the serving table, ordered a cup of black tea and a piece of cake.

He pulled from his pocket a small calico bag.

'Could I see the lady in charge?' His question was to Nell, who went to find Nora.

'There's some strange little man, like a leprechaun in there, wants to speak to the lady in charge. He has rings in each ear and talks like a real cockney.' Some of her mothers' sailor boarders had been cockneys. Nell knew a cockney accent and their strange dialogue.

'Let us go and see this charmer of Mary's and see what he wants.'

Nora and Bridget headed out into the tent. Billy was obviously enjoying his luxury of a piece of rich butter cake. He rose to his feet as the ladies approached.

'My name is Montez and Ma'am; I wish to support your work for the golden rule. Earlier I played a few tunes and my audience threw in a donation. I will play again soon before the crowd go home.' He delivered a flashing smile, and his small calico bag of coins, to the women.

'I wish it was more for your school, maybe we will pick up a bigger audience later.'

'Thank you, Mr Montez, we appreciate your generous work.'

Nora was feeling guilty about her lack of trust. Bridget joined in the conversation feeling justified.

'My daughter told me about you Mr Montez. She assures me you are the greatest music she has heard. But then she has only heard the conservative classics that we play,' Bridget said this with a smile, including Nora. Mr Montez shrugged and smiled.

'It was worth playing just to see her face, if she is the lovely serious child that spoke to me. I promised to play again. I won't play my wild gypsy rhythms this time, no sense in turning her ideas from what you teach her.'

He prepared to leave and gave them his winning smile.

'You may have a chance to join my next recital.' It was part question.

Half an hour later, the chords of an accordion floated across the lessening noise of the closing day. Mary was given permission to return to the concert stump. She took Janey and Thomas.

This time Billy Montez drew a much larger crowd of the tiring stayers. He struck up a bracket of Viennese waltzes, Mazurkas and conventional dance tunes. It was foot tapping rhythm that drew his audience. Many of them had little chance these days to listen to music or indulge in dancing. The rapport between the musician and his audience grew as they suggested tunes he may play. It was a grand finale to a great day. Bridget and Norah joined the gathered crowd. They too appreciated his skills on the accordion and then a bracket on the little mouth organ that came from an inner pocket.

'Well folks, it's time to end, if you have a coin or two for the hat, remember you are helping these wonderful children to have an education. Is there a final request?'

'Yes sir, please play your violin.'

Mary was amazed at the fact she had spoken up. She had slowly eased her way through the crowd, with Janey and Thomas attached to each hand.

'Why of course for you, young lady, I cannot refuse. In the case there, the old hey diddle diddle, would you hand it up please?'

Mary felt a sense of importance in her role and placed the black custom-made watertight box on the stump.

'Thank you. Now just a moment folks till I tweak it up to tune.'

Billy plucked each string in turn with the body of the violin close to his ear and was obviously content with the sound. He then lightly bowed each note. It only took a matter of seconds, then he faced the audience, held up the bow and asked for a request.

There was no immediate response, so Nora broke the silence.

'We will leave it to you, Mr Montez.'

'Well folk, a fiddle has as many moods as there are emotions. The day is ending so I'll borrow a nocturne from Mr Brahms.'

He launched into the haunting, melodic tune. The sensitive fingers and the old violin filled the clearing and audience with an engulfing sound. The tremolo effect of his fingers on the high notes surged clear, above and through the valley. When he reached the diminuendo conclusion, the soft but perfectly audible notes faded away.

His audience was under the spell of the pure sound, five, ten seconds and then their wave of applause. They clamoured for more.

'It's been a big day folks. I wouldn't have missed it for quids. Remember these children need a school. The old black cat would like a few more coins if you have any left.'

He motioned to the hat, worn many times in his magic roles, in many distant faraway places. It was battered but suggested different exotic worlds.

'Right, I know many of you have come from faraway lands. I'll wrap it up with Rabbie Burns, not one of my kinsmen, but possibly one of yours. Sing along if you will.'

He drew the bow and the simple musical setting of Auld Lang Syne filled the clearing. It held its own momentum. Soon the few proud Scottish folk found a voice and others too joined in, even if they didn't know all the words, they hummed along with the embracing sentiment of the melody. When the end came there was another burst of applause and many had an unashamed tear. There were many wanting to shake Billy's hand and coins clanked with momentum into the hat, so that many went home with completely empty pockets.

Nora, Bridget and the children waited until the crowd dwindled and then approached Billy with their thanks for his significant contribution. Norah spoke up.

'Mr Montez, I didn't believe Mary when she told us of what you were doing. I didn't believe her either when she told us how good you are. You are even better than she said, but I should have known. Mary has an exceptional ear for music.'

Billy Montez smiled at the group.

'It's been my pleasure. Since I've been wandering the tracks, there aren't many times that I can play to a human audience. Sometimes at night, out in the bush I just play softly to the animals, amazing that the wallabies and 'roos after a while seem to listen.'

He pulled another little calico bag out of his handcart and deposited the plentiful coins from the hat.

'Well, here we are,' and smiling directly at Mary he said, 'You make sure little lady that there is music in your school.'

They said their thanks and Bridget spoke up.

'After all is packed up the organisers and helpers are going to have tea here at the ground, why don't you stay and join us. There are plenty of leftovers and we would love to have you.'

Billy looked doubtful.

'Ma'am I'm a gypsy tinker not used to much company these days. Gypsies are often not welcome you know.'

Mary looked straight at Mr Montez with her calm serious eyes.

'Please Mr Montez I want you to come.'

The big day wound to an end under a young, rising quarter moon. A family of crows had worked late around the outskirts of the ground, squabbling over the bones and scraps thrown away by untidy patrons. With darkness, the loud carking of their disputes ended and they retreated to the dead trees up on a forest ridge. There were probably still pickings to arouse fresh interest in the morning. These black scavengers with their touch of iridescent green lustre, and sharp yellow rimmed eyes, always needed to be on guard. They were hunted by man and unpopular with other birds, yet they played their essential role as ever-working, carrion cleaning garbage collectors.

Some 20 or 30 men, women and children held their impromptu meal around the remnants of the spit fire, rekindled to boil their kerosene tin of water. Black tea was the communal drink where bush people came together. Most knew of each other, even if they had not met in the past. Distance was always a loneliness factor in a developing district such as the growing red earth plateau; neighbours relied upon any chance meeting to glean information of new or old settlers. The opportunity for distant neighbours to talk was a rarity such as the sports day provided. Usually it was of necessity, work, work and then more work.

Dick Hilardt, as treasurer of the day, was still counting his money. It seemed the effort would be better than their greatest hopes. The school would be a reality once a teacher was appointed. Many had used their abilities to make it happen. Some of the older children present no doubt had mixed feelings on the subject of a school. Their young lives were full of interesting happenings without the compulsion of book learning. Their freedom to roam and make decisions would soon be lost for a major part of each day. The parents knew school was the key to an outside world, but farm kids of eleven, twelve or more considered they could work like adults anyway. Why all this fuss? Why did they need a school?

Billy Mendez was escorted to the tea group by the women. Some of those present would probably have walked by on the other side had they passed the gypsy on the road. However, once told of his efforts by Nora, they welcomed and thanked him for his two contributions. These came to close on five pounds; a great help as many books could be purchased for that amount. He was soon pressed into playing a few tunes. He settled for the little mouth organ and old folk melodies of Ireland, Scotland or England. Music was a rare commodity in most of their busy lives, yet in most it woke deep buried scenes of other faraway places.

It was a happy end party; tired children went to sleep on parents' coats. For them it was the most exciting day of their young lives. The parents had opportunities to talk to other parents. Others found kindred souls to share a sandwich and cup of tea, or coffee, sometimes for the men a flask of well-hidden rum added a kick to the potion.

Bopper and Kate drifted to the outer fringe, close by a spreading fig.

'And don't you think I didn't see you making sheep's eyes at that flash sailor.' Bopper needed an eagle eye to account for Kate's suspected roving flirtation.

'Ah, big boy you know me. My job is to be pleasant to the lads; it sells plenty of grog and they soon get to the stage that their physical workings, well, they don't match their intentions. What harm can a girl come to in a crowded bar?'

She cast those big liquid eyes demurely at Bopper.

'Yeah, I'm not so sure about what happens in that back room of yours with a door that opens to the yard. Don't you forget what happened to that Italian Luigi. That oily dago won't be biting too well without his front teeth.'

'Ah, you're such a jealous lad, and let's face it, you don't own me. I'm my own girl.' She gave his massive arm a squeeze.

Bopper accepted the invitation and grabbed Kate in a beery bear hug that almost crushed the solidly built woman.

'Steady on lover boy, we are in company you know. I've already had a big day and you've had far too much beer.'

'Let us take a little stroll me lovely. I'll show you I'm in fine shape.'

'No,' said Kate firmly. 'I know you. Besides, there's all sorts of creepy crawlies in that undergrowth. Get it straight. All my clothes are staying well and truly on.'

They returned to the crowd. A frustrated Bopper joined the rest of the tug-o-war team to mix a little rum with the copious amount of beer still sloshing in his stomach. Romance would have to wait until Kate was in a more amorous mood.

The party broke up early. Most families had distances to travel, with children asleep in carts and traps.

'You are welcome to spend the night in our barn,' Jim Brewster made the invitation to Billy Mendez. 'Norah tells me she has asked you to tune our piano, so that way you will be close and handy.'

'Thanks Mr Brewster, it's real Christian of you, but I'm happy to pitch the old fly to the sky, it's a lovely night and the stars are my friends. I'll wander down for your piano tomorrow.'

Night settled in on the valley. Some alcoholic stayers slept on in whatever place their consciousness had deserted them. They would wake stiff and cold in the early morning, probably to the enquiring gaze of a timid pademelon.

The Johnson farm's grassy carnival clearing would once more be an arena for animal grazing.

Riordans to Tara - Dan a Carrier

The Hilardt property was slowly coming to some shape. The little cottage was more liveable. The two windows possessed curtains made by Carmel, the black cast iron stove was pulled apart cleaned and polished. Dick Hilardt had thrown in his primitive furnishings as part of the deal. Blackie, the strong black barb cattle dog with big, mournful brown eyes, was another free acquisition.

'Would you take him. He's been here since a pup and he's four years old now. He's a good old bloke and I'm sure he likes Nell already.

He'll be good company for her while you are away working.'

They agreed. Blackie, for days, kept looking for his old master but soon became attached to Nell.

Daniel ordered a new bed from Grafton and when it arrived in Ballina, Pat brought it up free of charge. The bed, tradesman made of local rosewood, complete with a heavy kapok mattress, was their one claim to luxury. They assembled it with pride, made it up with new linen sheets and were early to retire that night. They were happy with the comfort of their new bed and with the comfort of each other.

Dick had made it known that after the Sports Day, he would be heading back to the lights of Sydney. Meanwhile, he had an arrangement of being a semi- permanent boarder with Carmel. The bank had made good the loan to cover the deficit in Dan Riordan's cash supply. Money had changed hands and the Riordans were now owners of the block, waiting for registration of their purchase by the far away government authority.

Dan had a big fencing job on the Johnson property. He was up each morning early and rode across on Chief. His lunch in the saddle bag and some tea leaves in an old black billy. His skill as a post mortiser with his big, sharp chisels and ability to build efficient post and rail fences was sought after. On a good day with no stumps underground to slow his progress, he could construct 15 panels and be home by sundown. He intended to use Saturdays for making a neat home paddock that would hold a cow or two for themselves. Some of the land part cleared by Dick was already showing heavy growth of tobacco bush, inkweed and Lantana. This secondary growth meant constant brushing work until grass was established. The brush hook and axe would have to be constant companions once he could find time. There was no doubting the fertility of the land, everything grew apace.

Already Pat O'Reilly had thrown out feelers to Dan as to whether he'd be interested in part-time haulage driving.

'This business is growing and I'm having to knock back some jobs. You know how careful I am of my horses and I reckon you know how to look after a horse. It will take a while for you to learn to be a carrier, but I'm prepared to show you how I do it.'

'I'm interested Pat, I'll talk it over with Nell. I'd need to come with you for a while to learn. A day or two occasionally with no pay would be fine.'

Pat held up a work toughened hand and made it clear.

'No Dan, I'll pay while you are learning,' he said. 'Not as much as you now make in a good day's fencing, but enough that you won't be far out of pocket. At present our work is mainly collecting and distributing from incoming ships. As more settlers like you and I, produce crops it will mean carriers to take their produce to the shipping points. This plateau seems to grow anything but it's not easy to work the tracks to the river or to Ballina. In time there will be gravel on better roads. Meanwhile we haul when the weather allows.'

So, the die was cast for Dan to learn the carrying business. It was at times a nerve-wracking, long difficult job. The tracks were slowly developing to what could optimistically deserve the title of roads.

Some of the worst bog patches had been improved with the common cheap system of laying ti-tree logs crosswise, known as corduroying. This was a rough road building expediency and hard on wheels but prevented wagons sitting bogged to their axles.

Things could and did go wrong. Good horses and good equipment, as well as trying to see problems before they happened, were essential. Pat had developed an extra sense for meeting problems; he tried to give Dan Riordan the benefit of his experience. They did several trips together on the big wagon, and then several more trips with Dan driving the small cart with old Captain in the shafts, while Pat and the wagon carried the heavy loads.

'That old grey horse knows more about carrying than I do,' was how Pat put it across. 'If he stops and doesn't want to go, have a good look, there's always a reason. He's getting old but he'll teach you the job if you let him.'

Captain and Dan made several solo cart trips with light supplies from Ballina to Duck Creek.

'I never thought Pat would let anyone else drive the old feller. I'm sure they have two-way conversations. He must think you're very good.' That was how Barney Shaw at the livery stables greeted Dan when he arrived with a load of chaff and oats. 'I've yet to see a better man than Pat O'Reilly with horses, so watch and learn.'

He helped Dan carry the feed to the tack room.

'How about a beer?' Barney enquired of Dan.

'Thanks Barney but not this time. By the time we plod home it will be getting late.'

'Yeah Dan, that is probably wise, I've seen too many carriers with a thirst. Give our love to Nell, you are a lucky man. We hope it goes well for you. One of these days the wife and I will come and call.'

With the cart empty but for a couple of bags of chaff, Dan and Captain tramped east towards home. It would certainly be dark by the time Captain was fed and bedded down. Then it would be another half hour before Dan made it across to Tara and Nell.

The steady clip clop of Captain's shod feet and the rolling wheels made a rhythmic peaceful tune, a world apart, but not unlike the steady sighing of a ship under sail making slow way in a light cross breeze. So many nights on watch he had sat in this state of suspended time, part of, but superfluous to a progress completely out his control. Now his function was so different but it seemed in the deepening dusk that the cart and Captain, were masters of their destiny, and he was just there for the ride.

His thoughts roamed free as he watched the stars come alive. Venus soon rose bright above the western horizon and the overhead star canopy slowly increased in candlepower. He kept veiled the thoughts of the past and that last fateful sailing trip and shipwreck. He was busy and physical tiredness meant sleep came easily most nights. Nell was all he could hope for. She too, was always busy and they were happy in each other. His reverie came to an end as Captain turned into the lane leading down to Killarney. The old horse knew they were almost home and stepped out a little quicker. Dan jumped down, opened the gate and stood aside as Captain walked through of his own accord, stopped and waited for the gate to be closed. Many horses so close to the lure of stable and feed bin, would have continued on. Not Captain. He was part of a team; that was his training and his placid nature.

Over the next six months "O'Reilly-General Carriers" took on another horse, and a light spring cart. The increasing population of Lismore and more specialty shops meant an increase of carrying opportunities. Pat found with Duck Creek halfway between Ballina and Lismore, there were some jobs to be done not supplied by the river ships that made it all the way up the river from Ballina. It became common practice for Dan Riordan to spend at least a couple of days per week driving on the fast delivery scheme. Pat had purchased a part Arab, part Clydesdale, bay mare named Bonnie. She was capable of trotting long distances and making light deliveries where speed was asked for and the client was prepared to pay that little extra. It meant now Pat could often be collecting with the big wagon from ships in Ballina and Dan could be making deliveries around the area, wherever those deliveries were wanted in a hurry.

The men worked well together, and Dan was quick learner.

'You're learning plenty about this growing district Dan,' said Pat 'I'm only able to pay you a little more than you make fencing but you never know when what you are learning may be useful. Perhaps one day the business may grow enough for O'Reilly Carriers to want a partner.'

'I'm happy Pat,' Dan replied, 'It won't be long until the baby is due and I won't be able to go on long trips, you know that. I like the work and it is letting us pay off the money we borrowed. Nell is a great girl and never complains when I'm home late.'

The School and a Teacher

The school was ready to open in the Spring. It was a simple, spic and span little building, painted cream with dark brown trim around the windows and doors. There was a small veranda facing north, with two rows of metal hat and coat pegs, rather like highset metal teeth between wide awake window eyes. After the sports day, completion work went forward apace. There were sufficient funds to furnish and supply necessary double desks, stools, textbooks, maps for the wall, and incidentals that the school committee decided were necessary for their special seat of learning. Many parents helped with painting and finishing the building. Pat and Dan made a neat post and rail fence around the horse paddock, with a carefully swung gate that children could open. Many of the potential students would have to ride horses to school. Situated close to the end of the lane on a slight rise and at the northern extremity of Surreyville, it was the developing area's first big community effort.

Selection of a teacher was the all-important subject. They wondered who it would be and realised the choice would not be theirs to determine. Some parents of older children were strongly in favour of a male who would impart discipline to senior boys used to men's work. These freedom loving seniors would find book learning within the confines of a school an unwelcome restraint on their so far unfettered life. Some were happy and some unhappy when the Government Education Department in Sydney announced the choice of a Miss Wilkinson as teacher in charge. She was to board with the Brewsters and would have but a short walk to school. It was arranged that there would be a get together at the school on the Saturday night after her arrival, for parents and teacher to meet. It was expected most parents would find a way of being present to cast an eye over the lady to be entrusted with their children. No details were furnished other than name. There was much speculation as to who would eventuate to become this important but description lacking "Miss Wilkinson".

It was a two-way source of wonderment, for the potential teacher knew little of what she faced on the Far North Coast of NSW.

Edna Elena Wilkinson, with a large tin trunk, three medium size leather carry cases and a hat box, boarded the coastal schooner "Matilda" at Balmain wharf, bound for Grafton. From there she had to find an as yet unorganised land connection to Duck Creek Mountain. She had come to Sydney with parents and a brother from Liverpool, England in the late 1840s. That was twenty odd years ago. Now in her mid-thirties, this was to be her second venture aboard ship. The Matilda was a far cry from the big square-rigged clipper that brought the family from England. It looked incredibly small from the dock and only a trifle larger when she had negotiated the gangway to the deck. However, there was no turning back. She waved to her mother and brother who had accompanied her in a hired Hansome cab to deposit her, and the necessary luggage, on the busy wharf.

Captain Gillies showed Edna to the forward cubby hole that carried the flattering name of a cabin. However, the trip would only take two days with the favourable sou'east wind predicted to blow them up the coast.

They shared a common north of England accent, although the burr of Edna's speech had been blunted by the Australian outback.

'We'll be under way very soon Miss Wilkinson,' said Captain Gillies, 'There is little room for passengers on deck with the crew very busy on the sails until we clear the Heads. I'll ask you to stay in your cabin until we are out and the sails set. Then the mate will show you where you can find a place to be on deck when the weather is right. We should have a good trip, but I can't guarantee the weather, although it should be in our favour.'

'Thank you, Captain Gillies. I will try to be no trouble and keep out of the way.'

She settled into her foc'sil cubby-hole and listened to the sound of orders, winding windlasses and creaking ropes. There was the unmistakable smell of sailcloth, sisal rope, oakum caulking and the undefinable odour of a sailing ship. It blotted out the inland activity that she had experienced in the past twenty years.

She could have been back on the docks at Liverpool, waiting to take the tide down the Mersey on the big trip to Australia. Soon the gentle lift of the harbour swell, and the soft caressing slap, slap, of water on the ship's bow, plus the odd glimpse of movement through the minute porthole, meant they were heading down towards Sydney Heads. Edna sat on her bunk and wondered.

Fourteen years of age when she arrived in Sydney, the growing up process had been rapid. Opportunity for further schooling could only be achieved at some of the private schools of the city. This the family could not afford. Her father had been a clerk in a Bradford woollen mill and managed to find a similar position in the growing woollen brokers industry of their new city. The wage meant there was only enough after food and lodging for the younger brother to attend a school. Edna found employment with a North Shore wool broker as governess and general help for his family. She continued to read and study and three years later was recommended by her employer for the job of governess on a large inland sheep station. Here, years passed quickly. She became absorbed in the pastoral scene of a big station. Romance in the shape of a young jackeroo had brought the promise of marriage and a future.

It all fell asunder with the fall of a horse at a country race meeting. Before her eyes, the falling horses were unable to avoid his prone body. Carrying the weight of shock, she moved on. There were other stations in Queensland and South Australia, and she was governess to other people's strong healthy children. She immersed herself in those children and gave freely of herself. There were fleeting male friendships, offers of love that she retreated from, always at the expense of conflict with her own warm, human emotion. At times, in a lonely bed, she found it very difficult to explain to a healthy body her denial of its needs.

During a holiday in Sydney, she answered an advertisement for teachers in a newly formed NSW Government Education System. She was surprised when called for an interview, and even more surprised when told she was selected to be listed on immediate appointments for small country schools. A week later and here she was catching fleeting glimpses of passing water as her port hole window rose and fell. The Matilda gathered breeze in her sails and ran toward North Head.

Edna stowed the one carrying case she brought to the cabin and turned off the mental twitching that was part of this new adventure. She sat. Her body still but her mind racing, *where was this Duck Creek anyway?* Enquiries from Sydney sources said it was a scrub clearing, inland from Ballina amongst a vast plateau of rain forest. The area's claim to fame was it supplied valuable red cedar, this soft workable timber made into furniture and joinery, for many city buildings.

Edna felt it fitting to talk plainly to an infinite God.

'Alright God, if you know I exist, may this stupidity of mine be part of your great plan.'

The run up the coast was smooth and pleasant. A strong offshore sou' wester kept them under plenty of sail and making good time.

True to her word, Edna kept out of the way of a busy crew. She took meals in her cabin and made use of a rope coil seat between cabin and the main mast. Here she sat in the sun and read, watched the seabirds that came to check out the little ship. The gulls were a squabbily lot, fighting over galley scraps cast overboard. An occasional petrel or albatross drifted in to chase the gulls and a couple of schools of curious dolphins had fallen into line to swim with the Matilda. She was often able to see distant peaks of the Great Dividing Range, as the helping breeze allowed Captain Gillies to stay tight inshore. They were off the mouth of the Clarence by mid-afternoon on the second day. Edna was unsure whether to be glad or sad the trip was coming to an end.

The captain sought out Edna before he became busy with the task of entering the Clarence bar.

'Well, it went to plan,' said the captain. 'We've had a good run Miss Wilkinson, and we should be inside the river within an hour. Probably best you stay in your cabin while we enter. Conditions look all right but you never know with river bars. Thank you for being a cooperative passenger. I hope you find a way to that Richmond mountain where you are heading.'

'Thank you, Captain Gillies,' she smiled, 'I've enjoyed the sea trip. Most of my travelling in Australia has been by horse, usually hot and dusty.'

Their entry in past the small fishing village at the river mouth was without incident. However, Captain Gillies and the crew knew the dangers; no river entrance was to be trusted. The Clarence was the pick of the North Coast river bars, usually with good deep water and a predictable channel. Guided by the beacons on the banks, they still had several hours travel to reach their destination; the growing town of Grafton was well upriver. It would be dark by the time they tied up at the wharf.

Any ship arrival was an important happening and there were several interested parties waiting patiently on the wharf when the Matilda was successfully moored to the heavy, hardwood bollards on the long wharf at Grafton. Edna with Captain Gillies' help was able to hire a horse cab to shift her considerable gear to the Commercial Hotel. There she booked a room, settled for the night, and prepared to face the still formidable task of finding an overland trip for herself and her luggage to this nebulous Duck Creek Mountain.

Coach and Ship Travel

'Gor Blimey Miss, you gonna need a spare cart to shift that much luggage.'

"Shifty" Wheeler, the coach driver, who did twice a week return trips Grafton to Casino, suspiciously eyed the four suitcases, hatbox and a large heavy tin trunk. The small cockney scratched a large ear nestling beneath an old cloth cap and eyed the attractive young lady quizzically. He had sunk his small capital, accrued from bar work and tips, and found a backer to start his humble coaching business.

'Mr Wheeler, that luggage is an important part of my job as a teacher. Unless you can take it aboard with me, I will have to make other arrangements.'

Edna fixed her firm, but conciliatory, look upon the driver.

'Well, I suppose you be lucky, there's only two other passengers, maybe we can stow some of those cases inside.'

Shifty had no intention of losing a paying fare. Besides, Edna looked his most interesting passenger. The alcoholic commercial traveller, also on board, looked likely to spend the day sleeping off last night's love affair with a whiskey bottle, and the large elderly matron was an obvious pain in the nether regions, already bemoaning the quality of the coach seats. They provided Edna little competition. A couple of her suitcases could be handy to prop up the hung-over commercial traveller and keep him parted from the vocal matron.

The old coach lumbered north out of Grafton. The four horses in hand were matched pluggers who would raise a trot on the good stretches and walk the rough and hilly patches. He had a holding paddock at Halfway Creek. There they would change horses and hopefully reach Casino by dark or shortly after.

They reached the changing point at about 2 o'clock. A one room shanty and small harness room was all the amenity boasted. It was run by a half-caste lady named Renie, who kept a big, black kettle boiling for tea, and could supply damper and stew. The stew could contain wallaby, pademelon or bush birds; only the very fussy enquired too deeply into the menu. Most travellers were hungry and it was known that Renie's cooking utensils and rough crockery were clean. There was no reported food damage to travellers from her varied culinary menu. In fact, passengers spoke well of the cuisine.

She and Shifty had a friendship going that seemed to meet both their needs. Certainly, she was a vital cog in the business. Always, she had four fresh horses caught and waiting in the small yard. Her ability to handle a horse was well known on the cattle runs. Her previous man, Albert, three parts Aboriginal, was the best horse breaker in the district until a big mean sorrel seven-year-old came down in the yard and crashed him into a heavy round fence post. Renie dragged him to their hut and tended the unconscious man as best she could. She bathed his swollen forehead with water steeped in boiled ti-tree bush. Albert opened liquid, dark eyes around mid-night, gazed calmly at Renie and quietly life slipped away.

She sat by the body, wailing an unending, ebbing, flowing, soft nasal keening dirge until morning light reached the bush hut. A couple of the station boys helped her bury the body.

That was 10 years ago. Renie had knocked around a while doing cattle work on the "runs". She could handle a horse as well as any man. The offer had come of hotel kitchen work in Grafton and Renie had adjusted well, earning a reputation for hard work and honesty. It was there she met up with Shifty, when he came to work at the same hotel. They tried hard to disguise their no-frills romance. For a long time, no one saw a dark late-night shadow that flitted to and from Shifty's room. Always, she was gone long before daylight. Shifty marvelled at the fact he never heard her leave. Sure, he was a heavy sleeper and a night with Renie left him drained out, needing more sleep. She had the ability of her mother's people to melt ever so quietly into whatever space was available.

It was after a couple of years that he launched the idea of the coaching run. Renie agreed to be partner and went back to the bush and played her part well. She made a few shillings from selling her meals, Shifty bought the horse feed, and when in a generous mood handed over a little cash. There was no formal agreement and Renie knew Shifty would probably use her as best he could, then move on without her, if the business prospered enough to lead him somewhere better.

At the halfway stopping place, the travellers could make use of a slab walled pit toilet. Always, there was a dish of water and a bar of unscented soap. A rough table and a couple of stools stood on the small veranda, where the meal could be eaten and a short break enjoyed from the rough seating of the old coach.

It seemed half a day's jolting together of hips and shoulders along the rutted track, melded the three travellers of this trip to a form of rough unity. Mr O'Dwyer, the spirits traveller with a liking for his product, had improved in condition as the day progressed. Mrs Halley, the matron, was mission bound to visit "the prosperous run" of a daughter who was married to a "prominent" squatter. She even ceased after some time to espouse the value of modern comfortable Cobb and Co. coaches.

Edna let the travel experience flow over her and remained pleasant to her companions. She refrained from criticising the Shifty Wheeler transport; she had travelled in many tougher, rougher ways through outback, inland Australia.

It was a welcome arrival at Halfway Creek.

'Well, here we are folks, time for a break and a meal.'

Shifty opened the coach door and tentatively tested the humour of his human cargo. He had marked off Mrs Halley as a potential whinger but he was impervious to whingers, they were of no worry, once their fare was in his money bag.

'My good man, this wagon of your feels like it has four square wheels and those seats must be padded with stones.' Mrs Halley refused to be intimidated to silence. She clumped off to investigate the toilet.

Terrence O'Dwyer offered Shifty a nip from the sample flask of product in his pocket.

'Thank'ee but no, never take of the heavy water when on duty.'

Edna put a practised foot in soft leather buttoned boot to the iron step and athletically made the not inconsiderable drop to the ground.

A still warm damper, freshly cooked by Renie, was placed on the table. A heavy, black iron pot brought from the stove took pride of place on the rough, scrubbed hardwood slab tabletop. It wafted an appetising aroma from its stew content. A couple of lean, yellow dogs slouched across from the harness tack room and watched expectantly from five paces. Renie had definite thoughts on the role of dogs; they knew there was little chance of a handout from her before their scant evening feed. Sometimes they could scrounge a bite or two from softer touch travellers.

'It is half an hour only folks. We have to keep a rolling,' was Shifty's message as he went to change his horses for a new team.

He ran a practised eye over the four starters yarded by Renie. First, could he use the existing harness? The collars were the vital key. It didn't pay to match a nag with an ill-fitting collar or you had a sore shoulder that took weeks to heal. He reckoned this four would measure up to the existing sweaty collars so that saved time and effort.

A quick wipe with a hessian bag and on they'd go. That big baldy faced chestnut, with a fair splash of thoroughbred in him would have to be watched until he settled. He'd place him nearside back where he should settle well. The old roan gelding with the hairy heels of his Clydesdale forebears would make a good nearside leader, not fast or flashy, an honest reliable anchor point for the team.

They were ready for the road. Mrs Halley was first aboard with the help of a rough fashioned step loading block, cut from a bloodwood stump. She even seemed somewhat more resigned to the trip and spared her fellow travellers the praises of her past shared refinements. Mr O'Dwyer was a seasoned traveller. He found all forms of travel acceptable if washed down with an occasional nip of whiskey. Edna was looking ahead and already wondering about the final leg of her journey from Casino to Duck Creek.

It was night when the coach rumbled down to the crossing and then up and out of the shallow Richmond River that announced the small but growing village of Casino. They were booked into the shanty hotel. It now catered for the increasing number of travellers arriving to seek overnight accommodation. The two ladies were thankful to make the shelter of their small, but private rooms. Mrs Hallett had exhausted her complaints. Tiredness had taken over and her substantial bulk yearned for a bed. Shifty grabbed a young timber worker from the bar, with a promise of a free drink or two, to unload Edna's considerable luggage. It was stowed in the storeroom. Edna claimed her case with personal requisites and headed for her room.

Terrence O'Dwyer freshened up at the large crockery wash basin in his room, then he headed for the bar, sample case in hand. Work time had begun. Here there was business to be achieved. The publican was a good customer and hopefully would place a large spirits order. One country bar was much the same as another, the drinkers could be relied on to accept a free sample. Many a host usually responded well to a free sample and elaborate praise of an often threadbare establishment could work wonders. The O'Dwyer blarney could usually be relied on to wheedle a good order from a friendly barkeeper. He thought nothing of spending a pound on a night's good will; it was a gamble that usually netted handsome dividends. His reputation as a successful man on the track was making an impression on the brewery firms for whom he worked. Whether his hard-working methods would allow him an old age was not their worry. They relied on his orders and were prepared to pay a bonus when those orders were large.

The North Coast was a developing area of great potential, a predominantly male population of lonely, hard, physical workers not averse to having a drink. Hence, there was a need for the skills of Terrence O'Dwyer.

The logistics of the final leg of her journey from Casino to Duck Creek was a worrying challenge to Edna. There was no organised connection. Most travellers to the coast were male; they usually hired a horse and set out over the now well-defined track. Edna, at the suggestion of the publican's wife, was directed towards the Reverend Martin Baillie's house. It seemed a chance the Presbyterian Minister may have a suggestion. He travelled the road frequently and may know how her luggage and self could be transported.

Martin received her courteously at his residence and listened to her problem of transport.

'Ah, Miss Wilkinson, this area is crying out for education,' he said. 'May I welcome you. I was present at the first meeting where those good people came together with a common cause to build their school. It is wonderful that they have worked hard to achieve their goal and they now have a teacher. We will find the means for you to complete your journey. There is always a way.'

He gave her a confident smile.

'I could hire a horse and ride, Reverend Baillie, but my luggage is mainly to help set up the school, so that has to go with me.'

'Yes, the luggage is a problem,' he said. 'There is no carrier service by land, but there is a boat service down river from Irvington. That service could deliver the luggage and yourself to Blackwall. I know Pat O'Reilly would pick you up there if he knew when to meet your river transport. It is only a couple of hours' trip from there up the mountain to Duck Creek. That seems our best plan at the moment. Mr Cameron has a horse and cart that he uses to pick up shop supplies from Irvington wharf. I'll go and see what we can do.'

'It seems I'm giving you many problems but I gratefully accept your help.'

'Right, you wait in our parlour and Mrs Phipps my housekeeper will serve you tea and look after you. I'll go and talk to Mr Cameron. I'll soon be back.'

Half an hour later Martin was back. He smiled at her quizzically.

'The Lord is good and works in strange ways Miss Wilkinson,' he said. 'To-morrow, David Cameron is going to meet the *Susie* and if you don't mind riding in his cart, he will take you and your luggage. He will talk to Captain McKinnon. They are friends. I am sure he will persuade him to take you and the luggage to Blackwall.'

'I am very grateful Reverend Baillie and sorry to be a nuisance, but I knew I'd be relying on help to make this journey. How will Mr O'Reilly know to pick me up?'

'Ah, I've thought of that. I am due to make a trip to Ballina and it seems I'd better make that trip a little earlier than intended. Old Dundee and I will leave at daylight tomorrow and call in at the O'Reillys. The

Susie won't arrive at Blackwall until late afternoon. I'll have someone there to meet you, or I'll be there myself.'

Edna smiled at Martin Baillie. A trusting, friendly smile, that had won many hearts over the years. It belied the firm governess look she tended to normally fire at pupils or casual acquaintances.

'Well, I suppose, Reverend Baillie, my trust in God has worn a little thin at times. It seems he has blessed me with your help; so, I'd better do better in the future.'

Martin was in the saddle before sunrise. The morning was misty with the threat of showers. He wore the clothes of a normal bush traveller. If it rained, well, he would be wet and uncomfortable, as he had been many times before. His clerical suit, vest and collar packed in his oversize saddle bags, were there to be used when required.

David Cameron called for Edna and they set off for Irvington. It was an unusually early stop for Mr Cameron at the hotel. He delivered supplies there as ordered- that was his business. He disapproved of alcohol and although he accepted that Casino needed a public house, he was often outspoken of the behaviour that he witnessed there. The large tin trunk, four suitcases and one hatbox, were stowed in his cart. A flat board seat stretched across the front of the cart, this David Cameron and Edna shared.

Lochie, the old bay cart horse, knew the way to Irvington. It was a two to three hour trip at his steady walk. The track was through a heavy, black soil flat that could be boggy in wet weather. It was the way the Camerons brought in some, indeed most, of the store products they sold. The river from Ballina, or the steep track down from the tableland, these were the normal supply routes for Casino.

Small ships that worked the south arm of the Richmond, tried to work the tides. It was a very narrow river past Coraki, and difficult to make much use of the sail. Should the wind and tide be unfavourable a rowing boat and two sets of oars could keep a small ship travelling in the right direction. The *Susie* was at the little wharf taking on casks of tallow when the patient, honest Lochie and his cart pulled up at the planked surface, where sat the many needed goods to keep the Cameron store functioning.

David Cameron introduced Edna to the captain and explained her need to be transported to Blackwall wharf.

'I am pleased to meet you ma'am,' said the captain. 'You will realise we are not normally a passenger boat. We have no comfort to offer but if things go well and we catch the down tide at the junction, where the rivers meet at Coraki, I should have you at Blackwall before dark. I'll tell my crew to watch their language, but they are likely to forget if things go wrong.'

'I appreciate your taking my luggage and self aboard Captain. I will keep out of the way and keep my ears closed to what I shouldn't hear.' As an afterthought to assure Captain McKinnon that she was not a city shrinking violet, she added, with hint of a smile, 'I worked many years on sheep stations and sometimes came close to shearing sheds.'

The tallow from Tomki Station was winched aboard with the aid of a simple pole derrick and a hand windlass. One of the *Susie* deckhands helped load the Cameron goods from the wharf to the cart. Edna and David Cameron made their farewell.

'I trust it will go well for you lass; we will enquire from Reverend Baillie how your arrival worked out. He will see that you reach your destination.'

The reliable Lochie and a well laden cart tramped homeward, soon hidden by a bend in the river.

It was near high tide and a hint of helping westerly breeze meant Captain McKinnon was anxious to head down river with the first fall of the tide. The *Susie* had been turned before loading and they soon cast off from the wharf, with the rowboat acting as tug and four of the crew bending their backs to promote some initial movement. Out in the middle of the narrow stream the westerly found the small foresail and the *Susie* achieved steerage speed.

Edna sat on a case with her back against a cask and amused herself sketching the *Susie*. She was a capable black and white artist with many sketches, that one day she claimed she was going to convert to colour. The riverbanks in late winter were fairly bleak, the lean skeleton limbs not yet ready to burst buds on the trailing naked branches. The oaks that grew tall on the banks were clothed in drab, dark, brownish green needles. An occasional river gum graced the high banks.

It was a pleasant scene from the little ship that nosed its way down stream. It needed knowledge of the river channel to keep momentum without grounding. Edna was amazed at how close they came to the banks at times. On a couple of occasions, Captain McKinnon posted a man in the bow with a lead line to call the depth. The breeze held steady and although the river looped around many bends, a westerly could always filter through and tend the closely hauled sail to give momentum with help of the ebb tide.

They made the riverside village of Coraki, and here the river became noticeably wider. Yabsley's ship building yard on the edge of the river near the junction was a scene of activity. A wharf of reasonable size took pride of place in the middle of the village, but on this occasion, Captain McKinnon sounded the ship's hooter and continued through. The run in the tide was noticeably stronger and the *Susie* gathered speed. Captain McKinnon handed over the wheel and prepared to eat his lunch.

'Miss Wilkinson the menu is beef sandwiches and tea, you are very welcome to share. It's still a long way until you go ashore and there are no eating facilities at Blackwall.'

'Thank You, Captain, I do have sandwiches very kindly made for me by Mrs Cameron. A cup of tea would be lovely if it is no trouble.'

'Right Miss, I'll see you receive a cup of tea in our visitor's crockery. We can offer sugar but no milk.'

'You are too kind. The tea will be fine however it comes.'

The lad who brought the tea, smiled shyly at Edna.

'Your tea, Miss,' he said. 'The captain says you are going to the new school up on the mountain. My parents have a little farm near the track on the way up. My brother and sister will go to your school.'

'Thank you for the tea and thank you for telling me of your brother and sister. If you have any spare time, come and tell me about your family. I need to know something of my pupils. What is your name?'

'John Richards, Miss.'

'Did you have any time at school John?'

'Only three years. We came north from Newcastle when I was ten, and my mum tried to help once we went on the farm, but it didn't work too well. I can read and write a little.'

'John, just remember, it is never too late to learn and if you want some suggestions come and see me when I've settled in. Try to read everything that becomes available. If you want to learn, then reading lets you find a way.'

They passed the junction of the river with Bungawalbyn Creek and made good time downriver. The big sweeping semicircle bend of Swan Bay lead to a wide straight run to Woodburn. Here the larger settlement was on the north side of the river with some straggly buildings on the south side as well. There were other ships on the river, some much larger than the *Susie*. Captain McKinnon sounded the hooter and crews waved as passing was achieved. The riverbanks were much lower and a view of some of the land that stretched away from the banks was possible. Evidence of land clearing was easily seen. Some cultivated land with crops of unpicked ripe maize, and here and there a field of oats or barley, the vivid green a stark contrast to the winter browns of native grass and the wiry tall rush that grew on the banks.

The sun had fallen low in the west when Captain McKinnon came to Edna and smiled.

'We are nearly there, round the next bend Miss Wilkinson. I suppose we've been around so many bends, that you are beginning to doubt whether Blackwall will ever appear. Your river trip is almost over.'

Towards Journey End

They eased in and tied at the wharf. A large sawmill and a few buildings seemed to be the community of Blackwall. John Richards, the 14-year-old deckhand, collected Edna's luggage, and with another crewman, they manhandled the tin trunk and suitcases ashore. Next it was Edna's turn. A 10-inch plank sloped up steeply from their gunnel to the wharf. They looked doubtfully at Edna.

'Will you be able to walk up?' John's question made Edna determined not to show the doubt she felt.

'I hope John, I hope.'

Edna looked at the short distance, resolved not to look down, and made the few steps. The hardwood decking felt solid and friendly when she had successfully made safety of the wharf.

She wondered of the few persons on the little wharf, if one was waiting for her. She was relieved when it was a young lady of about her own age who came and made a smiling greeting.

'You have to be, Miss Wilkinson. I am Bridget O'Reilly. Reverend Baillie called about lunch time and said you were coming on the *Susie*. He offered to do even more and to be here to meet you, but I assured him he had done enough for now and that I can drive a horse and cart. So here I am.'

Captain McKinnon was now ashore and came up to the ladies.

'Ah, I suppose I am late to make introductions, but I shall anyway,' he laughed. 'Miss Wilkinson, meet Mrs O'Reilly. Mrs O'Reilly's husband is our most reliable carrier and I'm sure his wife will have it organised to take you up the mountain.'

'Well, Pat is away on a trip with goods for Lismore, so a few decisions had to be made,' said Bridget. 'The light cart and old Captain were at the stable, so it looked like I had best be carrier on this occasion. Captain knows the way on his own and he will take us home safely. Pat never lets me out on the road so it will be a surprise for he and Dan. They probably think it's men's work.'

Captain McKinnon smiled.

'If you bring your Captain up near the wharf, I'll have the luggage loaded.'

Bridget went and moved the old grey to a loading position. John Richards did the heavy work of placing the load aboard, so the weight was evenly over the axle. They said farewell. Bridget was keen to be off. She knew it would be long after dark before they reached Killarney. Fortunately, the track up the mountain was dry, and a half-moon would give some light to see them home.

'I'm sorry to cause this trouble, but there was just no way I could give an accurate time of my arrival. After Grafton no one could say how or when, or if I would arrive. It has all worked out better than I hoped.'

Edna explained her dilemma. Bridget reassured her.

'There is no problem at all. My children are being well looked after at the Brewsters, where you will be staying. Pat probably won't be home tonight and I am enjoying this little adventure. It's a bit like the times I spent with my da aboard ship to see the stars looking down, only here we can get out and walk on dry land.'

They headed out through the sandy heath country close to Blackwall. Captain stepped out well; he had little weight to pull and knew it was only the climb up the white clay cutting that was any hardship from a horse's point of view.

The women chatted. Both were probably surprised to find that their backgrounds, although completely different, were similar in that both knew the drama of a not strictly conventional background.

They found the gentle creaking of the well-greased wheels, played a quiet soothing tune to the late afternoon. The last pink smudge on a clear western horizon highlighted a flat wash of fading yellow with Venus already a white splash on the still starless sky. That westerly breeze carried a clear cool hint of mountain cold that made the women snuggle down into their warm collars. Soon the sky would reflect light from the moon already there, but for now it was a fast-fading outline.

The climb up the steep two-tiered cutting propelled them from heath and river plain to the magical world of rain forest. The once thought endless rain forest world was fast disappearing to the settler's axe. Tracts still sloped down to remind a night traveller that this was an ageless land of dark hobgoblin secrets. A flitting firefly, luminous fungi, the strong wing swoosh of owl or bat. These were home sights and sounds of that inner, mysterious world.

Bridget produced sandwiches from under their seat. Also, two bottles of drinking water were stored in the space. These supplies would defeat hunger until they made home. Edna was surprised to find she dozed off occasionally and would come back to consciousness wondering where she was. The last week had brought many scenes and situations that were leading to new life. Would she be a good teacher? A station governess was one thing but a 'school ma'am' was likely to be very different. Any way she was committed and determined to give it her best.

It was 9 p.m. when Captain swung into the lane that led home. He was not pleased to be turned into the Brewster driveway; this was not part of his routine. A warm stable and feed awaited just down the lane. He snorted and gave the reins an experimental tug, just to see whether this mug driver really wanted to make the strange turn.

'Come on Captain. Sorry old boy, but this is our turn for now. It won't be long and you'll be munching chaff.'

There was a reception committee. Jim and Norah Brewster plus Dan Riordan, and Mary, Janey and Tom O'Reilly. Dan placed a friendly hand on Captain's nose band. He knew the old horse would be keen to finish his trip. Jim helped Edna Wilkinson descend from the cart.

'Welcome to Duck Creek Mountain, Miss Wilkinson. We knew Bridget and Captain would bring you the last part of your journey.'

'The ladies will come with me, Jim, you and Dan will bring Miss Wilkinson's luggage to the veranda.' Norah took charge.

The children hovered on the edge, wondering what this lady would do to change their previously carefree lives.

'I'll only stay a few minutes.' Bridget was anxious to take her children home.

'You will have a meal with Miss Wilkinson, it is all ready to serve. Dan will take Captain home, so that you won't have to attend to him. Then you and the children can stroll home.' Norah had thought it out.

'Thank you, Norah, but no, we shall go home with Dan. Tom will be asleep if we don't go now. You look after Miss Wilkinson, and we will all meet up soon.' Bridget knew what was best for her children. They all headed off in the cart with Dan at the reins.

'How did you know what was going on?' Bridget demanded of Dan.

'Ah, I had feed for the Brewster cows; they told me the story, so I reckoned I'd stay until you were home.'

'That's good of you, Dan, but we'll help with Captain and get you home to Nell. Does she worry when you're away?'

'Ah she's a good girl and handles most things well. I reckon she worries a bit. We've agreed she'll go down to Ballina when it's closer to the baby's arrival. Carmel has Mrs Heggarty, the mid-wife, on standby.'

Captain was bedded down. The O'Reilly children were in bed. Bridget watched the embers of the cast iron firebox burn down, tiredness began to creep up, replacing the adrenalin flow of the day's planning. They had exciting news for Pat on the morrow. The big day drew to a close; a teacher had come to Duck Creek. It was the day that their community had dreamed would happen and had worked together to achieve.

Teacher Delivered - A Party

Saturday night open house at the Brewster home was assured of good attendance. Invitations were sent to all on the plateau with school age children and to those who had helped make the little school a reality. There was a buzz of excitement amongst parents and children. Some of the older children were playing unimpressed with the foisted prospect of attending school. There were boys twelve years old who could swing an axe like a man but were struggling to write down their name or add a simple column of figures. Girls who could cook a meal, darn a tear in a sleeve but were equally nonplussed as the boys when it came to book learning. Parents, usually mothers, had done their best to give some fundamental teaching. It was a struggle when their own education had often been just as lacking substance. They were determined to do better for their children. One and all had worked for the school and they turned up in force to meet the new school ma'am. Each and every child had been scrubbed, and warned with dire threats, to bring forth their very best behaviour.

A log fire was burning merrily away from the confines of Norah's garden. Pat had brought in a few logs of iron bark to mix with the off cuts of teak. The warmth soon made a haven in the late August evening chill. It was expected to draw the men like moths to a flame. Strong drink was frowned upon within the mixed company but some male guests would have a slim flask in an inner coat pocket for internal heating. A surreptitious nip of whiskey or rum would be shared with a like-minded acquaintance. They thought ladies on the veranda or in the Brewster drawing room would be oblivious to their misdemeanour. Not likely, but the ladies would do their best not to know, and all would be happy in an even-handed masquerade.

Edna Wilkinson had spent the week since her arrival setting up the school and making a timetable for six classes. She was unaware of the exact number of pupils to expect. Norah and Bridget had made lists of possible starters and it seemed a score of about twenty was possible. The double desks could accommodate 24 and, if future need required, there was even sufficient space to add another four desks. Her books, charts and maps were strategically placed around the cream painted walls. Slates and chalk at the ready, enrolment forms were there for the signing of parents, and Edna had perused her check list at least a dozen times. She was as ready as it was possible to be.

'Don't worry, Miss Wilkinson, it will all happen smoothly,'

Norah assured her with aloof English confidence. 'These children will be as putty in your fingers.'

'It's the waiting that's worst,' said Edna on the Saturday afternoon.

She was confident the children would not be that different from the inland station families she had taught, but there would be more of them, and her work would be under the scrutiny of a Government School Inspector. Anyway, Mrs Brewster was right, there was no use worrying. The die was cast.

By 6.30 p.m, a sizeable crowd had arrived for the gathering and Edna was kept busy meeting the families. Not all would supply children to the school, many who had helped at the sports day and fund raising were keen to see what this teacher, soon to be an important part of their community, seemed to promise. An invitation to Brewsters was always incentive to become social. Certainly, this was the grandest house around. Secretly, many hoped the day would come when a present slab dwelling was felled and replaced with something like this. It was a model for their hopes.

Dick Hilardt decided to make a trip up the mountain. He was due to leave for Sydney at an early date, when the first berth was available on a coastal ship that he felt had a reasonable chance of achieving the journey from Ballina to Sydney. It was an opportunity to say farewell to the people he had come to know. The money received for the selection block sold to Dan and Nell would dwindle all too fast if he didn't leave Ballina. There were too many willing helpers waiting to have a drink or two, or three or four, or many more! Dick knew his weakness but had no real incentive to drink less.

Norah buttonholed him on arrival at the party.

'Miss Wilkinson, allow me to introduce Mr Hilardt. He is leaving us soon but has helped considerably in achieving our school. As an educated man, he did much to balance our books and tell us what we could spend.' Norah bustled off, leaving them together.

'I'm pleased to meet you, Miss Wilkinson. I sincerely hope you have a happy stay at the little school. You really are about to become a very important person in the life of this community. It is great to think that these children will have organised education at last.'

Dick Hilardt possessed a friendly manner and smile. His black wavy hair was showing signs of grey above the ears. He wore his clothes as a man not out of place in shone shoes and neatly folded cravat.

'Mr Hilardt, I'm not sure that the responsibility I face is going to the right person. I will try very hard to teach these children, but my own lack of experience is a worry to me.'

'The parents are good people Miss Wilkinson, some rough and uneducated, but be sure of one thing, most will give you every support to see that their children learn and show respect. I reckon the education people made an excellent choice in you. People like the Brewsters, O'Reillys, the James will be there to give help should you need help. Bridget O'Reilly is a wise lady for her age, and I'll be surprised if you don't find Mary O'Reilly a student above the ordinary. She is a thinker that child.'

Nell Riordan, now very noticeably pregnant, arrived to serve them with a tray of food.

'Hello Nell, why don't you take a seat here with Miss Wilkinson and allow me to act as waiter.'

'Ah, Dick I'm fine. I feel well and the light exercise won't hurt me. Still Mrs Brewster would like a tray taken over to the fire and the men. I'm pleased you have had opportunity for a chat with Miss Wilkinson and I know Mrs Brewster has a list of parents to bring to the teacher.'

'Right, I'll be off as the bearer of food. I will be back Miss Wilkinson.'

Relieved of the tray, Nell sat briefly with Edna.

'We bought our block from Dick, he's out of place here. He knows so much yet never talks of himself. My ma says he hides in a rum bottle, it's probably best he's going back to the city. He's been helpful and generous to us.'

'It's a wonder a nice man like that hasn't found a wife, or that a wife hasn't found him.'

Edna mused that statement to Nell.

'My ma guesses at the secrets in Dick's life, but it's sure he won't be telling her, or anyone else from what we know of him.'

Norah kept a supply of parents filing up to meet Edna. She made sure that all were given opportunity to talk with the teacher and none monopolised her attention. The night went well.

Over at the fire, the men talked. Those with a little internal flask lubrication talked the most. The school and its attractive teacher one subject of conversation, timber, clearing, crops, livestock, talk to keep men busy. Bill Richards and Don Gordon were fathers with twelve-year-old boys smarting under threat of school. They had adjoining blocks on the cutting; their boys were not keen on the restriction of school and the men were not keen for the loss of valuable labour input on their farms. Don spoke his thoughts,

'I suppose it's for the best, but young Dave's scowlin' around like a just weaned calf. His mother's so keen on this educatin' business. She won't hear of his not going to the school. John's down on the river doin' all right as a deckhand, and he wasn't as useful or strong as Dave. No good me saying anything or she'd shut me out at night with old Rusty the dog.'

Bill Richards also had some reservations on losing his son for eight hours a day.

'I know what you mean, mon.' Bill was also a lowland Scot, frugal with his money and with his words. He made for him a long morose statement.

'Bonnie says we must buy young Malcolm a pony, but I've put me foot down at a saddle, a corn bag will do him fine. An' ye 'naw, I ain't mentioned it, but pony may get him home in time for milking in summertime.'

Bopper and Kate

The James had a flash four-wheel buggy, rather an oddity in the frugal battling community and fitting the station of leading village publicans. It had arrived dismantled on the deck of a coastal trader from Sydney and aroused a lot of comment on the Ballina wharf. Pat O'Reilly delivered the stripped down model in the big wagon. He had even helped Rupert assemble the finished job. True, its use was at the mercy of the roads but Rupert reckoned there had to be improvement in time. The track out to Brewsters was acceptable in fine weather, so to make use of the new twin seated vehicle, the James offered transport to Bopper and Kate to attend the school get together. It was quite a load on the back springs with the massive bulk of Bopper and Kate, definitely neither to be described as slim. Each time the buggy lurched into a hole on Bopper's corner it tended to lift the pole on the necks of the pony pair.

'You, big boy, need to go on a diet,' Kate hissed at her large boyfriend.

'Lack of lusty exercise is the trouble my pet.' Bopper rolled his eyes sorrowfully at Kate. 'You want to leave your door open more often at night.'

The conversation went no further on that tack. Bopper had hopes for when they returned that night. Having sown the seed, it was best not to push the topic any further at this stage.

It was planned for the get together party to end at 9 p.m. Parents with children must be home early, and the purpose of potential parents and pupils and interested residents meeting Miss Wilkinson would certainly be achieved by then. Some had long distances to travel, it would take two to three hours for Ballina visitors to return. Dick Hilardt had accepted an invitation from Pat and Bridget to make use of their spare bed for the night. It would give him a last chance to visit Dan and Nell in the morning.

The party broke up. Those stragglers left, including Pat, Bridget and Dick, helped restore the usually immaculate Brewster home back to its normal state. It ended with Edna and Dick washing and drying up in the kitchen. The time went quickly, they found it easy to talk. Dick arranged that he would call and say farewell on the morrow.

Rupert and Laura James dropped off their substantial passengers at Kate's doorway.

Bopper was very sober. He was a model of propriety. Kate's room contained a small stove which Bopper kindled to life and they awaited the black kettle to supply boiling water for coffee. It was cosy, with long friendly shadows walking the walls. Bopper reckoned it a good sign that Kate hadn't immediately bundled him out the door. He made their coffee and pulled a silver rum flask from his vest. He respectfully produced the flask with the question,

'How about a little nip of Nelson's blood?'

'Mmm well, just a small nip mind and not too much of that fire water for you, either.'

Kate conveniently looked away as Bopper added the rum, another very promising sign. He threw in a spoonful of sugar to mask the taste of her potent drop. They sat close on the old couch, warm, friendly, and fire crackled in the stove. Between the fire in the stove and fire in the O.P. rum, it wasn't long before signs of warmth flowed through Kate's well stocked veins.

Bopper couldn't believe his luck. Beads of sweat shone out from Kate's brow through her heavy mascara makeup. She found it necessary to peel off several skins of coats and woolly jumpers. *Don't push it*, he warned himself. He knew from past sessions with Kate, he had to bide his time. She could turn off real quick if her passion fire wasn't well kindled. He patiently worked at fanning that fire with respectful smooching. Their solid ample bodies carrying hot, healthy messages. It wasn't long before her kisses grew interested, then longer and stronger.

Bopper's capable soup plate hand ventured up from her ample waist, testing the lay of the land, stealthily climbing. Big, searching fingers reached, roamed and gently kneaded an exciting cloth-encased, prominent breast area. Still firm of texture, standing alluringly high from her powerful chest, his supple warm tradesman fingers snuck inside the ample bodice. His trying to ease the green satin topless dress slowly down, caused some halt to proceedings.

'Careful muggins, it's my best dress. Don't stretch it,' she warned him.

She wriggled sensuously, helping his downward pressure, until the dress bodice dropped and her breasts broke free: large, white, curving waves in the dim light. She exhaled a sigh that signified all was warmly well. Bopper breathed in the heady strong scent of perfume released on her ample hot body. His huge arms locked her naked chest against him, their lips met, in a kiss, where tongues sparred intimately. His fingers now confidently sought responses.

He went to walk her over to the bed.

'Not so fast, big lover boy,' she whispered. 'That old bed of mine won't stand it. You can make us a bed on the floor. Leave your clothes on the bed. I'll get comfortable and be right back. Blow the light out.'

Kate slipped behind a screen at the end of the room. Bopper made their love nest on the floor and waited in dim dark but for the glow from the stove. He began to wonder what was keeping her. Then a white blur skilfully found him, consuming him, swallowing him up. Kate's desires finding in him the strength she needed. Eventually she let him free.

'That should keep you quiet for a while boy-o.' She gave him an affectionate tickle and kiss on the shoulder, then rolled them tight in their swag of blankets.

At 4 a.m. the fire was long out and the floor cold. Kate woke Bopper, for her, quite gently.

'Time for you to be gone, my lad and don't wake all the dogs in the village. Respectable people are sleeping.'

Bopper gave her a playful smack on an ample bottom.

'You weren't so keen to get rid of me a few hours ago.'

He dressed and headed off into the pitch-black pre-dawn.

He was not one for deep thought, but Bopper confided to the awakening dawn, perhaps one day, he'd make an honest woman out of Kate.

The morning after the introduction party was foggy. The Riordan residence still seeped moisture despite the best efforts of Nell and Carmel to seal the cracks between the slabs. Dan and Nell were breakfasting at the old pine table, oatmeal porridge and toast, not very different to what Dan had known as Irish breakfast. They were up early to greet the coming busy day. They expected Dick as a visitor on his good-bye round. With the fire in the cast iron stove burning merrily, some condensation dripped down the walls. Pat had located a good source of clay near the creek and with this, they were slowly sealing out the worst of the weather. Nell had plans for placing cheap hessian on the inner walls and painting or whitewashing the surface.

'Just give us a little time, my girl and we'll build the grandest house on the lane,' said Dan. 'I don't want you working too hard. Your mother and the midwife have told you not to go lifting heavy weights and stretching too high. I'm going to have to tell old Blackie to make you behave yourself.'

Nell laughed and raised her eyebrows at Dan. The arrangement to leave Blackie with the Riordans had worked well. He took immediately to Nell. Dan was confident the dog would make sure no snakes came inside the house.

The old black dog tolerated Dan but looked upon Nell as his new master. He had even learnt that lying on Nell's freshly dug earth in flower or vegetable gardens was not acceptable. On the rare occasions that he was called to task for misdemeanours, his soft brownish yellow eyes held a pained expression that insinuated these footprints couldn't be his.

He was their indicator that Dick was approaching. He left the little front veranda at speed long before the horse and rider came into view.

'Stop that barking.' Dick's firm command restored peace to Brownie's hired livery hack. So, Blackie escorted them down to the cottage where Dan and Nell were already outside waiting.

'You've done wonders. Doesn't look like my untidy tragic domain anymore.' Dick tied the livery nag to the new front post and rail fence.

'Ah Dick, you should have found a wife for free labour.' Dan put a protective arm around Nell.

'The ladies weren't interested in me, only old Blackie would give me a pass, and he used to be as untidy as me,' Dick laughed.

They went inside, where once more Dick praised their work. The teapot and matching cups stood on a worked Irish linen tablecloth. Nell supplied morning tea. Dick felt satisfaction to see this young couple happy and proud of their achievement.

His mind was forced back briefly, out of his control, to a vastly different mind scene of a stately English home from his childhood. This was something he never allowed. The past was a closed book, not to be opened. It surprised him to find ghosts of other places could still sneak in over the drawbridge of his mind. It was on occasions such as this that flat, attractively shaped bottles repelled those skulking ghosts.

Without knowing his guest's errant spontaneous thoughts, Dan suggested he may like a nip of rum.

'How about it, Dick, a nip for old time sakes?'

The amber liquid smiled at him from Dan's squat necked bottle.

'No, I think not, this morning I'll give it a miss and enjoy Nell's special tea in her special cups, in a special room.'

Dick's answer surprised himself. These two couldn't know how the ghosts of the past had cast him back 30 years. Elegant silver, fine china, starched linen, an unobtrusive serving man; yet he felt this humble room with two young people searching a new life was far more important.

Dick gently tapped his saucer.

'A toast my young friends. To four of us.'

They lifted their teacups. and Nell found a warm, pink blush on her healthy young face.

'I hope it all goes well.' Dick smiled at them and looked around the room. 'It's a pity I hadn't built a better house to sell you, but let's face it, I'm not a carpenter, or a farmer. Don't ask me what I am.'

Nell looked at him with solemn grey eyes. She answered him, 'You are our friend.'

Nell had an ability to accept fact and not go chasing butterflies of fluttering possibility.

'Thank you, Nell and if ever you need that friend, make use of the forwarding address. Perhaps I may be able to help. Anyway, I want to know when the baby is born and how the Riordans are making out.'

They walked with Dick to the end of the lane. Blackie seemed at a loss to know which way to turn, but accepted Dick's firm "no". He followed Nell back without a real allegiance worry.

Hello and Goodbye

Lunch was at Brewsters. The well-equipped room, while a poor compromise for Dick's earlier fleeting insistent visions of his English home in a shady Sussex countryside, was what most colonials would call grand. He found he was seated beside Edna at the large mahogany table and once more they seemed capable of talking to each other. Once more he found an out of character decision and declined the offer of wine with his meal. He wondered when last he had refused alcohol twice in one day. What was more important he wondered why he had refused, when for twenty years alcohol had been a constant intimate companion.

'Do you have contacts in Sydney, Mr Hilardt?'

Norah wondered what this seemingly ill-equipped man would do in the city.

'Yes. I still have a couple of acquaintances, but I'll have to find work before too long.'

He didn't supply detail and Norah knew a hostess was not free to pry. Dick had always caused speculation as to his background, and he had never let down his guard. Even when grog freed his tongue, he did not talk of his past. It seemed he would leave them with very little known of one, whom Norah admitted to herself, was an 'interesting' man. She addressed him with a proposal.

'Now, Miss Wilkinson has been living with her books for the last week. She needs exercise. Why don't you two take a stroll down to the big fig tree? You, Mr Hilardt are one who could tell her what the rain forest used to be like.'

'Would you like that idea, Miss Wilkinson?' Dick asked, 'I would be happy to escort you and we would not go far. About my knowledge, it's commonly known around here that the rain forest was my master. My horse has to be back at the stable before night, so I must be on the track early afternoon.'

He smiled at Edna, half expecting her to refuse the idea. To his pleasure she agreed.

'Just give me a couple of minutes to put on some strong shoes.' Edna Wilkinson was a person who gave straight answers.

The big fig tree grew close to the creek in a remnant of beech and teak scrub. Its huge, buttressed roots clawed out into the tall trees up the hill, as a safe anchor, and then down to the clear running stream. The slant of the huge trunk toward the creek cast a vast umbrella canopy of foliage above the gurgling water. This part of the creek was always shaded, a cool refuge especially in hot summer. On a clear day, noonday sun shafts speared indistinct leaf patterns on the chattering stream below. When the yellowy brown fruit fig berries were ripening, flock pigeon fed in the top canopy, once careless of man, but the flesh tearing blast of shot meant they were now very wary.

Edna and Dick walked in under the presence of the tree. They eased their way out to the buttress that ran parallel with, and indeed made part of the high creek bank. From this vantage spot Edna had a clear view up to the canopy. Orchids grew in the limb crevices and vine ropes trailed down over the water. The only sound, a faint murmur from the running stream, then a whirr of wings, a bluey grey and white Wonga pigeon, not seeing the two humans, landed close on an adjoining buttress. It quickly spied its human companions and with consternation beat a hasty scramble back into the air. It whirred away, further into the secluded scrub. Edna summed up her thoughts.

'It's almost like a cathedral. I had no idea trees were so big. I feel like an ant.' She kept her voice low in deference. She was determined to peer venturously over the buttress and down to the creek below.

'Please take my hand. Mrs Brewster and the community will never forgive me if I were to lose you over the side.'

Dick kept the remark low key; he could see the effect the scene was having on his charge. She looked at him squarely with a hint of a smile on a serious face: he took the proffered hand and she leaned out to peer down under the huge buttress root. There dwelt a hidden world of ferns, orchids and clinging vines that clutched the stream bank, forming a cave of myriad greens that hid secure under the overhang of the giant tree.

Edna came back to the visual world above ground.

'There is so much plant life. This land of abundance is so different to what I found in the dry inland. Were there many trees and places like this?'

'Yes. This plateau was probably one of the richest and largest areas of rain forest. I suppose the name Big Scrub was given here for a real reason. When I came up ten years ago, there were some small clearings and many patches of scrub that seemed to stretch away for ever. Now the clearings stretch away and the remaining patches of scrub are rapidly being swallowed by axe and fire.'

There was a note of question and sadness in Dick's voice that Edna picked.

'And you are sad that when you come back again this will all be orderly farming land? It will all be gone.'

She made the statement-question softly. He shrugged.

'But who am I to expound my views? I dived in with an axe the same as all the others.' Then to lighten the mood. 'The trees were just lucky my pen swinging hands were softer than most of the other settlers. I grew tired of chopping down trees. At times I needed bottle courage to blot out the stories some of those suffering old timers hissed at me as my axe bled their life sap.'

'At least your eyes saw and acknowledged beauty that probably even my eldest pupils won't find.'

Edna recognised the sadness in this man and also that she was seeing something soon to be forgotten. She knew the strains farming ventures placed on families. Not enough money, not enough time, not enough physical strength to balance the time factor that dwelt with the land. Yet the farmer always lived on hope. Sometimes, not often, that hope was justified.

They sat, not talking, squandering time, their flat chair height buttress was an adequate seat. Out in the light of day the late winter sun struck the cleared land across the creek, helping the Brewster pasture grass to grow. Over here, under the tree, was a different world. For this, their moment, life's time clock ticked so slowly. This frozen spot of time was slowed to the present reality; both knew the present could not relate to the future. Neither moved.

That minute seemed an hour. It passed. The eyes of two mature persons met. Dick placed a hand halfway across the foot of space that parted them, palm upwards, seeking, offering. She sensed, saw the firm open hand, didn't move the touch of their eyes, but slipped a hand with strong firm fingers on top of the larger male fingers. His hand gently covered her female hand.

'Miss Wilkinson, would you become Edna, and consider me a friend?'

'Mr Hilardt, you are Dick and yes, I consider you a friend.'

They knew the time of their newfound friendship was brief. They sat another minute that seemed but a second. He kept it light; she preferred it that way.

'Well, Edna I rode up to say farewell to old friends. No one had the decency to tell me the new school ma'am was a young, attractive woman. My system can't stand the strain.'

She played the moment with a light response.

'Ah, I know you educated gentlemen. I bet you sweep all the country lasses off their feet.' He smiled, predominately a wistful smile.

'You know we must go back. It's cruel fate at its worst. Should I bolt with you into the scrub, they'd probably track us down, I'm no good as a bushman.'

'Think of the scandal,' she said. 'School would not open and the community would probably tar and feather their supposedly respectable potential teacher when they caught her.'

They stood. He turned her toward him, lifted her face and gently kissed her. Their lip touch so soft yet transmitting its message. Neither allowed their depth of feeling to show. This splash of time and place presented unsought, was their secret. It was now time to emerge to the light and reality. They must return to hosts who could not be allowed to suspect anything from an overdue absence.

It was a small farewell cavalcade that walked down to the corner of the lane where the waiting school was ready to know the sound of children. Dick led Brownie's hired hack, the O'Reillys had come up to wave "God Speed", the Brewsters and Edna Wilkinson, all in attendance. They watched him mount. He turned and waved to the answering hands that fluttered near the school.

These people were all his old friends but the dark-haired Edna standing a little to one side held most of his attention. She caused him unexpected excitement, tinged with sadness, tinged with gladness. Why? It was so long since he had turned his back upon that disease labelled love. It was so long since he'd made a decision to live without the comforts but claims of women. He had not expected this farewell trip to untie phantom feelings long defeated. It all appeared straightforward until practised disciplines vanished with something that called to him through Edna. He had easily withstood the painted, practised women who had willingly displayed and made their charms available; they could be purchased and turned away. This person with clear grey eyes was different. Without trying, she had caused him to forget lessons he thought well learned. Would he come back to his senses? What was she thinking? Was this malady his alone?

They were soon gone from sight. He trotted briskly toward Ballina.

Bridget walked beside Edna as they made their way back down the lane. The children, Pat, and the Brewsters were in front. All had taken a final survey glance of the school to make sure it was truly in readiness for 9.30 a.m. tomorrow.

'Is it really only ten days since you picked me up at the Blackwall wharf? It seems an age ago already.'

She brought a light reply from Bridget.

'You know there is nothing like being busy to make the time fly. The school looks ready to welcome your pupils. You've done a great job. Don't worry, just let it happen. Norah or I will help anyway you feel it possible.'

School Colour Problems

It was on the Wednesday, two days after school opened. Miss Wilkinson had marched her nineteen charges inside and all had been given writing tasks, the only sound was the unmusical nasal gritty squeak of chalk on slate. Edna was neatly placing sums with varying degree of difficulty on the big blackboard.

'Miss Wilkinson, please Miss,' Mary O'Reilly spoke softly, with her right arm held skyward.

'Yes, Mary. What is it?'

'There are two people out at the veranda Miss.'

Sure enough, a glance through the window, proved Mary's information right.

'Carry on with your writing children.' Edna closed the veranda entry door behind her as she went out.

The space immediately in front of the veranda was empty, but out of view of the classroom, near the end wall stood a dark woman, and a lighter skinned girl of about ten years of age. Both dressed in clean but cheap calico dresses. The pair stood self- consciously still, looking at the ground.

Edna greeted them, 'Hello, my name is Miss Wilkinson. I'm sorry there is nowhere inside where we can talk, but this is fine, if you tell me what I may do to help. For a start, please tell me your names.'

The dark lady looked up briefly but found it too hard to meet Edna's smile and looked down again.

'I'm Rose, this Pearl. My man, Yan, told me, bring Pearly, see can she go to school.'

'Would you come to school each day, Pearl?' Edna spoke gently to the child, who made a big effort and looked briefly at the teacher.

Pearl nodded her head and said a clear, 'Yes.'

'How far away do you live?'

'Out that way. About one hour.' Rose pointed west.

'Who would sign the book giving me authority to teach?'

'Me, no write. Yan writes, he will sign your book.'

'Right Rose, you bring Yan, before or after school. Once I have the authority Pearl will start school next day.'

They nodded, turned and quickly walked back down the track.

Edna hurried back to the classroom. She knew a couple of the bigger boys would already be finding things more interesting than writing to make use of her absence.

'Did you get rid of them boongs, Miss?'

Angus James was her biggest and oldest pupil, 13 going on 20, and considered he knew all things that he needed without this school bother.

Edna was expecting trouble with Angus, but not this early in their relationship.

'Angus, you will not refer to dark-skinned people as boongs in this classroom, or I hope anywhere else. Bring me your writing so I can see what you have done so far this morning.'

He reluctantly squeezed out from under his too small half of the desk and proffered the rectangular slate. His task of, "It is a fine day." was only half scratched in an untidy scrawl.

'You would have been better occupied doing your work, Angus, than watching out the window. Go back, wipe it off and start again, and please, this time with more care.'

The large lad took his petulant bulk back to the desk. Edna knew he would not be slow to find a future opportunity to even the score. She wondered what the general reaction would have been if the half caste Pearl became a pupil in response to her offer. She looked a clean, tidy, well-behaved child. It would save any possible problems if Pearl, Rose and the unseen Yan, decided it was too hard and didn't return. Yet Edna hoped, and felt, she would return.

That afternoon, Edna told Norah of her visitors and asked if anything was known of the family, as they had not been mentioned in any of the exploratory student lists of possible children drawn up with the help of locals.

'I do believe Yan may be a scrub faller that Jim employed for a time, several years ago. He was a European, probably from the Balkans. We found out very little about him. Jim said he was an excellent axeman but would never talk at all other than to ask what was required of him. It's more likely Pat O'Reilly would know of them than anyone else around here.'

'It is best I find out something of the background if it is possible. I saw Pat go past with the wagon just after school came out, so I'll walk down and see what he tells me.'

Edna found Mary, Jane and Thomas seated at the dining room table working at the small tasks given for homework.

'Hello, come through,' was Bridget's call from the kitchen.

'Sorry to worry you Bridget but I wondered if Mr O'Reilly may have some information that would be useful to me.'

Bridget laughed, 'Ask him. He seems to store all sorts of information as he wanders around this plateau. Just head up to the stable, I think he's changing a set of shoes. I'll carry on with the scones, if you don't hurry, they should be ready when you come back.'

Edna followed the track to the stable. The not unmusical clink of a heavy hammer on hot iron indicated Pat was at work. The big, roan Clydesdale sensed Edna's presence and whinnied softly.

'He's a smart lad that one. Has an eye for the ladies. Those girls of mine think I don't know they sneak him goodies. To what do I owe the pleasure Miss Wilkinson, I hope those children of ours aren't a problem already.'

'Mr O'Reilly, your children are a delight. I may have the offer of another pupil. Norah and Bridget thought you may be able to tell me something of the family.'

Edna told Pat of the visit to the school by the shy, dark lady and daughter. He stood straight from his farrier task and stretched his tired back.

'Well now, that's very interesting. It just goes to show, even though we thought our list preparation of potential students was thorough, we slipped on that one. They have been around since the little girl was three of four. Their shack is down on the escarpment, probably we didn't consider it as part of the area when we drew up lists. Anything I can tell you is mostly the scraps that have come my way. Would you like me to come down to the house?'

'No, Mr O'Reilly. Just a few facts, such as whether you think the father and mother would try to see the child attends school. Whether the father could sign his name. Gossip doesn't interest me, but at times its best to know of circumstances that may affect the child's learning.'

'Alright, well I know Yan is able to sign his name. I know that he and Rose have a constant relationship, and it does not surprise me to find they want Pearl to attend school. Years ago, I picked up Rose and Pearl and gave them a lift almost home. Pearl was five or so and had a badly cut foot. Rose had carried her for miles to a bush nurse who had stitched the wound and she was carrying her back home. At first, she refused to climb on the cart, but Pearl's need got the better of her mistrust. Yan goes anywhere he can to find timber falling work. That's not as easy as it was, even five years ago. Rumour says the man has a past, but that's not unusual in the bush. I've carried a stove and goods for him. He always pays and gives me an impression that in his own country he had an education. The only other thing I could tell you, with a word of warning, is that some parents may not welcome a part Aboriginal child, but rest assured the O'Reillys would be right behind you.'

Edna gave him a quizzical smile.

'Thanks for that. Probably they won't come back, if they do, and give me signed authority as parents, I'll accept her. There is nothing I know of in my rules to say that I can't.'

'Good luck Miss Wilkinson and I hope it works out.'

Pat bent to his task, continued to thump the big heavy shoes into just the right shape for each foot, which the patient roan Clydesdale lifted on command.

Edna returned to the kitchen. The warm air dripped the lingering one-off scent of newly baked scones. To the invitation she said, 'Now you know I can't. Mrs Brewster will suspect at once if I don't do justice to dinner.'

She threw up arms in mock horror at the sight of the buttered scone coated with gooseberry jam.

'Norah doesn't have to know. The walk home will clear a space. The mental strain of those children demands we keep you strong.'

Bridget presented the scone and Edna praised her culinary work.

'Just one of my skills, you see why I'm getting fat.'

The casual observer would not have called Bridget O'Reilly fat; she still looked remarkably young and trim.

Pearl the Pupil

When Edna arrived at school the next morning, she was surprised to find Rose and Pearl plus the unmet father already present. He was a tall man with unkempt but clean, greying hair and a roughly cut beard. His clothes were old, well darned working drill, clean and probably the best he owned. His boots were heavy and oiled. He was a man of indefinite age, probably fiftyish.

'This Yan.'

Rose made her introduction and stepped well back to allow Yan the right to conduct the conversation.

'I'm pleased to meet you, Yan. The children won't arrive for a little while so we will go inside.'

Once inside, Edna produced the big book containing parents' information and signed by at least one parent. Edna explained briefly what would be required, emphasising that attendance and good behaviour was the one essential that she required.

'My English not good, but I understand. Pearl is taught to do what told. I will sign your book.'

The signature added to the list of nineteen names was Jaroslav Yanohavovich. The writing was neat with some letters formed differently to English. He looked at her.

'I just known as Yan, but that is my name. Rose and I have been together many years. Understand please, no wedding. Pearl is our daughter. We want to see her learn; we will help.'

It was agreed Pearl would start school that morning. Edna assured them that she would look after their daughter.

Her parents said farewell to Pearl and headed back down the lane. Edna did some quick thinking and decided to place Pearl in the same desk as Jane O'Reilly. They were the same age and perhaps Pearl would benefit from the bubbly outgoing Jane. Leastways she knew that opposition to Pearl was not likely from the O'Reillys. This was more than the storm clouds she expected to gather with Angus James.

Edna made a low-key introduction of Pearl to the class. She made them say a communal, 'Good morning, Pearl,' and the school day was underway.

The morning work session was mathematics for the four groups. First tables, then there were simple problems written on the blackboard. It seemed most of the bigger children had some idea of adding and subtracting figures and their general mathematical skill was better than their ability to read and write. Edna had decided to keep them in age groups for at least a week or so, before deciding the grade of work to which they were capable. The group of five 10-year-olds, seemed capable of tables up to five times, but Pearl shyly shook her head when asked whether she knew about tables.

'You can write down the sums anyway Pearl.' Edna decided she needed to find out whether Pearl had any idea of writing figures.

It came as a surprise when she inspected the work, to find of the 10-year-olds, Pearl's slate with its four simple problems was neatly written and her answers correct. The more surprising since one of Jane's answers was incorrect, so she had not received help from there.

'That's very good, Pearl.'

She made sure not to embarrass her with too much praise. There was time enough to find how her sum skills had been developed. At least, she seemed to have a good chance of keeping up at mathematics.

By the end of the morning, Edna had discovered the little dark girl was very lacking in spelling and using words but probably bright and quick enough to stay with the age group. There was certainly a story somewhere in her past. It seemed almost certain that Yan had tried hard to give his daughter some basic skills.

Some of the children spoke to her at the morning break. Some made sure they avoided her. She watched them play and Jane stayed close by her as a shield. Lunch was a bigger problem as it had been agreed the O'Reillys, being so close, could go home. Pearl sat on her own and ate the two damper sandwiches from her calico bag. Edna was relieved to see Ann Richards, after a while, came up and talked to her. Ann was of the same age group.

At 3.30 p.m. when school finished for the day, it was a scramble for home. About half of the children, the ones from a distance, had a horse or pony to ride. The small horse paddock had no water point, but there were streams on most of the bridle tracks so that horses could be watered on the way to and from school. Edna called Pearl aside and gave her a battered pre reading book, one of her own from the days of being a governess.

'Show it to your mum and dad, Pearl, and they may be able to help you learn the letters. You've done well today.'

Pearl didn't look up. but smiled shyly.

'Your maths is good, Pearl. Who has showed you how to do sums?'

The little girl rubbed a bare foot on the ground. 'My dad.'

'Tell your mum and dad you've done well. I hope you like school.'

Pearl headed off on her three mile walk home. Edna knew it was an ongoing daunting task for the little girl. She knew that before long there would be children who would delight in telling Pearl that her mother was "black" and so was she. All she could do was hope most of the children would support and help her difference. She was not very dark; her features threw heavily to Yan, her Baltic region European father.

Nell and Progress

Winter drifted slowly away from the plateau. The nights were still cold with a touch of early morning frost in the creek hollows, powdered white icing that browned any grass and crisped black the low leaves on vagrant lantana. Yet the sun fought its way into the sky each morning with a little more warmth and determination. Peach trees wore close cropped pink curls on their leafless arms and torsos, dark evergreen oranges shook white fists of sweet-smelling blossom. Worker bees loaded with nectar flew many trips back to their home hives. Some scrub trees were breaking to bloom, the rain forest teak and carrobean carried a sweet-smelling floral tribute. Spring: was a time of awakening activity on the Duck Creek plateau.

Nell had watched Dan ride off to do a day's fencing for a neighbour. She attended to the early morning chore of feeding the Riordan poultry. They were housed in a small slab shed with a sapling perch a couple of feet above ground level. Dan had arrived home a couple of months before with a wriggling corn bag. It contained a white hen, named Snowy, a black hen named Sooty and a nondescript speckled part bantam named Queenie. The fourth member of the poultry cavalcade was an indignant golden Chinese Bantam rooster, with feathery legs, and an attitude, whom Dan had been assured would answer to Napoleon. They had been on the verge of becoming chicken soup in the household of a gentleman who was keen to protect his often attacked garden.

Dan listened to the abuse and asked,

'How much do you want for them?' of the irate owner, who was evicting them, axe in hand, from his cabbage patch.

'They are yours for two bob, if they go now, and I'll throw in a bag to take 'em in.'

Dan made his delivery and left with a squirming bag of chooks.

Nell welcomed them to the family and Dan had the unwanted job of building a chicken pen.

What Napoleon lacked in size; he made up for in volume. The first hint of light in the sky was enough for him to produce a tenor serenade to the morning. Occasionally, if the breeze was from the east, he could catch the bass challenge of Brewster's big Black Orpington. The following arpeggio fired off by Napoleon, made Dan roll over in bed and mutter dire threats upon his carolling rooster. Despite a laying box in the corner of the shed, they still awaited the first new laid egg. Dan had even purchased a small bag of expensive out of season corn to stimulate the egg production.

Only this morning he had said to Nell, 'Tell that noisy boasting spalpeen down in the shed, to get his harem on the job. Otherwise, it'll be the guillotine for him.'

'You are a vindictive man. He doesn't lay eggs.'

'That's right me girl, you be on his side. He's supposed to do things to those old girlfriends of his that inspire them into action.'

'Just be patient.'

As Nell threw in the feed, she felt the child in her womb moving strongly. She was aware of spring in the air and the changes of her own physical climate. She was large with the growing child and her breasts were developing rapidly. The Ballina mid wife had checked her dates and development. She had assured Nell the baby would not come for another six weeks. Dan had insisted she be ready to go to Ballina and her mother's by the end of September.

She eyed off the strutting Chinese golden bantam rooster. He was resplendent in his new spring suit. His short stocky legs completely feathered with gold epaulets, and his comb flamed a fiery cherry red. Nell thought she had better deliver the message,

'You are not popular. The master of the house demands an egg for his breakfast. You had better talk to the girls.'

Nell conscientiously felt she had done her best and returned to the house. There, Blackie greeted her with courteous attention. He seemed to be very solicitous of her lately. She reckoned it was imagination, the old dog couldn't know of her 'delicate' condition. Anyway, she had never felt better, other than her bulk was a problem to move around. She found Blackie a source of friendship and comfort. He kept her very much in sight and they usually walked down to the little creek each afternoon. Of late, she had been curtailing their walks to the big sprawling teak tree about halfway. At first, he would continue on expecting her to follow, but now he seemed aware that this was the distance of their trek.

The vegetable garden was in the throes of winter and suffering from her inability to pull out weeds. She had a wooden box that acted as a low seat and enabled some weeding of the carrots, beetroot and onions. The cabbage plot was close to producing hearted specimens and the weeds were not affecting their growth. Potatoes planted in the autumn had withered tops and were brown, already Dan had raided some bushes to harvest the smooth clean butter-coloured tubers. He proudly declared them better than the Irish praties of his boyhood. Plans were circulating in his head to use one of the gently sloping creek flats for a commercial crop of potatoes when he could achieve cultivation of the friable red earth. Pumpkins planted anywhere on part cleared land thrived and soon ran over lantana, tobacco bush, inkweed and any of the other naturally occurring weeds. Crows claimed some of the spoils but pumpkins were not considered of much value as an aid to the plateau diet. Nell kept a big old saucepan on the stove that usually contained a pumpkin stewing, seeds and all. This she fed to the chooks.

Honey, the six-month-old jersey calf that had been a gift from the Richards as a wedding present, also consumed boiled pumpkin as part of her food quota. Nell had become a real farm girl and found companionship with her animals.

Also, she had been given books to read by both Bridget and Norah. She set aside part of each afternoon for reading and already she was becoming much quicker at the task. On hearing of her effort to become a reader, although the school years had been few, Edna Wilkinson contributed a small, battered dictionary. This Nell treasured, a possession perhaps only second to Dan. She was now into the habit of passing on her newfound knowledge. Dan often gave her the chance of catching him out with a word meaning that was unknown to him. He was pleased to see her efforts to become a reader, and happy to let her use him as a testing ground. The eight months of their marriage had flown and they were happy in the farm life, and in each other.

Nightmares that could and did grip either on occasions were becoming less frequent. The savage unexpected sexual attack that caused deep bodily and mental trauma had eased with her physical love for Dan. However, there were oppressing panic dreams when rough hands and male genitalia corrupted her body in an agony from which she would awake sobbing in a shivering cold sweat. In these rough times she found Daniel's warm sheltering arms always a haven of relief that restored practical sanity. The dreams were becoming less frequent; she prayed for a time when dreams of that terror happening would leave for ever.

Daniel had his own demons to excise. He would be on the deck of a sailing ship that plunged into engulfing waves and didn't come back to the surface. The shadowy white face of his friend Sean would be there with a stiff fingered hand extended just out of reach. Then another green roller would force his breathing to stop and when he thought this wet green world was eternity, he would awake with a gasp, his lungs clawing, rasping for breath. It was from these journeys of despair that the warm soft arms of Nell clutched him. He suffered that his arms had failed to reach Sean. At times tears and sobs shook his body.

Neither mentioned these night demons in the light of day, but both knew the debt they owed the other. Both were prepared to be a reliable crutch for each other as long as it took.

Yes, Nell had in her young life achieved maturity far beyond her years. She was not looking forward to the approaching time when she was to return to Ballina. This baby that used her taut stomach for internal drumming practise, was being awaited eagerly by all her friends at Ballina and here on the Duck Creek plateau.

Birth of Sean

Several weeks later Nell was ensconced at Ballina. Although dates said the baby was not due yet, Bridget and Norah had insisted she make the trip. Rupert James had told Dan months before that the buggy was at his disposal when the time came.

On the Sunday afternoon, Dan rode Chief into Duck Creek, left him at the stables and borrowed the James' ponies and the buggy.

When he arrived back at Killarney, there was a send-off committee of Brewsters and O'Reillys. The suitcase that contained Nell's essentials and clothes for the baby were stowed safely on board.

'This is all too soon,' argued Nell. 'I'll be in Ballina for weeks waiting, with Mum fussing around, and I should be here looking after the animals.'

Bridget took Nell by the arm and steered her to the buggy.

'It's best this way Nell. The risk of you going into labour with Dan not around is too great. You know that Dan would not want to go to work and leave you; it would be too much worry for him. You are lucky to have your ma close at hand, so in you go.'

'We know we won't look after the animals as well as you do, but they will be all right. Mary and Janey will come over at the weekends and Pat or I will see everything is well when Dan has to go away.'

It was on the Wednesday night that her labour started. Nell had felt a little odd at tea. She retired early to the spare room on the pretence of reading by candlelight. The first pain exploded through her body at about 11 p.m.

Carmel sent Tom around for Ma Geddes, the midwife, at 2 a.m. when the labour pains were consistent.

'I don't know why babies won't wait till morning,' Ma grumbled, but she dressed and accompanied Tom back through the cool, starry morning.

At 4 a.m. Ma and Carmel were worried. The pains were consistent but the baby didn't seem to have moved into an imminent birth position.

'We could wait a little longer, but perhaps if we are going to need Doc Mason, now is the time to bring him in to have a look. At least he should have had some sleep.' Ma was worried.

Tom was summoned once more and tramped down the long main street that fronted the river. The doc's little cottage was one of the more solid buildings.

'Alright, alright,' Doc Mason responded to the knocking on his door. 'Ah, it's you Tom, what's the problem?'

'Sorry Doc to wake you, but Nell is having the baby. Ma and Carmel are not happy with how it's going. Could you come around?'

'When did she start having pains?'

'About 11p.m. last night.'

'Right, you head back. I'll dress and be right around. Five hours isn't long for a first labour but if Ma thinks I should have a look, she must have her reasons.'

Doc arrived.

'Well Nell, this, having children, is not all that easy, eh?' Doc patted the girl's hand.

A contraction shook her body and sweat soaked her brow.

'It will be all right, lass.' He worked his experienced hands over her swollen belly.
Stood up and turned to Ma and Carmel.

'Mm, it's time for a cup of tea, I'll be out to the kitchen.'

A few minutes later, tea in hand, he addressed the women.

'That baby seems slow getting into position. I suspect an arm is twisted forward. Probably I'll have to try and push it back into the right position.'

Half an hour later he smiled across at Ma.

'Yes. That feels better. The head is able to move down now.'

He gently wiped Nell's brow.

'Things will happen now, next pain you shove hard and if you work with the contractions, it won't be too long.'

At 6 a.m. the baby's head was visible and with the aid of instruments and skilled fingers, an eight-pound boy entered the world. Ma slapped his bottom and he responded with a strong howl of protest.

They placed him on Nell's breast and towelled the blood off his skin.

'He's dark,' was Nell's comment. His hair was black and his skin still red but with an olive hue.

Doc Mason examined him carefully.

'He seems fine to me. That shoulder I had to push back may need watching, but it should be all right. You did well, Nell, but you're a sensible, strong girl.'

How to get a message up to Dan was the immediate need. He would probably be surprised the baby had arrived so soon, but they knew the relief he would feel.

It was a couple of days later when Dan arrived to view his son. The week he had spent without Nell had been busy, the days spent on a fencing job, but he found the nights long without her. Blackie also wore a permanently mournful expression once Nell was gone; he kept watching down the road hoping for her return.

Dan saddled Chief on receipt of the information and let the chestnut work off some of his pent-up energy in a quick trip to Ballina. They had talked of names but agreed to wait and see before declaring a name for the baby.

Carmel embraced him on arrival.

'Ah, Nell will be all right now that you be here.'

Dan looked quizzically at his mother-in-law.

'Is there anything wrong?'

'No Dan, no, but she will be all the better to see you.'

Nell was breast-feeding. She laid the baby on her tummy and

hung on to Dan with strong arms.

'It's good to have you here,' she whispered in his ear.

'I suppose I get second place now,' he chided her.

'No,' was all she said, but tears shone in the clear grey eyes. 'Take a look at him.'

Dan did as bidden. His experience of babies was very limited. The mop of black hair and olive skin was a surprise, but he made no comments other than to praise Nell and the child.

'He looks fine to me and so do you. Was it very bad?'

'Not really, once Doc Mason did a little work he came along fine. I want to come home.'

'What do you call him?' Dan asked.

'Well, just baby, but we talked of Sean if he was a boy, so what do you think?'

'Sounds fine to me, and Sean was dark, so that's settled, Sean, he is.'

Nell put him back on her breast and he attached himself with gusto.

'He knows how to suck, and my milk is starting to flow, so he's happy if his stomach is full.'

Dan sat by the bed and watched the feeding process.

A week later and Nell was home at Tara. Both Carmel and Dan had tried to persuade her to stay on longer at Ballina, but Nell insisted she was fine. Once more, Dan borrowed the James buggy. This time it was a family that made the trip up the cutting and out to Tara. Once home, Dan left his family and returned the buggy. Rupert set up a strong free OP rum for him on the bar, when he returned the rig.

'Here's to Nell and Sean.' They drank the toast.

'I'll come and build that back fence for you, no charge.'

Dan thanked the James and reclaimed Chief from his temporary stable. The horse was keen to be home and loped over the few miles in no time.

Over the next few days there were visits from the O'Reillys and Brewsters. They came bearing presents. The homecoming of a baby was a lift to the small community. Dan worked around the block for Sean's first week home; he and Blackie kept a close watch on Nell and Blackie viewed the baby with aloof suspicion.

Nell plunged back into her routine of farm jobs.

'You want to coddle me,' she accused Dan. 'Back home in Ireland I'd be out digging praties before the baby was a week old. Don't worry, I'm fine. I'll be careful.'

On her first morning back, she insisted on rising early and feeding the chooks. After dumping their mash in the small tin trough, she glanced in the nesting box. Two eggs, one brown, one white, sat neatly in the straw.

'Why you've welcomed me home. Good girls and may I say it's not too soon. Well Napoleon, at last you have something to crow about.'

Dan was outside preparing tools for the day's work. Nell took a saucepan added the water and popped in the eggs for boiling. By the time Dan arrived in, the cooked products were sitting on a plate in front of his chair.

He acknowledged the farm produce with surprise.

'Well, begorrah, what do you know? Those overfed feathered spalpeens have produced something at last. Mary kept telling me when she fed them, that they would lay soon. She will be pleased to know they have welcomed you home. One for you and one for me, we share alike. '

So, Tara as a produce farm, boasted its first eggs.

The Brewsters had arranged with Bridget for either Janey or Mary to come across every second day with fresh milk for Nell. The Brewsters now had three big red Durham milking cows and assured Dan that milk for Nell and Sean was freely available. The Riordan baby was a source of interest for the neighbours, most of the farming settlers were older and already had established families. If anyone raised eyebrows that the baby's arrival was less than the customary nine months, nothing was said within the hearing of Nell's friends. Life had slipped into a new dimension for the Riordan family.

School Has Problems

The school year drew toward a close. Three months since the opening had been challenging and mostly rewarding. Edna Wilkinson had come to terms with most of her pupils and parents. Those of the older age groups were finding the chore of attending school a little easier to accept. They had the hardest task of trying to achieve a scholastic level that matched their age. This was difficult. The older boys could do many farm tasks beyond their years and likewise the girls were able to look after younger children and cook or sew quite well. The grind of learning mathematical tables and intricacies of sums, plus the use of words and grammar, was a slow process.

In families where parents had a reasonable chance of helping their children, there was good progress. Some parents had little schooling and found it difficult to read a simple sentence. For these, helping children with homework was too difficult. Edna tactfully only asked that parents see children did some homework. It was up to the student to ask for help at school. Some did, but some of the older children were too proud to ask, when many of the younger ones could already handle that task. It was a basic problem of bringing education for the first time to the area. Following children would start younger and be on an equal footing.

Mary O'Reilly took to learning as a duck takes to water. She was prepared to read and soak up knowledge. She was also prepared to help any child who asked her assistance. It was apparent to Edna, that Mary, without any formal school attendance was in most subjects of suitable standard to attend secondary school. Of course, there was no secondary school, so the O'Reillys would soon have another problem to face.

Pearl was an interesting child. Still very shy and sometimes absent from school but making progress far beyond what Edna had expected. Her ability to master sums was a constant surprise; she was more advanced than Jane O'Reilly and Ann Richards. Reading for her was proving a problem, but she was making progress and at times Mary or Jane would quietly give her help. Edna avoided making an issue over the days Pearl did not arrive at school. She knew the young girl's home circumstance could cause problems that would not have an easy answer. The distance she was walking each day was in itself a problem. Her parents had bought her a couple of blue check gingham dresses and she was always neat and tidy. She did not wear shoes, but about half of the pupils followed that fashion, so if her feet were tough enough to do the miles, that was no problem.

Angus James and a couple of others made remarks about Pearl, but not where Edna could hear. The group games played at recess and lunch included all who wanted to participate. For some weeks, Pearl would only watch from a distance but eventually with Jane's help, she was brought into activities. She was very nimble on her feet and a fast runner. So far, Pearl was making good progress.

The day things turned sour was a normal Wednesday. It was early December, a hot morning with an afternoon storm seeming a distinct probability. On Wednesdays, as a concession to sport, the children had an extra hour tacked on to lunch, when they could play an organised game. This day they were playing cricket, a new game for most of the children. One of the fathers had crafted a couple of small beech wood cricket bats, and stumps and Edna had managed to acquire a rubber ball. With cricket a team game, all the school played, usually teams were picked by two of the elder pupils. The captains for this occasion were Angus James and Mary O'Reilly. Edna usually supervised to ensure fairly equal teams. Angus was by far the most proficient player, and always managed to be in the winning team.

Angus and his team made 50 runs. Mary and the opposition only had thirty with Pearl and Thomas the last two left to bat. It was an unwritten law that only underarm was bowled to the smaller children. Pearl and Thomas were steadily making runs against the weak underarm, so Angus decided to bowl again himself and finish the game. His underarm was fast and accurate, a couple of catches were dropped to Angus's annoyance.

'Butter fingers,' he yelled at Janey, when she dropped her second catch. 'Why don't you try?'

He lined up Pearl with the next ball fast and straight at her shins. She managed an edge of the bat and it flew away from the wicket. They ran two.

'Right its overarm this time,' he snarled at Pearl. 'No boong is going to beat me.'

'You know the rules, no overarm to those two,' Mary intervened.

'Just you watch.' Angus went back and raced in to deliver the ball just as fast as he could. The stumps went flying. The game was over and

Angus was once more the winner. He didn't have the good sense to leave it there.

'There, how about that you little black bitch? Why didn't you hit that one?' he yelled at Pearl.

Angus did not realise that Edna had come out from the school and was watching. She had seen his bowling overarm and heard his remarks to Pearl. So far, she had tried to avoid confrontation with Angus, hoping he would come to accept Pearl as any other schoolmate. This was too much.

'Angus, come inside with me. Now. The others stay out and continue to play.'

Edna escorted the slouching Angus to the schoolroom.

'Well, Angus, you tell me why you behaved like that. You are my oldest pupil and I expect you to set an example.'

Some of the bluster had left the teenager but he wasn't going to apologise.

'She shouldn't be here at our school,' he mumbled his defence, but didn't look Edna in the eye.

'You tell me why Pearl should not be at this school, Angus.'

'She's a part boong. My dad says this school was built for white kids.'

'What don't you like about Pearl? Why do you think she is different to the other children?'

'My dad says boongs are dirty, they don't wash and they have diseases.'

'Is Pearl not as clean and tidy and polite as the other children?'

Angus looked sullenly at the floor.

'I expect an answer Angus, what actual complaint do you have about Pearl?'

No answer was forthcoming.

'I'm sorry Angus, you leave me no choice, you either apologise to Pearl and agree to treat her as any other school pupil or I will cane you in front of the school and send a note home to your parents telling them why I punished you. The choice is yours.'

There was still no answer.

'I must have an answer, Angus. I would like you to apologise and the incident will be forgiven and not mentioned again.'

'I won't apologise to her,' Angus mumbled the words.

'Right, stand in the corner until the school is assembled.'

Edna brought in the pupils and sat them at their desks.

'Children I am sorry that a fellow pupil has to be disciplined for rudeness but I have no choice. Angus is to be caned because he was rude to Pearl. I heard what was said and I have no choice but to discipline Angus.'

Angus was stood in the clear space. Edna armed herself with a four-foot-long dried lawyer cane produced from behind the world atlas. It had been collected as part of the school equipment but until now, not used. Edna administered two swipes to each hand with a well-coordinated aim.

'Sit down. You will take a note home to your parents.'

It was apparent that Angus was well able to stand the minor stinging to his fingers and probably considered it far preferable to an apology. He returned to his desk stoney-faced and did not speak for the rest of the afternoon.

Edna was pleased when 3.30 came. She would have liked to think the incident was dealt with and forgotten but she had a feeling that repercussions would flow. The James family was prominent in the community and had worked hard for the school. The note sent home with Angus explained he had been rude to a fellow student and refused to apologise. She asked that his parents explain to him the need for courtesy and said she would be pleased to discuss the matter with them.

A brief note arrived back on Monday morning, saying Rupert James would pick up his son at 3.30 and would talk with Miss Wilkinson.

The day passed without incident. Pearl was not at school. Angus was quiet but attentive to his schoolwork. Edna was in fact pleased with the progress Angus had made during the term. It had been difficult for him to start school at 13 years of age.

Rupert James was on time. Edna dismissed the children for home and suggested to Angus he wait outside until his father was ready to take him home.

'Please come in Mr James. I am sorry it was necessary to send a note. Angus has done very well with his schoolwork but I felt it best that you know of my worry about his attitude to a fellow student.'

Edna offered Rupert the chair at her table, but he declined, so both stood.

'I'm afraid, Miss Wilkinson, that when we worked for this school,

I did not expect Aboriginal children would be allowed as pupils.' Rupert made his statement calmly.

'Mr James, it is a public school and my wage is paid by the government. Any parents who present their child clean, well behaved, and prepared to learn, make it obligatory for me to accept the pupil, if there is seating accommodation. Pearl Yanohavovich meets all those requirements. Do you have an objection other than the child is part Aboriginal?'

The colour rose markedly in Rupert's florid English complexion.

'I do not serve Aboriginals at my hotel so I do not see why they should be allowed at school with my son.'

'What about Yan Yanohavovich, Mr James? Would you serve him at your hotel?'

'Of course I would, but not his wife.'

'Do you know Pearl, Mr James?'

'No, I expected to see her today, but it seemed she was not at school, so what about her attendance. Angus says she does not come all the time.'

'She has a long way to walk, her attendance, work and behaviour are satisfactory to me.'

'Well, Miss Wilkinson, Laura and I have told Angus that he must do what you tell him. We have also told him to ignore the Yanohavovich girl. I am not going behind your back, I will be speaking to other parents and I will see what their reaction is to a black kid being a pupil at our school. I consider you made a bad decision in accepting her as a pupil. That is all I have to say. Good afternoon to you.'

That interview was probably what Edna expected. There was nothing to be done except wait. She determined to write a written report to the Inspecting Department at Grafton. It was an unpleasant way to be finishing what had been a great start to their first school year activity.

Edna knew Rupert James was a popular person in the community and could probably influence others. She would have to await developments. Her immediate concern was that Pearl had not arrived at school, after the weekend break. She hoped she would be there tomorrow. Edna was determined not to let one unpleasant incident undermine the good things she had observed happening in Pearl. It was obvious Yan had been helping with her homework and even her English and writing were steadily improving. Her mathematical and drawing skills were outstanding.

Edna walked down to O'Reillys and sought out Bridget. She felt it likely the children would have mentioned the outburst of Angus and his problem with Pearl.

Bridget was in the kitchen, ironing school clothes. She had two heavy cast flat irons that heated on the stove top. A blanket on the table made a temporary work platform.

'Come on through,' was Bridget's cheery answer to her knock, and Thomas' called out information, 'It's Miss Wilkinson, Ma.'

'I hope you can spare me a few minutes Bridget.' The friendship of the two women had developed since their immediate rapport on the cart trip home behind old Captain.

'Take a seat, I'll finish this blouse and then we'll have a cup of tea. Thomas, you go and help the girls milk the cow.'

'You probably know something about the discipline situation that arose last week?'

It was a question.

'Yes, a little. Pat and I didn't want to pry, but I think we heard enough to know that you had to act. We were very sorry that you were forced to a difficult decision.'

'Well, I have spoken with Mr James, and while he has told Angus that he must obey, he has voiced his opposition to an Aboriginal child at the school. He is going to petition other parents to find opposition to Pearl. The most worrying thing to me is that Pearl was not back at school today. She has been doing so well and I don't want her intimidated by Angus.'

Bridget folded the blanket back from half the table and made a pot of tea. There was always healing or wisdom power in a pot of tea. The women drank the brew and Bridget smiled at Edna. She reflected thoughtfully.

'It was always going to be touchy. You know Pat and I will support you all the way. We would expect there are others who would take our view, but there would likely be some to support the keeping out of an Aboriginal.'

'Yes, I know the attitude. Many of the stations I worked on didn't even consider Aboriginals to be people, but I hoped things might have been better in a new area like this. The main reason I came over is that if Pearl isn't at school tomorrow, I will go to see her parents. I need to know how to find them.'

'It could be tricky Edna. They live further around the bluff we climbed that night when we came up the cutting from Blackwall. I haven't been there; I know there is no real road and the tracks still run through some standing scrub. We had better talk to Pat, he's been in with the small cart, so there is a way, but we don't want you getting lost.'

'I can't just wait and hope she comes back to school. She has been doing so well and obviously Yan has been helping all he can. Her maths is as good or better than most children her age and she is trying so hard with reading. I feel that if I can explain that Angus' outburst shouldn't happen again, at least they know I want her at the school. When will Pat be home?'

'Probably not until late tonight. I will talk to Pat and send a note with Mary in the morning. I'm sure he won't be keen on your going on your own.'

Edna made her way back to Brewsters, still worried and nothing resolved.

It was 10.30 p.m. when Pat had the horses bedded down and rescued his warmed-up dinner from the top of the stove. Bridget came out from the bedroom and kept him company while he ate.

'This is unexpected, you should be in bed. What sort of a day has it been?'

Bridget told the story of Edna and her resolve to go looking for Pearl and her parents.

'Hmm, you were right, it's not the sort of trek she should be making on her own. If Pearl doesn't turn up tomorrow, I'll go with her tomorrow afternoon. I'll be home by 3.30. We'll take the light cart. Probably it will be after dark when we get back, but that's no problem.'

Mary delivered the note with Pat's proposal of help to Miss Wilkinson. Pearl was still absent from school.

With the cessation of lessons in the afternoon Edna headed up to Killarney. In the interest of speed, Pat put Tar the young roan Clydesdale on the light cart; he was capable of maintaining a steady trot on the better parts of the track. It was about an hour before they branched off the used road and worked their way south east through the last plateau before the escarpment.

'I'm sorry, Pat, to inflict this on you.' Edna and Pat had said little while the cart rocked along at a trot. Now with a steady walking pace and the quiet of the scrub around them conversation was possible.

'Don't even mention it. You know Bridget and I are willing to help any way we can. Pearl deserves a chance. How many parents agree with the James I don't know; with luck we won't have to find out. It's not much further.'

They came to a clearing in the scrub. Its residence building was a humble slab hut, built originally by a cedar cutter and then improved slightly by an old slab and shingle splitter who lived there until his death. That was when Yan, Rose and Pearl moved in as occupiers. There was then no owner of the land as it was a steep forest and scrub plateau not yet officially applied for as a land grant. Yan made an application with the Land Board and became registered owner.

A mongrel, yellow dog, lean and furtive loped out from shelter of the lean to, from which acrid smoke oozed. The dog contained a fair splash of dingo in his background. He didn't bark, just circled the cart in wide, wary circles.

When they were close to the dwelling, Rose and Pearl came out. The sight of visitors was unexpected and their obvious shyness was disconcerting. Rose refused to look at the cart, while Pearl in her mother's company, followed that lead.

'Hello, Rose and Pearl.' Pat knew Rose would remember him from their previous trip in with the cart years before. 'Miss Wilkinson would like to talk with you both.'

Pat helped Edna to the ground. She found the foot step with her lace up leather boot, took his hand and descended nimbly.

'I was worried that Pearl hasn't been at school,' Edna spoke slowly and softly to Rose. 'She has been doing so well, I wanted to find out when she will be back.'

'Yan away working.' Rose made the statement, then with eyes downcast she continued, 'Pearl say she not wanted at school, and she no want to go.'

She looked up, a fleeting glance before casting her eyes back to the earth.

'I want Pearl at school. The other children want Pearl at school,' Edna stopped, then continued, 'They won't be so unkind again.'

She walked over to Pearl.

'Pearl, please come back to school tomorrow.' She took the little girl's hand and smiled at her.

'Why you are my best pupil at sums, we need you. Your dad would want you back at school.'

Pat had led Tar and the cart away from the group; he didn't want to make their shyness worse with his presence.

Edna kept hold of Pearl's small hand and spoke gently to Rose.

'You want Pearl to learn, Yan wants her to learn and I'm sure Pearl wants to learn, so tomorrow, will you see that Pearl comes to school? There is only another week of school and then there are holidays.'

Rose made a big effort and looked shyly at Edna.

'She go if she want.'

Edna turned her attention to Pearl.

'Please Pearl, we need you for our little play on the last day. I'll see you tomorrow, now, is that right?'

Pearl looked up briefly.

'Yes, I'll try.'

Pearl's answer was soft but clear. With her hand in Edna's, she looked more like the pupil and less like the little bush lubra. All she was wearing was a calico shift. Her hair needed washing and her fingernails were grimed with red earth. Edna was confident that should she return tomorrow it would be a tidy Pearl not the rough bush child of the moment.

Pat brought out a package of eggs. Bridget and Janey had sent them with a little note attached. Rose accepted the gift with little expression, but Pearl smiled and said to thank them for the gift.

It was time to go. They headed back into the gathering gloom of the forest. Pat wanted to be back on the defined road before darkness set in. This they achieved with little time to spare. Even for an experienced bushman the rainforest after dark was full of tricks. It was a slower trip home at walking speed. Little was said about the visit. Both knew that problems lay ahead, but Pat admired the initiative and skill with which Edna had tried to solve the problem.

The early night was dark, with few stars. An occasional large, brown owl swooshed by on powerful wings, and an odd pademelon caused Tar to snort a nervous protest.

'Thank you so much for taking me. I'd have found it hard coming home in the dark. The O'Reillys have been good to me,' Edna spoke her thanks.

'We help each other in the bush. We are pleased and lucky to have you as our teacher.' They journeyed slowly on with the soft rolling crunch of the wheels the predominate sound.

'I received a letter from Dick last week. He said to remember him to his friends.'

'How is it going for him in Sydney? Dick Hilardt was well liked here and we were sorry to lose him.'

Pat kept any surprise from his voice at the information that Edna and Dick were writing letters. He let his mind flash back to the afternoon of Dick's departure. Yes, it made sense.

'He is working in a shipping office and says that he will be tripping around at times.
It is probable that Grafton will be a port of call. He says Ballina is not popular for passengers as too many ships strike trouble on the bar.'

'Well, you can tell him there are always beds on the plateau where he could spend a night if he comes up. He'll probably find it a bit hard to become a city slicker. Thanks for telling me that you heard from Dick.'

Life

They arrived back at the Brewsters. Once more, Edna handled the step down from the cart. It crossed Pat's mind as he continued down the lane, maybe the O'Reillys should think about purchasing a sulky. Nothing flash like the James buggy, but it could prove useful for tripping around. The carrying business was going well. After Christmas it may be possible to offer Dan Riordan at least three days a week driving. There was too much work for one driver. He plodded home, wrapped in thought and settled Tar in his stall. Bridget was keen to hear the news of Pearl and they talked while he ate his dinner. Later, he told Bridget of Edna's news of Dick Hilardt.

'Now don't go getting romantic and sounding wedding bells, but it seems there must have been some attraction,' was how he finished that bit of news.

'She told me she was engaged once and the lad was killed. We don't want to lose a teacher, but it would be great if those two got together. Strange that they met when it was time to part.'

Bridget mused on the good news.

'People need people. It is lonely in bed on your own,' she smiled at him.

Pat thought, *she looks seventeen.*

'I'll help you wash my dinner things, then perhaps I'll see to it that you are not lonely in bed.' He saw the pink glow of her cheeks as she tossed her dark auburn locks back.

'It's not safe to encourage you Irishmen, you take advantage of a poor colleen on any pretence.'

The washing up was soon finished.

In their bedroom, quietly he shut the door and pulled her into his arms. Their lips met in a lingering kiss of need from which they didn't break. Free hands undressed each other. Slowly at first, then with urgency, clothes fell to the floor. Standing locked together, savouring the stillness and its ripples of communication until the fire of active passion needed the support of their bed. Culmination of their love making came with timing and spontaneity. Spent, they clung together, released, at peace. Words were unnecessary, irrelevant and they drifted into sleep.

Pat awoke before daylight; Bridget was still asleep. The soft warmth of her generous body made the bed a holy shrine. Ever so quietly he slid out from the warmth. With a smile hovering on his lips, he picked up their scattered clothes and stacked them neatly on the bedside chair.

He dressed and tiptoed out to the kitchen. He knew from experience that the slight squeak of the door opening would probably have Bridget awake.

A lamp lit, and the fire kindled, he brewed tea and went back to the bedroom with tea and several scones.

Bridget lay where he had left her but he knew she was awake.

'So, you sneaked out from me, did you?' she whispered at him. 'Think you can win my favours with a cup of tea?'

Without answering, he picked up the woollen button up cardigan she had been wearing the night before off the chair and handed it to her. She wriggled into it before emerging from under the bedclothes to take her tea.

'Now that you are part decent, I'll join you for tea.'

They drank their tea. He kissed her gently on the forehead and left the room to start his long busy day.

Education –The Way Forward

It was a relieved Miss Wilkinson who saw Pearl coming down the lane. Jane O'Reilly had obviously been watching and ran to meet her friend. Pearl was dressed neatly in a gingham dress, unironed but tidy. The black hair that had looked so unkempt the previous evening was combed flat and still wet from a morning washing. She and Jane stood at the corner of the back row when it was time to assemble. They were the last to enter the classroom.

With only a week to finish the school year, Edna had planned a short play for the children on the last afternoon. Parents were invited to attend. The Brewsters had offered to supply half a dozen book prizes to be allocated at the teacher's discretion. All of the past part year's operation would have been perfect but for the cloud that hovered regarding the James' objection to Pearl. Edna wondered what would happen should Pearl's parents attend the school closing. She was determined that all the children would take a part in the play.

The afternoon arrived. Parents and interested persons were to be at the school by 1.30 p.m. and it would be finished by 3 p.m. It was planned to use the school veranda as the stage, the children would come for their part presentation from inside. The audience would sit on stools outside. Fortunately, the weather was kind.

Edna commenced at 1.30. All stood while they sang *God Save The Queen*. The visitors sat on the outside stools, while the children sat on the veranda. She welcomed them.

'It is rewarding to see that so many parents have made the effort to attend,' she smiled at the audience. 'Our first part year is over and I am proud of your children. They will only succeed at school with your help and support. For the older age pupils it has been difficult to settle in to the routine. They have done well.'

'Mr Brewster will make a presentation of awards. We will then present a short play in which all the pupils have a part.'

Jim Brewster mounted the veranda steps.

'Ladies and Gentlemen, welcome. We are proud of our school. It took much effort to make it a reality and it will always require our support. Miss Wilkinson has spared no effort in presenting education to the children of our area. We know the long hours she spends in preparing lessons, her dedication and her effort to see that these children will be able to have a start in learning.

'My wife and self have no children, so we decided to give these book prizes as encouragement to the pupils. Miss Wilkinson chose the books to suit each important category. We will see each year that these awards are available.'

The books were resplendent on a small table, The colourful covers contrasting with the white starched tablecloth supplied by Norah Brewster.

Edna instructed her pupils, 'If your name is called, stand up and come forward.'

'Best overall senior student: Mary O'Reilly.' Mary made the few steps to the front, collected her book and shook hands with Jim Brewster.

The procession continued as Edna called those to receive the books.

'Best overall junior student: Neville Morgan.'

'Most improved senior student: Anthony Richards.'

'Most improved junior student: Pearl Yanohavovich.'

'Best at Sport: Angus James.'

'Most helpful student: Jane O'Reilly.'

When the presentation was complete, Edna thanked Jim and said there would be a five-minute break while she organised the play.

The play was a simple presentation of Australian life. There were gold miners, bushrangers, sailors, farmers, stockmen, teachers, a nurse, a doctor, a lawyer, a bank manager, a carpenter.

Each had a make-believe item of equipment or clothing to depict their occupation and a few words to say to indicate what they were. They also carried a small cardboard sign turned inward that was turned out when they left the stage so the audience could read their occupation when the presentation was over. There was much laughter, at some of the make-believe characters and all managed their parts, sometimes with the help of audible prompting. Parents were proud of their children, and the time flew so it seemed no time until it was 3 p.m. Edna Wilkinson declared an official completion of school until February, next year.

The Yanohavoviches did not arrive, but Pearl performed her role as a nurse and was clapped as much by the assembly as any other performer.

Rupert James found a brief opportunity to speak with Edna before going home.

'Miss Wilkinson, you have done well. I have not changed my opinion of an Aboriginal at the school but the girl seemed presentable today. We will see what happens next year.'

'Thank you, Mr James,' was all Edna contributed to the conversation.

She was busy catching and talking with all the parents who had come. There were some absentees but there were also nonparent friends of the school who swelled the number. It had been a very satisfactory first end of year school function.

Billy Montez - Music Leavening

Norah insisted the O'Reillys and Riordans call at Surreyville for afternoon tea.

'We won't delay you long, but I will be insulted if you don't come. It will give Edna a chance to relax after all she has done and I want a chance to nurse young Sean.'

So, they settled on the veranda.

Sean Riordan was growing fast and Nell coped with the strains of motherhood. His sallow, dark complexion under a mop of black hair was something of a shock to those who knew both parents, but Nell and Dan were proud of their son.

The gathering on the veranda was extravagant in their praise of Edna and the progress made at the school. She insisted she was only doing her job, that there was a long way to go before their school could be considered an established unit.

'We will wait and see how the James protest about Pearl develops,' was how she summed up her worry over that subject.

'Ah, I think it will soon be forgotten. Pearl will be accepted for what she is, a very intelligent little girl.' Norah voiced her confidence. 'It's a pity the parents didn't come today.'

'Perhaps Yan will make the effort one day, for Rose it would be just too difficult. The transition to white people culture is for Rose a distance away. I hope we give Pearl that bridge across,' Edna musingly spoke her thoughts.

The day drew to its close. The O'Reillys and Riordans went home, leaving Edna and the Brewsters to prepare for dinner. After dinner, Edna pleaded tiredness and retired to her room. She had the luxury of a kerosene wick lamp by which she was able to read and prepare lessons. Tonight, there were no lessons to prepare. She sat at the little cedar table and pulled from the drawer the last letter from Dick. It had only arrived up from Ballina yesterday and though she knew the contents, she read it again. He was coming north on a company ship bound for Grafton, then Ballina and then perhaps to the Tweed. He reckoned they would arrive before Christmas and that he was certainly going to visit Surreyville, either from Grafton or from Ballina. He made no secret of the fact that she was main reason for his journey back so soon to the plateau.

Edna looked at herself critically in the dressing table mirror. She was into her late thirties; there were numerous little crow's feet wrinkles appearing around eye corners. It was a presentable face but she was sure that even ten years ago no one would have considered she possessed any real beauty. Thomas, the young jackeroo so tragically killed, had paid her lover's compliments but they were young and in love. She had reconciled after his death to being an 'old maid'. True, there had been plenty of advances. Out in the bush,
white women were a short commodity and men were quick to make the most of what was available. She had literally wriggled out of the clutches of amorous station managers looking for casual relaxation with the governess, when their wife took a city holiday.

Now, out of the blue, there was a man who was interested in her. She had expected the pulse raising magic of that unexpected kiss under the big fig tree would fade quickly for both. Dick was in a city where she was sure there were women available and looking for a presentable man. Why should he want to come back to a place he was quite keen to leave? What were her own feelings, anyway? The school was a rewarding challenge and she expected to give it a few years. Having remained "manless" until now, surely she could forego the sex thing. According to many women, it was much overrated. Children? Well, she could indulge the mother instinct looking after other people's children. She smiled wryly to herself, it had to be an advantage to send them home after school. Then the thought of those happy minutes with Dick Hilardt came back. Undeniable too, the language of a healthy body that sometimes brought her awake at night with dreams and feelings hard to deny!

She sat and wrote her reply letter, newsy and friendly, promising nothing. If Dick was going to pay a visit in the course of his work, well, that was his business. Her dilemma over Pearl and the problem of the racist reaction she mentioned, she had no idea of Dick opinions on the subject. Indeed, she had no idea of his reactions to politics, religion, many of the things that made the persona of an individual. Perhaps like many people of English descent he looked upon Aboriginals as stone age people, with little hope of making a transition to white man ways. She passed on Pat O'Reilly's message that a bed was available at Killarney.

It was ridiculous to think much about Dick; her life was interesting and self-sufficient without the complication of romance.

Billy Montez trundled his two-wheel cart down from the ranges. One more day and he could be in Casino. His trip west over the Great Dividing Range had taken him along the tableland sheep and cattle stations. Sometimes there was work, sometimes the station owner threatened to unleash the station dogs if he did not keep moving. Often at shearing time his skill at hollow grinding the blade shears made him welcome and brought in a few shillings from around the sheds. The average shearer was capable of keeping his blades sharp. The 'guns', once they had used shears, expertly hollow ground to a razor-sharp edge by Billy Montez, were willing to pay for his skill. They knew their flying hands were less tired at the end of the day, and that more snowy white gaunt merinos, carrying less crimson flowers of blood, were propelled down the chute. Speed was money and high tallies prestige that flew a message from shed to shed.

Then there was the station wife. Some had excellent pianos and were looking for a tuner. This was Billy's favourite task. Once he had satisfactorily tuned a valuable instrument, the news filtered out, and even a gypsy with that recommendation was welcome at the next station. Knives and scissors always needed sharpening, but small tasks did little more than supply tucker, perhaps a little silver money. A gypsy tinker out on the track was not likely to become rich. The skills and nature of Billy Montez allowed him to follow the nomadic life of his forebears. He was at peace with his circumstance and did not envy the squatter or any person of affluence. He trundled his little handcart, found a station shed for sleep when the rains came down, or slept under the white daisy stars when the summer skies smiled. His old violin that lived in its heavy waterproof box at the bottom of the cart, sometimes it was brought forth when the weather was fair. Usually, companion music came from the little brass coated reed harmonica that lived with him always in an inner waistcoat pocket. It supplied a tune either for him or the timid bush animals.

At the foot of the range, a large tent mining camp straggled back from the river. The creeks that fed into the mighty Clarence in its upper arms yielded considerable gold. Chinese and miners of many races had fought up through the gullies, washing, sluicing, trapping the alluvial gold. Several deep shafts had been sunk into the basalt ranges and gold still produced that signature fever tune of hope and despair. Billy Montez drifted into the outskirts of Drake with the western sun long behind the brooding dividing ranges, but night still a space away.

A rough tent fly, away from the main concentration of miners, caught his attention. The elderly miner, with an alert bouncy little fox terrier bitch, was producing savoury smells for an evening meal. The old iron pot dangled over an open fire, a cauldron of unknown delights. From the dress of the miner and an intuition for picking origins, Billy had guessed he was northern English.

'Hello friend. Is there a place around where an old tramp hulk could drop his pick for the night?'

Billy approached the miner tending his potential dinner. The glow of the slow burning red gum fire was contained in a fireplace of several well-placed river rocks. The camp and the man in his dungarees and grey flannel were tidy.

'Well, Spot doesn't seem to be threatening you much, she be a better judge of travellers than me, the ground away from our camp has been knocked down a bit. Help yourself, Spot and Geordie at your service.'

'Thank you to Geordie and Spot. I'm Billy, I'm a traveller but I'll be no trouble. As you can probably see from my rig, I'm a tinker. Anything to sharpen, I'll do it for you later, no charge, it will pay for my ground rent.'

'When you set up, come back. Our stew pot will stretch for a traveller from Bell Bows.'

Later, the two men talked of distant times, distant lands. An unwritten law of communication in the bush was no personal questions were ever asked. Another unwritten law of the mining fields was that a drifter never asked whether a miner was finding pay dirt or just river gravel. When the conversation had flagged to a natural conclusion, Billy pulled the little harmonica from his waistcoat.

'Like a tune?' He tapped the reeds on his knee.

'Yes. The only music around here is when the lads get drunk and gargle out a terrible sad tune fuelled on far too many nips of watered down rum or some worse poison.'

Billy Montez sent folk songs and shanties of the old country, floating out on soft night wings of melody. Shadows of the campfire embers danced outwards. Then he made the perfect, bittersweet lilt of nostalgic Romany campfire tunes sit on the still smoky air, tunes that had drifted on the Magyar plains, and were centuries old.

Geordie dragged at his clay pipe. Spot sat, head tilted askew trying to find this unusual voice that came from the small brass appendix to the visitor's lips. She crept closer to Billy's legs and wagged her cropped tail. He ceased playing, tapped any moisture from the reeds, and let the little dog peruse the source of music.

'You are good. Spot reckons so too. Please don't stop yet.' Geordie smiled at his guest.

Later when they turned in from the recital, all three seemed to feel the night was well spent.

Two days later Billy walked the road from Lismore towards Ballina. He rarely carried an itinerary in his head. The strength of his situation was that he followed the vibes of a place as they called him. He remembered the big sports day, months before. He wondered how the little school was functioning. He turned right at Duck Creek and followed the red soil road towards Surreyville. The Brewster piano, he felt, was an excuse to lead him down the shady lane. It was a fine instrument and he was keen to see how his tuning had held. In the coastal climate instruments suffered much from the rapidly changing humidity.

He made his way to the back entrance of Surreyville. It was late in the afternoon, Norah busy in the kitchen heard the knock at the door. She saw him.

'Why hullo, Mr Montez. Where have you come from? Take a seat here on the veranda.'

Norah, as always, was polite, but a tinker, though she rated Billy an unusual tinker, well there were norms of behaviour that still had to be observed.

'Thank you, Mrs Brewster. I'm just travelling down to Ballina, thought I'd drop in and see how the piano is holding tune.' Billy still stood on the bottom step.

'Ah, Mr Montez, that is kind of you. To my ear the piano is fine. You did an excellent job. Please take a seat and let me mix you a cool fruit drink from our very own lemons.'

'That is kind of you Mrs Brewster. The day has been warm but I've recently walked down from the tablelands where it's much hotter.'

Billy took the proffered seat on the solid veranda chair. Norah scuttled off to prepare his drink. She was soon back with his lemon refreshment in a long glass and a large piece of butter cake, resplendent on white china plate.

'You are too kind, Mrs Brewster.'

Billy handled his plate and glass with the aplomb of a dining room connoisseur. Norah returned to kitchen duties. He enjoyed his drink and cake. When Norah arrived back, he praised her for the repast. He made to leave.

'Would you like to assure yourself the "Lipp" is well, Mr Montez?'

'I would be happy to Mrs Brewster, but I am grimy from the road dust. I would not presume to enter your drawing room.'

It was then that Jim Brewster arrived from milking the growing herd. He welcomed warmly his gypsy guest. Back home in Surrey he would have walked speedily with nose held high to the other side of the road at the sight of a maligned gypsy.

'Why, you are welcome to camp in the shed,' he said to Billy. 'There is water and soap, Norah makes sure I'm clean before I venture inside. The O'Reillys wouldn't forgive us if we let you just wander off.'

'Well, that's settled.' Norah took control. 'Jim, you go and invite the O'Reillys up for early supper. I know Patrick is at home as the dray went past earlier. Mary will make sure they come if Mr Montez agrees to play his violin.'

Billy just smiled and gave a gentle shrug of his wiry shoulders.

'It seems I will do as I'm told.'

Later, with the O'Reillys and Edna Wilkinson present, a very different looking Billy Montez carefully tuned his violin. Washed, shaved, his black hair slicked down, hiding the salt and pepper specks of grey, dressed in black satin slacks and big sleeved black shirt with a red cummerbund around the waist, he looked the part of the true Romany fiddle player. The outfit he wore, was a carry- over from stage appearances in faraway places. It was another of the surprises that lived in a waterproof bag rolled up tight in the bottom of the handcart.

He had carefully checked out Norah's Lipp and declared it close to perfect. Then he had Norah give him the basic four notes for the violin. He slowly brought the old violin to pitch, his sensitive fingers bringing each gut string a little closer to the note.

'It's a hard life on the track for a fiddle. Even though its case is well insulated against weather with Merino wool, the temperature changes are tough on an instrument.'

There was no attempt at apology in Billy when finally, he reckoned the violin was close to concert pitch. He played a few simple scales to make sure his fingers were working, then smiled at his small audience.

'Perhaps we'll go with a few simple airs, while Arabella and I warm up.' In deference to his hosts, he played some pastoral tunes and jigs of England then crossed the sea to Ireland. He stopped. He looked to his hostess and suggested that maybe she would play for those present.

'Mrs Brewster, we would love to hear a tune from that fine instrument. I'll play a little more later if you wish.'

Norah looked a little surprised but agreed she would play one piece if Bridget or Mary would also perform.

'Bridget is perhaps more capable than I am Mr Montez, but I know she will say she never has time to play, which is true, but if I play something short, we will see from there.'

She sat at the instrument and with the competence of a good pianist, a couple of short tuneful Mozart sonatas tinkled through the room. They all clapped enthusiastically and Norah beamed at her small audience.

'Right, that's enough from me. You are very kind. Now who is going to be next? Why not Mary? She has been learning a minuet and I know she could play it for us.'

Mary, in her normally quiet competent way, agreed to play and the simple tune on this good instrument sounded fine.

'That was wonderful, who knows where someday you may perform.'

Billy beamed encouragement at the rapidly growing girl. Soon she would be a young lady, even in the months since his first contact with the family, Mary was growing up.

It was Edna Wilkinson who asked Billy Montez to play music of his Romany forebears.

'I will try to fire my unused hands, but Miss Wilkinson, two things you must realise. I was brought up in Cockney London. Gypsy music is the heart and soul of a roving people. As the blood flows, so does the music. I will try.'

The tune that came started slowly, nostalgic, searching, reaching for something far away. As he played, Billy seemed swallowed into a different time and place. Eyes closed, the instrument took charge of the musician and the tempo rose, drawing the powerful, slightly off-key minor chords that hammered the mystery of searching what was distant.

The man that played seemed to shrink into the flamboyant clothes that gave him a powerful persona. A crescendo of musical poetry that held the drawing room spellbound. It ended, almost abruptly. The sound still ebbed after Billy held the old Pambrico wooden bow distant from the singing strings. He opened his dark eyes and looked anxiously at his audience with an almost imperceptible shrug of the shoulders.

It was Edna who broke the spell of silence after the musical resonance had finally bounced, ricocheted, and faded from the solid teak walls.

'Thank you, Mr Montez. It has been a rare privilege.'

Billy smiled, a trifle self-consciously.

'Ah, I rarely have the chance to play these days. I stick with my pocket orchestra to turn out a comforting tune. Yet it takes the weeping strings to tell the struggles of my people. And of course I'm only half Romany, so you must be thankful for my cockney mother, who never wandered too far from bell bows.'

They enjoyed an early supper. The O'Reillys tramped the short distance home and Billy Montez retired to the Brewster barn.

The next morning, he thanked the Brewsters for their hospitality and headed back down the lane. It was a snap decision to take the turn down to Riordans. He had liked the young couple and thought maybe there was something he could do for them at Christmas. Blackie hurtled out to confront him, but a sharp command from Dan brought him back to the slab veranda.

'I was passing through; thought I'd drop in and say good day.'

'You are welcome, Mr Montez.' Nell, who had joined Dan at the front gate of the small garden, spoke.

'Come in, you must be able to enjoy a cup of tea with us after your walk.'

'Thank you. A cup of tea would be fine. They tell me you have a boy. My congratulations.'

'Yes, he is growing fast.'

Nell pulled Sean from his cot and showed him to the visitor. He was wrapped in a shawl that she unwrapped to display her son. Much of the black mop of hair had fallen out, but his olive skin and dark brown eyes, seemed out of place with his fairish parents.

'Ah, he's a picture of health.'

Billy's eyes took in the small, brown triangular birth mark below the hairline on his forehead but made sure his observation was unreadable to the parents. Strange, that birthmark was often on Romany people. Well, who knew the antecedents of many Celtic people. After all, both these parents were Irish.

'You know, there is a little something out in the cart, that will be his for a Christmas present.'

Billy came back with a little tin whistle.

'It will be a little while, but maybe someday the lad will make a tune.'

Billy gave the whistle to Nell and bid the family farewell. He headed off trundling the little hand cart. Dan walked with him to the corner of the lane, where Billy and the track headed on towards Ballina.

Death of Pat O'Reilly

Pat O'Reilly had cleaned up his work before the Christmas week, determined to have a few days at home with his family. The carrying business was growing rapidly; he felt that soon he would employ Dan for at least four days a week.

'I'll have time then to do a few jobs on the farm,' was how Pat put his planned future.

'Perhaps. You'll get sick of us in a couple of days and be back on the road,' was Bridget's comment, but she knew her husband was becoming tired from the draining nature of the life he had lived over many years of hard work.

'Hmm, it will probably depend how much you nag me.'

Pat knew his family would appreciate his spending more time at home.

There was still a patch of standing scrub to be felled. He had spoken with a few contract fellers but had it in mind to finish the job himself. There were trees he intended to work around, rather than go through in a face and destroy all timber as had been the case with most of the Big Scrub clearing.

The monkey rope vine around the big teak tree looped several times and made it across to a nearby tall blue fig. The ground floor was a mass of ferns, lawyer vine and stinging trees. Pat had decided to leave the blue fig and several smaller cedar and white beech. The teak had to go. There was plenty of good timber in the straight barrel, it would be handy for use around the farm.

He had made his decision how the tree would fall. It was a gentle slope and he aimed to deep scurf the bottom side so that it would miss the fig and fall clear of other surrounding scrub inmates. It looked a straightforward job. He needed to bring the tree down so he would be able to snig the log when trimmed to an adjoining open paddock.

Whether Pat had any warning there was a problem when the teak commenced its fall, was later discussed, but never known. It fouled just one limb of the fig, shearing the branch but throwing it on a trajectory that brought it crashing down on the axeman. If he saw it coming, it would have been but a fleeting instant of realisation. It would have been but a split second, far too late for any evasion. Who knows the time value of an instant in that situation?

Jim Brewster heard the teak fall. Knowing the intent of Pat and wanting to discuss the milling of the log should it be sound, he sauntered over to the patch of scrub. He began to worry when he heard no sound of movement or action. He called, several times.

'Hello Pat!'

Still there was no sound.

Gripped by foreboding, he fought his way in past the fallen teak. The scene that met his gaze was to remain with him ever more. The axe was still clutched in the lifeless hands of his friend. Pat was prostrate on his back and it was only when Jim checked for signs of life that the massive damage to the back of the head became visible. The branch from the fig lay not far from the body. Still shrouded in vines the big teak lay exactly on the angle and in the place Pat had intended. Jim, deep in shock, closed the eyelids and covered the face with his coat. Reality claimed him. He staggered out of the scrub in a stupor of shock and disbelief.

Should he go straight to Bridget? There was no help for Pat, his death would have been instant. No, he decided to first get Norah. She would help him with the ordeal they faced.

It was half an hour later that Jim, Norah and Edna walked up the driveway to Killarney. Bridget met them at the veranda. One look was enough.

'Is it Pat?'

The question needed no answer. Norah put her arms around Bridget trying to quiet the shivers that ran through the younger woman.

'Is he dead?' Again, the question needed no answer but had to be asked.

'Take me to him please.' Bridget was too calm, too composed.

Her next request was to Edna.

'Edna, will you please stay with the children.'

Miss Wilkinson tried to muster them inside, but Mary was quite firm.

'No, I'm going to my dad.' Norah looked questioningly at Bridget. Bridget nodded and took Mary's hand.

'Yes, let's go.'

They took a blanket and set out the long, but too short, distance to the patch of scrub.

Bridget and Mary knelt by the man they loved. They prayed in their grief, the common prayers of their Catholic faith ingrained through Bridget's convent years.

'Hail Mary, full of grace–.' Jim and Norah knelt with them in silence.

An hour later, back at the house, it was Bridget who took control.

'I want him at rest here in the house. I'll help carry him back.'

'No, Bridget we will organise help and do whatever you want.'

Jim was going to head into the village of Duck Creek just as soon as he felt he could be spared.

'Norah must stay with you and the sooner we tell Dan and Nell, the better.' Jim looked at Edna.

'Would you be able to go across to the Riordans, Edna?'

'I could save a lot of time if I rode. It's a few years since I've been on a horse but I'm sure I can manage. Mary will help me saddle Shamrock.'

Jim took Edna aside.

'If you find Dan at home, it could be best if he would go into the village after he has helped me bring in Pat's body. He could find Bopper and get him out here to build a coffin.'

At the stable Edna caught Shamrock and, with Mary's help, found the saddle cloth and saddle. She looked speculatively at the long skirt she was wearing. That wasn't going to be suitable for riding astride Shamrock.

'Mary, would there be any old clothes of your father's that I could wear?'

Mary nodded.

'Yes, he always left something down here at the stables.'

She went into the feed room and came back with a pair of dungarees and a long-sleeved shirt. Always the ever-practical Mary, she carried an old pair of his riding boots.

Edna took the clothes. She shed the long skirt, petticoat and blouse. On went the rough blue shirt and then it was a case of into the trousers and pull them up over her long-frilled drawers. She adjusted the stirrups to an approximate length.

'Now, Shamrock you be kind to me.'

The old horse snorted in disbelief. Mary gave him a handful of chaff to chew and Edna made a good swift mounting. She eased him once around the small yard and then followed Mary down to the gate. He accepted the strange light weight on his back and knew at once that the hands on the reigns were experienced. They set off at a trot that soon lengthened to his mile-eating easy canter.

Rallying Round

Fortunately, Dan was home working with Nell in their vegetable garden. The shock numbed them for many seconds, then Dan quickly saddled Chief and sped off for Killarney.

'I'm coming too.' Nell grabbed necessities.

She collected the needs of baby Sean. These minimum necessities were placed in Edna's saddle bags. Nell had worked out a way of carrying Sean in a type of sling; they walked together until the fork in the road. Then Nell insisted Edna leave her to finish the trip.

'I'll be right and you need to be there for the children.'

Edna made it with confidence back into the saddle and let Shamrock head for home with a lengthened rein.

This wasn't real. It seemed a bad dream, but they knew it had to be worse before any relief could be expected. They were in that immediate shock that demands action above thought. Pat O'Reilly was part of their lives, he was their rock. He was a leader, they all owed him something. The sad day passed as a rapid succession of events; it was almost as if they were in a play scene that would end with a return to normality. People came, did what they could and went back to their own environments.

The next day dawned a clear summer morning. It was Friday and

Sunday was Christmas day. It should have been the "happy" time of the year, but not this Christmas of unexpected tragedy.

There had been no rest through the night at the O'Reillys or at the Brewsters. The necessities of death meant that Pat's body be brought home, cleaned and prepared for burial. The rallying of the community meant that long before sundown on the previous afternoon the important people had begun to arrive. The news spread through Duck Creek with rapidity. Dan's calm but almost tearful announcement caused great shock and then an immediate rallying of the forces. Bopper, as makeshift coffin maker and undertaker, was found and despatched with his tools of trade in the James buggy. Kate, though many thought the James barmaid tough and a lady of loose morals, insisted she go with him to be of assistance. The James agreed.

It had to be, that with death, especially in summertime, burials took place quickly. Rupert James asked the question of Dan, 'When and where shall Bridget bury him?'

'Bridget says that he will be buried on Killarney. She would like a priest but that probably won't be possible.'

Rupert James mused.

'It may be of use, I heard there was a travelling French priest went down to Ballina on one of the river boats. They say he has a little organ that he carts around with him, causes quite a stir. Could be, he's still in Ballina.'

'Thanks for that Rupert, I'll head down to Ballina, I'll let Nell's mum know and check out the priest.'

Rupert James' hotel bar provided much information. He wanted to help in any way possible with this sad situation.

'There's a traveller going through to Casino this afternoon. I'll see if he'll drop a note off at that Presbyterian minister, Baillie. He always asks how the O'Reillys are if he calls in to get food for his horse. Doesn't grace my bar but he's a good bloke from what I hear.'

'Could you let me have a sheet of paper and I'll write the note?' said Dan. 'I know him and I know how good he was to me after the shipwreck.'

That task done, Dan headed off for Ballina. Rupert James promised to get word to Killarney of what Dan was trying to achieve in searching out a possible priest.

Men of the Cloth

As usual, Carmel knew what was cooking in Ballina. She was shocked at the news and vowed to be at Pat's funeral even if she had to walk. She knew of the visiting priest.

'I know Father Schurr was to go back up the river in the morning. He's staying with the Kellys. We'll go and see him.'

The French priest, still fairly new in the district and finding his way around the Catholics and any others who wanted his help, listened to the sad tale from Dan and Carmel. A tall, slender, middle-aged man, he nodded slowly. Sudden death was by no means new to a priest who had served in the West Indies islands and in this colony of New South Wales. Fevers, starvation, violence, crashing trees, spears, knives – Abbe Schurr knew all forms of death. Death always left its heavy human residue of grieving.

He spoke calmly, 'I am sorry for your friend. He must have been a great man and I will pray through the night for his family and friends. For him there is no more that I can do after this time of death, but I am sure he was loved by God. His soul will be at rest and he will live for ever in that family of which you tell me. Perhaps, if I can find me a horse, I can delay my trip up the river for a day and conduct a burial service tomorrow afternoon. I serve God where and when I can without a strict timetable.'

A sad smile hovered around the thin ascetic lips. He promised to talk with Brownie at the livery stable in the morning. He blessed them and bid them *bon soir*.

The night at Killarney had been for Bridget and the children a heavy footprint of pressing sorrow that tramped them down in a clinging bog of unreality. Pat was brought back to the house. Bridget, despite the efforts of her friends, insisted upon helping in the cleaning and dressing preparation of her husband. Kate carefully insisted she take the task of cleaning and binding the shocking wounds to the rear of Pat's skull. The tenderness with which she handled a terrible task, tears flowing from her eyes that many thought hard, was something Norah would not forget. When all was done, Pat lay in state upon a bed from whence he would be transferred to the coffin Bopper was carefully crafting from Killarney teak.

Bridget gathered her children, asked that they be left in privacy, kneeling around the stark white bed to pray a vigil rosary and say their farewells. The calm of the family had effect on their friends and neighbours; there was no need for words. Bridget and Pat's life together had been one of work and love. Pat O'Reilly through his work as a carrier had become known and liked by all throughout the growing pioneer district. His success was such that he had admitted to a few the time had come to slow down and enjoy his fertile little farm.

How could this overwhelming tragedy be just? Some muttered, 'Where is your God?' Yet it was obvious that Bridget was not asking that pointless question.

So, morning came. Dan had returned through the night. He waited until Bridget was up and bustling with the stove at daylight. He came to her, took over the fire lighting, told of the trip to Ballina and that there would be a priest. He also told that he had written a short note for Martin Baillie. Bridget placed her hand on his arm and thanked him for the long ride he had undertaken.

'Thank you, Dan, we are lucky to have wonderful friends. I know Pat would like Martin to be present. It will be a long day, but we will be all right.'

At this stage reinforcements arrived in the kitchen. Several minutes later Jim and Dan came back to call Bridget aside.

'Where do you wish to lay him to rest Bridget? We will prepare the site wherever you say.' Jim spoke gently.

Already there was a burial area outside of Duck Creek looking down over the ocean, but Bridget was determined for Pat's body to go back to the soil of the property on which he had toiled so hard to make their home.

'When Pat cleared the northern ridge, he left three trees in a triangle, a cedar, a beech and a "maiden's blush". I'd like the grave placed between those trees. He took much trouble to save them. They will appreciate and look after his body.'

They went and inspected the knoll and found it to be a place of quiet beauty, only a quarter of a mile from the house. The decision made, they returned to the deep red soil with shovels and the work commenced. Bopper was the authority on grave digging and the job was soon under way. It was expected the police sergeant from Ballina would arrive during the day for the formality of a visit to the death site and the filling in of a death report.

Interment was to be about 3 p.m. This should give time for friends to arrive and allow them opportunity to part return to their homes in some daylight. Cooking was underway to provide food after the service. Any idea of numbers present had to be a wild guess. Pat would be buried before many friends would hear of his death, but it was known some would hear and come to pay respects. The bush had its own means of communication.

It was 7 a.m. Friday morning that Martin Baillie, eating his morning rolled oats, heard a knock at the door of his Casino cottage. His housekeeper opened the door with a reproving frown. She did not approve of visitors at mealtime, especially at breakfast mealtime. Martin knew she was looking after him carefully, but at times he wished she wouldn't frighten some of his tough visitors with her brusque greetings.

'Well?'

One acid word was all she fired at the dishevelled handyman from the hotel. He was not likely to be a welcome guest. Hotels were works of the devil, and she had seen this miscreant looking worse for wear on many mornings.

'Sorry Ma'am, but a letter for the reverend,' said Tim O'Neill. He looked quite sober.

'H'mph, give it to me then,' was all she said.

She carried the letter, somewhat soiled, in her fingertips to Reverend Baillie.

'Have your breakfast first,' she commanded her charge.

Martin Baillie ignored the instruction and opened the envelope. She watched him carefully for she was distrustful of any message that came from that den of iniquity. She saw his face whiten and the strong fingers reacted by tapping the table. He glanced over the message again.

'I have a funeral to attend near Ballina and will leave almost immediately. I'd like you to go over and tell Donald Campbell that I have gone, I should be back for the Sunday service.'

'You can do little good charging over to Ballina. Dead is dead,' was her cryptic comment.

Martin pulled on his riding clothes. He threw clean shirt and clerical clothes in his saddle bags, caught and saddled the new grey horse he had been given and set out for Killarney. His mind was overactive. He knew the grief it must cause the family. He knew the high regard he felt for Pat, ever since that long ago day when the two met on the Clarence-Casino track.

'Lord, how could you allow this to happen, but give his family strength?'

Thoughts flooded his mind, but he had seen enough of death to know that once you started trying to find answers, it was a slippery slide of recriminations and God was the boss. All he could do was try to relieve the immediate poignant sorrow of death.

The O'Reillys were his friends. Pat for a start, and then his pretty, younger wife crept into his heart. He assured himself, the vision of Bridget and the children that sometimes flooded in unannounced was certainly not an occasion of worry. It seemed that despite the best efforts of his flock, they did not come up with a wife that filled his expectations, so he looked fated to the ongoing attentions of Mrs Phipps, his guardian housekeeper. He had no idea of what he could say or do, but he knew that it was a must for him to offer what help was within his feeble power. His thoughts were for Bridget and the children. Mary was fast approaching that transition from childhood.

The big, flea-bitten grey gelding, arranged by David Cameron, from an adjoining station squatter, was a good horse. He loped along well. Martin had christened him Cardinal. He reckoned the long, solemn roman-nosed equine face carried an appearance of disdain. His hours in the saddle gave opportunity to remain fit and he was able to work over many a contentious sermon whilst striding along on a free rein. This morning, he felt much at a loss as to how he would find the funeral scene. He realised Bridget would try to find a Roman Catholic priest, but that may be difficult. He wanted to be there in case he was needed for Bridget's sake and for the memory of the Irishman whom he knew was his friend.

The newly arrived Abbe Schurr had sought him out in Casino and seemed a man prepared to be friendly. He was there like himself to be an itinerant man of God. It was approximately one week ago that Martin had heard the French priest was heading down river by the trading boats with his small portable organ. Where he would be by now was anyone's guess. It was hard for a clergyman to make an itinerary and keep it; needs of a struggling scattered people was always how you found it on the day that you happened to be there.

The brief note penned by Dan Riordan, gave no strict time for a funeral, but Martin knew a body must soon be consigned to the grave in hot weather. There was no waiting for mourners to arrive. He paused briefly to give Cardinal a spell at the Lismore crossing and to eat the lunch prepared for him by a disapproving Mrs Phipps. He smiled wryly to himself, recalling her cryptic wisdom.

'Your work is with the living. The dead is dead.' He could not entirely agree.

When Abbe Schurr had made his way around to the livery stable the morning after Dan's visit, it was a shocked Brownie who heard the news. His first reaction was one of surprise to find a strange clerically attired priest strolling into his feed room. When told of the purpose for the priest's need of a horse, he sat on one of the big wooden bins in a state of disbelief.

'Ah, I'm right sorry to hear this. He was a good honest toiler, and a bonny man with a horse. To see him with his team was a pleasure to watch.'

Brownie needed a heavy drag of nicotine to steady the shock, then plaintively,

'Any fool could chop down a tree, why didn't he leave his axe at home? There's but a wee few who could handle a horse like Pat O'Reilly.'

He cast an eye over the suit clad priest.

'I've just got me a trap for hiring out. I'd like to pay my respects at O'Reilly's burial, so Father, I'll get you there and back if you would care to travel with me.'

Arrangements were made for them to set off out up the mountain long before lunch.

Ashes To Ashes

It was a morning of great activity at Killarney and Surreyville. Perhaps they were over catering for they knew that many who would wish to be present would not make the 3 p.m. deadline. Bridget's friends tried to shelter her and the children from the harsh reality of the day but Norah, Nell and Edna knew the need for tears and sorrow had still to come.

Bopper and Kate had transferred Pat to the solid, but tastefully made, teak coffin. Bridget and the children had knelt a last time in Pat's presence before the lid was finally closed. All was in readiness for the afternoon service and the cortege to walk up the hill.

It had been Bridget's wish that Captain and the old original cart would be the final transport for the man who had been his master and friend. Pat had spent so much time with the old horse.

By 2 p.m. they commenced arriving. The neat paddock that fronted Killarney began to fill. On foot, on horseback, in carts, in sulkies, they arrived, dressed for respect in their sombre best. Most were carrying thought of some past favour or good service performed by Pat O'Reilly.

Abbe Schurr had made himself known to Bridget and family, and to those loyal neighbours who were ably supporting them. Martin Baillie, sweat stained, arrived with a half hour to spare. He freshened up and changed to his clean shirt and clerical clothes. The French priest, realising that this clergyman was a friend of the family, went back to Bridget and asked whether Martin could be the one to speak of Pat. She looked at the two men, took Martin's hand briefly in welcome and thanks. She nodded in assent.

At 3 p.m. from the steps of Killarney, already the afternoon sun was casting some shade. The plain oiled teak coffin on the low east facing veranda was flanked by candles burning at either end of the casket. Family and close friends sat on chairs stretched along the veranda length, whilst a big congregation gathered on the ground level around the steps. Abbe Schurr held his hands wide to the big crowd.

'My friends we will begin. Spiritus Sancti, Oremus,' and with Dan acting as altar server holding a battered black Latin text of the Catholic burial rite, the quite short burial service was reality.

The almost musical drone of the incomprehensible age-old Latin service of Requiem spread out over a sombre crowd. Hatless men, women with hair tied up under their best dark headwear, and a sprinkling of restless children brought because there was no other option. Many of these witnessed a Roman rite of requiem mass for the first time.

At conclusion of the mass, Abbe Schurr motioned Martin Baillie to join him at top of the steps and introduced him as clergy and a friend of the family.

'Reverend Baillie will pay brief tribute to his friend, and I am sure a man who was friend of you all.'

Martin Baillie looked out over his audience. His still, strong Scots accent was in sharp contrast to the soft French-toned speech of the officiating priest.

He told quietly of his meeting with, and help from Pat, on that lonely track many years before. How he had watched with sincere interest as the O'Reilly family prospered. He told of his affection for the family and his sorrow for what had befallen Pat. He emphasised that just as Pat O'Reilly had helped him so Pat had helped many others and that they must be grateful for his part in making the community grow. Perhaps there comes a time when a man's work is done and even though no one expects it, God calls him home. He concluded, 'What we can do now is support his family and be thankful to almighty God for the life of Patrick O'Reilly.'

The walking crocodile of mourners climbed the hill. They followed the old grey Clydesdale and the well- used cart led by Dan. Captain seemed to place each foot in meticulous respect to the master and friend with whom he had shared a bond of trust. At the graveside, he stood in firm attention whilst the brief interment took place. The pall bearers placed the casket on ropes in the grave and final prayers were said. Rich red earth, that was built on the mould of countless aeons of rain forest, rattled down on the teak coffin.

Pat O'Reilly was laid to rest.

There was a move from the graveside by the majority of travellers. They needed to set out for their homes with as much daylight as possible. Refreshments were laid out at the front of Killarney in order to help the travellers on their way. The immediate part of the family's terrible ordeal was drawing to a close.

The long day found its conclusion. It was dusk. Most of the crowd, except the special friends, were gone. Perhaps a dozen lingered on the cooling grass and front veranda. They were determined to be on hand for the family as long as they could be of service. Would exhaustion allow Bridget and the children to sleep later that night? Who knew? Edna had decided to stay and be on hand for what help she could offer.

Martin had accepted offer of a bed from the Brewsters provided he could leave without fuss early the next morning. His farewell to Bridget, Mary, Janey and Thomas was brief. What could be said? Yet he knew his presence had been welcomed by the family, he assured them he would return in the not too distant future.

Abbe Schurr and Brownie had headed back to Ballina in company with Carmel and Tom O'Rourke. In a day and a half, the world had changed and a whole raft of decisions would soon have to be faced. For now, the present was a calm vacuum after the storm of mental upset and the oppressing reality.

The few remaining friends sat on the veranda making sure Killarney welcomed the coming long night of the soul as gently as possible for Bridget. Soon, with the exception of Norah and Edna, they would go their ways. Over cups of tea, they sat and silence of a still summer night settled down. The crickets crackled a soft song and a mopoke called for his mate over in the scrub.

Then from up on the hill, the gentle clear notes of a violin, descended on settling drifts of cool air. They knew who the fiddler would be, although none had seen Billy Montez in the considerable crowd. The tune was a timeless Romany lament that ebbed and flowed in the broken minor key of gypsy music. At the distance of the player, only a clear evening and the gentle drift of a sighing breeze made audible contact possible. At times the haunting notes clothed them, at times their imagination carried the tune when it failed until the sound waves gently flowed back. Darkness and silence took over.

Phantom chords of choice travelled with travellers as they took their thoughts home. Life and another day's chores would be there on the morrow.

Sad Welcome

The trip up the coast had been smooth with the breeze a steady southerly. Dick Hilardt leant on the deck rail of the small trading brigantine, *Saucy Jack*. As the company man on the little ship, he had little to do whilst at sea. At their one day visit to the Clarence, he had been ashore and talked with the shipping rep about matters of company policy. It would remain to be seen whether the book work improved. It was now mid-afternoon and leaning on the rail waiting for the Ballina bar to become recognisable, he was hoping they would be able to enter. The skipper had assured him that they should make it into Ballina. The bar should be favourable. It was his intention to stay until after Christmas day. He wondered what the reaction of Edna had been to his letter. Would she want to see him or would his visit be an embarrassment to them both? Only one way to find out, perhaps he was just suffering a rash, middle-age itch. He'd heard it did happen at times, even to careful people.

A whistle from the captain at the wheel and a pointing hand signified Ballina was coming up. Dick peered inland through the surf haze. Yes, he supposed that headland was off Ballina, the low rocky cliff that guarded the entrance. Every man to his trade, that low rolling surf seemed to offer very little in the way of a welcoming track to a landlubber like himself. Well, if they didn't make it, then that would solve his problem and the doubts he carried as to whether he should be calling upon Edna.

Captain Collins worked in close to the bar. There were no flying black balls on the pilot's trapeze and the making tide should promise enough water if he could pick the best channel. A tug service was now operating but Captain Collins reckoned the task looked as easy as Ballina bar ever presented. He picked what looked a sensible entry path and stood out to sea. Tacked around, called for sail, waited for them to set and fill, then ran for the bar. Dick joined the sailors wedged firmly amidships awaiting any orders from their skipper or mate. They drove in, skirting the headland with enough speed to carry the break. Inside, Captain Collins lifted a left thumb at the mate in triumph and as signal to furl most of the sail. Every entry to Ballina caused most sailors to say a silent prayer of thanks, either orthodox or of their own form. Too many men had lost their lives in the last thirty years, perhaps the new tug service would be of some help.

They worked upriver from the bay to the growing town and were granted a mooring at the wharf. Only one other ship was in Ballina to spend Christmas. This was Christmas Eve and it was certain the crew would be good customers to one of the towns three pubs.

'How about a tot of rum?'

Captain Collins pulled the mate and Dick to his small cabin. It was half an hour later that Dick broke free from their threesome. He had decided to make his way around to Carmel Flaherty's, perhaps her lodging room would be free, at least he would catch up with the local news. There was nothing like a tot or two of rum in the bilge to make a man's load seem more acceptable. He tramped down the street with his heavy canvas kit bag feeling much lighter. His knock on the door met a surprised greeting from Carmel.

'Why, by the saints of old Ireland, if it's not Dick Hilardt. I thought you would be safely celebrating in the fleshpots of Sydney. Where did you drop in from?'

Carmel beckoned him into the small parlour-dining room. She motioned him to one of the straight-backed chairs with a serious facial expression that worried him.

'Have you heard the sad news?'

Dick shook his head, wondering what to expect.

He sat in stunned silence after Carmel dropped her bombshell. She was not one for hedging round the subject. Within a minute of arrival Dick was aware of the turmoil that had burst on his old residency area. When he spoke, it was with emotion.

'I wish I had been here. Not that I could have done anything. Somehow, I'm finding it hard to believe. Pat did all things so well. How are Bridget and the children? What will she do?'

'Who knows?' replied Carmel. 'Bridget is strong and Dan Riordan could possibly keep the business afloat with his experience; but who knows? It's not easy when you lose a husband. I found out from experience.'

Dick nodded.

'What's my chance of hiring a bed for the night? I'll head up and see what is happening tomorrow.'

'Yes, the room is empty. You'll have seen there's not many ships in at the moment. I'll have warm water in your jug and dinner is at 6.30. You'll probably be out on the town for Christmas Eve?'

He shook his head.

'Thanks Carmel. No, I think it will be an early night for me.'

He probably didn't see the lift of Carmel's eyebrows as she left the room.

Why would Dick Hilardt turn up from the ocean, when he had made it clear not many months ago that he was only too pleased to brush the red soil off his toes? Ah well, his money for the room would be handy. Certainly, she felt for Bridget, nothing was easy about being a widow with a family. Yet Bridget would not face the financial battle that had been hers. Had it not been for the help of Tom O'Rourke that no one was supposed to know of, they would have been hungry many times. Carmel was a realist and reckoned there would have been plenty to guess that Tom was more than just her lodger. She smiled to herself. Their relationship was between them, God and their very occasional confessor. The rumour mongers could go hang.

Christmas day dawned clear on the plateau. It had been late when those left at Killarney through necessity went to bed. Bridget gathered her children into the big cedar bed that Pat had fashioned with his own hands. They needed to be together and surprisingly sleep had captured them. Bridget woke with the dawn, gave thanks to God that the children were sleeping -a sleep of exhaustion.

'Lord, give me the strength to carry this load.'

Ever so carefully, she eased her way onto the floor. The kitchen stove still had warmth; she added small kindling which she knew would catch.

It was Christmas day; the children's presents had been packed a week before with Pat's help. She eased them down from the big cupboard. Hopefully, even Mary would not wake for some time yet. Things must be done. Myrtle, the jersey cow, had to be milked. Mary had been insisting for a time that she was capable. Maybe it could be another chore for her. For now, Bridget silently eased out into the cool morning. The big bucket sat on its shelf. She took feed from the shed and went to find Myrtle. The ground mist puffed up in wispy patterned breaths from the pastured earth, a joyous morning brutally unaware of her sorrow.

As she returned to the house, the sound of activity in the stables made her look to see what was happening. Dan was feeding and watering the horses.

'Ah Dan, you shouldn't be working so early on Christmas day. Thank you, and a Happy Christmas.'

'Bridget you should not be milking the cow this morning, I would have done that next.'

She shrugged.

'Life must go on. I intend to do what Pat would have done, where I can. I'll be talking to you soon to see whether you will continue working with the business. Too soon today, but we know clients have to be looked after. I am so lucky to have friends.'

She went inside with the milk.

The kitchen was a hive of activity. There was the smell of toast and freshly made tea, strengthened by an unusual coffee aroma, the favourite beverage of Norah. Christmas greetings were exchanged. Norah said,

'After breakfast we will go to Brewsters, all of us. I know it will be a difficult day Bridget, but we need you and the children with us, so please let Jim and myself make that decision.'

Norah, Edna and Mary were in charge of the kitchen and Bridget took the opportunity of placing the wrapped presents on the dining room table. It all now seemed incongruous, books for Mary, a dress for Janey, and a bat and ball for Thomas. The new pocket watch Christmas present for Pat remained hidden in her wardrobe. It would be a long day.

When Dick made his way around to the livery stable, it was not with great enthusiasm. He didn't claim horsemanship as one of his attainments. True, he could manage a horse if the nag was cooperative. It was necessary, either that or walk if he could not find Brownie. The old Scotsman was late on the job feeding his horses. He had felt it necessary to knock over a good quantity of malt whiskey to make use of Christmas Eve, and this clear Christmas morning his head was far from clear. He knew Dick, but theirs was normally but a nodding acquaintance.

'Happy Christmas, Mr Brown.'

'Ay, same to you mon. What brings ye back to the rivers?'

'Well, I came in yesterday on the Saucy Jack. I heard the bad news about Pat O'Reilly from Carmel Flaherty, so I'd like to go up and pay respects to my friends.'

'Ay, a great shame, a gud man and a horseman to do me heart good. He'll be missed.'

'How would I be for a horse to hire?'

'Mr Hilardt, I'm in the business o' hiring horses. The old grey plug gets most o' the travellers around. Not quick ye know, but he'll make it there and he'll git ye back.'

'He'll do. I'm in no great hurry. The Saucy Jack won't be looking for a tide before Tuesday, so I'll take him slowly.'

'Ah could ha let ye have me new trap but it's booked out for tomorrow.'

'No, the old grey will be fine. We are friends.'

Life Flows Onward - Dick and Edna

Christmas dinner at the Brewsters was fated to be a sad occasion. Yet there were streamers and the trimmings. Bridget insisted Pat would want his friends and his family to carry on with their lives. However, she insisted early in the afternoon that the family were going home. Together they would attend to the farm chores.

'Our friends have been wonderful, we could not have managed till now without you, but we have to pick up our lives and work is the way we will do it. We have to manage without Pat, hard as it will be.'

Bridget marshalled the family and refused to let the Christmas gathering break up. The O'Reillys tramped home.

They were not long gone when Dick and Brownie's steady old hack turned in at the Surreyville gate. They welcomed him warmly. He insisted they tell him if his presence would make it harder for the little community.

'No Mr Hilardt, you are a friend and welcome. Bridget insisted on going home not long ago. Leave her a couple of hours and I'm sure Dan would like an excuse to go over and help with the animals.'

Norah spoke for the group and insisted he wash and be seated, so they could supply him with a late Christmas dinner.

Edna helped serve his meal and when that was on the table, sat opposite. They both felt a restraint. Perhaps it was just the emotional tension of Pat's tragic death, perhaps it was that the reality of his visit clanged mental alarm bells for both. They kept it low key.

'I can see why I travelled around up here on foot.' He smiled quizzically at Edna and added, 'There's some that sits on a horse easy, but there's some like me that find it hard work.'

She told him how she had ridden Shamrock over to Tara.

'Well, you are much better than I am. It is not exciting pushing a pen but perhaps that's all I'm cut out for.'

'Ah, you sell yourself short.' Edna looked at him quietly.

What was the story to this man?

They chatted about the school. He seemed genuinely interested in

Pearl, and wanted to know whether Edna expected her back for the next school year. It seemed he had met Jan on a couple of occasions but knew nothing of Rosie.

'Usually, white men walk away from black women and the children they father, so Yan has shown something to earn respect. There is probably education behind him from my brief encounter with the man. Who knows what brought him to this plateau and his job as a scrub faller. There is probably a story, and he is a quiet man not likely to tell that story.'

On completion of his Christmas meal, Dick insisted on helping Edna clear away and wash the dishes.

'You know my domestic record is not good. When everything became used in the shack, I'd boil up my old black kettle and give them a quick scald. Just as well Blackie was not the fussy kind of dog or he would have walked out on me.'

Edna spoke quietly, 'I saw plenty of men in bush homesteads who did it that way. At times men and women have different priorities. I've seen it tough you know, the outback is not lush and green. Most of the time dust puts a dull cover overall. Then that odd time when rain falls, the brief contrast of green and growth spins a fickle magic that keeps the real bushies going until the next drought knocks them down again.'

'I haven't been far from the coast, so you know what makes this vast country tick far better than I do. Perhaps one day. For now, I'll visit the ports as part of the company services, and hope the little ships sneak in safely.'

They finished restoring order in the tidy Brewster kitchen. The 10 minutes of working side by side helped, still the doubtful thoughts as to whether their wavelength of mutual interest was there. No denying it. It was pleasant to be together.

Later in the afternoon, Dan asked whether Dick would like to stroll over to Killarney with him. It was decided Edna would go also just to check on the children and to see whether there was anything with which she could help. They found Bridget and the children doing the afternoon chores with the animals. Dan took over the feeding routines for the horses in company with the children and Edna. They left Bridget and Dick to return to the kitchen.

'I'm so sorry Bridget. If I still lived up here, probably I could have been of use. It is little use my saying anything, but you know how I feel, how we all feel. Perhaps if you have any business or book problems, I could be of use there. I'm sure the likes of Dan will supply the work to keep the business going. Jim Brewster too, is a sound man.'

She laid her hand lightly on his arm.

'Thanks Dick. All my friends have been so good. The years with Pat were so wonderful, it will take a while. I'm strong and still have Pat's love in our children. We will be fine. He kept the books, but I think we will have enough to carry on. I can drive a cart you know, and I'm not about to let his work disappear. We will keep the wagons on the road for now, carrying goods and see what happens as the children grow older. I can't keep Mary here much longer; she needs a chance of education. She is a thinker. Probably the convent in Sydney where I was educated will be the place.'

Dick Hilardt nodded.

'This area will grow and your school is certainly the first big step forward. It will only take some roads and useful crops for the farmers to make the area go ahead. It's gone forward rapidly even in my ten years. The time will come when there's a decent entrance to the river.'

Bridget shrugged slightly and Dick saw the slow smile that Mary had received from her mother.

'Yes. We will be fine. It will take time but there's nothing like work. Should I need financial advice, well perhaps I could be lucky, Edna may still have your address.'

The sideways glance Bridget gave him seemed to indicate that perhaps his interest in Edna was not the complete secret he chose to believe.

The threesome headed back to Brewsters. Dan, Nell and Sean still had to walk home and attend to the chores at Tara. It had been agreed Dan would ride across to Killarney on the morrow and he and Bridget would draw up an immediate plan to meet the needs of O'Reilly Carrying Service: they would keep operating for its many customers.

Dick occupied the man's room in Brewster's shed for Christmas night. He would set out back to Ballina at some time next day on Brownie's old grey hack. The Brewsters claimed that the events of the past few days had taken a severe toll on them and headed for bed early.

'There are fresh sheets and pillowcase on the side table near the back steps,' Norah instructed Dick. 'Edna will see you have a light. There is a dish and water in the room. We will see you for breakfast. May you sleep well.'

Dick and Edna were left to occupy the formal Brewster living room. Their aloneness weighed heavy. Dick sat on one side of the large mahogany table and Edna on the other. A big kerosene fuel lamp threw out light from the middle of the table. As with kerosene lamps, the wick charred a black crust and a resultant wisp of smoke eddied up from the fluted glass. Dick reached across and turned down the flame. This reduced the smoke.

'You are not afraid of being in a dull light with me?' He smiled across at Edna. 'It seems Mrs Brewster must think I can be trusted.'

Edna surveyed him steadily. There was hint of a smile around her attractive mouth.

'That's all right for Norah, she's gone to bed. I'm the one alone with you in the semi dark. We too need an early night, you know.'

Dick nodded, his face softened, calm in the reduced visibility. Not a handsome face, but a face with character. The frequent specks of grey in the dark hair coloured back to black by the room's dim light. He placed a hand with strong well-kept fingers, palm up on the table and slid it slowly across to the middle.

'Perhaps Miss Wilkinson, you may think it safe to meet me halfway. It is a big solid table.'

Edna held his gaze. Then to her discomfort, felt the colour rise in her lightly made-up cheeks. She was thankful for the low light. When it seemed he must surely be thinking that his approach was not to be met, Edna placed her gloved hand on the table.

'As you say it is a solid table.'

She slowly removed the glove from the turned down palm and pushed the soft doeskin further down the expanse of table. She extended her hand, on an arm covered in a long-sleeved lace-edged blouse and placed it in his hand. Neither spoke, nor did Dick attempt to pressure her slim, firm fingers that did not refuse his approach. It was reassuring communication for both.

The seconds ticked long. Pressures of death held Edna in the guttering light flame. She had thought, after witnessing the death of her young love so many years before, that life's end would never again shatter her being with that devastating extent of consuming content. But the death of Pat and her close involvement, even to the extent of helping with a lifeless body, had grabbed her once more.

It seemed something in the touch of a man who wanted to offer help, and probably love, released a coil spring of emotion. Soundless tears welled from her eyes, washed down her cheeks. Those tears glinted a sparkling stream in the lamplight.

She was grateful for his silence. The tears stopped flowing. She looked up and his face came back into a fuzzy washed view. There was caring pressure from the strong fingers, his wordless expression of concern. He leant across the table, eased out the crochet-edged linen handkerchief clutched in her free hand, and carefully wiped the drying tear trails from her downward cast eyes. His touch was gentle, reassuring and strangely necessary.

'Are you all right?'

'Yes,' she smiled at him. 'Thank you. I am dull company, I'm afraid.'

'It's been too tough a time for all concerned. Perhaps you had better pack me off to bed.'

He rose, released her hand, came to her side of the table and carefully brought her to the perpendicular.

'Right ma'am, show me to my lodging.'

Edna collected his sheets and pillowcase from the back table. They soundlessly opened the door and headed over to the adjacent shed, with its neat add-on room.

'I can manage, you know,' this comment from Dick, when they reached the open door.

'No, I'll make your bed. You strike a match and light the candle which is sure to be here.'

The candle offered a warm, shadowy glow, pulling in the room's simple shapes as intimate bed fellows. Edna made the bed with a teacher's precision.

'There. Sleep tight, now I must go.'

Dick took her hands and held her at arm's length.

'That bed would hold us both with no room for demons of the night,' he whispered. 'You could stay.'

She looked at him squarely.

'The trouble is, it would be too easy for me to stay, but it's not to be, not tonight.'

She led him from the intimate little room back out into the safer space of the passageway. At the house steps she opened the back door, with a firm grip of his hands in hers, she lifted her face to his and gently kissed him.

'Now you go,' she said. He lingered. She shook her head. 'We'll talk in the morning.'

She pushed him away and went inside behind the protection of the door. Neither went quickly to sleep. Both sets of arms felt oddly empty.

Boxing Day morning flowed swiftly upon the household. The opportunity for Dick and Edna to be on their own proved elusive, too difficult. Soon it was time for him to go, and Norah guessed there were things that this couple may have still unsaid.

'Why not put on some walking shoes and walk down the road with Mr Hilardt? It's a great day and perhaps we won't see him again for a while.'

Dick said his goodbyes to the Brewsters. Edna walked with him down the entrance way from the lane to Surreyville and out onto the road that would lead him back to Ballina.

The bright warmth of a summer day soon caused a thin layer of perspiration to attract an occasional fly as their unwelcome travelling companions. They walked side by side. Dick looked straight ahead.

'Only to the main road, it's all I can let you walk. But I don't want to ride off into the distance again. Perhaps the first time, we'd just met, I couldn't be sure. Now, Pat's death, the fact I lay awake most of last night and all I wanted was to feel you with me, there's something that's laid me low. I'm not a callow youth, I thought it best I live a life on my own. Now I don't want to be on my own, I want to be with you. Will you marry me? It's said.'

They walked on. After a while Edna spoke, 'Dick, when I was young, I was in love with a man, killed before my eyes. To me, my chance of romance, love, family, all seemed gone, too remote. I wandered around and looked after other people's children and I thought I was happy. I came here and I am happy. You have woken something in me I thought was not for me again. Thank you for the honour you have offered me. Please don't push me for an answer now. Perhaps I'm selfish, yes. I think I love you but let me think. I will write you an answer.'

At the crossroad, Dick took her in his arms and they savoured the embrace. He placed a thumb and forefinger under her chin, their lips met, offering, sharing, communicating. When they broke away, he smiled.

'Well, Miss Wilkinson. I'm going now but I will be back. Just don't you find another bloke.'

He mounted and turned the old grey toward Ballina. Edna didn't trust herself to watch him go. She turned, started the trek back to Surreyville and did not dare a last look as he left.

Forward Time – Mary to Sydney

The heavy, all devouring, starched habit of Mother Cecilia rustled up to the counter of the shipping office. Hers was an impressive, no nonsense approach.

'Young man, would there be any news of the *Firefly* from the North Coast? I am expecting a student and her luggage when your ship finally does arrive. I was assured it should be here by today.'

The shipping clerk became very used to fobbing off public enquiries as to when a ship would arrive. Shipping often did not run to schedule. He was apt to have an appropriate answer, that involved wrong wind, thick fog, or other vagaries of nature. This was his second visit from a nun in the past two days. Definitely unusual.

Yesterday, he had found the young Irish sister with a wisp of red hair that, unbeknown to her, had escaped from her severe veil. She was very timid and prepared to rapidly retreat, once told there was no news. Today, he felt this large, forbidding, elderly, also Irish nun, probably with authority and a hint of long-term colonial exposure, was not about to leave until an answer was supplied. She was obviously concerned as to the arrival of her expected charge.

He opened the big ledger of shipping, then ran a finger down his carefully scribed list of names.

'Yes Sister, the *Firefly* out of Grafton, should be here today. She will berth at Balmain wharf. I am told there is a fairly strong southerly off the coast so it would not be a fast trip down.'

'And that's all you can give me?' Mother Cecilia fixed him with her direct look, reserved for pupils not doing their best.

'Later, in about two hours, we should have a report of the ships in sight. I hope the *Firefly* will be listed.'

The clerk politely offered that carrot of information. He had a reputation for his repartee, he would have liked to suggest she use her influence above to find the whereabouts of the *Firefly*, but he was not without discretion.

'Thank you. I shall return in two hours, young man.'

Mother Cecilia flowed out of the cedar-fitted office. She was rather like one of the many ships under full sail pictured on the walls.

The *Firefly* beat down past the heads until she had enough astern in the wind to enable her to run for the harbour. Not a large ship, but she boasted a passenger cabin that on this voyage was occupied by 14-year-old Mary O' Reilly. It had been a sad parting from her mother on the wharf at Grafton. Mary was sure her mother could not continue on and prosper in the carrying business and looking after the farm animals without her help.

Since her father's death two years before, she had been a resilient prop for her mother and siblings. Mary's life had been a mixture of study and work. She was very capable of handling situations that would have tested others twice her age.

Although Bridget had shed tears at night in her lonely bed at the thought of Mary leaving Killarney, she was determined that it must be. It had been delayed a year longer than it would have, had Pat lived. A letter written six months before to the Sisters of Mercy at Rosebay had brought an enthusiastic answer from Mother Cecilia. Of course, she remembered Bridget Foggarty; it was such a pity she had not completed her education. Of course, she would consider it a privilege to take charge of her daughter Mary's education. The die was cast.

It was an unsure Mary, with her mother and two boxes of luggage, that arrived in Grafton to catch the *Firefly*. Bridget had purchased a sulky

and a smart bay pony. This was their longest trip by far. The road from
Casino was now more vehicle trafficable, except in wet weather, and
Bridget was determined to avoid Mary's crossing out over the Ballina
bar. So, the adventure of travelling, and opportunity to do most of the
driving of Major the pony, went some way to appeasing Mary's trauma
of leaving home.

They arrived at Grafton in good order, with only an hour to wait
for ebb tide and the ship to sail down river. It was a restrained farewell,
Mary refused to melt into tears.

She clung briefly to her mother.

'No tears. I'll write when I arrive. You tell Janey and Thomas to
do their jobs or they'll have to answer to me when I come home on
holidays.'

Standing at the wharf rail waving as the *Firefly* cast out into the
wide Clarence was too much for Bridget. The tears ran down her still
almost unlined cheeks. She had arranged to stay the night with a friend
of the old days. She would head back to Killarney in the morning.

To Rose Bay Convent

'Take a line,' the bos'n of the *Firefly* bellowed at a hand on the wharf.
He twirled the light, lead weighted pilot line in his expert fingers, and
pitched it accurately to the heavy wood decking of the wharf. It landed at
the wharf hand's feet. The sisal hawser followed out off the capstan and
soon the *Firefly* was attached to bollards fore and aft.

'Well, missy, you seemed to handle your first sea trip very well.
It was running a bit of a chop too but the mate said you ate your meals
and came on deck. We'll see that your guardians are here to meet you
when we put the luggage ashore. I'll not be turning you loose in this big
city until they arrive.'

Captain Perrett had been told a little of Mary and promised to see her delivery to the nuns was safely in order.

'Thank you. It was wonderful,' said Mary.

She felt the hardest part was about to begin, but her mother's assurance had been given that Mother Cecilia was not as severe as she would at first appear.

With the *Firefly* secured, and the gangplank laid to the wharf, two habited nuns came into view from the dockside waiting room. The large portly figure of Mother Cecilia was closely followed by a slim, tallish figure well disguised from view, and keeping a deferential couple of paces behind.

Captain Perrett escorted Mary up the gangplank to the dock. He was not at all sure about nuns but a ship's captain had to be versatile, He removed his gold braided cap and bowed to Mother Cecilia.

'I am pleased to introduce Mary O'Reilly ma'am. I assured her mother that she would be delivered personally by me to your care.'

'Thank you for your care and courtesy, Captain. We will collect her luggage to the cab we have waiting and proceed up to the convent. May God keep your ship and its men safe in His ever-caring charge.'

Mother Cecilia despatched Sister Benedictine to bring the cabbie to start carrying. Captain Perrett bent a finger at a sailor to help the cabbie. Both boxes, and the trunk, followed by the two nuns and Mary, left the wharf.

They made their way through the busy streets and soon arrived at the convent. The cabbie was commanded to deliver the boxes inside the strong, wrought iron gates of the high stone outer fence. Sister Benedictine was sent to sound their arrival. The polished brass doorbell echoing in the depths of the convent brought a postulant and housemaid to act as porters. The nuns and Mary entered by the huge, heavy, cedar door, and the well-oiled heavy lock clunked behind them. Mary felt this must be what it was like to enter a gaol.

'I shall talk to you in the parlour Mary and after that Sister Benedictine will show you to your room. Follow me.'

The convent parlour smelt strongly of an oil and turpentine furniture polish, books and a touch of carbolic cleanliness: all defined themselves in the family of odours. Subdued light gave the brooding statues aloof watchfulness as they peered from their corners at the stiff chintz covered sofa, to which Mary was directed.

Mother Cecilia was now prepared to focus full attention upon her newest charge.

'I was sorry to hear God so suddenly called home your father. It must have been very difficult for your mother and she has told me how you have helped. She seems to think that your schooling, although sparse, will see you equal to girls of your age. We shall place you in a class of girls of your age and see how you cope. If necessary, you shall have extra coaching. WE believe in producing young ladies from here who fear the Lord and make good wives or servants of God,' she said.

'Sister Benedictine will be your scholastic and spiritual advisor. Prayers are at 6.30 each morning in the chapel.'

The interview was over. Mary dutifully said, 'Thank you mother.'

The bell was rung and Sister Benedictine glided into the room, smiled at Mary and motioned with her index finger. Mary followed. It was just too much for one day; her mind was in a state of watchful suspension.

O'Reilly Carriers and Progress

Bridget O'Reilly sat at the table, allocated in a corner of the home living room as her office. Her wage books, dockets, invoices, all neatly pigeon-holed and in order of attention. It had been a battle to run the carrying business and maintain a steady growth. Dan Riordan had agreed to be her full-time leading hand, in charge of the big wagon and the heavy jobs.

She had approached John Richards and offered him a full-time job as her offsider with the view that he would later become a driver. He had worked with her, from Pat's death on one of the carts, doing the heavy lifting, and looking after the horses. Some twelve months later, she and Dan felt he was capable of working on his own, and he had proved to be honest, reliable, competent, and old for his years.

It had caused quite a stir when Bridget notified all her customers that the business would continue with herself as the second driver. The gossip mongers predicted failure, they predicted it would not take long and the business would be sold or given away.

'Plain daft. That crazy woman won't last a month.' Bob Beames was quick to pass his opinion around the Ballina dock. There were others who agreed, but at least they were prepared to give her a chance and see what happened.

They were surprised. She and old Captain may have been slow, but they always delivered the goods. Bridget allowed herself few concessions.

The long, flowing auburn hair went before the scissors. The resulting short, red bob was covered by a wide-brimmed felt hat, much to Norah's horror. She wore overalls, long sleeved shirts and light serviceable men's boots. Strangers who passed her on the tracks, probably did not know the driver was a woman. She threw herself into the task and the therapy of work. It helped ease some of the nightmare of Pat's death. Her friends and neighbours helped but all had busy lives of their own. It came back to Bridget and the children to support each other. And this was what they did very well.

With Bridget on the road, there had to be provision for housework, cooking, cleaning, all the things considered to be a woman's real tasks. Edna came up with the suggestion. What about offering Rose a job as help to the O'Reilly household? It floored the ever-resilient Bridget.

'What does she know about housework? Would she be reliable? Would she want to take a job?'

There were many questions and Bridget admitted to herself, the fact Rose was black, not the least of those questions.

'Well, you need domestic help. It's too much for you, and Mary probably does too much now. Talk to Mary, she knows Pearlie and may know something of her mother. Mary is wise for her years, see what she thinks. You can't be a carrier and a housekeeper too.'

The seed was sown. Rose had not forgotten the kindness of Pat O'Reilly. She reluctantly agreed to come on trial if Yan approved when he came home. It was an arrangement that worked out well for all concerned.

Many eyebrows lifted and many feigned shock that Bridget O'Reilly would leave her children in the hands of a "gin". The children and Rose were soon firm friends. They slowly taught and widened her range of English, although she would shrug and say, 'Too hard.'

As a housekeeper, she kept the cottage spotless and learned to cook European meals. She and Pearl took to staying in the man's room out at the stables through the week and went back to their shack on the escarpment at the weekends.

Bridget and Dan employed Yan at times, when they could afford to have scrub felled on Killarney and Tara. He was prepared to do the felling as they wanted it done, and capable of working around the trees they wanted spared. It gave the Riordans a chance to make progress with Dick's block.

Nell was a keen farmer with a real skill at growing things. She planted fruit trees and grew wonderful vegetables. She also read slowly all the literature she could accumulate about horticulture and was so proud when she produced her first successful limb graft on a peach tree.

Her large garden soon boasted a plot of sugar cane. The Johnsons had some acres under the ribbon variety, and willingly allowed Nell a few stalks that were soon growing rank and tall under her care. Potential sugar farmers were listening with interest to the thought of growing cane and crushing the stalks for sugar. There were many small cottage industry mills springing up down on the riverbanks and "Johno" Johnson was sure this was the crop to bring stability and growth to the Duck Creek plateau.

'You mark my words, Nell; this is the crop to make us money.'

Johno had listened to Reverend Thom and Abbe Schurr. He had gone to the Clarence and brought home cane sets. He was adamant.

'The pesky birds can't eat sugar cane, and it grows wild on this rich soil.'

The Riordans' second son, Matthew, was born when Sean was 12 months old. Nell had much to do. Dan was seldom home now that he was the full-time supervisor for O'Reilly Carriers. It was Nell, with Blackie faithfully at her heels, who mostly looked after the farm chores.

The school went forward with Edna proving to be a competent teacher. It brought fundaments of education to the plateau's children and a newfound optimism to the settlers. Her acceptance of Dick's proposal had been by often unreliable ship's mail, and this saw him later return to Ballina, setting up as the growing town's shipping agent. Her answer to the Christmas proposal had been the briefest letter to pass between them.

'Dear Dick, if you still want me as a wife. Yes.'

They were married a year later. Edna was replaced by a Miss Cavanagh. The Hilardts went to live in a growing Ballina. The little school at Duck Creek flourished as more land was cleared on the plateau and real farming enterprise began.

Other areas were also looking to establish schools as their pivot point of community and there was talk of an actual church to cater for spiritual needs. Men of the cloth, such as Abbe Schurr and Martin Baillie, were constantly on the move trying to meet some of the needs of a growing population. Church services and Mass were celebrated wherever a setting could be found when a clergy person made the infrequent visit.

Work, Life, Humanity

It had been a wet autumn. The Richmond had swollen and flooded on several occasions, but this time it looked as if a major flood was well on the way.

Despite the gravelling of many roads, O'Reilly Carriers had been battling to supply their customers. The wear and tear on vehicles and horses was so much more in wet weather, not to mention the operators. For the past week Bridget had been back on the road, filling in for John Richards who had torn an arm muscle and was forced to take rest. She had taken the light cart and two horses to Ballina, aiming to bring needed supplies from a recent ship. She hoped to take a load of essentials up the mountain. As a fill in for John, Angus James was found as an offsider for Bridget. He was a big, strong youth, with a liking for his own way, but so far Bridget had kept him under control, with help from Rupert, his father.

'You do what you are told and no back chat,' had been Rupert's order to his son, when Bridget had picked him up for the trip.

They loaded early in the afternoon at the wharf. Bridget reckoned the road would only get worse with the steady rain, and there was the threat of heavier falls to come, so she wasted no time in heading for home.

Captain was no longer a full-time worker but Bridget had brought the old horse on this trip to lead the young Clydesdale, John assured her was going well. She knew the hill climb could still be tricky and difficult once ruts cut through the sparse gravel. They struggled up the cutting with what was only a light load of mostly staple supplies for Duck Creek. At one stage, they lurched into a deep hole and Captain kept the load balanced when his young offsider momentarily panicked. Angus and Bridget both threw their weight onto the sunken wheel. They pushed and levered with bars, eventually the horses won against the gluey earth and the cart came out, like a reluctant cork from a bottle. At the top of the cutting Bridget insisted on giving Captain a good rest.

'Ah, let's keep going, it's not far home now.' Angus was cold, wet and covered in red mud.

'No way Angus, Captain saved us from real trouble; he needs a rest.' Bridget was not influenced by Angus and his desire to be home.

She knew how much work and time it would have been to unload had it not been for the restraining influence of the old horse.

She too was wet, cold, and muddy to the skin, but at least she knew now they should eventually make it home. The rain was pelting down and it seemed, was not about to stop. There was a strong, cyclonic northerly cutting across their main line of travel.

It was almost night and thankfully they were on the last slope down into the village. The black night's fingers were fast choking to death the dismal leaden grey afternoon. A lone rider came up from behind the cart.

Bridget became aware when the horseman was alongside.

'Is that really you Bridget? I was told you had given up driving. At least I would have hoped that you weren't out in this sort of weather.' She recognised the voice.

'Hello Martin. It's a while since we've seen you. We're a driver down at present and Dan is probably only on the way back from Lismore. I'm all right. Don't forget I climbed masts on sailing ships and I'm fit. Angus here is my power supply.'

Martin Baillie dropped in beside the cart.

'Well, we are nearly to the village, I'll help you unload.'

Martin and Bridget had not met up for nearly a year. At times on his infrequent trips down to Ballina he wanted to take the time and diverge to Killarney, as he used to in the first couple of years after Pat's death. Perhaps he enjoyed those trips too much, he told himself, but there was the excuse that he was able to supply spiritual comfort and friendship to the bereaved family. Now that Bridget's life had returned to a constant plane, he had been keeping away. He pulled his grey mount in beside them and they tramped up the street to the storage shed that carried the prominent words 'O'Reilly's General Carriers', on the big double doors.

The rain chopped into eyes, mouth, and nose, with an icy burning bite. Savage wind squalls packed solid the downward fat raindrops, and thumped them, ground parallel like sharpened spear thrusts, on any bare skin.

Bridget jumped down from the cart and rummaged in her leather belt pouch for the big heavy key. Martin motioned to Angus to act as head side ostler to the horses, while he helped open and hold the heavy wide door on the windward side. Bridget put her hand lightly on Captain's nose band and the old horse slowly led in the procession. It was a welcome relief for three people and the two horses to be folded into the calm of the big shed.

On a side bench, Bridget found a couple of prepared lanterns and a tin of wax matches. The phosphorous match scratched to life as the head rasped across the roughened bottom of the tin. Its meagre light flare was a wonderful welcome contrast to the inner blackness. She lit the lantern wicks and dropped the mechanism of the enclosed glasses. The shed became an oasis from the outside cyclone, an odd eddy of searching breeze still fought its way in, but the contrast of in and out was dramatic. Bridget felt it was now possible for Angus to make home.

'Angus, once we unload, you'd better make it home. Your parents will be wondering where you are.'

'What will you do? It's not going to be much of a trip home for you unless that wind drops. Mum would give you a room in the hotel for the night.'

'Thanks Angus, but I don't like leaving Rosie and the children unless I have to. Anyway, let's unload, perhaps the wind will drop.'

The cart's load was soon neatly stacked along one side of the shed together with other goods left there by Dan when he had continued on to Lismore. It would be easy to make local deliveries from here when the weather abated. Half an hour later, Angus was free to return home.

It left Bridget and Martin to decide on what to do next. There seemed to be a lull in the rain, although the wind still howled from the north.

'I'll lock up and head for home,' said Bridget. 'The horses will be better off in their stable and although Rosie has sometimes looked after Janie and Thomas when I haven't made it home, it's only an hour from here. What will you do Martin?'

'I am going to see you safely home. Then I'll come back and stay at the hotel.'

'I would be all right you know; you don't have to come with me, but if you can stand being wet and cold for another hour, well there's always a bed at Killarney.'

They backed the cart out onto the road and trudged toward Killarney. It was about 9 p.m, and the rain bucketed down again. They made it slowly up the driveway with the sight of a welcome light burning in the living room. They went straight around to the stables and undertook the bedding down procedure for the horses. Rosie appeared out of the gloom.

'Plenty bad night missus. I told Thomas and Janey you may not get home. They in bed asleep now. Big fella kettles full of hot water on the stove.'

'You've done well, Rosie. Thank you. You know Reverend Baillie; he will stay the night. Make up the bed in Mary's room.'

Rosie busied herself back in the house. Martin and Bridget unharnessed the horses. The steam rose briefly from the wet horses before a cooling chill started to set on their soaked hides.

Martin shed his coat and with dry chaff bags rubbed up the hair on each horse to quicken the drying and threw a bag blanket over each. Bridget prepared ample feed in their bins. She knew Martin was a capable horseman, but without any prompting from her, he took to his tasks as if they were what he did all the time. Expertly, he cleaned out their feet and painted the soles with a mixture of tar and mutton fat from the bucket that hung on a hook.

The tasks in the stable were done in companionable silence with the lantern glow drawing them in. Although both had worn oilskins, the driving rain had long soaked through all their garments to the skin.

Bridget knew it was important to follow the same procedure with themselves as the horses. They needed hot water, use of the big tin washtub and warm, dry clothes.

'Martin, you are good at your job. O'Reilly's Carriers could write you a reference as a skilled stable hand.' Bridget smiled at him. 'However, it is now time you dried out yourself. You know the O'Reilly bathroom, help yourself to one kettle of water and I will find you some old clothes of Patrick's and leave them at the door.'

Seeing he was about to protest; she held a finger to her lips.

'No arguing or I withdraw your reference.'

They headed back to the house.

Bridget found clothes of Patrick's, stacking them at the bathroom door. She had meant long ago to give Pat's clothes away but, in the end, had just kept them in a spare wardrobe. Did she feel disloyal in lending some to another man? Not in the case of Martin. She knew Pat would have appreciated the way he helped and there was always an easy bond of friendship between those two very different people.

She made sure there was food warming and retired to her bedroom with a tin dish and plenty of hot water. It was necessary to do what had to be done with what was available. She lit a lamp, closed the door, checked the children were sound asleep in the next room, and shed her wet clothes. The big towelling washer charged with hot water and her best scented soap, soon made her feel better, tired but content that the challenges of the day had been met. She rubbed herself dry with the big fluffy towel and was surprised to see her dim, naked reflection in a dressing table mirror, was still not a bad shape. Hard work had always agreed with her. She dressed quickly, oddly guilty that she had been pleased to observe her flat trim belly and firm well shaped buttocks. Vanity was a sin.

The nuns had often lectured on the sinful attractions of the flesh! Her short hair was rubbed dry but left uncombed.

Back in the kitchen, Martin had made their tea. He was busily toasting a couple of bread slices. He looked up and the clear-faced, short-haired, completely robe-covered young woman that met his gaze, caused a baffling turmoil of his senses. He hadn't planned to come here and he knew quite clearly now that there were reasons why he could not come here. They prepared their meal from Rosie's warmed leftovers: to people who had been cold and hungry for hours, it smelt like a feast. Seated at the table, Bridget smiled across. 'Grace,' she mouthed the word. Martin sat in silence for a moment then placing his hands in the supplication of prayer.

'Lord, we thank you for this food, for your care and protection. Amen.'

They ate in silence. Yet it was a warm silence of togetherness. Outside, the wind howled a terrible wail and the cyclonic symphony featured intermittent drum rolls that pounded a crescendo of hammering banshee hands on the tin roof. From the open door of the old black cast iron stove, an orange glow of blood wood embers gave out the invisible odour of fire. Warmth pulsed as a friendly occupant of the room. The friendly comfort of a turned down kerosene light found the dark corners with a touch of simple solace.

Their conversation was of the common place. Bridget told of her family. Martin asked questions as to Mary. He was genuinely interested and pleased to hear she was a top scholar and showing much promise as a violinist.

Bridget smiled at him.

'You know Mary, she has her own ideas. At first the discipline was a shock. Even now, she misses her freedom. She has made friends, but still thinks we are incapable of running Killarney without her.'

They washed the dishes. Martin insisted on helping and the task was soon done.

The proximity of a man helping with chores brought thoughts of Patrick flooding back. Patrick was gone. Did she still need more than what her busy, successful life was offering? Probably those thoughts came with the weather, the low barometric pressures of the day, and the completely unexpected arrival of Martin out of the storm. She added a solid hunk of wood to the sinking embers; it caught and new flame pictures danced in the firebox.

'Well, we'll let that block burn down and then we had better turn in.'

Bridget placed two chairs side by side, so the warmth and scenes of the fire could be shared by both.

'Now Martin, tell me a little of you. Janey was only saying the other day that we hadn't seen Reverend Martin lately, so you'd better think up an excuse for the morning. They will be delighted to see you.'

'I have been busy. Each time I go down or up from Ballina, I seem to be trying to meet an appointment.'

He told the truth, but knew it was only a half truth.

'We are talking of building a church somewhere in the area. The trouble is some of our people want it in Ballina, some want it up on the plateau. There won't be enough funds for two, so a decision must be made.'

'You may have to ask for the wisdom of Solomon, I'm sure a church will serve the people very well in either area.' Bridget asked a question. 'Do you still have contact with your family back in Scotland?'

'Yes, my mother is still alive. She writes sometimes of my brothers and sister. My father is dead, a married brother runs the little farm where I was a barefoot bairn. They are country folk. It all seems so far away and so long ago.'

He stopped. Thoughts back on the lowland border moors, while he watched the wandering patterns of a fire that burnt hard eucalypt instead of dried peat.

'At least she has the comfort of another generation of bairns.' He added it as an afterthought.

Bridget looked at him with that firm eyed contact her eldest daughter had inherited.

'You should have married, Martin. Catholic priests can't marry, but your faith recognises marriage for a clergyman can be a good thing. I've seen you with my children, I know you would give a family love.'

'Hmm, you sound like Mrs Cameron.'

Martin hoped his bantered reply would not give away his real thoughts. Then without weighing his words, 'The trouble is, you don't look like Mrs Cameron.'

The hint of a smile softened Bridget's face, devoid of any make-up, framed by its short tousled red hair. To Martin, she looked so young. He didn't know her age but guessed it to be similar to his own. The lavender scented soap that had scrubbed away the mud of a day's work, radiated from her skin with the warmth of the room. His flying thoughts escaped, before he could apply a brake.

'Yes Bridget, Mrs Cameron makes me think of my mother, but you send very different thoughts through me. You probably guess, I have had nothing to do with women at the physical love level. I am still a virgin, that has to be peculiar for a man my age. Once, when I was home on holidays from college, there was a girl with the necessary experience and charms, prepared to change all that in a hay loft. I often wondered after, why I didn't throw my clothes off and let it happen. It may have been better.'

'I'm sorry Martin,' she whispered. She looked down momentarily but then caught his eyes and smiled once more. 'I should have been more tactful.'

'No, don't be sorry. You may as well know why I haven't been dropping in lately. For a long while after Pat's death, I felt it was all right for me to come and stay and offer any comfort that I could. It seemed right and natural. Then it reached the stage that the more I saw you, the more I wanted to be in your company. I had the crazy thought that one day you may see something in me that awoke something in you. Not the love you had for Pat, but a different love that saw me as a man to start with anew.' He took a deep breath.

'There! It is stammered out. I had no thought of telling you. Not thought through, but I've told you my secret. It had to be said. This storm, our meeting has made an opportunity I didn't expect, or plan to happen. It just happened.'

They sat in silence. Then Bridget spoke.

'Martin, I didn't know. For the first couple of years, I would not have woken to the reality, but then perhaps I should have shown some imagination. Truly, I don't know whether there could be a combined future for us. We could not be youthful young lovers, but neither are we too old to feel the need and fulfilment of physical human love. In my life I have only had one lover and that was my husband. Our love was wonderful and will always be part of me. One thing I know, Pat would not begrudge my loving someone else, should it happen. He was a loving, giving person. Our children were God's gift of recognition for us.'

Silence continued. It was Bridget who spoke again. In a lighter vein, she offered wisdom.

'Now, Reverend Baillie, can you imagine what the good matrons of your church would say, if they thought an Irish catholic widow, was making sheep's eyes at their favourite pastor. It would be a scandal from the ranges to the coast. How do you answer that sir?'

He raised his hands in question.

'At the moment, I don't know. For a start, I'm not in the presence of the matrons or the men of the kirk. I'm in your presence. I need you to tell me straight that you are not shocked and going to throw me out in the storm for admitting that I love you.'

'I won't throw you out in the storm. Love is not something of which to be ashamed. But you have to let me think out this predicament. Cocoa, and then its bed for each of us. It's not every day a woman is told by a good, attractive man that he loves her. I do not treat it lightly.'

They sipped warm cocoa made on the milk that Rose had left in the big, galvanised bucket. There were so many unthought out questions, so many new problems that this stormy night had opened for them. Yet, there was an exciting comfort in the proximity of each other that certainly added things not thought of but an hour before. What of the problem of their differing faiths, could that be reconciled?

Bridget shut the stove door. She went back to the wardrobe and rummaged out a pair of pyjamas. Opening the door to the room with bed prepared for Martin, she beckoned him to the door. She held out the pyjamas, as he took them, placed an arm lightly around him. She reached up with her lips quickly before he had time to fully realise what was happening and kissed him softly. She felt the tension in his taut, well made and muscular frame. He was a strong, solid man.

'Martin, I want to be your friend always, and do you know, I don't think it would be at all hard to be your lover. Now to bed and God bless you. Let's pray for wisdom.'

The thoughts of both blew in direction-twisting chaos with the moaning, circling, cyclonic wind. Maybe it was the result of prayer, maybe the result of exhaustion, eventually sleep shut out the wailing wind and a torrent of unanswerable questions.

With morning came an easing of the weather. The old black stove kindled back to life by Rose, welcomed the emerging family. As was her habit, Bridget woke, dressed quickly, looked in on her sleeping children, and joined Rose in the kitchen.

'Better morning missus. Big fella storm blow real hard.'

Next to emerge was Martin. His greeting look to Bridget was one of doubt, silence, hope, conspiracy, all those specks of human feelings that twirl in a fast, spinning centrifuge of unsure emotions.

'You slept well?'

Bridget's question was the path to normalcy, commonplace, smoothing an avenue for conversation. He was saved an answer by the emergence of Janey. Always a will o'the wisp of action and decision. She spied Martin with pleasure.

'Well look what the storm blew in, we thought you had forgotten we lived here.'

She made a dramatic curtsey. Jane was nearly 13, maturing as she emerged from childhood. Inclined to flit from action to action, she helped on the farm, did her chores, was doing her schoolwork at a satisfactory level, but her interest was not the serious application of her older sister. Indications were that she was not an outstanding scholar, but confident of her ability to meet the needs of what any moment demanded. She played the role of meeting immediate expediency well. Bridget planned that she would join Mary at Rosebay convent.

Thomas came out rubbing his eyes. He was beginning to look like Patrick. School, he tolerated, but he was happiest doing the farm chores and already under Dan's tuition was capable with a horse. He was allowed to ride Shamrock when the old horse had first been ridden by another rider. They were developing a rapport, and he was learning rapidly from the needs of a responsive swift moving animal.

'Hello Reverend Baillie. I'll feed your horse as I feed the others.'

Thomas retreated to attend his round of greeting hungry stable friends.

Events of the previous evening were, by necessity, pushed away to meet the humdrum needs of the morning. They gathered for breakfast. Bridget looked at her family in company with Martin, in a new way. Could it work? They would have to play it cool for now. Martin would have to be prepared to wait an answer as to their future. Perhaps he would realise the problems of their differing faiths and his commitment made too large a problem. She smiled inwardly at the seven-day wonder of the community if it became reality that Martin Baillie, eligible bachelor of many Presbyterian matronly dreams for a daughter, was courting the cart driving Catholic widow. Perhaps she should just say, "No". It was that the only sane, sensible option.

Then the nagging thought, did she wish to be sane? Did she wish to grow old without knowing again the love of a man? Love could always be a risk. Yet, she had climbed the shrouds of a sailing ship, and accepted that different risk. Later, the risk involved in marrying Patrick was also accepted, and without a backward step she had followed and helped in his plans. Life was full of risks.

Mary, Music, News

Mary O'Reilly stroked a last vibrant note from the "A" string of her violin. She let the melody gently fade into the big, deep, convent music room and then she looked at Sister Benedictine.

'That was really good Mary. You are starting to feel the melody as I'm sure Mr Brahms intended when he wrote that rhapsody. Your practise is showing the results you deserve. You have a talent, but talent is nothing in a violinist unless they are prepared to work, and work, and then work some more.'

Mary and Sister Benedictine were spending extra time at the music room, in preparation for the school concert to be given in another two weeks. The Irish sister was an excellent teacher and musician. As a girl in Dublin, she had performed at a high level as both pianist and violinist, and then turned her back on a musical career to become a nun. Most thought it a sad end to a promising career. She sailed to a colony that had only been a name. Australia was a faraway, huge, pink-coloured island on the world map, hanging in the Dublin convent.

After five years in Sydney, she found her life to be not that different as a teacher in a Sydney convent to what it may have been had she stayed in Ireland. She nurtured a dream to "head up country" and serve with Aboriginal people, but up till now the order was making full use of her musical ability. Mother Cecilia met her occasional enquiries with a stock answer,

'In God's time, Sister. To be sure, you are doing God's work here in educating young ladies to have musical refinement in this rough colony.'

So, Sister Benedictine worked on with the small strata of Catholic girls whose parents could afford to pay significant fees for senior education.

'Do you think I have ability or am I just another competent violinist?'

Mary had come to depend on Sister Benedictine. Being Mary, she believed in asking and receiving straight questions and answers.

'At the present time you are a competent violinist,' Sister Benedictine replied. 'Remember, you have only been playing violin for three years. Your progress has been very rapid and you have capacity for work. There are times I hear in your playing an ability to feel and portray music that is more than competent. It could be that God has given you ability well above the ordinary; it will depend on how your technique develops and how much you really want to be a top musician.'

When Mary returned to her room, shared with two others, Cath Lonergan greeted her.

'How's the virtuoso? Big Ben wouldn't waste her time on the rest of us. By the way there was some mail, my parents even wrote to me for once, and there's always a letter for you.'

'What are you growling about? Sister Benedictine has you singing in the concert, and I've heard her say you have a good soprano.'

'Yes, I suppose she thinks I can't completely wreck her choir.'

'Ah, stop grouching, you don't know when you are well off. Where's my letter?'

Mary retreated to a spot near the window. The light was fading but Mother Cecilia had strict rules as to when lights could be lit.

The letter contained three pages, two from her mother, and one shared page from Janey and Thomas. She digested the page from her sister and brother. Their writing was improving, but it seemed neither was really into writing. They both were happiest as active doers. She turned to her mother's neat round legible hand. The first half page was of the normal things, how the business was going well, how the new jersey cow had a calf, how the flowers were growing in the garden, and then Mary read with disbelief, stopped, took a deep breath, and read again, mistrusting her eyes.

There is no easy way to tell you this news. I hope you will be happy but I will certainly understand if you are not. You will be the only one to know at this time and if you really disagree, please tell me. Martin Baillie has asked me to marry him. I had no idea that he felt that way about me. We had not received a visit from him for almost a year, at times, I wondered why? Then when the truth came out that he was keeping away from Killarney, because he was sure that the subject must be avoided, my first reaction was to be sorry for his embarrassment.

Then it surprised me to find that I do really care for Martin, not as I cared for your father, but in a way which could make for a happy marriage. I said that I must have time to think. The problems of religion are very real. I will always remain Catholic and Martin has done much, great work for his Presbyterian faith. Many people rely on his ministry. Since your father's death, you have been more than a daughter, you have been my friend as well. I relied upon you so much. So you, Janey and Thomas are my first concern, but I am not an old woman yet, and you are mature enough to know that has its problems. You will make your way in the world in time. I pray every day that it will be a happy way.

The business and the farm have kept me busy, but Dan is capable of running the business. I have made up my mind to accept Martin's proposal, if he feels he can handle the problems that would come with our marriage. I need to know whether you have objections or think we would be doing a foolish thing.

Mary sat quietly. Her stunned shock probably showed on a face that was practised at avoiding emotion.

'Hey, are you all right? Nothing wrong at home, I hope.'

Cath realised her roommate was more serious than normal.

'Yes. I'm all right.'

Mary's answer explained nothing. There was no way she could confide at this time in the bubbly Cath. She continued to sit in withdrawn silence.

The possibility of her mother marrying again, was something to which she had not given thought. But why not? Her mother was still young, an attractive, healthy woman in her mid-thirties. Later that night, before lights out, she worked on her reply to the momentous letter.

Dear Mum,
Well, it was surely a surprise, but why not? It will take a while for me to comprehend but as you know I have always liked Uncle Martin. That is probably what I shall continue to call him. He and Dad were so different but they remained friends. There will be plenty of comment from people around, and from Uncle Martin's Presbyterian congregations and superiors, but if you both feel that marriage will bring happiness: your eldest daughter approves-I love you. I don't think I will tell Mother Cecilia, not yet anyway. The idea of an ex-pupil marrying a protestant minister would certainly be "an occasion of sin". Sister Benedictine would handle it without trouble. I hope Janey and Thomas are grown up enough to take it calmly.

The concert at the church hall is next Saturday. I have been practising hard with Sister Benedictine giving me plenty of work. At times, I feel it is sounding all right and that perhaps the audience will be satisfied. At least, it may give me an idea as to whether there is good reason to persevere with the thought of trying to be a violinist. The ease with which Billy Montez made a tune from his old fiddle, probably lured me into thinking it was easy. Now I know it is all hard work.

Differing Viewpoints

'Och mon, av ye taken leave of your senses?'

David Cameron reverted back into the broad accent of Scotland in times of stress. The bombshell calmly dropped by Martin, that he was going to marry a widow with a family, caused the old storekeeper consternation. He had often thrown none too subtle hints that Martin, whom he had grown to look upon almost as a son, should be married. The Camerons had even introduced him to several eligible, attractive, well brought up young Presbyterian ladies in the hope of it firing a spark of matrimonial interest. Now he was turning his back on sanity and wanting to marry an Irish Catholic with three children.

'And just how do ye think you will be able to serve the Lord, being married to a Catholic woman? If you be determined on this do ye think she may be prepared to follow our ways and give up the papacy? Perhaps the scandal would settle down.'

'I'm sorry to alarm you David, you've helped me so much. Should you know Bridget, I'm sure you would like her. I would not think of asking her to renounce her faith, and indeed I know she would not. She would not interfere with my work for the Lord.'

'Have you told the moderator of your plans?' David demanded.

'I have written a letter telling of my plans and explained the situation of Bridget's family and faith. So far, I have not received a reply. I am confident my work here in the district for eleven years will count for something. We are planning to build one and probably two churches in the near future and my pastoral work was recently favourably commented on by the moderator.'

'Maybe, maybe. I'll be interested in his reply. If you take my advice, you will reconsider this proposal. Have you thought it through? To me it seems sure to be disaster for you and for Mrs O'Reilly. Where would you live? There has been talk of a manse to be situated near one of the new churches.'

'Well, it would save the cost of a house. My intention would be to continue travelling, to attend and supply service to those needing marriage, christening, burial and to supply regular services when and if the churches are built.'

'Mon, there are too many problems. A clergyman's wife has to be part of his work. How would your proposed wife, who runs a business, and has school age children, attend to duties as a Minister's wife? Especially when she is of different faith, and as far different as possible, being Roman Catholic. Don't rush into this marriage laddie - think about it, pray about it.'

There was no easy resolution to the impasse. When Martin finally received his reply from the moderator in Sydney, it was a much stronger version of the conversation recorded with David Cameron. There were no half measures in the reply.

'You are no callow youth, give this woman up. We would have to consider seriously whether scandal caused by your marriage to such an unsuitable person would debar you from clerical duties. Why throw away an important career in the service of the Lord, by such a rash decision?'

Martin had known that his love for Bridget would cause much comment, but he had hoped for an element of tolerance. He had hoped his years of riding the trails of a developing district would have caused at least understanding from many. It seemed this one omission from complete observation of selfless duties to the Protestant faith in the area meant he was condemned.

Had he cultivated sexual liaisons with women, this would have been tolerated as mere natural human transgressions, to be regretted but to be expected. Because he had lived a celibate life and chose to offer marriage to a lady of high moral character, he was to be considered unfit for his dedicated vocation of helping people to know the touch of Jesus Christ. He accepted David Cameron's advice of prayer, but the result of prayer did nothing to change his viewpoint that marriage to Bridget should not be a reason for giving up his calling to follow Christ as a Presbyterian minister.

The news that Martin Baillie, respected Presbyterian minister and eligible bachelor, had sought the hand of Bridget O'Reilly in marriage, and that she had said 'Yes', caused a hot topic of conversation. There were those who said, 'Good luck,' and those that said, 'It can't work, they are old enough to have better sense.'

Bridget and Martin

It was some time after Mary had been told the news that Bridget told Jane and Tom, and then her close friends. The big decision came as a surprise to all, but they pledged support.

For Martin, the decision soon brought forth the reality that marriage to Bridget would see the end of his tenure as the Presbyterian Minister to the area. He had been given two ways of keeping his job: don't marry Bridget or have her agree to being a non-practising Catholic. He was not prepared to discuss either option. His dismissal would be effective fourteen days before an announced marriage date. There were many persons to whom he had ministered that wished him luck and thanked him for his caring service. David Cameron, although firm in his view that the marriage decision was a bad one, was still gracious enough to say,

'Ye will always be welcome in our house, my boy, and its right sorry that I am.'

The decision was made and Martin hoped that as news value he would soon be forgotten.

It was an early September spring day, a probing westerly wind whipped up dust from dried cart tracks and sent dead leaves scurrying skyward with no purpose but to float back slowly to earth. Martin and

Abbe Felix Schurr met on the lonely road between Casino and Lismore. The men of the cloth had grown to know each other and sometimes their paths crossed. Usually, the Abbe favoured river boats as his means of transport, but he was a capable horseman when the occasion arose. Today the priest headed east with the wind driving his mount onward, its tail tucked in underneath from the following strong gusts.

From the other direction, Martin plodded toward Casino, his trusty grey head low and eyes half closed to the buffeting wind. They met on the road and pulled up.

'I have the fairer direction today, Martin, you have to beat into the gale.'

'Yes, it's a raw breeze but we'll make it to port, God willing.'

'We could find some shelter behind that thicket, and I could offer you a cup of coffee from my flask.'

'That sounds all right to me.'

They rode in on the lee side of the thick tea tree thicket and 90 per cent of the westerly whistled high overhead. It gave a welcome relief from the raucous wind. The horses were tied to useful limbs and the French priest worked at his large saddle bag. He produced two small ornate silver mugs, a large flask and a small flask.

'I could add a drop of good Jamaican Rum, if you would let me?'

'No, Abbe, even though you no doubt have heard I am to be sacked. I'll stay off your West Indian firewater.'

The sugared coffee was hot and strong. They sipped the brew with pleasure in their refuge from the road's windy world, which was but a few paces distant.

'I'm sorry to hear you will be leaving the job as pastor of your flock. I know how much you have achieved for the people of this area and there will be many outside of your faith who will miss your caring service. I fancy the Lord will still find much use of your many abilities.'

'Thank you. You also, no doubt, have heard that Bridget O'Reilly has agreed to be my wife. Perhaps you would be prepared to perform the ceremony, in about two months' time?'

'*Mais oui*. I would be honoured to do that. Be assured I shall pray for happiness for you both. Have you discussed with Bridget the wedding ceremony?'

'No. She said she would be prepared for just a civil ceremony, but I realise her Catholic faith is all important in her life. I would not ask her to deny what she has been brought up to accept.'

'Ah, it is good that you take such an attitude. Believe me, there will still be much for you to achieve as a servant of the Lord.'

There was little more to be said on the subject.

'We will be in touch.'

They left their shelter and faced the blustery howling dialogue of the waiting rampant westerly wind. A wind that threatened to sap dry and blow away the faint hint of any venturing green grass shoot that was brave enough to appear in a slow waking spring. Eventually, spring spread a benevolent carpet of green.

The December wedding day came. It dawned hot and clear. Abbe Schurr had agreed to perform the ceremony on the big veranda at Surreyville with about twenty guests in attendance. A time of 2 p.m. had been arranged and the married couple were to travel by sulky to Ballina afterwards. They would spend a few days at the newly built Australian hotel and then, after their brief honeymoon, return to Killarney. Martin was to become a working partner of the carrying business. The whole business arrangement had been discussed with Dan. He and Martin felt they could work together and it was agreed there was still room for expansion in the carrying business.

'I will become a lady of leisure, practising the finer qualities,' Bridget quipped at her friends. 'No more overalls and boots, no more short hair and broken fingernails from lugging bags of grain.'

Yet Bridget O'Reilly, soon to be Bridget Baillie, had thrived on the hard work since Patrick's death, nearly four years before. She was still slim, young-looking and carried an independent assurance from her proven ability to mix it in a man's world. Of the wedding there were many critics, out of Bridget's hearing, but having made her decision, the knockers could have expressed their sentiments to her face. It would have caused Bridget no loss of sleep. Her close friends and family had recovered from the shock and were happy when the wedding day arrived.

Mary and Nell Riordan were her attendants, and Dan Riordan and Tom Flaherty attendants for Martin. His work within the growing north coast villages made Martin Baillie, on a broad scale, well known and a popular man. He was always available to help any who asked for ministry or advice. His taking of a Catholic wife and his forced withdrawal from the Presbyterian ministry had sparked much discussion and some bitterness. Many thought his sterling work for Christ in all weathers, always with care and good humour, should have been enough for him to be allowed a choice of whether he stayed or left the ministry. Others felt any minister prepared to marry an Irish Catholic should be dispensed with as quickly as possible. Still, others liked Martin for the man he had proved himself to be as a pioneer of the area, and they didn't give a jot about church matters.

The Campbells had accepted an invitation to the wedding, even though David Campbell had strenuously urged Martin not to go ahead with the marriage.

'Ye know my sentiments mon, but I be close to family as ye have in this country. We'll be there and pray God gives ye long life and happiness. I do na ken how ye'll be as a carter, but as a man of the cloth ye did a bonny job. There will always be a meal place for you at the Campbells.'

Friends and Family

Mary O'Reilly had arrived home from school for the wedding. She was met at the Ballina wharf by Edna and Dick Hilardt, and she was to stay the night at their River Street house. The *Firefly* had been lucky to carry a prevailing southerly up the coast and crossed in on a rising tide just before dark. When tied to the wharf, a stout gang plank was shoved across the space, and Dick, as company agent, boarded the small ship. His task was twofold, to collect the ships bill of loading, and the young passenger to be his guest. He doffed his hat to Mary and turned to the captain.

'Is this charming young lady, Miss O'Reilly? I was sent to find and welcome a schoolgirl, perhaps there is another passenger?'

Mary fixed him with her cool stare and just a hint of a smile around the corners of a rather large, expressive mouth.

'It is good of you to meet me Mr Hilardt. I hope Mrs Hilardt is well.'

'Yes Mary, she is fine, and is out there on the wharf to escort you to our little home for the night and looking forward to your city news.'

They left the captain to arrange a hand cart for a large, strong chest. That chest contained clothes, presents, and Mary's violin. He assured her, all would arrive at the Hilardt's within the hour. Mary hitched her long flowing skirt, above the medium heeled soft leather buttoned boots and nonchalantly walked the 12-inch plank across a six-foot gap from ship to wharf.

Edna took her hand as she stepped ashore. Then she stood back a step, to take in fully the girl who had changed a lot in twelve months, since she had last been home on holidays.
She put her arms around Mary and kissed her on the cheek. The child Edna carried at eight months plus of pregnancy was a very pronounced package between them under her ample pleated skirt. Very obvious, but Edna looked well and was overjoyed to welcome Mary.

'Ah Mary, my star pupil has grown up. The four years have treated you well. It is so good to have you for a night. Perhaps you are too tired for talk, but there are so many things I want to ask. You may not get to sleep early. For now, let us walk slowly home, it's not far from here. Dick will be along later when he's finished his business with the *Firefly*'s captain.'

They linked arms and walked away from the wharf, along a finely gravelled oyster shell foot path. The Hilardt home adjoined the small shipping office. River Street, the commercial hub of Ballina was boasting quite a few shops with a sprinkling of houses. Grog shop hotels had moved up a notch in class with the new two floored impressive Australian Hotel.

Ballina was growing and agitation for improvement of the dangerous river entrance was ever an ongoing topic of conversation.

The Baillie-O'Reilly wedding competed with the weather as a hot December topic of conversation. Of those who missed an invitation through lack of room on the Brewster home veranda, some were known to have voiced doubts as to the sensibilities of the union.

A Wedding

Two p.m. sharp, with the attendants lined up on the well-prepared veranda, Norah at the piano struck up the wedding march and Jim

Brewster escorted Bridget to the table set up as an altar. Abbe Schurr stood her beside the waiting groom. Mary O'Reilly and Nell Riordan, her attendants, were stylishly dressed in flowing blue gowns, a foil for the simple deep cream outfit Bridget had chosen. The service was soon over. Those acquainted with a Catholic Nuptial Mass were surprised at the brevity of Abbe Schurr's contrived, constructed service. He performed his duty with the utmost solemnity, as it was not a mass, and obviously out of respect for Martin and the few Protestant friends present, he kept the service short and simple. He also used English as well as the standard Latin prayers, so that all knew the basis of the wedding service.

While bride, groom and attendants signed the civil papers, the veranda was rearranged for the wedding breakfast. It was planned that the guests would leave for their homes no later than 5 p.m. Jim Brewster as Master of Ceremonies kept to the plan. Guests and the newly married couple went their ways with much daylight still in the closing day.

There was still a last glowing thumb print of western light hitting the river as Martin and Bridget's horse jogged into Ballina. They had no need to illuminate the sulky lights. A room booking at the new Australian Hotel had been made weeks before, an open-ended booking, they did not intend to have a long honeymoon.

They swung into the hotel yard with its three-box stable.

'Whoa boy, you are a good lad.'

Martin jumped down, removed their two cases and took Bridget's hand, while she found the step with her smart tan boot.

'May I be of assistance Mrs Baillie.'

'Thank you, Sir.'

Bridget took the firm hand and demurely descended.

They both knew that as a working carrier she was very capable of jumping four feet down from a moving cart with sure footed agility. She played out the charade for the stable lad, who was waiting to attend to Major, the smart bay Welsh breed pony. Another hotel worker took a case in each hand, led them to the entrance and across to the reception desk. The cases disappeared upstairs to their room while the publican's wife booked them into a part used page of the large, new, leather-bound register.

'Welcome Mr and Mrs Baillie. We will be honoured to look after you as long as you decide to stay with us. I am Lyn Foster.'

Bridget chatted a moment with Mrs Foster as Martin signed the book. They agreed that a tray with light refreshments be sent up to number three and they would attend meals in the dining room on the morrow.

Getting to Know You

It was a big airy room with doors out to a balcony that carried a sweeping view of the river. Bridget shut the door, took off her smart hat, moved a couple of long hat pins from her now shoulder length regrowth of red hair, and sat wearily on the edge of a large attractive bed. She patted a space beside her and beckoned Martin

'Well Mr Baillie, we are at last alone in a hotel room. I am your wife. How do you feel about that?'

'Och Mrs Baillie, perhaps it's a dream, ye be just a figment of an Irish leprechaun with playful ways. I like what I see but I'm trained to be suspicious of what those Irish leprechauns may conjure up.'

He looked at her with a serious, shy half smile.

'Do ye think it likely an unpractised old man like me will be of use to a lovely colleen like you? I'm scared lest I fail you. That part of me works I know from some of its dark night explosions, but I'm just plain ignorant.'

Bridget gently took his hand in hers.

'Let's get a few things straight. You are only three years older than me. We are neither what you call young, but God willing there are good years of life left in each of us. I know you are not an experienced lover; it doesn't matter. You love me and we have interests in common. We are not going to rush anything but I'm a woman, and I've felt the desire in you that will awaken with love and proximity. You know I loved Patrick in all ways. Our sex love was special and always will be, but you and I will have the chance of a special life, too. I was only a girl when I married a wonderful, mature man. He brought me to life gently. We just made sure we were honest with each other and I soon grew to awareness. We will be all right.'

A discreet knock on the door broke the silence and announced the supper tray.

'You are a very special lady, and God was good to bring us together.' Martin looked at her steadily then said to the door, 'Coming.'

He went to receive the tray.

After their supper, arm in arm, they decided to stroll down along the river. Several ships, all of which Bridget knew, were tied to the long wharf. She told Martin a little of what they carried, and something of the masters who controlled these small shipboard communities.

'That shoaling bar is still too dangerous, but things are better than when we first arrived on the plateau. One of these days there will be a safer way in for this river. Perhaps we may see it. My growing up years on a ship makes me think like a sailor.'

He answered reflectively.

'Yes, I know the need. I buried far too many young seaman bodies, and I'm afraid it continues on for clergymen. It seems being a sailor is a tough life.'

Bridget gave his hand a squeeze.

'I know how well you did your job, and so do those who remember your kindness.'

They headed back to the hotel, nodded to the doorman and went back up the stairs to room three. The proprietor John Foster came across to his doorman.

'You can knock off soon Wal. The Baillies won't be out again tonight, or I wouldn't be if I had a looker like that one to take to bed on a wedding night. The missus was telling me a little of her story, I hope she finds the ex-parson to her liking. Seems she was not afraid to pitch in and work when O'Reilly was killed. It doesn't seem to have done her any harm.'

Their room had a large kerosene lamp and once the balcony doors were opened, an odd brown moth fluttered into the light. The night was humid, sticky warm. Heat lightning played off the coast, silhouetting in its flashes, a heavy, bubbling, off-shore, water-laden "wool pack" storm cloud. That cloud could find the shore with cooling of the land.

'Too hot to shut the doors. We'll find our night things and put the light out.'

Bridget turned out her long, cotton nightdress. She sat at the dressing table mirror to brush out her now shoulder length, kinky, auburn hair. Martin found his brand-new striped pyjamas, laid them on the bed but made no effort to change. There was shyness for both of them. Her hair finished and face washed, Bridget sensed it best to snuff the light to undress. They were able to change hidden in the room's new cloak of darkness.

'Do you say night prayers? I do.' Bridget spoke softly to the blurred outline that sat on the bed.

'I used to, but lately I've been slack.' Martin acknowledged.

'Well tonight we pray. Please, we pray for each other in our own way. God will hear us.'

In silence, they knelt and in silence, they prayed. Bridget finished with a sign of the cross and waited the few seconds for Martin to finish his conversation with God whom Bridget was confident listened to faithful servants.

'Thank you,' she said simply. 'Now to bed. It's been a long day.'

They made it under the supplied covers. The bed carried blanket and quilt above the linen sheet, on this warm night it was oppressive, too much.

'What do you think husband? It seems too many bed clothes to me,' she asked the question lightly.

'In summer I rarely have more than a sheet, sometimes not that,' Martin answered.

Bridget arose, neatly folded the quilt and blanket. She dropped them on a bedside chair and returned to the big, soft bed.

'So, is it "Good Night"?' she whispered, leaning across the solid body beside her, kissing him lightly on the lips. She went to slide back to her side of the bed, but a strong right arm came up and held her firmly to his chest. His lips found hers in the night shadow, gently but with obvious intention of not letting her go. Their kiss grew with increasing strength and a left arm closed from the other side. She found herself firmly and pleasantly held.

'Is this the way you say goodnight?' she whispered, 'Throw off the sheet. I'll stay where I am.'

The sheet found the floor. Both Martin's arms came back even tighter around her waking body. Proximity called an all-important message. They became one. Nature must soon speak its force within this her husband. Little time. She felt his surge of pleasure. Strong arms locked her tight in triumph. It seemed all too few short seconds for their woken union. His strength relaxed. Bridget snuggled down tightly upon him. Their heartbeats, and sweaty clothing bound them as one.

They lay in silence, but for the thump of pumping hearts and in tune rapid breathing. She felt him about to speak and gently laid a finger to his lips.

'No words. Rest, feel and thank God,' she whispered gently.

The warmth of the night and used passion held them together. Drenched in the sweat of their release, strength of need gone, gently she slid down his side and brought her head on the pillow beside him. Both were still dressed in some form of clothing. Martin refused to let her out of his arms.

'I love you. I love you. I love you. Was it all right?' His voice was deep, anxious, far away.

'I love you too. Of course, it was wonderful.'

'I had no idea. Thank you so much. Do you think I'll learn?'

'I don't think you have much to learn, but I'll agree to continue the lessons.' She kissed him. 'Now I think it is time we slept. There's plenty of time in the future to practise.'

Still together, happy in the feel of their proximity, mental and physical tiredness took over and they were soon asleep.

It was an hour before dawn that the threatening storm came in off the sea.

Martin arose quietly, closed the balcony doors and returned to bed and the almost magical presence of this soft, wonderful, warm shape that was his wife.

Bridget felt him arise. As he arrived back in bed with a clap of rumbling thunder, she whispered,

'We are being given a stormy welcome to Ballina. Remember that night we came in out of the storm at Killarney?'

'What do you think Mrs Baillie?' he asked.

'I think you remember. I hope there are no ships close to the bar tonight.'

They lay pleasantly, side by side, while lightning and thunder played outside. Sleep did not return. Vivid flashes sparked the room bright as day. They snuggled together, awakening. His lingering kiss chased tiredness from parts thought put to rest for the night.

'Am I being too greedy?' he whispered in her ear.

Her answer was to lie in even closer. She whispered back, a smile in her voice,

'We could take our clothes off this time.' She kissed him gently. 'There's no hurry at all,' she whispered.

She soaked up the pleasure of his lovemaking. Demanding,

giving, their consuming totality of feeling spread, bathing them in a total immersion.

A huge flash of lightning lit the room, followed by a crash of thunder, that even shook the crockery on the washstand. The thunder pulled a trigger to that most intimate part of her. It masked her cry of pleasure, and final release of mind and body. She felt the flood ease, and their body rhythms slowed to normality.

As the storm tuned odyssey faded, she locked him tight on soft used compliant breasts. Skin, sweat glued in delicious afterglow of peace, they melted naked, completely spent, together.

'Well,' she whispered, 'you see now, I'm a wicked, wanton, greedy woman.'

'Don't say that. You're the most wonderful, warm woman. Offering love that I thought would never be for me. Thank you for marrying me. Perhaps, I will learn with a teacher like you.'

They lay floating, enveloped in their cocoon of extended time.

'Well, we'd better sleep or we'll look as if we had too little sleep at breakfast.'

'Ah, and when did you worry about what people think or say? I feel beyond sleep.
Ye know Bridget, at last, I think I'm alive.'

In exhaustion they slept. The drenching storm rain unheard by their ears. It came as if washing away their past, preparing a seed bed for life together.

It was fully light when Bridget awoke. She knew Martin still slept a sleep of exhaustion, his breathing strong, even. Gently, she slipped from under his binding arm, and felt achievement that he didn't stir. She made her way to the porcelain toilet facility and relieved her bladder. Carefully, silently, she moved back to the chair and reclaimed her nightdress. The storm had passed. Weak soft, low sunlight was hitting the outside balcony. The balcony door opened silently to her hand and she took a deep breath of the riverside air. Martin slept on. She gently covered his nakedness with the sheet and still he did not stir. She felt the protectiveness of a mother, and wondered, by no means for the first time in her life, at the mystery of female emotions.

She thought of her family and asked God that they be safe, happy and well. She thought of Patrick and their life together; she felt no sense of betrayal for breaking a three-year physical denial of sexual activity that his death caused. She had no problem with her awakened passion that came as wife to Martin. She felt Patrick would approve; he had taught her to love. He would read it as a sign of their wonderful unrestricted love together. Martin slept on.

She extracted rosary beads from their case and silently stood watching the early morning and the beauty of a washed, clean river. She fingered the beads, counting through the decades of the Joyful Mysteries in tradition of her convent upbringing, and her deep, living faith. At the conclusion she felt Martin's eyes watching silently from the large bed. She went, sat on the edge and gently kissed him.

'Good morning,' she whispered.

'Hello lassie, ah must be a poor sight to wake up to. I'm pleased you covered my ugly nakedness. Thank ye. Is it still all right to be my wife?'

'Yes, it's all right. I like it. I think you may have even read that message not so long ago. That's answered your question. By the way, nakedness is not ugly, nor is the lawful relationship of man and woman something to be ashamed of acknowledging. I think God worked out a good way of making sure the human race increased.'

She went to the chair, recovered his striped pyjama pants and flicked them backhand to him. Went to the passage outside their door and brought in a large jug of hot water left there by the morning maid. She was thankful that another container was still there for Martin.

Sand, Sea, Life

'Good morning, Mr and Mrs Baillie.'

Lyn Foster stood at the foot of the hotel stairs receiving her half dozen house guests to Sunday morning breakfast. Her smile was warm and welcoming. Discerning woman of the world eyes read in their brief glance what men would not see.

Last night she had been impressed with the fashionable appearance of Bridget. She had been told a little of her expected guests. The tragedy of Patrick's death and the way his wife had coped with men's work. She heard also of the good works of Martin Baillie and of how his decision was made to give up ministry, in order to take what his superiors considered an "unsuitable" wife. It was a love story with a difference and she admired their initiative.

'Please, I'll show you your table and Maggie will bring a menu. The early morning storm was severe for a few minutes. I hope you were not too disturbed.'

'Thank you, Mrs Foster. We were very comfortable.' Martin turned upon her the attractive smile. A smile that had melted many matrons.

'We were fine. I've climbed masts at sea in storms worse than that,' Bridget said gaily.

Mrs Foster did not quite take on the sense of that statement. She knew this handsome mother of a grown-up daughter had been, for a period of time after her husband's death, a hard-working carrier. She had not been told that she was once a sailor. Anyway, there was a bloom to her this morning that she read and envied.

That clergyman is a lucky bloke, she thought to herself.

The Baillies sat and enjoyed their breakfast.

Later in the morning, dressed in their most casual clothes, they were ready to take the gig and Major from the stables.

'We'll go around and visit Carmel,' said Bridget, 'then we could go across North Creek past the cemetery and have a walk on the beach. I'm sure Mrs Foster would make us a basket with a cold lunch. I'll go see her while you organise Major.'

Mrs Foster was in accord with the idea.

'Just give me 10 minutes and we will have something ready. My that's a smart skirt. With your figure it's perfect.'

'Well, my young neighbour, Nell Riordan, made me this. Good, isn't she?'

Lyn Foster admired the work. Then she laughed.

'But my legs, unlike yours, need covering right to the ground these days.'

She went to arrange their picnic.

'Ah, but it was a great wedding.' Carmel greeted her guests.

'We won't stop long; just thought we'd drop in on our way to the beach.'
Martin went with young Tom out to the back bench where the lad was

cleaning a big catch of fish.

'You look wonderful my girl.' Carmel ran her experienced motherly eyes over Bridget. In her matter-of-fact wisdom, she smiled at the young woman.

'A woman does not often land in a marriage bed with two good men. Your Pat was one of my favourite men. At times, he made me feel quite weak, but I'd be sure he never had eyes for anyone but you. I wondered how you'd be with Martin. My Celtic second sight sees the answer is pretty plain my dear. I thank God for your happiness.'

'I've been lucky Carmel. It's a shame another good husband hadn't come for you.'

'No good crying over spilt milk. I haven't completely dried up yet or joined a nunnery, still have me moments you know.' She winked and patted Bridget on the shoulder.
'I'm pleased to see young Nell is making out. He's a good lad that Daniel. One day, she or I may tell a story that you probably can guess at, but don't know. Thanks be to God she has a friend like you. Life can play some queer tricks.'

Martin came back from admiring the fish. Carmel insisted on a quick "cup o' tea", before letting them jog off following the river to its mouth.

They crossed over on the little ferry punt. There was strong talk in the town that a bridge across North Creek was high on the agenda of the growing town's progress.

Major was hooked to a stout hitching post when they came to the cemetery on its small rise at the entry to north creek. The grave for Sean, Daniel's Irish friend and shipmate, had been furnished with a simple headstone. His mother had written to Daniel from Ireland and he had arranged that last task for his friend. Martin and Bridget stood quietly at the grave. Bridget made a Sign of the Cross and took Martin's hand.

'Please say a brief prayer.' She waited.

For a time, Martin stood. Was it still his calling to pray at cemeteries? Then he found unsought, almost in spite of himself, a steady flow of vocal thought that he had always found entrusted to him. His soft Scottish brogue mingled with the searching chatter of busy gulls and seabirds. He concluded:

'Heavenly Father, grant all whose bodies lie here or in the ocean, safe rest and peace until called by you. Amen.'

Thoughts that flowed from his inmost being.

He stood silently. Bridget, who had moved back a step, rejoined him. She placed her hand in his and felt the welcoming, needing, strength of his fingers. Nothing was said, then by mutual consent they returned in silence to the waiting Major.

There were no other visitors to the small, unfenced cemetery. Bridget hitched her trendy calf length skirt and climbed nimbly from the sulky step to the tray and seat. Martin untied Major, handed Bridget the reins and sat beside her. She kept the reins and clicked Major forward. Soon they were climbing a sandy track up the steep hill. On its eastern timbered side, the hill lurched down toward the wide shallow river bar. They were heading north to one of the close headland locked bays, with white sand and rolling surf. The cart track they followed was used mainly by fishermen or occasional devotees of beach combing. Following the many wrecks on the bar at times amongst the flotsam, there was a harvest of useful bits and pieces. Very few people saw a beach as a place of leisure. It was barely acceptable for men to strip to their trousers when fishing; the thought of a woman beach bathing was not to be contemplated.

At a solid banksia tree close to their selected beach sand dune

Major was hitched, unharnessed and given a ration of chaff, sent along by Jimmy the stable boy. Then it was the turn of Bridget and Martin to spread their lunch under the shade of the wind-battered banksias. The hypnotic, sleepy symphony of a half out falling surf was too much. After they had worked around Lyn Foster's adequate hamper their body clocks collapsed. They drifted away in isolation, a couple of shore seeking sea nymphs in their own sandy hollow. More than an hour later, Bridget awoke from her pillow of Martin's arm. For a moment, she gazed at the unfamiliar scenery, the lullaby of the ocean seemed to have hosted a time spent dream that she was back lazing noonday on her father's little ship. Martin awoke and held up his arms. She shook her head and laughed,

'You are a lazy man. Up, we're going for our walk. No need of shoes on the sand.'

She threw her light kid boots in the sulky and waited for Martin to leave behind his heavy footwear. Then, as an afterthought, demurely she commanded him to look the other way, wriggled out of her skirt length slip and added that also to the sulky.

'Come on I'll race you to the surf.' She sped off and he followed, confident that he could soon catch her.

It wasn't until they reached the hard sand that he overhauled this red-headed wisp. She had in one short day offered him horizons he hadn't believed existed. She just smiled and beckoned him to the water, now flat low with very little surf break.

'Good sir, will ye paddle with a shy young maid?' She firmly took his hand and they walked into the delicious, cool water. The floating foam painted shade patterns through the shallow water on the sandy beach floor, ever coming, ever going, as the waves washed their feet.

'Have you had much to do with the ocean?' Her question was serious.

'Almost nothing. I suppose I am scared of uncontrolled water. As a child, the lochs of Scotland were far away. To learn to swim never seemed an option. Here in Australia, my crossing of water has mostly been on the back of a good horse. So, you see, ye have bought a complete landlubber.'

'Well, I'm not a Greek sea siren but let me lure you out a little deeper. Hitch those trousers up your legs. I'm not about to wet my nice new skirt so look the other way.' She hitched the bottom of the skirt up knee length into her frilly pantaloons.

'This surf is friendly and nearing low.'

She took him out, 20 or 30 yards, through a shallow gutter, onto a flat sandbank where the waves crept up to knee height. She smiled at him; his confidence grew. What right had he to be afraid in the hands of this wonderful woman?

After a while, they headed back to dry sand and walked along the shore toward the northern headland. Bridget picked up a couple of excellent leopard kauri shells on the high tide mark.

'Thomas loves shells. These will be a great present for him.'

She showed and explained many of the simple shells that littered the tideline to Martin. Hand in hand they wandered the wonderland of flat untouched beach. Pristine clean, a sand slate never to be quite repeated by the next tide.

The sun was dropping low to the west when they came down the steep hill to the ferry and from there across a fairly narrow North Creek. They followed the well- worn riverbank track back to Ballina. Red streamers of sinking summer sun shook fire over the sand bars soon to be merged with deepening river channels of the making tide. On the far southern bank, heavy tidal mangroves etched almost black against the sky, bled their heavy dark presence into the river.

'Stop,' she said, and after a moment, 'Thank you husband, it's been a wonderful day.' Bridget squeezed one of Martin's hands upon the reins and snuggled a little closer. He took his eye off his driving and smiled seriously at her.

'It has been **the** most wonderful day of my life.' He left unsaid what flooded his being.

Jimmy the stable boy took charge of Major, He seemed to have developed a liking for the friendly. smart pony.

'I'll dry him down, see he has a couple of small drinks and feed him right. He'll be fine with me.'

They bid him thanks and headed for a clean-up and change for dinner.

'That lad could be handy in the future,' said Bridget as they headed up the stairs.

Dinner was roast fish and vegetables. Lyn Foster took charge of their needs and found both Martin and Bridget easy to talk with. She warmed to the easy-going red head. There was no pretension with her, unlike some people who felt they had substance in this fast-growing river society.

'Would you let me bring a bottle of wine with our compliments?'

Lyn's question caused Bridget to glance enquiringly at Martin. While they rarely touched alcohol, she and Pat sometimes had a glass of wine after the children were in bed. She decided to let Martin answer. He thought a moment and then smiled at Lyn Foster.

'It's kind of you Mrs Foster. You are looking after us too well. As a Presbyterian minister I did not drink wine and I suppose I hadn't thought of changing the habit, but some things in my life must change. Would you and your husband join us when convenient to you and we'd be happy to share your offer.'

Lyn left to speak with her husband. Bridget smiled at him.

'You handled that well,' she said. 'I would not have minded had you said "no" but they have tried so hard to make us comfortable, it would have seemed a little ungrateful. Wine is not one of my bad vices anyway.' She kept it light and squeezed his hand under the table.

'Och woman, you did na tell me ye had vices. Na you have me worried. Tell me.'

He tried to fix her with a mock, firm pulpit glare but she gave him her most demure smile.

'A woman is entitled to her privacy.'

They chatted on comfortably and when the other guests left the dining room, Lyn and John Foster appeared with a wine bottle and glass tray. Lyn introduced her husband. The Fosters had only been in Ballina a short time, coming with the opening of the new hotel.

They talked of the growing district and it seemed they had already met up with their fellow publicans, the James, who told them a little of hotel-keeping in the area. Bridget now knew why Lyn seemed to have taken a special interest in them. John Foster poured their wine and proposed a toast

'To Mr and Mrs Baillie, long life and happiness.'

It was a pleasant interlude, but the Fosters were busy people and the Baillies were happy to retire.

They had an invitation to lunch the next day with the Hilardts.

The birth of Edna's baby was drawing close and she was keeping very much at home, other than the trip up to the wedding.

When they were in bed and the light out, the day's full agenda, that had started very early, seemed to indicate they would sleep. Bridget knew she was probably still the steering force of this fragile learning time. They kissed pleasurably and she turned gently till her back and his front spoke lightly together. Soon they slept a sleep where dreams of many things kept them company from deep wells of stored experience.

"C'est La Vie"

Morning came to their consciousness with discreet bumping sounds of the hot water jugs being delivered outside their door. For an instant, Bridget wondered just where she was, then the strange room and the man sharing her bed slotted into a present sharp reality. For so many early, lonely mornings after Patrick's death she had merged out of that dream sleep, expecting, wanting to feel his presence, until the hard shattering truth would strike that she was alone in their beautiful cedar bed. She would hit the floor, pray briefly and shove herself into the work pattern of a new day.

So, she hit the floor. Offered her prayers and thanked God for his gifts. Then she knew Martin was awake for he had moved over to her side of the bed as she had left. She stayed on her knees and looked at this, still so new, husband. They smiled at each other and she laid her head on his chest and his strong, firm fingers stroked through her thick, soft hair. They had no need of words, for each discovery of the other brought the new day to life.

'Hello,' she whispered to his chest.

His hands gently turned her face upwards. Lips meeting, they kissed. Bridget had not planned that kiss to start urges flowing, but it seemed, flow they did.

'You are more intoxicating than wine, I want to drink you up.'

He felt the tremble of her awareness and the new strength of being sexually male flowed through him. As she stood in a moment of indecision beside the bed, he was beside her on the floor and wrapped her tight. His background meant he hadn't seen a naked woman other than in paintings, and that enticing lightning flash in the recent storm had kindled a need to look upon his wife. He needed her visual completeness. He needed to know and partake of her complete beauty.

'May I look at you?' his voice choked with emotion.

Would she think him peculiar?

Bridget looked at him steadily, undismayed and sensed his need. She smiled uncertainly. Slowly he lifted the loose-fitting nightdress over her head. In the full light of day, despite her telling him there was nothing wrong with nudity, she felt immediate shyness as the garment lay on the flowered linoleum floor. He stood at arm's length and his hands wandered the wonderful warm living texture of her soft skin. His eyes feasted from waist up, lower parts still covered, protected by knee length loose frilly cotton night pants.

Quest started, he sought to know what made a woman, and particularly this woman. Competently, lightly, his hands pressured down the broad waist band. She wriggled out of the pants shyly, doubtfully, as he eased them down to her knees. They fell to the floor. His eyes roamed her completeness. Hands ever so gently ran over the areas his eyes could now see. Bridget appreciated his gentleness. She was shy under this searching play in broad daylight, but she loved him. She was his wife; the call was his.

He drank in the reality of this intoxicating new visual knowledge. Touch spoke back wonders of the human female form. Here was definitive truth. He felt the tremor of her shyness. It was a strange vacuum of time, neither spoke, brief seconds ticked by that completed his awareness of the female form. Gently he kissed her forehead.

'Thank you.'

His masculinity carried new knowledge and protectiveness. Her fingers touched the black curly hair on the back of his neck, as she would a child. Instinctively, she felt his need for now was complete. This strange, almost spiritual contact brought them close. Perhaps even closer than the exploding, unexpected orgasm that gifted their early love-making. She felt her decision to marry Martin was right. They needed each other.

'You now know all of me Martin. I love you. I've offered all I can.'

He sat on the side of the bed and cradled her naked form gently in his arms. She felt protected.

'Thank you. Five minutes ago, I wanted to use my awaking hungry manhood. Your gift of letting me make love with my eyes has given me awareness. It is enough for now, is it enough for you?'

'It is enough. I love you Martin, more and more I feel safe with you. God willing, we'll make love in many ways, many times. I appreciate the gentleness of your eyes, your hands, and your mind. I'm a lucky woman. Now we'd best get ready for breakfast.'

She broke the magic and gave him a playful shove.

'At least we won't need all the hot water this morning.'

Edna led them into the neat parlour of the simple Hilardt cottage.

'Dick will be home any minute now, and we'll have lunch. It is all ready and waiting. I am an efficient housewife now.'

Edna took Bridget's hands.

'My you look well. It seems crazy, you don't look any older than your stunning daughter, Mary. You look as if marriage to Martin isn't doing you any harm either. Dick seems to have taken a few more grey hairs waiting for this baby; it should not be much longer.'

Dick arrived home, shook hands with his guests, and ran his arms around Edna's large expanse of baby.

'Hey, he kicked,' he said solicitously and kissed his wife.

'She uses me as a dance floor,' Edna said with a shake of her head. 'The sooner out of there, the better.'

They sat and talked. Bridget made sure Edna sat while she served the ample food.

'I'm taking a few hours off,' Dick announced. '*The Raven* is off the bar and could get in on the tide so I will go in to the office later if that happens. Would you like to come for a row with me across the river Martin while I pull the crab traps? Those two would be happy to pack us off for an hour.'

'It sounds a good idea to me. Teach him how to row, he's a real landlubber.' Bridget patted her husband's knee under the table.

'I'll come if you tie me in,' laughed Martin.

Later when the lunch things were washed and the men had left, Edna and Bridget sat side by side on the chintz couch.

'Well,' Edna demanded, 'are you happy with that man?'

Bridget met her questioning eyes. She smiled a telling narrative smile into the ex- teacher's probing look.

'The answer is yes. We'll be fine.'

Edna just said, 'Good. You deserve the best.'

'What about you?' Bridget fired at her friend.

'Oh, I was plain lucky to find a man like Dick. I was prepared to be satisfied as a teacher. A scholarly 'old maid' was my destination. Being married to Dick brought physical love entirely new to me. I thought that went out the window when my fiancée was killed so many years ago. Dick woke a demand in me that I've had to put on hold until this baby comes, only because he thinks I'm fragile. I still feel him beside me at night and that bottom part of me doesn't feel at all fragile. Am I strange?'

Bridget took her hand.

'Let you into a secret. When I waited the final weeks for Mary, I had the same worries. No, you are not strange.'

Dick had his crab pots across the river under a mangrove overhang. There was a large buck mud crab in each. He cautiously steered them into corn bags and securely tied the tops.

'One of the benefits of knowing the fishermen, they give me the waste fish to bait the pots. The rowing across is good exercise but I don't like leaving Edna on her own anymore. I won't rebait them at the moment. Would you like to row back?'

'Thanks, I'll give it a miss. You want to get home this afternoon. Another day you can try to teach me.'

They rowed back over the spits with water rising rapidly and a few pelicans still fishing the shallows. Soon it would be too deep for their scoop-like beaks to trap the small fish.

'It'll soon be all over. If you want me, send a message. We will probably soon be back at Killarney. This is a short honeymoon,' Bridget whispered her message to Edna as she and Martin left the Hilardts to stroll home.

'Is it very hard having a baby?' Martin asked the question as they walked arm in arm up the street.

'There is extreme pain but you forget it pretty soon. It's wonderful to feel a baby in your arms.' Bridget answered his question honestly, seriously.

She knew it was asked in that vein.

'Women have been getting pregnant for a long time, we usually survive,' she added her postscript with a sunny smile.

'You could get pregnant from the other morning, couldn't you?' There was concern in his voice.

'Yes Martin, but I don't think I will. You see, I'm too close to my menstrual period. I'm not afraid of being pregnant again. I'll take it as it comes or as God sends it.'

He gave her fingers a loving squeeze. It was no wonder he had not been able to visit Killarney for a long time before that fateful meeting on the road. She just overwhelmed him with honesty. She was different to the women who had formed his background; they hedged cautiously around the important things of life.

That night after dinner, at Lyn's request, Bridget played the hotel's attractive piano. Bridget still played well, although she knew practice over many years had been far too sparse. The new book of popular selections, that sat on the lid, contained many of the simple melodic Mozart sonatas. These she had learned back in her final school days at the convent. It was a Lipp iron frame upright, slightly out in some notes from a rough trip up from Sydney in its crate. The small audience who gathered were amazed at how good she was. Lyn shook her head when she finished.

'Mrs Baillie you have many talents. Thank you for letting us hear how good our piano can sound.'

'I'm just an amateur, it is a fine instrument but slightly out of tune on some notes. I know just the man to bring it to perfection. If he ever wanders in to see us, we'll steer him towards Ballina.'

Bridget wondered whether Billy Montez would arrive back on the plateau; it had been a long time. She knew the part gypsy would soak up and appreciate Mary's convent-trained violin playing if he had a chance to hear her progress.

Seated at the dressing table, taking the pins out of her hair, she smiled at the reflection of the dark man standing behind her. Ever since, and probably even before, that night they had arrived with the storm, wet and cold at Killarney, she had felt chemistry that flowed between them. She had wondered. Was it just made of loneliness and healthy physical attraction? Should she risk tarnishing the blessings that she already had received through marriage to Patrick, blessings probably more than many women ever found.

Now, after only three days together, she felt it was good. This man too, was special.

He took the brush from her hand and gently, firmly brushed out the heavy curls from their rolled-up position. Thoroughly, he did the job till her hair fell around her shoulders and she enjoyed the peaceful sensation of his care. He put down the brush and finished the job by gently using his fingers as a comb, through her hair and down her neck and upper spine. There was no need of conversation. His touch sung psalms of love, there was prayer, sexuality, understanding, vibrant, alive in this fully clothed proximity. Time ticked by in intimate passionless contact, both felt it could go on forever.

Not so. Soft, friendly lamplight threw secret shadows. The wordless idyll progressed, waking thoughts, sensations, desires. Inevitable, in growing anticipation, they slowly undressed each other. They sought and found consuming completeness. Eventually, bodies spent, they did resort to comfort of their excellent bed.

In soft light of dawn, Bridget felt the slight flow from her body. Quietly, she rummaged for a towelling pad, brought just in case. But she had been confident they would get through their honeymoon week. Back in bed, she hoped Martin had not awoken, but his hand sought her.

'Are you all right,' he whispered.

'Yes, I am all right, but my period has come early.' She gave his hand a squeeze.

'I'm sorry, you deserve a "well" wife for your honeymoon. Men have to put up with women's periods later. It shouldn't be on a honeymoon.'

He didn't answer straight away, but eased her head up on his chest and shoulder.

'You found out this morning how little I know about women,' he said, 'so long as a period does not make you too unwell, don't worry for one minute about me. You are the most wonderful, loving person that God could have given me. Since our wedding, that seems so long ago, you have given me everything. I wanted completeness, oh so desperately, but I had no idea. I knew my body worked, and that it wanted to prove its masculinity but I had no idea how I could be worthy of you and give you pleasure. You've led me and helped me. Your beauty, understanding, sharing, has set me free. Just let me look after you and love you in all ways.'

He felt the slight shake of her shoulders and her warm tears flowed on his skin.

'I love you too, Martin Baillie. If God is willing, there is so much more of our life to come. I wanted my body to give all it could through our honeymoon.' She stroked her fingers through the thick hairs of his strong chest.

'Just having you there is enough lassie.'

They lay in warm companionship until the maid had delivered their hot water jugs. Bridget arose, sorted their rumpled discarded clothing of the night before. She knelt with rosary beads and prayed in thanksgiving and for protection of her family.

She remained on her knees facing Martin. She smiled at his serious face.

'Do you have any problem with my prayers?'

'I have no right to have problem with your prayer,' he replied, 'just keep praying that prayer will come back to me. You are an educated lass and you know that Protestants mistrust many Roman Catholic doctrines. Your ability to love makes me happy and sure that your standing with God is real. I will never try to stop your prayers.'

He leant across and brought her back to his shoulder.

Gently he ran lips and fingers ever so gently over any skin to which he had access. They didn't speak verbally but their eyes met and spoke. When they had washed and dressed. Bridget sorted their used and clean clothes.

'Well, Mr Baillie, we have two more days of clothes left, unless I prevail upon Lyn to use her laundress. Also, I may have to destroy a towel to handle my new condition, so we'll have to make a decision as to when we go home.'

After breakfast they decided on another picnic trip with Major and the sulky. Bridget reckoned they had best make the most of their days left. They followed the northern sandy track, further out than before until they gained access to a beach leading to a vast area of flat tidal washed rock. Major carefully picked a way through the banksia and creeping dune plants until they reached a narrow dune front leading down to the rocks. Major was taken from the shafts, unharnessed and given his chaff. The tide was more than half out and with a flat sea, already a very large area was a drying haven for every type of seabird.

Bridget mused.

'Perhaps we leave our boots on the rocks. It could be hard on bare feet. Are you happy to have our lunch down there?'

'You're not going to be happy until you make me a beachcomber.'

He took the basket in one strong hand and Bridget in the other. They slid down to the beach and made the short distance to the rocks, where they sat on a comfortable seat height basalt outcrop. Their lunch was washed down with lemon flavoured water. The gulls fought noisily for scraps. Bridget named for him the oyster catchers, a couple of varieties of snipe, even an overhead wandering albatross. It soared enquiringly above, checking the human visitors.

'How do you know so much?' he demanded.

'Any long-term sailor can recognise sea birds and fish. Take heart, Mother Cecilia reckoned my mathematics left a lot to be desired.'

'I'm pleased. You make a peasant Scotsman like me feel inadequate.'

'Let's walk out and see some of the rock pools. You can help, for I'm not up to my normal jumping form today.'

'Are you sure that this exercise is good for you?' he demanded solicitously.

'Look Martin, women have been having periods since Eve. I can handle it. I just feel a little annoyed with my body for being inconvenient.'

He protectively held her close and ever so gently stroked her tummy.

'Don't you criticise your body. I love it and you. I won't hear a word against it.'

Even Bridget marvelled at the sea life in the pools as they slowly walked out over the tidal rock pools. There were sea urchins, anemone, star fish, many seaweeds and little fish that flashed bright colours. She gave him a task of collecting several kauris and striped cone shells from the shallows of one pool.

'Will you come back with me again and we'll bring Thomas? He'd think this was wonderful. I'm not sure that Janey would be interested, she'd probably be better left with Edna in Ballina.'

He enjoyed her enjoyment and couldn't help thinking how different she was from the young 'ladies' of his clerical life contact.

'You have done enough. We'll head back to shore.'

Bridget did not argue; slowly they retraced their steps.

On one crossing, he saw her measuring off the long step. He scooped his right arm under her knees and lifted her effortlessly.

Choosing his spot carefully, he took her across like a child in his arms. He kept walking away before she laughingly demanded to be put down. She kissed him and he tasted the beautiful salt taste of her lips. Was she a sea nymph after all? They made it back to the sulky and he knew she was tired.

'You just relax while I make a few adjustments.' She rummaged around in her small bag and headed off into the trees. When she came back, she took in the concern on his face.

'It's all right, but you men have it pretty easy.' She leaned against him and spoke in a matter-of-fact tone, as he guessed she would to an elder daughter.

'We are never quite sure how much we will bleed early in our period. I should make it back all right on the new pad I have put on. Don't look so worried, I wouldn't have missed our trip on the rocks for anything.'

Another Bridget

It was about four when they arrived at the hotel stable. Jimmy was on hand to take over Major. He had a message to deliver.

'Mrs Foster asks that you see her, Ma'am.'

'Thank you, Jimmy.' Then, as she watched the lad's greeting of the pony. 'Have you driven with reins, yet?'

'I haven't had a chance yet, Ma'am.'

'Would Mrs Foster let you go once around the block with Mr Baillie?'

'I don't know Ma'am, but I only have Major to attend to now.'

Bridget smiled at Martin.

'Take him for one spin of the block. Perhaps you'll let him drive into the yard.' She gripped Martin's hand. 'I'll see Mrs Foster and tell her the trip won't take more than five minutes.'

She watched them out into the lane and went to find Lyn Foster.

'Ah, thank you for finding me.' Lyn Foster was talking in the kitchen.
She followed Bridget to the empty dining room.

'Mr Hilardt was here about an hour ago and asked me to tell you the baby may not be far away.'

'Thank you. I'll go down as soon as Martin comes back. I hope she has the midwife ready.'

She told Lyn Foster of Jimmy and Martin's trip around the block. Lyn smiled.

'He'll be over the moon. I think he has a tough life. He never seems to want to go home. You are a kind person, Mrs Baillie.'

They were back in the stable when Bridget went to collect Martin.

'He drove like an expert,' Martin said seriously.

There was a beam of pleasure on the lad's thin face. He was firmly brushing the pony's smooth coat.

They headed for the stairs and Bridget gave him the news.

'I'll just get right and we'll get down there.'

'Are you up to walking? he demanded.

'Stop fussing.' She squeezed his hand.

Back in the room she went to her case and came out of it with an unused towel.

'Here, something useful you can do. Tear that into four pieces. There is a pair of scissors if you need them. Then make yourself scarce. Go and tell Jimmy we may need Major again later.'

He produced what she wanted and left as directed. Not many minutes later, they were walking down the street.

Dick answered their knock.

'I'm pleased to see you both.'

He took Bridget in to Edna and came back out to the front room and Martin. It was easy for Martin to sense the worry in his companion.

'She'll be all right,' he offered lamely.

'That's what she says, but she does not look at all right now.'

Dick shrugged his shoulders and tried to relax. He tried to smile at Martin.

'I don't know much about these babies. It seems easy enough to get them in there but darn hard to get them out. Ma Geddes and Doc Mason are away somewhere, I've left messages for them to come.'

In the bedroom, Bridget assumed her efficient work mode, after putting her arms around Edna and kissing her gently on the forehead.

'When did the spasms start?' she asked.

'About three hours ago.' Edna looked questioningly.

'There's probably a long way to go yet before it happens.'

'You know all about this. I'm afraid I don't know much and Dick is a mental mess already.'

Edna winced in pain as a longer contraction shook through her. When it subsided, she gave Bridget a weak, sweaty smile.

'Just my luck that the experts are out of town.'

Bridget ran her hands over the swollen abdomen, noting the baby was already down very low.

'Back in a second.' She went out to the men.

'Dick, go around and see whether Carmel is home. Tell her what's going on, she will be around in no time.'

'Martin, you take over in the kitchen and have plenty of hot water ready on the stove.'

She read the consternation in his face and kissed him.

'Your other job is to pray, I know you can do that, just keep telling God we want this mother and baby safe.'

She heard the low moan from the bedroom and flew back to her post.

Once more Edna was wracked with pain. This baby was probably not waiting for midwife or doctor; she hoped it would wait for Carmel. She packed pillows under Edna's knees and gently worked dry towels under from her bottom down. Obviously, the baby's fluid bag had been broken for some time. She breathed a sigh of relief, at least there were plenty of clean towels. The washstand held a large floral jug and dish. She grabbed the jug, opened the door.

'Martin,' and he was there. 'Half full of warm water, for now it's only for me to wash my hands and arms.'

She carried it in and carefully washed in the warm soapy water. Once more, Edna was in the pain of a contraction. Bridget waited for it to ease and carefully felt the swollen opening of the birth canal. Her fingers could feel the baby's head pushing down. She knew with womanly instinct a couple of good pushes and this baby would be out. *Where was everyone?* Obviously, Dick was looking for Carmel.

She put her head around the door.

'Martin. Hot water in whatever you have for containers and if Carmel doesn't arrive in the next few minutes, I'll need you in here to help me.'

Another contraction brought forward the birth.

'The baby's coming. Edna you are doing fine. Only a couple more pushes.'

She tried to sound calm. She'd glimpsed the table set up with scissors, thin cord and a large button. Edna had done well. Bridget knew she at least needed someone to pass these items after the baby arrived.

Come on Carmel where are you? Her lips worked of themselves.

'Holy Mary, Mother of God, help us now.'

Edna cried out as she pushed with another huge contraction. Bridget felt the baby coming, grasped and firmly eased the slippery, precious bundle from its mother's womb. She felt it moving strongly.

'Thank you, God,' she breathed, and the tears flowed from her eyes.

'Edna, look. She is a beautiful little girl. I want to let the cord come a little more.
Martin here, please,' she called him. He came. 'What do you think?'

In amazement, he looked at the blood-flecked little girl, his first reaction not to look at the naked mother in her complete exposure, then it didn't matter.

He felt an outpouring of love for them all. Especially this wonderful woman who was his wife, with her tears dripping down her nose onto the little girl. He felt a surge of happiness, brought back to reality by Bridget's instruction,

'Now, soon we'll have to cut and tie the cord. Martin, you lift Edna a little and put more pillows behind her, then she can hold this squirmy bundle, while we have things ready.'

It was at this stage that Carmel and Dick came unheard through the open door. Dick in a stride was at Edna's side.

'There,' she whispered, 'I told you she was a girl.'

'Saints be praised you three have done fairly well.' Carmel took the baby and wiped any mucus from her mouth and nose.

'She looks right fine to me.' She gave Martin a special, warm smile.

'You be a useful man, that's unusual, but we women still have a few jobs. Stay if you like, then you can trot out the grog.'

Martin looked at his wife, she was pale but triumphant. He knew the relief it must have been when Carmel arrived.

'Take Dick out for a little, while we clean up.'

'We would have managed it all well enough,' she whispered, so that Martin alone heard.

The cord was cut and tied. They warm sponged the baby and placed her on Edna's full breasts. Then Carmel eased gently on the placenta afterbirth. It was still not ready to slide completely free of the exhausted womb. They sponged Edna and put a sheet over her.

'Well,' demanded Carmel, 'what is her name?'

'I'd better have a conference with Dick. Send him in for a minute.'

Carmel and Bridget left the parents and the squirming baby together and went out to join Martin for a moment.

Dick joined them.

'Her name is Bridget,' he announced.

Bridget Baillie looked up, unspeaking: tears of achievement; tiredness; comprehension sought release from her eyes.

They were all having a cup of tea when Doc Mason arrived.

'Congratulations,' he said, 'I didn't want another difficult birth today.'

They left him to inspect their work and check the afterbirth. He joined them outside.

'They both seem fine. And how many babies have you delivered

Mrs Baillie?'

'That's the first Doctor Mason.'

'Well, you did a great job, and congratulations to you and Mr Baillie on your wedding. I'll come around in the morning and check all is well.'

'Would you like a whiskey, Doctor?' Dick's question brought a smile from Doc Mason.

'Why not Dick?'

He eyed appreciatively the good quality bottle of Scotch and the top-quality glasses. Dick almost filled the glass, before Doctor Mason lifted his finger. He rejected the water jug.

'Right,' he said, 'here is a toast.'

'To the Bridgets - both of them.'

He raised his glass and drank it down.

'I must go. That's fine whiskey. I suggest you all have a nip, even the mother in there, a small one would make her sleep.'

He left them, looking warily at the bottle.

It was late when they walked back to the hotel. Carmel had decided to stay the night with Edna, just in case any problem arose.

'Young Rosie is capable of my house duties.'

Bridget was happy to make their room. It had been too much for one day, but she was still uplifted by the happy result.

'I'd best put a towel under me for the night. I don't want to risk soiling the bed with blood.'

They lay side by side. Martin spoke with a degree of concern,

'I don't know about these babies. I don't think I want to put you through that pain,' he said solemnly.

'Rubbish,' she said and kissed him, 'that birth was perfect. Different, but it is good, as the final climax of sex is holding your baby in your arms. Thank you for praying, that's why we made it.'

Her head cradled in on his arm, sound sleep covered them swiftly.

At breakfast the next morning, Lyn Foster beamed at them both. The news was all over the village, probably increasing their skill with every telling. Dick Hilardt, as shipping agent, was well known. He would have many offers to toast the health of young Bridget.

Before they came down, Martin and Bridget sat on the side of the bed and decided to return to Killarney late in the day.

'It hasn't been long enough, but we know each other now.' She smiled at him and squeezed his hand.

'I'd like to keep you to myself for ever, but I know we have to go back.'

He held her gaze.

'No man was ever given a better honeymoon.'

'I'm not complaining either, you know.'

After breakfast they walked down River Street and checked on the Hilardt family. Carmel had them under control. All was well, baby

Bridget not waiting at all patiently for Edna's tight breasts to start supplying milk. She had sucked down a mostly boiled water mixture from a bottle. Edna was worried that her milk was not flowing.

'You'll soon be milking better than a dairy cow,' Carmel promised her. 'They can get by without me at home for another day, by then you'll be fine.'

Bridget Baillie picked up her namesake and placed the small, wrapped bundle in Martin's arms.

'Here, my girl, get to know your Uncle Martin.' Then to Edna and Carmel, 'We are going home this afternoon. I think you'll soon have a visit from the girls when they know the news. We will call in on our way home. Dick will probably be here from his work by then.'

.

Killarney and Home

The sun tucked low under the western tree line as they turned into the lane winding down to Killarney. Close together, conversation dispensed, each heavy with tiredness and thoughts. On this plateau changes had come apace. There was now in this home habitat, much open country, some under crop, some under grass. Sentinel tops of tall timber were declining. It was a guard line pushed back, melting amber spots in the dusk of evening. Bridget reined in Major; the pony shook his head in frustration, he could feel home. They watched the sun's last lingering kiss of colour creep away. Gone.

Allowed to continue, Major snorted and stepped out keenly to join his friends in the stable. The high decibel treble of Mary's violin drifted up the lane, Bridget picked the Brahms tune and she smiled across at Martin.

'Welcome home, husband, it seems you now have an acquired family.'

The melody stopped mid note and Bridget sensed they had been spotted. Confirmation came with the sight of three figures, a reception committee, heading for the gate. Bridget drove through, then reined in the frustrated Major.

'I'll drive him home.'

Thomas gave his mother a quick kiss, acknowledged Martin, took charge of the reins, waited for them to hop out, and let the pony trot off.

They spread across the track; Bridget hugged her daughters. Jane walked at her mother's side and Mary between her and Martin.

'Have you managed all right?' Bridget asked.

'Of course we have,' said Jane, 'That Mary thinks she can boss us around just because she comes from the city.'

'Someone has to start making you useful,' said Mary.

She turned to Martin, with that smile so like her mother.

'You are home early Uncle Martin, are you giving her back?'

He put his arm firmly around Bridget.

'No Mary, I've decided I'll keep her.'

Dinner was a happy meal. Martin quiet, letting his acquired family become used to his presence. He knew there would be pressures but he was determined to respect their rights. They talked late. The girls and Thomas delighted that Miss Wilkinson had a baby daughter.

'Why is she Bridget?' demanded Jane.

'Well, we were there when she was born,' said her mother.

She gave no further explanation. They didn't push the matter further.

When her children went off to bed, Bridget and Martin sat on a while. He sensed that taking him to her bedroom was not going to be easy for Bridget.

'Time for bed,' she said.

She reached across and took his hand.

They blew out the dining room light and closed the bedroom door behind them. Bridget laid out night attire from a drawer, not worrying about her travelling case. Martin found pyjamas. They changed and blew out the light. She took his hand and knelt by the bed. He felt the downward pressure of her hand and he knelt by her side. He felt her sign of the cross and her arm around his waist. Her inclusion of him in her relationship with God touched him deeply. He couldn't analyse his feelings. It may take time. He knew he loved God, and he knew he loved this woman. He prayed it would all come together.

December warmth dripped out of the night. They lay on top of their sheet.

'Martin,' she whispered, 'this is a brand-new bed. The bed that Patrick made for us is in Mary's room. Patrick would not have minded us making love on that bed but I think it is better this way.'

He said nothing but gently kissed her.

'Anyway, it will be some days yet before this bleeding stops and we are free of that nuisance. If it's too warm being close just move over, it's a big bed.'

He stayed close, warmth of the night more acceptable, than loss of contact with this newfound treasure.

In the cooler hush of morning, before the roosters started crowing, still predominately asleep, he cuddled into her back and drank a sub conscious swig of her proximity.

Dan Riordan - Work

Dan Riordan was up at dawn. He planned a trip down to Ballina with the heavy wagon. There should have been a couple of ships in over the bar during the past few days. The weather had seemed favourable. He had returned the night before from a Lismore trip and John Richards had gone on for Casino with a cart order. He had the fire going, and hoped Nell would stay in bed as she had been up several times through the night to Catherine. However, he was not surprised to find her beside him in the kitchen.

'I'll have your breakfast ready and sandwiches for lunch, if you want go and saddle Chief,' said Nell.

'Ah, he's in the small yard so it will only take a minute. I'd rather help you here, I'm sorry I've been away so much lately. It should be better when Martin gets back. Perhaps we could have a few days off and just loaf.'

'It sounds good Dan, but I'm all right you know. At least we have money coming in and I find it relaxing when I have time for the garden and the trees.'

'You're really the farmer, Nell. Perhaps one day I'll be able to do the things you want done, at present being a carrier keeps me busy.'

He put an arm around her waist.

'It's been a battle but we're getting there. Will you keep me as a husband?'

She laughed. 'Maybe, not much offers around anyway, so I'll keep you a while longer.'

He kissed her. Held her close and didn't want to go to work. She pushed him to the table.

'Sit down, you need your breakfast. Martin and Bridget are the ones on a honeymoon.'

She brought the porridge pot and spooned it to the bowl. His arm went around her drape- covered backside at table level, and his fingers lingered in a gentle pinch.

'Eat your breakfast and then you are out. Its work for you,' she said with pretended severity.

Since the birth of Catherine, their relationship seemed to have strengthened. Only on rare occasions did the old fear and hurt trauma turn her to a shivering wraith of her normal self. She loved him for his care and understanding and tried to fight the odd attack of depression that crept in unannounced.

She knew, they both knew Sean was the result of her nightmare rape, but they both loved him as their son. She knew neither wanted to admit their suspicion. He was a handsome, dark, olive-skinned child, intelligent but at times moody and subject to tantrums. Mathew was a solid little fellow, fairish and quiet, but a wanderer now that he was walking. Catherine, just twelve months younger, was fair and usually smiling at the world. The three children loved each other and hated being separated. The Riordans were a happy, normal family.

Dan cantered across to Killarney stable. It was fully light. He was surprised to see the sulky and Major home; they hadn't expected them for a few more days. He fed and harnessed Tar and a big new baldy faced black they called Midnight. There were now six Clydesdales; old Captain only went out on the road when they needed his wonderful, steadying influence. He worked willingly for any of them but Dan always felt he was still looking and waiting for Patrick.

Before he was ready to trundle out the wagon, Bridget was beside him in the stable.

'Hello Daniel, don't you sleep? Thought you'd better know the news. Edna and Dick have a daughter. I'll go over later and tell Nell and Norah. Those girls of mine won't be satisfied until they have been to Ballina.'

'Why that's great news, Mrs… Baillie.'

Bridget noticed the pause in Dan's address. She took him lightly by the arm.

'Do me a favour Daniel, call me Bridget. It won't be too hard.'

Then she thought she'd better ask, 'Is it all going well?'

'Yes, it's close to Christmas and we have many jobs. I've been keeping your logbook up to date. It's a great idea, check it later and see that we are doing it how you want.'

'That's good Dan, I'm sure it will be a help.'

'I hope to be back before night,' then an embarrassed afterthought, 'You and Martin had a happy honeymoon?'

Bridget held his eyes and smiled. Open, honest, no means shy or coy. She knew his question was of honest concern.

'Thanks Dan, for asking. We are great.'

He headed off. The familiar hauling language of well-oiled harness and crunch of heavy wagon wheels greeted an awakening dawn. It was working music so often prelude to a new day.

Bridget closed her eyes a moment; she was glad no one could see that those green eyes were very moist. She took the big logbook back to the house with her for perusal of what was happening with O'Reilly Carriers.

Martin the Carrier

Martin had the fire going, and the big kettle was boiling for their tea. Bridget guessed the children, or at least Mary, was keeping out of the way. She knew Mary, once home, would have drifted back to her habit of early waking and rising. Bridget knocked softly on Mary's door.

'Tea is made.'

'Thanks. I'll be out.'

Mary arrived. Her pyjamas covered under a shapeless drape. She was growing tall, her breasts fast developing. Her copper-coloured hair almost a copy of her mother's.

'Those other two loafers sleep half the day.'

She sat opposite Bridget and Martin.

'I've been getting up and seeing things are organised before I drag them out. Thomas is good with the horses and animals. That Janey, if she's coming back with me after the holidays, well - perhaps Mother Cecilia will sort her out.'

'We heard your playing when we entered the lane, it was a good welcome home.'

Martin looked at his acquired daughter. She raised her eyebrows a fraction.

'I'm practising to the schedule Sister Benny has tied around my neck. I still don't know whether I'm any good, or whether I want that form of slavery.'

They chatted on.

After breakfast it was agreed they visit the Brewsters and then across to Nell. The news of the Hilardt baby would soon arrive on the plateau anyway, but Bridget wanted to be the one to bring it to near friends.

Martin was to check out the work schedule and find where to slot himself into the workload. He read the business diary and a forward list of definite booked jobs. He was keen to be started. There was still much to carry before Christmas. A job from Wardell wharf up to the Johnson farm caught his eye. A double disk plough was waiting the steep trip up the cutting and across to Johnsons. He reckoned it a job requiring some time to load and tie, then a matter of hopefully a right height bank, or planks to put it down at destination end. The roads were dry. Now was the time to climb the Meerschaum Vale cutting. It was a job for him. As it was school holidays, he would ask Thomas if he wanted to be a helping hand and overseer.

Martin made his preparations. Bridget and the girls came to bid farewell before they headed off visiting.

'I'll take some lunch and collect Johnson's plough from Wardell. Do you think Thomas would want to come?'

'Ask him and take your time.'

Thomas was keen. They cut sandwiches for themselves and prepared a halfway feed for the two horses.

'Who do you think we should take?'

Martin knew the eleven-year-old boy could probably sum up the horses they needed better than he could. Thomas was sure in his opinion.

'Captain needs a walk and Spud goes well with him.'

They harnessed the two horses. Martin lifted aboard a couple of strong planks, various ropes and tie ropes and a small hand winch just in case. They were outfitted with overalls. Bridget's small men's model didn't need much turning up for Thomas, an old straw hat completed his outfit. They took to the road, Thomas handling the reins.

Bush Telegraph

Norah was overjoyed.

'This calls for celebration. Janey, please go and tell Mr Brewster he is wanted. Don't tell him why.'

A few minutes later, a worried looking Jim Brewster puffed around the corner. Norah immediately told him the news.

'We have a baby,' she said in triumph. 'Right James, we need a bottle of wine.'

Out came the quality crystal glasses. The girls joined the toast.

'To baby Bridget!' unaware of the real reason for the choice of name.

Bridget knew Edna would tell Norah enough of the story soon

enough, she felt happy to let her wait.

'We will have a party Christmas Eve,' Bridget announced as time came for them to set out to the Riordans.

'Why not let James take you across in the buggy?'

'Thank you, Norah, but no. I'll be getting fat and these girls need exercise.'

The sun was very warm when they approached the Riordans. Blackie ambled out to meet them, wagging his tail in pleasure; these were his friends. Nell was out working behind the house in her vegetable garden.

'Hello, this is a surprise. I didn't think you'd be back yet.'

They told their news, and the girls took over the care of Sean, Matthew and Catherine, leaving Bridget and Nell to retreat and gossip in the kitchen. Nell demanded details. Bridget gave some, but still omitted that she delivered the baby.

'I'm so pleased it went well. I thought Doc Mason was going to need a tin opener to get Sean out.' She shrugged her shoulders. Then she said with pride, 'My mum will see they are well. I bet Dick is a proud father; it's great news.'

'Yes, he's over the moon, I hope he's not drinking too many toasts.'

'Ah well, he seems to have stayed very sober for Edna. He'll be right.'

'We won't stay long, Nell. It's Rose's day for housework tomorrow, but you can't always be sure with Rose. There's heaps of washing. I told Dan this morning about Edna but I wanted you to know as soon as possible.'

'And you and Martin are happy?'

Bridget leaned toward her and took the girl's work worn hand.

'Yes. I told your good husband the answer to that question, but he may not pass it on.'

She liked Nell, the girl was honest like her mother. Bridget smiled at her.

'You know I wondered too, but it was wonderful. We are happy. I pray the children accept him in time. Tom has gone off with him today down to Wardell, so that's a good sign. Martin wants to pitch in and work. I know Dan has been doing too much, and looking at the work schedule, there is plenty to keep them all busy.'

They chatted a while then inspected the garden and Nell's thriving orchard. Much of the block was still scrub. What Dick had originally cleared, Nell, with some days from Dan doing the really heavy grubbing, now had under grass. She wanted more cows. It was apparent she thrived on the hard work.

It was hot. Hats pulled down, perspiration soaking their clothes, they made it back to Killarney. Cool drinks and a sit on the veranda, they felt better.

'Perhaps we should have let Mr Brewster trot us over in the buggy.'

Bridget wanted her daughters to be self-sufficient but knew that just because she had climbed high masts and tied off sails, this was no reason to push them too hard. Yet it pleased her they didn't complain but tramped stoically home for the best part of an hour.

Making a Carrier

Martin and Thomas took the horses from the cart at Wardell. There was shade under the riverbank fig tree, where they could attach nosebags for feeding time. First, a small drink demanded a trip over to the public trough. Once the horses were right, it was sandwich time and they enjoyed their lunch of corn beef and leftovers.

They went across and found the wharf manager.

'Good to meet you Mr Baillie,' said the manager. 'I hope it all goes well for you and the business. O'Reillys have been good carriers for the district. Mrs O'Reilly did a great job to carry on after Pat's death and she deserves the best.'

Martin quietly nodded his head and signed for the Johnson plough.

He decided it best to remove the disks from the plough before starting the loading operation. He was on his back removing the large reverse thread retaining nuts when he heard Thomas talking with someone that he obviously knew. He finished his task and slid off the two big disks.

'Uncle Martin, this is Mr Yanohavovich and Pearl.'

Martin wiped his greasy hand and offered it to the tall, grey-bearded man. He knew about the part Aboriginal family.

'Hello, I'm pleased to meet you. I've met Rose and it is good to meet the rest of the family.'

'Call me Yan. I help load that plough. It looks heavy.'

'Thanks Yan. I'm going to winch it up on the planks. Thomas and

I will be pleased of your help.'

They set it up ready and Yan watched the wheels carefully as it inched up. Soon it was in the tray and anchored. The plough was tied off securely so there was no chance of its rolling in any direction.

Yan and Pearl had walked down from the escarpment to pick up three new axes that had arrived on the same boat as the plough. Martin insisted they place the axes in the cart.

It was time to start the trip for home. They tramped out west into the heath leading towards the range and past a big sawmill. The reins tied and Captain setting a steady pace, the four walked along behind the horses. It was very warm on the sandy heath track. The roots of many shrubby plants ran as a mat of surface veins on the sandy track. Some straggly shade was overhead where stunted eucalypt and ti tree formed an intermittent canopy.

'Smell that honey,' Pearl said to Thomas. 'Want to come and find the hive? It won't be far away.'

'All right if I go with Pearl?' Thomas asked of Martin.

Martin smiled and nodded. The two were of a height. Pearl was two years older. They disappeared in the ti-tree.

Pearl followed the heavy scent of heath honey until her sharp, very dark, near black eyes picked up the odd working bee returning pollen laden on a common line toward the nest.

'Wait, we'll just sit and see where the bees go.'

They sat close under a squiggly gum. Her brown arm pointed the sight trail.

'We follow, it's not far now. Listen. Hear.'

At first, he didn't pick the sound but as they sat in silence, the low pitched, vibrant,
 whining hum of the working nest, separated from the other heath sounds, and crept to his untrained ear.

'Yeah. I hear.'

They crept in close to feverish activity in the hollow fork of a large paper bark.

'We won't go close,' she said.

They watched the hive activity in companionable silence. Mission achieved; they had found the busy honey loaded colony.

'Better catch them up now,' said Pearl.

They headed back across the heath toward the track. When they reached the sandy passageway, 'They are not far in front,' she said and swung toward the distant hills.

'How do you know?' Thomas asked.

'Those roots, still standing up.'

She showed him the signs of the cart passing that her keen eyes read.

Martin and Yan had walked along, much of the time in silence. Martin was surprised by this man. He lived in the bush, had virtually cut himself off from what Martin's Australian contacts would have called civilisation. Yet he spoke with calm authority. He had even committed what to them, was his complete destruction by having a liaison with an Aboriginal woman. This the righteous Europeans considered but a fraction up the ladder from bestiality or sodomy. Martin felt there was a story in this quiet man's past that only God knew. Yan aired a thought,

'I thank your wife and Miss Wilkinson for Pearl being at school. She is good girl and clever.' He shook his head. 'Not easy for dark skin person with white skin person.'

'Pearl is not very dark, Yan. She is a pretty girl.'

'Probably worse. White men only want dark, pretty girls for quick love, not marriage. I worry for Pearl. Perhaps if she have enough learning.' He shrugged, and left it unsaid.

'You are all welcome at Killarney. It seems Pearl and Thomas get along. Bridget says Pearl and Jane are friends.'

The children caught them up and told eagerly of the big bees' nest. They tramped on as the sun angled away to the west. The horses, their pace set by Captain, moved toward the white clay cutting where a climb back to the plateau would begin. Today the track was dry and easy.

At the fork of the road that wandered a little north of west, Yan and Pearl swung to the left; the group parted. Yan, with three heavy axes upon his strong shoulder and Pearl swinging lightly beside, they quickly disappeared out of sight

It was the next track, on top of the white clay cutting that led around to Johnson's property. Martin and Thomas tramped on. They came to a free running creek of soft, clear water. The horses were given a drink, Martin and Tom splashed their faces and arms. It wasn't much further. The Johnson farm was one on the plateau of size. Johno Johnson was known as a keen farmer. Mostly, it was flattish land of soft, deep, dark reddish soil. Martin had called some years ago after the big sports day that boosted funds for the school. The Johnsons practised faith of the Church of England, but Flora Johnson was a lowland Scot like himself and spoke with the soft brogue of his childhood. They had welcomed him with the invitation to come back again at any time.

Clem Johnson was an ambitious man who had tried most crops since settlement on the block. He was now increasing the sugar cane area and already had made some primitive experimental sugar with a crude, crafted mill of hardwood rollers. He saw a future in the sugar industry. Hence, he awaited his double disk plough that would make for faster preparation of his well, set out rectangular blocks. He now had sufficient ribbon variety for setts to make larger plantings. He saw the cart coming, recognised O'Reilly horses and called out to Flora.

'It looks like the plough is coming. Better have a cuppa tea ready while I take them over to the unloading bank.'

Clem greeted them and ran an interested eye over his most modern piece of equipment, before recognising the driver.

'Why it is Martin Baillie. We heard of your wedding. Congratulations.' He looked at the sweaty overall clad ex-clergyman with some surprise. 'We knew you and Bridget O'Reilly were married but I didn't think you would be the driver so soon.'

They tramped on another 100 metres to where there was a cutting that could be backed into to allow the plough to be pulled off. Martin used Captain only and the old horse inched back into position with the tail board down. It was a better unloading platform than Martin had expected and soon the plough was sitting on the ground.

'I'll replace the disks on their shafts, Mr Johnson. I thought it best to take them off for the loading.'

'That's good enough, you've done your job. My boys can put the disks back and I'll see they make sure the bearings are fully packed with grease. You've done well. Flora will have a cuppa ready on the veranda when we get back.'

They left the horses in a patch of shade and walked over to the

Johnson veranda. Flora greeted them with warm interest.

'Ah, but it be good to see ye Mr Baillie and you too, laddie.'

Martin answered, 'This is Thomas and he has steered me through my first job.'

Thomas drank down a large glass of water and passionfruit juice.

'Thank you, Mrs Johnson.' His manners and smile were well taught and polite.

They didn't stay long. Martin knew it would be dark by the time they were home.

'Now that you're one of us on the mountain, I'd like to talk to you about sugar, but you are now anxious to get home. We'll visit one of these days. Do you have a bill for me?'

'No, Bridget will send you an account, and yes Mr Johnson, we will talk one day.'

They left.

'What you reckon Flora? Will the clergyman and that dynamo, Bridget, be all right together? I bet he's learned a bit already.'

Flora eyed him sternly.

'They deserve to be happy. I'm ashamed my church threw him out for marrying a Catholic. I am sure it will be a good marriage. She's a good woman; look at the manners of that boy. He is a credit to her and Patrick O'Reilly.'

Another Christmas

Dinner was late at Killarney by the time Martin and Thomas had bedded the horses and bathed themselves. It was a slow meal and there was much to talk about. After the dishes were done, Mary took her violin to the front veranda and her finger exercises flowed to the night. Thomas was soon for bed, for him it had been a big day. Likewise, Jane soon left Martin and Bridget alone at the table. He told her of their meeting with Yan and Pearl and how the children had gone following bees to their nest.

Martin said of Yan, 'He seems a good man and he is trying to give his daughter a chance in life.'

'Yes,' Bridget nodded, 'Edna said she was gifted at mathematics. She must get it from Yan. Miss Cavanagh says she is doing very well at school and there has been no real trouble for her since Angus James left. The others seem to accept her, probably some of the parents look down at her, but I hope they say nothing to their children. I've thought about Pearl, I'm pleased you are interested. I'll talk to you soon with an idea that came to me. I try to make it easy for Rose to work here. She was there for us and so good when Pat was killed. She and Pearl ran things well when I went away to be a carrier.'

A week to Christmas and Killarney was a hive of activity.

The carts and wagon were leaving every morning to catch up orders and make deliveries, many from the big shed in Duck Creek village. Bridget had worked out a schedule that O'Reilly Carriers should clear their backlog by Christmas Eve. All they needed was fine weather. Martin worked as long as the other drivers and Thomas was keen for another trip away as his offsider.

Mary issued her ultimatum in search of a trip to Ballina.

'Mum, I want to visit the Hilardts at Ballina. That Bridget will be grown up before I see her. I can drive Major.'

'I know you can drive Major, but I would prefer to come with you. Would you tolerate your mother? The three of us could make it a full day and do our Christmas shopping.'

'I suppose you can come. I need some money, so you had better come. That is, if we go to- morrow.' chimed in Jane.

'I'm pleased I'm some use.' Bridget raised her eyebrows; it seemed these girls were fast gaining independence.

Martin Learns the Realities

The wharf at Ballina was a busy scene. Two ships had made the most of a flat bar, a rising tide and early morning daylight, to enter and dock. Goods were coming off and commodity piles were growing on the smooth tallow wood decking.

Bob Beames and a couple of small cart carriers were already completing a load, when Martin and the big wagon arrived for loading to some of the more distant places. He parked clear of the wharf entries, went in to check with the wharf manager what was for O'Reilly Carriers and to check with the ship masters. It was his first trip to Ballina with the big wagon, he had to appear confident. Thomas had sought permission for the trip, and Bridget knowing she and the girls were also heading for Ballina had agreed.

'Hey you, Sky Pilot, you be too close to the entry. You want'a learn the rules,' Bob Beames bellowed rudely to attract attention of all on the wharf.

Martin looked at him calmly. He knew of Beames and it seemed Beames knew of his connection with the business.

'Good morning, Mr Beames. I thought I had left plenty of

clearance from the entry. How much clearance do you need?' Martin answered calmly.

'Enough. What I says is enough,' snarled Bob. It was a combination of too much grog the night before and anything to do with O'Reillys, turning his florid complexion the colour of cooked beetroot.

He continued to snarl, 'Are you going to move?'

'No. Not unless I am too close and I don't think I am.'

'If I have to get down from this cart, you'll wish you'd stayed a parson. I'll pelt your carcass in that river and we'll see whether you bloody well walk on water.'

By this time a crowd of hangers-on had arrived. The sound of Bob Beames roaring at someone, or something, was not unusual. However, this was a little different. The ex-reverend, if not known, was known of, and they thought here was an opportunity of entertaining action. Beames usually only bellowed, but they knew the O'Reilly colour scheme made him see a shade of red that matched his complexion.

Dick Hilardt was on the wharf checking a load with the *Sophie's* master and heard the rumpus. He took no notice of Beames' tantrum until he saw it was the O'Reilly wagon in his sights. He hastily sought Splinter Clifford, the wharf manager, and steered him toward the growing crowd.

'What is your trouble, Bob?' Clifford asked.

'Can't you see that obstruction parked near the entrance. You must need glasses. What do we pay you for?' Beames spat the words at him.

Splinter Clifford made it to the entrance, looked quizzically at the wagon and carefully stepped off the number of strides from the ample entrance to the back of the wagon.

'It's not me that needs glasses, Bob. That wagon is no problem where it is parked.'

'Yeah, that'd be right. Anything to do with O'Reillys is right, anything to do with a battler like Beames is wrong.'

He wagged his finger at Martin.

'Just you be careful Parson or I'll flatten your nose so good that flash wife of yours won't know it.'

He gave his long-suffering horse a smack with the reins and, still muttering, left the wharf.

Martin went about his duties and Thomas remained at Tar's big roan head. The little crowd of wharf hangers-on melted back to previously boring methods of killing time.

'That livened up the morning,' Dick Hilardt smiled at Martin.

'I think he may have blood pressure,' was all Martin said. 'I had to find you anyway. Bridget and the girls will be down later. How are Edna and Bridget?'

'Good. Good. Edna will be delighted. I'll slip home and tell her after I sort out a few details here. When do you think you'll have your load and get away?'

'No idea, Dick. This is my first wagon trip,' he grinned. 'Could have been my last if Bob Beames, had his way.'

'Ah, he's all bluster - unless he just has the right amount of grog aboard to make him dangerous.'

Martin checked out their freight and talked with the ship masters.

Plenty for Duck Creek area and two stoves for the Lismore side of the settlement. He wondered whether it would all go on in one load. He supposed that was the skill he would acquire with time and practice. They placed the wagon up on the wharf, Thomas taking position at Tar's head.

'Would you like to earn some money for Christmas?'

Martin went over and put his question to a couple of able-bodied layabouts. He guessed they must have a reason for being present.

'What you got in mind, Mister?' The skinny youth took a long drag at his cigarette, eyeing Martin warily.

'That wagon requires loading. I could speed up the job with help. There are two stoves to go on first at the front, then various other things.'

'What you reckon Skeet?'

'Yeah Butch, why not?'

The wagon was lined up close to the stoves. Thomas talked softly to the horses, rubbing in turn their big soft noses. The strong planks went in position from wharf to wagon tray and Martin laid out the big, wide, leather lifting straps. He left Skeet and Butch a strap each while he took a strap in each hand. They took the weight and worked a stove onto the planks. Slowly they eased the stove up until it was on the wagon floor. The task repeated with the second stove, they were then worked into a position at the front of the wagon.

It was then a case of moving along the wharf collecting, recording, marking their list. There were bags, tins, boxes, tools, wire, many goods Martin could not identify. The wagon was filled until he felt it was a load. He knew experience and practise would make it easier to know when the right load point was reached. He determined to err on the light side.

He smiled at Thomas.

'Do you think we have enough?'

Thomas looked over the load.

'Yes.'

There were still goods on the wharf for O'Reillys but Martin felt what was left could be put next day in the light cart.

'Right boys,' he smiled at his waiting work force, 'does five shillings each sound fair?'

He did not know what casual work on the wharf usually paid. They had worked well for more than an hour. He did know some labouring jobs only paid 10 shillings a week, so he thought his offer more than fair.

'That's fine, mister,' Butch seemed the spokesman. 'We'll work for you anytime.'

Martin counted out the money. They moved off the wharf. He thought of leaving the wagon parked and going around to see whether Bridget and the girls were at the Hilardts, but he decided they had best lumber off toward home. It would be a long day by the time deliveries were made and all the off- loading completed into the big shed. Once there, it would be a case of moving it out at first opportunity.

Shopping and Friends

Bridget decided to call at the Australian Hotel and see whether they could leave Major and the sulky at the stables. It was only a short walk down River Street to the Hilardts.

'Hello Mrs Baillie, it's good to see you,' Lyn Foster greeted Bridget. 'How can we help?'

'I wondered whether we could make use of your stables while we walk down to see the Hilardts.'

'Of course. Jimmy will look after that pony of yours. He only has a couple of hacks there at the moment.'

'Thanks. I'll pay when we pick him up. It probably won't be until mid-afternoon. My girls want to go shopping and we will go and see Carmel Flaherty.'

Bridget found the girls talking with Jimmy. He had already taken Major out and was rubbing him down.

'He remembers me,' Jimmy smiled. 'You be a good lad and I'll give you some real good chaff. '

'He knows how to smooge people on side our little Major,' Mary laughed at the lad who was probably her age. Jane joined in the conversation.

'He tries to stand over the big horses at home, even has success with some. Not old Captain though, he just slowly walks through him.'

Bridget looked at the young stable hand.

'Thanks Jimmy, Mrs Foster said it was all right, and we will be back this afternoon.'

'I'll look after him well Mrs Baillie.'

Abraham's Emporium occupied a prominent place in River Street. It boasted a sign "We Sell Everything". It was a sweeping claim. Zaccary Abrahams, about fifty, swarthy faced, peered through heavy gold-rimmed glasses.

His sharp, black eyes looked out over a long, hooked nose, and gave him an appearance somewhat of a perched predatory eagle. Yet he was known as a fair man, prepared to give value for money. He habitually wore long, sweeping meticulously clean, heavy, calico aprons; the big waist pocket held tape, scissors, knife, and a note pad with pencil attached. He hovered close to the big door off the front street waiting to usher in any potential customer. The sight of Bridget and the girls coming down the crushed oyster shell footpath, brought Zac to a state of keen alert. It wasn't often potential sales of the calibre that could be here came down the street of Ballina. He grabbed his broom and tidied the already immaculate entrance.

'Good morning, ladies. We have some fine Christmas gifts.'

He knew Bridget from her days on the cart, in overalls with hat or cap covering her cropped hair. He had thought her attractive then, now dressed well, with long, red hair down to her shoulders, he had not been mistaken.

'Good morning, Mr Abrahams. These are my daughters. Yes, we could be interested in looking at some of your wares.'

He ushered them inside. They wanted some present for Bridget Hilardt and maybe this was a chance.

'Perhaps a baby plate or cup Mr Abrahams.'

Bridget's request sent Zac scurrying up his step ladder to a top shelf. He came down with a big box that he sat on the strong, clean pine bench. He rummaged inside and proceeded to unpack the various "bunny" plates, feeding cups and bowls.

'These are very best quality English china.'

He rubbed them attentively with a soft cloth and sat them back on their pink tissue paper wrapping. Zac walked down the inside of the long counter, and busied himself so his customers could discuss in privacy. When he came back, they had placed a bowl, a plate and a mug side by side.

'How much for these Mr Abrahams?' Bridget smiled at him. 'You are right these are very nice, but they may be too dear for us.'

'Ah Mrs Baillie, they are not dear for the quality. Five shillings, three and sixpence and two and sixpence. Together they are a lovely set and I will sell you the three for ten shillings.'

'All right Mr Abrahams. Will you pack them for us.'

'That I will and I'll give you a plain white card to go in the box.'

He came back with a card.

'While you write on the card, I'll pack them carefully.'

Bridget handed over her 10 shillings.

'There are many things here in my shop Mrs Baillie. Clothing and the like if you wish to look.'

'When we have paid our visit, we may come back Mr Abrahams.'

'My prices are competitive and I look after my customers.'

They smiled and thanked the Jewish merchant.

Their knock on the Hilardt's door was quickly answered by Edna.

'Dick told me you were coming.' She kissed her visitors and ushered them in.

'Where is she?' Jane demanded.

'Asleep in her crib. She will wake for her feed soon. Go and look.'

The girls needed no second bidding. Bridget and Edna sat in the little drawing room.

'Is it all going well being a mother?' Bridget asked.

'Yes. We are managing fine. Carmel keeps her eye on us. Dick is very good and does his best to help. He even seems to have weaned himself off drink again, now that the excitement has settled down.'

The girls came back in.

'She's beautiful. You did well. We can't wait for her to wake up.'

'Don't worry it won't be long. She likes her feeds.'

They gave Edna their gifts.

'You've been too kind.' Edna had tears in her eyes.

'Did your mother tell you that it was her task to deliver Bridget?'

'No, she certainly did not. She tells us nothing.'

Mary put her arm around her mother.

'So that's why she's called Bridget. Gee Mum, you are even better than we thought.'

'Ah well, she was ready to arrive and wasn't waiting any longer. Edna was the clever one. And Martin, we needed him; he threw in some useful prayers as well as hot water.'

'Gee he must have been a nervous wreck,' said Janey.

Baby Bridget was busily working on extracting her lunch time feed from Edna's breasts when Dick arrived home for a meal. The girls put out lunch and told him how the Riordans were faring. He was always pleased to hear that the Riordans were making progress with the block.

'Blackie looks after the three children and Nell as his full-time job,' Jane told him.

'Nell gets things to grow better than anyone else on the plateau. She has all sorts of fruit trees that are bearing fruit and her chooks and cows always seem to do the right thing.'

A visit to Flahertys and another venture into Abrahams' shop saw the afternoon well gone when they reclaimed Major and set out for home. Many small parcels filled the sulky luggage box and the girls considered it a satisfactory day.

'We could do this again before we have to go back to school,' Mary told her mother.

'I am not made of money,' Bridget informed her daughters, 'But we may have to shop for clothes for you both to take away to school. Nell will make your uniforms but it is probably easier to buy much of what you want.'

They met up with Martin, Thomas, and the wagon at the first lane. The cavalcade made it through the gate and around to the stable. John Richards was there filling in the book of his day's deliveries. He was an honest reliable young man, keen to learn and to do a job well.

'I'll help with the horses,' he told Martin and Bridget.

'No John, you've attended to your horse and harness. You get on home. There are plenty of us, and morning will come quickly.' Bridget was firm. Mary stayed with a dust coat over her street clothes, while Bridget and Jane went to prepare the evening meal. The parcels could stay at the stables overnight.

'Did Dick tell you about Bob Beames?' Martin asked later when there was a lull in conversation around the table.

'No. He only remarked that you'd taken a load and got away early. Bob does not like O'Reillys so he's not likely to be polite to you.'

'Well, he does not seem to be a good judge of distance. I'm happy to keep out of his way, but perhaps, when he's more sociable I'll try to have a talk with him.'

'He's a difficult man,' was all Bridget said.

Everyone was ready for an early night and it wasn't late when Martin and Bridget made it to their bedroom. Light out. She started to undress.

'You should be ready for sleep,' Bridget said in mock censure, when his arms brought her into an embrace that needed no words. The fire grew. They lay as one body. Messages spread. Asking, coaxing, seeking, demanding, yet desiring to give, not just to take. Completion came. They remained spent in each other's arms.

'I love you,' he whispered.

'M'mm. Go to sleep. You need your rest; you are a working man now.' She snuggled into his side.

Blunting the Edges

Lochie Paterson was a lowland Scot who had settled on the Big Scrub plateau after the 1861 Robertson Land Act made selection possible. His block was a good one, well-watered by a constant creek. The cedar had brought an early cash flow, and he was smart enough to seek out and market the many other good timbers that most settlers just felled and burnt. Often settlers wasted much good timber in their over- riding ambition to clear, burn and bring the rich, red soil quickly under maize.

He had learnt fundamental wood working skills in Scotland before seeking a new life in NSW. Employment as a joiner in Sydney was his introduction to the many timbers that came from the northern coastal region. He had worked hard, trying, testing, asking questions of tradesmen, and forming his own opinions. The keenly sought red gold, *Toonis Australis*, was the fashion symbol of Australian joinery, soft, easy to work - and easy to damage. He found planks of beech, rosewood, the different teaks, the pines, silky oak to be all good timbers and an open book of learning for Australian cabinet makers.

It was a job down on the wharves replacing a couple of split teak planks high in the hull of a coastal trader, that made him aware of Ballina and the Big Scrub plateau from whence the high rainfall timbers came. He sought and found a couple of white beech planks in a timber yard that he felt would make a good repair on the ship.

'Are ye happy for me to use these beech planks?' he asked the Master of the damaged ship, Captain McKinnon.

'You are the shipwright, not me mon. Beech is used plenty I've not heard any problems. Go to it, we want to get back out to sea. How long will it take ye.'

'Give me a useful offsider and I could have you out tomorrow.'

'I'll gi' ye two and take me coat off m'self if ye can do it that quick.'

The job went well. The beech planks cut, curved, and pegged

home to the ribs, were snug and tight. Lochie found the pale, yellow, close grained oily timber a pleasure to work. They tapped home the long strings of oakum sealing into the seams. By lunch time of the next day, he was packing his big tool chest.

'Are ye happy with our deal?' Captain Mckinnon asked.

'Yes, your men helped, not a hard job. Would ye take me up on a trip to Ballina when I can get time off?'

'That I could, and willingly if ye be prepared to risk the Ballina bar.'

Lochie Paterson took his trip. He looked, liked what he saw and eventually was a successful applicant for the block he called Inverness. He built the house and married Bonnie, daughter of a Sydney Presbyterian Minister for the church they both attended at the water side suburb of Balmain. In time, they moved to the coastal Duck Creek plateau and prospered through hard work.

It was approaching midday when Martin with Spud in the cart, made their way down the track to Inverness. He had unloaded several items to other places north of Duck Creek and now only the big cast iron stove remained with him in the cart. He realised the Patersons were probably hoping it would arrive to cook their Christmas dinner. Martin wondered whether to avoid what he knew would be a difficult meeting and leave this delivery to Dan or John. No. He decided he would not shirk his meeting with Lochie. He would see the stove to its destination. The Paterson home had been a regular call on his ministerial round; he had stayed with them overnight on several occasions. He knew Lochie, a church elder, had been vocal in condemning his marriage to Bridget, and adamant there was no place for a serving Presbyterian minister with a Catholic wife. He knew Bonnie would dutifully follow her husband's lead, but he wondered whether she felt as strongly on his shortcomings, as did her husband.

Lochie saw the O'Reilly Carriers cart coming down the track. He recognised the solid form of Martin well before his arrival and stood hands on hips awaiting the cart.

'Whoa boy.' Martin descended from the cart reading his reception.

'I thought the stove could be handy for Christmas.'

'Kind of ye to be sure.' Lochie's hands still sat belligerently on hips and he had a face of granite.

'So ye have a new boss. Looks like she keeps you busy. How you going to get that stove out?'

Martin eyed him off calmly and kept animosity from his voice.

'I suppose that depends on whether you are prepared to help or not Lochie. I have planks and a winch and can put it down right where I am, or where you tell me. I would be very happy to help put it in your kitchen if that is of assistance to you.'

It was then that Bonnie arrived.

'Hello Martin. It's good to see you and its good of you to bring the stove so promptly. I did not really think that I'd have it for Christmas. O'Reilly Carriers are prompt. Why not come and have a cup of tea before you get it out. It looks very heavy to me.'

'Thanks Bonnie. It depends on Lochie.' He looked steadily at the dour Scot.

'Tie up your horse. Ye can unload later at the steps.'

Spud was tied to a tree and Martin made use of the dish of water offered by Bonnie.

The Patersons had four small children from six down to twelve months old. They lined up on the veranda to watch this big occasion. Martin had christened all four and was genuinely interested as he asked Bonnie of their progress.

'Robert should be going to school, but it is a long way for him to ride on his own over to your school. There could be one closer soon. If not, we will have to find him a quiet pony.'

'Miss Cavanagh is a good teacher and very interested in her pupils,' Martin addressed Bonnie.

'H'mph we'll work it out,' said Lochie.

There was little conversation at the ample table. Martin knew Bonnie wanted to talk, but it was obvious Lochie was silently voicing his protest about what he saw as betrayal of a minister's sacred duty. The somewhat quiet meal ended.

'Thank you so much Bonnie.' Martin excused himself.

He backed Spud over and laid the stout planks to the veranda.

'Its heavy, Lochie, if you have no problem, I'll pull it on to the veranda with the winch.'

Martin found a suitable anchor point and eased the stove onto the planks and then slowly to the veranda.

'Lochie was wondering how he was going to get it on the veranda. You've solved that problem. Maybe it could be going now to cook our Christmas dinner.' Bonnie's thanks caused her husband to scowl even more deeply. He retreated to find his cheque book. When he had gone, Bonnie smiled at Martin.

'He'll come around you know,' she said softly. 'I hope you and Bridget are very happy.'

'Thanks Bonnie, we are happy.'

Lochie returned, wrote a cheque in silence. Martin gave him a receipt, climbed in the cart and started for home.

'Happy Christmas,' he called to the waving children.

Well, he allowed himself a wry smile, it was not worse than he expected. He knew the reception would be cool in many families who had once looked forward to his arrival.

Bond of Humanity

Billy Montez had come down across the dividing ranges, his itinerary always a day to day happening. To those who sometimes asked what steered his course, his reply was, 'I'm a little trading ship that runs with a friendly breeze.'

He could tinker tools or resuscitate a musical instrument wherever it happened. His needs were few. In the handcart always a tight bundle of clothes for an occasion; sometimes that bundle may go a year without being needed.

His normal attire was all of strong cloth that he could skilfully mend until the time came for replacement. The boots he wore always perfect fitting soft hide that enabled his neat feet to walk where he asked. They were the one item of his attire to which Billy paid due deference. His feet were his motive transport, they must be kept in good order. There was a felt hat for winter, a straw for summer.

Attire always neat, manner always polite: that was Billy Montez.

It was three days to Christmas. Billy had grave doubts as to his religious affiliation. Was Christmas important to him? Well, he liked the manger story. Sometimes at night under a bright canopy of stars, he pondered the subject. There was a battered little Bible in his tin box, which he sometimes read. His strange life gave hands on contact in a world of beauty, of greed, of pain, of kindness, of birth, of death, of reality. It honed an awareness that life was a great gift. He acknowledged a cockney gypsy was likely to be a spiritual vagrant, but at times he felt an inkling, of what that Jew Jesus had taught by example. He felt it was all a little too much for Billy Montez. He would follow down toward Duck Creek- perhaps he would drift into the little community where he'd been welcome in the past and see how their lives were heading. He knew the community would sorely miss Patrick O'Reilly.

He reached Casino in the afternoon. The Camerons' little shop may have a few trinkets he could buy as presents. There should be children where he was going, to receive a Christmas gift. He had faith in children.

'Good afternoon, Mr Cameron.' The little shop was empty. David Cameron peered at his customer.

'Good day to ye. I know ye don't I?'

'We met a few years ago. Billy Montez, tinker and a drifter, that's me.'

'Ah mon, I remember, you're a great musician. Can I help you Mr Montez, or ha' ye just dropped in for a chat?'

'Have you any little children's gifts for Christmas? I hope to make Duck Creek, just thought you may have something.'

'There's a box with a few odds and ends somewhere.' He called out, 'Maisie.'

His wife arrived.

'What have we for children? This is Mr Montez.'

They produced a box, brushed dust off the top. In it were skipping ropes, hair ribbons, combs, a pocketknife, picture books. Billy chatted with the Camerons while Maisie Cameron wrapped six items he carefully selected.

'Can ye afford eight shillings?' David Cameron asked.

'That's no problem, Mr Cameron.' Billy produced the money.

'Would you join us for a cup of tea Mr Montez?' Mrs Cameron appreciated the generosity of the polite gypsy.

'Thank you, Mrs Cameron, if I'm no trouble.'

Seated at the table, they chatted and Billy praised his hostess's home-made cake.

'I thought to call on the Reverend Baillie, would he be home?'

'No. But if you be going to Duck Creek, you will find him there. He is no longer a minister. He married Bridget O'Reilly recently. He is now working as a carrier.'

Mrs Cameron gave him the information.

'Thank you, that is news. I hope they will be happy. Thank you for telling me. It was the sad time of Patrick O'Reilly's death when last I was in this area.'

'Ah, Baillie was a good minister; they tell me he is doing alright as a carrier.'

David Cameron left it at that and Billy Montez took his leave.

Christmas Gifts

The last few days before Christmas saw O'Reilly Carriers on the road, cleaning up the jobs. The big shed at Duck Creek was about empty and Bridget had told Dan Riordan to take the week off after Christmas.

'I don't want to see you back before the New Year.'

The Riordans planned to stay with Carmel for a few days. Nell had been persuaded that her neighbours could look after the animals while she was absent. It would be their first break away from Tara. Rose and Pearl would move in while the family were away. Any goods that arrived in Ballina by ship could wait until the first trip down between Christmas and New Year.

The weather all the week had been sticky hot and Norah Brewster was worried lest the Christmas Eve party attract a storm that was overdue.

'Don't worry Norah, there's nought you can do. Even you can't organise the weather,' Jim Brewster assured his wife.

They had decided to put up tarpaulins for the occasion as they had for the wedding. Martin Baillie was coming early in the afternoon with extra ropes and tarps to help with the job. Bridget and the girls would be there with the final cooking and setting up. Surreyville was used to social occasions and Norah was in her element checking off the details. She had a willing helper in Isabel Cavanagh. Edna's replacement was a dedicated career teacher in her fifties. It seemed unlikely that she would forsake her profession for any personable mature male, but at times Norah worried. Miss Cavanagh had settled in well, and the school would be full in the coming year.

After breakfast at Killarney, Martin went to the stables and packed a cart with tarps and ropes for the party annex. Seeing that her family were occupied, Bridget made her way over to the stable.

'Checking that I'm working, huh?' Martin threw in another tarp.

'Yes, can't have you loafing. But I want to talk to you on our own.'

He smiled at her. 'I'm listening.'

'It's about Pearl. I've had it in the back of my mind for a long while that perhaps we could send her to Rose Bay with Jane. I know there is a lot to be thought out, perhaps it is not a good idea. I want your opinion after you have given it your best consideration. No answers yet. You are to think of all the pros and cons that go with my wild idea.'

'Perhaps there is no answer, but I'll think, and we should pray for wisdom.'

'All right, King Solomon, something else you can do in your spare time.'

She stood close to him behind the cart and lifted her face. He kissed her lips, her nose, her forehead. She wriggled out, and round the cart.

'I'd best be gone.'

'Delilah,' he said softly.

'Sean, why is Blackie barking?'

Nell, busy packing clothes for the family holiday, sent the sturdy three-year-old to investigate. Obviously, Blackie was not very perturbed, it was not his demanding bark. Sean scampered out to their small front lean-to veranda. He came back.

'Man. Small cart.' Sean did not say much, but he was starting to string words together.

'Right. Good boy.' She left her packing and went to the veranda, half expecting an O'Reilly vehicle. She straight way knew their visitor.

'Why Mr Montez, it's good to see you. We sometimes wonder where you are.'

'I too, wonder how my friends are at Duck Creek. Your son was a small baby when I was here last. Look at him now.'

'Come in and make yourself comfortable while you meet my family; I will make a cup of tea.'

'You have done wonders with your little home, and you must have the best garden I've seen for months. It is good to see life has treated you well.'

'Ah, I've been so lucky, God gave me a good man. He should be home soon. There's a party at Brewsters late this afternoon, you will be a great Christmas present for us all.'

'Do you think I can come uninvited?'

'Yes, and you are now invited. They would never forgive me if you didn't come.'

Nell proudly showed him her children. Then she showed him their orchard and her two pens of chooks. White Leghorns for egg supply and the big, speckled Plymouth Rocks as potential meat birds.

'You really are a farmer, Nell.'

She told him the news of Edna and Dick Hilardt and baby Bridget.

Also, the marriage of Bridget O'Reilly and Martin Baillie. He admitted his visit with the Camerons, and his gathering of that news about the Baillie wedding. The rest Nell reckoned he would find out for himself later. Billy Montez soon excused himself and walked on down toward Surreyville and Killarney.

It was Mary O'Reilly who spotted the little handcart coming down the lane. The Brewster kitchen was a hive of activity and Mary, with a position near the big window cutting up sandwiches, looked out with envy toward the open space and sunshine of a fine afternoon. She wanted to abandon her task and fly off to meet her Gypsy friend but decided to follow protocol and seek permission.

'Mrs Brewster, I think it's Mr Montez coming down the lane, may I ask him to the party?'

'Of course, we haven't seen him for years. I hope he'll stay and work on the piano later.' Norah smiled at the girl. 'He will wonder who the young lady is.'

Mary headed across the grass paddock to the lane.

'Hello Mr Montez. I knew it had to be you.'

'Mary O'Reilly, it is, but it isn't. Just stand a moment and let me look. Why you are more beautiful than your mother. Is it really so long since I came down this enchanted lane? Mary, I want to know all about you.'

'Yes, Mr Montez we will talk. Mrs Brewster knows of your coming, she let me off sandwich making, to come and invite you to the party. She hopes you will look at the piano.'

'I cheated, Mary. Nell Riordan told me of the party, so I already snared an invitation.'

As they walked up to the house, they were joined by Jane, Thomas and Pearl. Billy Montez knew those vibes luring him back to Duck Creek were still in tune. It was a place of friendly people, like a safe harbour for a storm-tossed ship. It called him back

A couple of hours later, he put the front and top back on the Brewster Lipp and placed his long tuning tool and his tape cutters back in their box. The big dining room was empty but there was a buzz of activity in other parts of the house. He sat and carefully listened to each note as he worked up the keyboard. Perhaps, still not quite perfect but much, much, better. The recent years of humid coastal climate had caused problems that would take more time to restore full potential of this fine instrument. He closed the lid on the ivory keys. Many of the Brewster guests were arriving. He sought out Norah.

'It sounds much better now. Before I leave the plateau, I will finish the job.'

She ran her hands over a couple of simple scales on the keyboard.

'Mr Montez, you are a wizard. I did not realise how bad this piano was until I tried it now. Please feel free to use the room out in the shed. There is hot water and a towel. Come and join us when you wish. The food and guests will be out on the veranda and under covers on the lawn.'

When he joined the guests later, it was as the suave colourful gypsy, not the cockney tinker. His bundle of black satin clothes had shaken free of most creases. He wore the red silk cummerbund and a cravat carefully knotted added a striking contrast. His black, wavy hair carried a much greater sprinkling of grey, the deep-set dark eyes gave a hint of seeing both outward and inward. Billy Montez carried a visual imprint of his lineage. He was a performer, not needing the props of wealth or stage. His story line carried onward by the genealogy of a thousand years of roaming on-the-spot performers.

He found Bridget and Martin to offer his congratulations and good wishes.

'I'm sure you deserve each other and I see many years of happiness will be yours.'

The party went well as did most functions hosted by the Brewsters. The food circulated freely with Jane, Pearl and Gwen Richards, young waitresses seeing the guests had well filled plates. A table stocked with some bottled alcoholic drinks and non-alcoholic punch was set up on the lawn. As day faded, the hurricane lanterns took over under the tarpaulins, casting friendly shadows of goblin gloom in some corners.

Jim Brewster tinkled a fork on his glass.

'Friends. Tomorrow is Christmas and it is our pleasure to wish you all the compliments of the season. We know some of our guests with children will not stay late so now is the time to say that Norah and I are delighted to have you with us. It is a happy surprise to have Mr Montez arrive this afternoon, most of you know him from his efforts when we were fundraising for our school. Those who don't, will realise later when he performs for us, his musical abilities. So, enjoy yourselves, and Happy Christmas.'

Norah took over his place on the steps.

'What is Christmas without some carols. So let us hear how we can sing. Miss Cavanagh will play for us from the drawing room, the tune should drift out. See how we go.'

Isabel started up with *Oh, Come all ye Faithful*. Norah gathered a few to the veranda stage and they sang the carol with gusto. The strong baritone of Martin Baillie balancing the majority soprano voices of the women. Billy Montez pulled his harmonica from an inside pocket, joined the piano, lifting volume of the tune. Soon, most were singing. They ran through half a dozen carols and people joined in, people who at the start, said as matter of course, 'Not me. I can't sing.'

'There I knew we could sing,' said Norah, and added, 'Mary O'Reilly, home for the holidays, has agreed to share her violin skills with us.'

Mary used the veranda as her stage and picked up Isabel's accompaniment to a Brahms violin solo. She played with confidence and skill, her strong young fingers working the tune and accurately hitting the notes with practised ease. She let the final lingering minor chord drift away. The applause of her small audience was enthusiastic. Billy Montez climbed the three steps and stood beside her.

'My friends. This young lady has a wonderful musical skill. I heard her play that fine piano in there when last I was here some years ago. That she has progressed so far with a violin in this short time amazes me.'

Mary looked at him steadily.

'Thank you, Mr Montez. It was you that made me want to try when I first heard you those years ago. Now it is your turn.'

She handed over her fiddle. Billy took it, holding the instruments neck between thumb and index finger. To her he said, 'Arabella is by the piano. I tuned her while working on the Lipp, please bring her out.'

He took Mary's instrument and ran the bow lightly over the strings, finding the notes and taking in the feel of the instrument, tucked it under his chin and started playing an old Gypsy dance tune.

When Mary joined him, carrying his age darkened violin and bow, he stopped. She held out his old instrument toward him. He smiled, shook his head.

'No. You play. Arabella will sing for you. This one is fine for me.

Mozart sonatas. You know, them just let your fingers follow.'

They played and the people, the veranda, the night, all drifted away. So many times, his fingers had coaxed, caressed, brought to life the *anima* soul of his old violin. Now his ears listened to other young fingers that skilfully caressed the old ebony fingerboard. He led, he joined, and imperceptibly, he followed. The music flowed. Mary O'Reilly lifted and soared into the purity of melody, by the flowing resonance of the instrument. She had the eerie feeling that the notes were coming of themselves, in front of her busy fingers.

It was probably a quarter of an hour that they played together. Even people listening with no great appreciation of music hung on the notes with pleasure.

When they stopped there was silence, then applause and many requests to play more. Billy looked to Mary, she shook her head, sweat beads glistened on her forehead, her fingers felt incredibly used.

'Thank you. Perhaps Mr Montez would give us one more number.'

He took Arabella.

'Just one. We'll finish with your great Christmas hymn *Silent Night*. May we all have a Happy Christmas.'

He let the haunting, simple tune of spiritual hope soar through those still present. Some voices took up the carol. Then it was over. People were anxious for home and to be ready for Christmas in the morning.

Billy Montez distributed his packages wrapped by Mrs Cameron, to the Riordans, to Tom and Jane O'Reilly, one to Pearl, and a couple to the young Richards children. He agreed to join the Baillies for Christmas dinner.

The tidy up process was rapidly attended to, and Norah insisted the Baillies and Mr Montez join the Brewsters for a drink and a piece of her special Christmas cake.

He found Mary.

'You will play, just for me before I head off on the track,' Billy smiled at her. 'Your talent has given me happiness. And it has solved a great problem. I am not prattling idle praise, whoever has brought you so far in such a short time must also see your talent.'

Mary told him of Sister Benedict.

'She has put much time into me but has been honest. She says being a top-class musician often demands too high a price. I have one more year at school to see where I am heading. People frown at female musicians outside of a home parlour, so I probably have no real future as a performer.'

Christmas day carried with it the tempo of a dry, but humid north coast summer. Toward late afternoon, a distant bank of cumulus cloud lay as flattened, sugar-browned meringue on the western hills. Perhaps tomorrow a storm would brew. Mary and Billy had wandered away toward the creek. A big teak log beside the creek acted as a seat to anyone wishing to listen and watch the clear water bubbling over the stony ford.

They sat on the log and watched the water. Billy Montez spoke carefully to the girl beside him.

'It has been for me a happy day. I chose my nomad life and it suits me well, but I know there is a price to pay. I am growing old; it does not worry me. I have no wealth for folks to squabble over. My kin are in another world and probably untraceable so where my body will lie at death is in the future and does not cause me worry. Many of my Romany forebears would lie in strange, unmarked graves; it has ever been the lot of my people. There is only one possession that I worry over, it deserves a caring owner, and that's where you could help. I want you to take Arabella as my Christmas gift to you.'

'I could not Mr Montez. Your violin is part of you.'

'Mary, that is exactly why you must. I will be happy knowing the instrument will be played and looked after. When I die, probably on some lonely track, the violin could be destroyed because no one would expect an instrument of that quality in a gypsy tinker's cart of junk.'

'What about when you want to play?'

'I can pick up any old instrument and coax it into shape, so that it would sound fine. Did you feel Arabella suited your fingers?'

'It seemed the music just floated out. It was uncanny. I have not had that feeling before.'

'Arabella was crafted in Cremona in the mid-1700s. Her maker's mark indicates an apprentice of Stradivarius. Believe me, she could take you far.'

'You will have to let me talk to my mother. Perhaps if you took my instrument?'

'No, you need a spare and that's a nice violin. I'll find a fiddle that will travel comfortably with me. You would make an old man happy by my knowing Arabella was with someone who could feel her voice.'

It happened that way.

Rose and Yan

The subject of Pearl and the convent school in Sydney came to the Baillie table a couple of weeks after Christmas. Bridget and Martin decided the family should offer thoughts on the idea of Pearl Yanohavovich going with Jane to the Rose Bay convent.

Mary thought a while.

'I have doubts, it was hard enough for me. Pearl is bright enough to handle the work but how would she be shut up in a convent? Would she cope? How would Rose be without her? Jan would be in favour; he would want to give Pearl her chance. It is generous of you Mum but let them make up their own minds. It is not to be your decision.'

Jane came out with her flippant approach.

'I'm not keen on going myself. Maybe if Pearl goes and we don't like it, we could run away. I agree with Mary it's for them to make up their minds.'

Thomas gave his wise contribution.

'Pearl knows and sees many things that we can't. She likes to learn.'

It was decided the Yanohavoviches would be approached with Bridget's idea and left to form their own important decision.

They waited until Yan was having a time at home between his clearing jobs and invited the family over. Rose was still employed at Killarney for at least one day a week and Pearl often came with her to help or spend time with the O'Reilly children. So, it was agreed, they would come for Sunday lunch and the proposition of Pearl going away to school be introduced. The proposition was made. Rose and Pearl looked to Jan for an initial answer to the suggestion.

'It very generous. I don't know. I would have to pay some of cost. Do you think nuns would take our Pearl?'

Bridget could only answer that an approach could be made, if the Yanohavoviches decided this was what they thought best for Pearl. She expressed her opinion that she thought it was probable the convent at Rose Bay would accept Pearl as a student.

It was agreed that an approach be made to the convent, and if they agreed, then Pearl would go. A reply came back from Mother Cecilia. Yes, she would take Pearl. The weeks slid by.

All too soon the end of January saw feverish activity, with Nell Riordan busy making uniforms and some of the underclothes for Pearl's school wardrobe. Pearl was saying little about the huge change of circumstances about to descend upon her. No longer would she be free to wander the bush and rain forest. Her ability to track and find the forest animals and to know where they would be feeding on the fruiting trees, would be lost in the city. Pearl hoped she would be accepted and find satisfaction in the white man's world. She was old enough to know her life held problems of her birth. Rose had said go, but Pearl was worried at leaving her mother.

The holidays sped by and it was arranged the three girls would leave on the *Aphrodite* from Ballina on the next Wednesday. Weather and bar permitting, the adventure for Jane and Pearl would commence. Mary was a seasoned sailor and could try to keep them from harm. The Sunday lunch at Killarney was for the Yanohavoviches and Baillies to come together and check that all was ready. After lunch, the girls and Thomas decided to walk down to the big fig tree on the creek bank. There it would be cool from the heat of the day and Thomas took a tin, a couple of long strings and some meat scraps. Sometimes the big yabbies would hang on long enough to be trapped in the tin.

Thomas worked his lines down into the deep water. Yabbies soon started feeding but dropped off before he could work them over his submerged tin.

'Want to try?' he said to Pearl.

She had taught him how to coax the yabbies up and he knew she was better at it than he.

'I'm not supposed to get dirt on my dress.' But she lay close beside him on her stomach, took a line and became absorbed in the task. In no time she had a couple of big yabbies in the tin.

'Just ease the meat away very gently.' She guided his hand and the string, making sure his touch was slow and steady. They trapped another yabby.

'It just takes practice; you can do it.'

'I'll miss you, Pearl.'

'I'll miss you too, Thomas.'

They decided three big yabbies were enough and gave up their fishing.

'Let's go up to the sand bar and get cool,' Janey suggested.

They walked up along the bank to the bend where the fine, predominantly milk coffee-coloured sandy gravel settled when the creek was in flood, leaving a place to walk out into the water. Even Mary took off her shoes. The girls tucked up their skirts and they ventured knee deep in the cold, running water. They had been coming here for years and knew it was safe on the gravel bar. The depth increased quickly as the water colour deepened to green in the big pool. Bridget had taught Patrick to swim off the sand bar and given all her children basic "dog paddling" lessons, but they knew not to go swimming on their own.

Rose had taught Pearl to swim at an early age. She came from generations of water-dwelling people who swam and dived from when they could walk. Pearl had swum naked in this and many other pools, when she was sure no one was around. Her body seemed as one with the soft, caressing water. She could dive deep, viewing the underwater world of settled stones. That was her secret. She knew future nude swimming was out now they were sending her off to a convent for education.

They paddled for a while and let the caressing clear water wander around, talking to their knees, cooling, whispering seductive messages. Then it was time for home.
But then even Pearl knew very little of her mother.

Rose had an affiliation with the sea. She came from the local coastal tribe. For thousands of years, they had wandered the coastal belt between shore and range, where fishing, shellfish gathering, spearing the big stingrays and swimming were normal lubra functions. As a girl, she had swum naked, unashamed, relishing the caress of the salt water on her developing body. Past puberty and reaching the age of sexual maturity she was given, as it had long been planned, to a warrior of the tribe. Unfortunately, he had grown cranky, scarred and old, but he was still an important boss elder of the tribe. When he could not achieve sexual relations with the girl, he blamed the teenage virgin for his lack of virility and accused her of sleeping around with some of the young bucks. This was totally untrue; she had obeyed all the sexual taboos for girls of the tribe. Cruelly, he disowned her, beat her to a pulp with his nulla nulla, and threw her out, all because his sexual functions were finished.

Battered, bruised, scorned and abused, she fled inland from the tribe. She sought solitude in the dense scrub hinterland to try and heal her injuries. Those injuries were extensive, because not content with pounding her ribs and face, her ravisher had repeatedly abused her virginal vagina.

For two days she lay near a clear, running stream. She used big, soft, green leaves of the cunjevoi and a patch of white clay to cover and heal her external abrasions and bruises. Soaking in the cold, clear water, the burning fever pains of her internal injuries were temporarily eased.

She was able to gather a few berries and roots but was constantly hungry. Fever from her festering internal tears set in and a near constant delirium took over. In the dream world, she was a piccaninny again, back in the rough bark family gunyah. She saw the big grey and white fish eagles circling, perching in riverside trees; she felt they would soon swoop and pick her up in strong claws, then it would all be over. Deeper she shrank into the rotting leaf mould under the root stanchions of the streamside tree.

Close to death, her body was shutting down. It would soon have fed to the rich, organic mulch, had Yan, in his searching out millable cedar trees along the rambling small creek, not stumbled upon the unconscious girl.

At first, he thought she was dead, but as he watched, he noticed the slight movement of her chest. He took in her exterior injuries, the leaves and the mud she had been using to treat them. Those injuries looked clean. Feeling the hot, dry nature of her skin, he recognised the deep fever that possessed her body. He wondered why.

There were no Aboriginal people in the immediate area. He knew too, that most white people in his situation would walk away, making sure not to see an injured Aboriginal. But Yan couldn't just leave her here to die, without trying to help. Certainly, she was only a girl, and looked like she had been healthy before whatever disaster had befallen her. His crude slab hut was a little further up the creek, only about half a mile. Perhaps he could carry her. He stowed the big saw and axe in a suitable root buttress. There was no track as such, so it would be slow carrying her back to his camp.

Several times on the way to the shack, he laid her down, took a brief rest. Once she moaned quietly and made sounds that were probably in her language. Other than that, she lay inert in his arms, not that heavy but awkward to carry. Eventually, he brought her in through the hut opening. His only furniture was a primitive bed, axe fashioned, covered with soft branches for a mattress and a heavy grey wool blanket. Perhaps she would be more comfortable on the ground but he laid her on the bed. If she survived, well he could knock up another bed until she was better. For now, he felt she must be kept comfortable until he could find the cause of her fever and hopefully bring it down.

Jan had knowledge of ailments. He had needed fundaments of first aid many times in his forty years of life. He had learned about fever from practical experience. The last time had been years ago on his trip to Australia. Severe fever contagion had swept their ship. He remained healthy and his nursing skill, most of it learned as a soldier, helped earn him praise from the ship's captain for his unrewarded effort. His life, to all whom he had met in Australia, was a closed book: some speculated as to his past but he kept that story his own possession.

Brought up in Serbia, he had been a soldier, a non- commissioned officer in the army at Belgrade. In his mid-twenties he had struck up a tempestuous love affair with a merchant's daughter. She was dark, passionate, and a few years younger than he. She had been the driving force in a relationship, leading him to an engagement and they planned to marry. He was posted away for army exercises in the country; his unit returned days earlier than expected. On arriving back, he went to her parents' house where she lived in a small attached self-contained villa. There was no response to his knock at the door. He made his way to her villa entrance, afire to surprise her, take her into his arms. Through the narrow, open hallway, he made for her chamber and burst in through the open door. This brought into sight her bed. He was stunned. She and one of his unit officers were naked and copulating, an oblivious mix of arms and legs. First, there was the shock, then a hot rage grabbed him. He entered, slamming the door behind him.

'Come back later,' the lieutenant snapped at him.

She disengaged herself, rolled out of bed and fled behind the high canopy.

Army protocol said a sergeant could never question an officer, but

Yan was prepared to throw his career out, with this finding of his two-timing fiancée. In the heat of anger, he snapped at the lieutenant.

'Dress and find your sword! Or I'll see you have nothing left to prod with again.'

Yan used the point of his sword and tossed random scattered pieces of uniform from around the room to the officer. He speared her silk pink underpants from one part of the room and her ornate blouse from another and flicked them to her.

'Put them on!' he gritted at her cowering form.

He stood with his back to the only door, watching them struggle into clothes.

'Be reasonable sergeant, I'm your officer. You can't demand satisfaction of me. I'll have you arrested. It is best we forget this happened.'

Yan balanced the long sword lightly in his right hand.

'That's right, but you'll have to get out of this room first.'

When the officer had most of his uniform on, Yan picked up the officer's ornate, jewelled sword and threw it on the bed. The lieutenant grabbed it and flew at Yan in the confined space of the room, but he was far too slow. Yan sidestepped and drove his own sword, deep into the officer's shoulder, the jewelled sword clattered back to the floor. Blood gushed from a deep, debilitating wound. She screamed in terror, but Yan scowled at her.

'Pack up that arm. Get a surgeon. If he doesn't bleed to death he may marry you. I won't.'

Two days later, Yan crossed into Austria and continued down into

Italy. Years later, he made it to the other side of the world and Australia.

Yan was usually a mild, calm man. Once Rose was on his bed, he lifted her head and tried to ease a little water into her mouth. He was heartened by the fact that she swallowed several times. A fire lit and a kerosene tin container of water meant he could bathe and clean her body. Methodically, he worked cleaning her recently matted hair, her face and chest scars and the bruises he felt under her soft dark skin. These all seemed to be doing well. The cause of her high fever must be hidden somewhere else. The bathing process continued down. It had to be done, gently with her turned on a side, warm water and soap he bathed her lower back and buttocks, then laid her face up. The warm water worked over her smooth, flat belly. He noticed a stir of pain as some of the soapy water spilt down between her legs. She stirred but lapsed back into an unconscious state.

It was no use being squeamish. Very gently he placed her legs slightly apart. Damage and a nasty discharge from her vagina seemed to be an obvious reason for the high body fever. He wondered whether she had suffered a miscarriage, but abraded external injuries seemed to indicate the damage came from the outside. All he could do was try and keep her clean and bathe down the temperature. His few bush remedies included a salve based on goanna fat and an aloe cacti that grew wild and freely available. This he used as gently as he could. She moved several times but settled back to her twilight state. Only some fifty yards away a big stand of cunjevois would be useful. It started a long, caring and watching brief until she regained consciousness.

Humanity to the Fore

So, his battle to save Rose began. Late on the second day, he felt she was a trifle cooler. He kept working small quantities of pigeon broth, and at times, water into her mouth. She seemed to have a desire for life and swallowed liquids. He slit the outside skin off the cunjevoi leaves making thin moist suppositories that he was able to work inside her torn and battered vagina. The wide-skinned leaves he used as exterior pads. He kept her bathed and clean. During the second night, he heard her stir. Immediately he was beside the bed. Two big liquid black frightened eyes roamed the shack in the dim lantern light. She made as if to try and jump up, but he took her wrists firmly, shook his head and smiled kindly at her. Terror shone in those luminous eyes; she lay back on the bed, resigned to her fate, just looking at his hands.

There was no chance of verbal communication but he grabbed his ointment tin, placed some of the content on his fingers and gently rubbed it into the hard bruises on her arms. She settled, seeming to receive his message that he was trying to help. Sometimes she glanced briefly at him with frightened but intelligent eyes. He felt she was aware he would not hurt her further. He sat with her through the night and felt the fever breaking out of her body. Could he be sure she wouldn't try and escape like a frightened half healed animal? He brought her broth and some well boiled meaty pigeon legs. After a while, she chewed a couple of pigeon bones and he felt confident he was winning the battle.

He was now hopeful she knew he was trying to heal her injuries.

It took days before she could leave the hut. Her physical functions started flowing, blood laden but slowly returning to normal. She abandoned herself to his care. The shock of waking in the hut had been accepted. After many days, Yan tried to show by signs that he must go back to work and that he wanted her to stay in the hut. She nodded. Their sign language was starting to cover basics. At least now, if she fled back to wherever she came from, there was a fair chance she could live.

The cedar came crashing down near the creek. Yan sawed off the top and started trimming away the branches. When he looked up, there was a strange but welcome sight in front of his eyes. She wore one of his old shirts, the tails of which fell almost to her wasted knees and her wire thin legs. In her hand was a billycan of warm stew. She put it down in front of him and stood back. Yan smiled at her.

'Thank you.'

He said it slowly, several times. He saw her lips move, trying to feel and copy his words.

A deep clear pool further along the creek was his bath area. This she found. She shed his shirt and swam in its depths. It seemed her eventual recovery had begun. There was no doubt in his mind she had been shockingly abused and he knew she must still be suffering much pain. He thought she would probably melt away into the bush one day while he was at work and that would be an end to this strange interlude. Perhaps that would be a good result.

It didn't follow that way. She took to cleaning the hut. Cooking rough meals and with the use of twine and pigeon or turkey flesh, fished the deep hole for big, dark yabbies that he didn't even know were there. These she cooked in the fire coals. She watched and soon learned to make dampers, and proudly showed him each new achievement as she assumed her new skills. He had knocked together another rough bush bed. She continued to use the original one.

Other cedar cutters he had met up with in the past, boasted of their lubras' sexual charms, but claimed they were totally lacking in hygiene, and useless around the camp. That description he found all wrong. She watched closely when he washed his rough clothes. Soon she washed the blanket off her bed, his old shirt, that was her entire wardrobe. She kept even her hair clean. Washing his clothes when he changed to his second set became her chore. Always, she went well away from the house for her toilet. The months slipped by and she seemed fit and well. They were now able to understand each other by signs and a few basic words were even starting to function as dialogue between them.

Rose showed no sign of wanting to leave him. At times now, she even looked at him risking a shy smile. One day he arrived home at night to find tea ready by lantern light, and Rose with short-bobbed hair. She had found the big scissors, using them with great effect. Then by the way her hair shone almost purple in the dim light, he guessed she had really soaped and washed it in the creek. Her nervous grin was a shy enquiry of his reaction. She risked a brief look at him with big, dark eyes. He smiled at her.

'Nice,' he said.

She knew he recognised her efforts, her smile widened further and she put out his tea.

Jan found himself looking at her with different eyes. At first it worried him. She had put on weight, was now well rounded, well covered, her legs no longer skinny, her hips had broadened and she moved with easy flowing grace under his old tattered slitted shirt tails. Her firm pressing breasts filled out its twin pockets. It was a long time since he had lain with a woman, and that had been a paid for, not very pleasant commitment. The last one had grabbed his money, quickly worked him to ejaculation, then thrust him out into the night to make way for another customer.

Should he be seeing this primitive black girl as attractive? He had decided to steer clear of women when he cut himself adrift in the scrub. There had been no sexual stirrings whatever when he had carefully tended her torn, intimate areas. He knew the extent of her hurt but had no idea how or why. Was she recovered now; how could he know? He thought he sensed a new awareness in her approach and how she viewed him, but he could be reading her wrong. Was she agreeable, needing, and seeking love making too? He had no way of finding out. He couldn't ask her. The fact she showed no sign of going back to her own people was peculiar.

Under no circumstance would he force himself upon her. They continued on together, accepting a strange non-touching union.

Every night he went to bed tired from a heavy day's work with axe and saw.

One night he woke, not sure when or why. The hut interior around him was impenetrable black, in the heavy shrouds of dark contrast thrown by an outside sinking moon. Some light and shadow crept through the room. He felt, rather than saw, her presence, in the deep shadows near his bed. Her warm, dark, naked shape stood close, looking down at him. Spontaneously, with no planned thought, still half asleep, his hand reached across the space, finding, touching, resting, on the soft, warm luminous silky shine of her thigh. There was no movement away from him by that shadow beside him. She waited for his reaction. She was immobile, impassive, making no move to back away, or come closer. With her keen hearing, he felt sure she would hear the eager pounding, pumping of his heart. She remained there unmoving, waiting.

His hand moved of itself, gently stroking her outside thigh, his fingers wandering over the curve of her buttock. She seemed to find in that caressing touch a message she awaited. He felt her turn to face him, coming slowly closer. Her hand took his and guided it. Her voice was a sound of the night, strange, soft, guttural, deep, "Raaght," a low, basic night bird sound.

She led his fingers to her previously mutilated zone of privacy. The area he had bathed, poulticed, treated with such care, when she had lain, fevered, abraded, torn, festered, close to death. She now felt to him attractive, needed, waiting, offering herself. It seemed a liberal coating of goanna fat and aloes added to the natural lubrication of her body. There could be no misunderstanding her intention. She now stood closer and he breathed her presence.

'Sure?' he asked.

'Raaght,' she breathed her low invitation again. It seemed she was offering, proving, telling him that she was better.

'Thank you.' Softly she spoke her first learnt two-word phrase.

His arm encircled her, until she stood against him beside the rough bed. She came to him confidently now and, in one smooth movement, slid in beside him. Then she melted beneath him, helping his aroused strength deep into her willing, prepared body. Uncomplicated, she offered and asked of this man who had given her back life, to now fill her with his need.

She clung to him briefly after his rapid urgent love-making exploded within her, then made as to return to her own rough, bough bed. But he kept her at his side. They slept together from that night. Their sexual need, dependency and mutual respect, grew apace.

Rose learned how to swing an axe or work the other end of a crosscut saw. She found cedar trees that he did not know existed. She worked with him all day, willing to love him to their exhaustion, long into the night, or, at any time, in any place of secluded dim daytime depth, should their need stir.

Probably, there had been lasting internal damage deep in her uterus, from that first near death cruel assault. Rose only conceived once. That was Pearl, and even then, many years later. It had to be some strange fluke of nature's goodness that it happened at all. The egg and sperm that bonded to make Pearl, somehow managed to survive, travel to its place of safety and grow in her womb. It was totally unexpected but welcomed by both of them. Often through the pregnancy she insisted Yan's hand measure her expanding life carrying belly with pride. Proof for her of their meaningful, complete, love-making.

Eventually, Rose told Yan with signs and limited words the basic story of her abuse.

When the time approached for birth of their child, she wondered about seeking the surviving remnants of the coastal tribe. Some of the old women would probably remember her and assist at the birth if she asked their assistance. She and Yan discussed it in their limited word conversations. He read the fear still present from her ill treatment and forced flight, those many years before.

'We'll manage,' he told her.

'Thank you,' she squatted beside him. Her heavy stomach dropped low to the ground.

'Know how,' she said, and smiled at him.

He made a rare trip to the village at Ballina. He bought a bag full of things. Yards of material, towels, sewing gear, disinfectant, soaps. Not the normal gear for a scrub faller. The storekeeper wondered but saw no need to mention the scrub fallers strange order.

Rose went into labour during the night. By early morning, the baby's head was down in position and Rose followed her people's method of squatting to give birth. She and Yan eased out the slippery bundle that was Pearl. She held her baby up by the feet, gave her a sharp smack that prompted a loud yell from the wrinkled small face. Yan cut and tied the cord, sponged off the blood and mucous, and put the baby in Rose's arms. Even in the dim light he could see the little girl's much paler coloured skin against her mother's full black breast. They laid her in a towel, examined her proudly, minutely; she was perfect. The afterbirth came away. Rose was keen to be on her feet, but Yan made her stay on the bed, brought warm water, with a hint of antiseptic in the mix. He bathed and carefully dried her spent body clean of blood. He insisted she rest on the bed. Gently he sponged, and her white teeth glinted up at him in appreciation. Her hand took his, and to his surprise, she laid her full lips briefly on the back of that big, strong, gentle hand. Kissing had not been a part of their love-making; briefly she offered him something new. He responded, leant and kissed her forehead, his lips tasting a trace of sweat and antiseptic. Yan felt good. There was pride in his fatherhood.

Was there a God after all? What had caused him to find the dying dark girl, heal her, and made him grow to love and need her?

The years slid by. Yan, Rose and Pearl were a family, moving around the edges of the Big Scrub, wherever trees were to be felled, was his work area. Unlike most white men, ashamed of their black women and children they produced, Yan registered the birth of his daughter. Proudly, he claimed fatherhood of Pearl and identified Rose as her mother. Rose stayed away from her fast-diminishing coastal tribe, but taught Pearl many of their ways learnt in her childhood.

When the farming settlers started moving in, work became plentiful for Yan. They found his ability with axe and saw cleared them an area to cultivate or grass over, far more quickly than they managed themselves. As the Big Scrub clearing was achieved, Yan found the primitive cabin and small, steep block, given up by its settler, way out on the fringe of the escarpment. He paid the price in cash and made sure it was legally gifted to Rose and Pearl should anything happen to him.

It seemed to them, not that many years had passed.

New Pupils for Rose Bay

Yan and Rose left the outfitting of Pearl to Bridget and Nell. They came across on the day of the uniform try on. Yan insisted on paying all the costs. The two new scholars were fairly similar in size and Nell had made the long, dark green uniforms to the same pattern with a few modifications. Already, Pearl was sprouting a bust line while Jane was more solid than Mary had been at the same age. Probably, she would end up shorter and more like the build of Patrick.

'Right, let us see how these uniforms are now.'

Nell Riordan took the girls to a bedroom and supervised their dressing. She pulled, pushed and hitched.

'I think that's right enough. Just don't grow too fast.' Nell walked them around. 'Now show your mothers what respectable young ladies you are.'

Bridget smiled confidentially at Rose.

'She'll be fine, Rose. Be proud of her and yourself, you have done a great job.'

The Brewsters and Miss Cavanagh also arrived to comment when the girls emerged complete with large cream straw hats.

'Really it's remarkable, they look grown up,' said Norah.

It was agreed the uniforms were right, they were admired and sent back to change.

Miss Cavanagh gave them a dictionary each and the Brewsters supplied two large books of well-known English literature. Bridget didn't let on that she doubted the Irish nuns would have much call for English literature. It was still a battle for Pearl to read fluently, hopefully the books, any books would help with her battle for words.

It was only left now for the packing to be done and luggage sent down by cart. Tuesday would see O'Reilly Carriers swing into action. It would take two carts and the sulky. Yan was going to see his daughter off. Rose declined.

'You go. I stay.' They both knew she stayed away from Ballina, with its many memories. Pearl and Rose made their farewell on the Monday night.

'Live white man way. But you no forget Rose.'

Rose's simple desire for her daughter caused Pearl to grab her mother.

'Of course, I no forget.' Tears were not far from Pearl's dark brown eyes, but she knew tears were not part of her mother. She held

Rose's arms.

'I'll write. Dad will read you my letters.'

'Thank you.'

Rose still gave her first and favourite phrase much use.

Tuesday threatened rain. Showers came. Tree lined lanes wept onto the red soil roads, staining the rolled wheel tracks a darker mahogany ochre. The cavalcade set out equipped with coats, tarpaulins carefully draped over their belongings. Martin and Yan were in the first cart. Dan, Mary and Thomas in the next. Bridget with Jane and Pearl to leave last in the sulky and hopefully get there first.

The dreamed reality had arrived. Education from the little school was now reaching further afield. Bridget breathed a prayer to the rolling rhythm of the wheels, for her family, for Pearl, and specially for Rose left behind.

The *Aphrodite* lacked the beauty of a ship clothed in sail but as one of the first steam assisted coastal ships, she started a new era. Her engine power meant it was possible to work even Ballina bar under most conditions. Captain Peters wanted his passengers aboard early Wednesday. He hoped for favourable conditions on the ten am high tide. Luggage for the O'Reilly girls and Pearl Yanohavovich was stowed the previous afternoon while his passenger list waited to be filled the next morning. Mary, he knew, she would know what was required of coastal ship travellers from being a passenger on several occasions.

The girls said their goodbyes. Pearl took her father apart from the group.

'Look after Mum.' She held him briefly and then rejoined the other travellers.

'Good morning young ladies,' Captain Peters greeted them, and helped them up the gangplank. He smiled at Mary clutching Arabella.

'I hope these two are sailors like yourself. The mate will show you to your cabin.'

Seeing Bridget and the others of the group on the wharf, he joined them assuring the worried mother that he would do all in his power to deliver them safely.

The Hilardts and Carmel Flaherty became part of the wharf farewell party. The scenario was of interest to even uninterested hangers-on. Three local girls were off to the city for education. Some raised eyebrows, unfortunately it would be a topic of conversation that one was a despised "half-caste" going to a posh city school. What next?

'Just make sure you work hard.' Carmel didn't mince words with the travellers.

She knew how much Bridget would miss both her daughters; she hoped sending Pearl was a good idea. Time alone could answer that.

Bob Beames happened to be picking up freight. He sounded off on the subject to the usual wharf lay- abouts and anyone else prepared to listen.

'Seen everything now, I have. That crazy O'Reilly woman is sending a part Abo kid off with her snooty girls to that posh tyke convent in Sydney. They'll probably make her do the scrubbing before they mate her up with one of those randy Irish priests.'

Even the lay-abouts didn't seem to want to listen to Bob's sick wisdom. They knew there was no chance of getting a few shillings out of him for work. He owed them all, threatening to "knock their blocks off" if they suggested payment for long past employment.

Steam was rapidly climbing in the boilers and once the tide rose past half in, there should be clearance on the bar. The morning bled grey clouds, with little doubt of showers and probably a strong chop at sea.

At 9.30 the *Aphrodite* stood out from the wharf. Her paddlewheels thumped the water, stirring the muddy river bottom; she made off slowly into the rising tide. The girls stood near the foredeck rail waving vigorously, while the send- off party followed down the wharf. Soon *Aphrodite* was well out in the river. An intermittent tooting on the whistle shook a new tune of compressed steam over the township of Ballina, letting all know that she was on her way. It was a different, more strident call than the tinkling of ships bells on sailing ships that these whistles replaced. Uneventfully, the ship followed the pilot's designated channel, turned and ran out through the bar surf. Soon that surf close to the lighthouse lay behind. The *Aphrodite* steered a course to the south.

'I think I'll go back to shore.' Jane held firmly to her bunk, wrestling a churning stomach.

'Ah, you'll get used to it,' Mary reassured her sister. 'What about you Pearl?'

'I'm all right.' Pearl walked around the small bunk, finding her balance.

It was a slow trip down the coast. The short, irregular chop made it often unpleasant. Jane missed the first couple of meals. Pearl was growing used to the movement by breakfast of the second morning. Mary was quite at home in the conditions; she tried to keep them cheerful. By the time the *Aphrodite* made it in through Sydney Heads the girls were ready to watch the growing residential bulk of the city crowding down on the harbour shores. How could there be so many people? They docked on the busy wharf area where horse drawn traffic flowed continuously up to the city. It was a scene of undreamed activity for the two newcomers.

A waiting Mother Cecilia and Sister Benedict whisked them into a large hansom cab. They sat upright, pinned in propriety, gaining eye boggling glimpses of activity, and a never-ending bustle. Here, suited men and fashionable women walked the pavements. Their cab clip-clopped along with its passengers locked in their insulated comfort.

The big cedar double doors of the Rose Bay convent gobbled them in and clicked behind them. Jane and Pearl were ushered into the parlour for their welcome and instructions by Mother Cecilia. Of course she made no specific reference to her first Aboriginal student.

'We will look after you well,' she finished.

She tinkled her bell and dismissed them to a starched, young postulant.

Mary, given leave to proceed to her room, found Cath had arrived back the day before, draped on her bed, busily writing.

'Hello, hello. Studying so soon, I'm pleased you've decided to start working.' Mary and Cath had a relationship of verbal armed neutrality. 'I hope you had a great holiday.'

'Hello, my mother superior. I had just the most wonderful holiday. There was this wonderful, handsome boy staying on the next station. I'm writing to him now. I'm sure I'm in love. Do you want to hear about it?'

'I will anyway, so I suppose the sooner the better.'

Mary stowed her small hand luggage and Arabella. She sat on her bed, this was forbidden in daytime, but probably safe at the moment.

'When is the wedding and does he know about it?'

'You can scoff, probably jealous. Perhaps I won't tell you after all.'

'Please yourself. I'll survive without your fantasies.'

Story of the holiday romance flowed out. He was a final year student at the big catholic college over at the other side of the city. His parents owned "thousands and thousands of sheep". The stolen snatched moments of hand-holding bliss came bubbling out.

'The last night there was a dance. We sneaked out around the big water tank. I knew he wanted to kiss me, so I gave him every chance. When he did, I just went all weak. I tingled all over, but we had to get back in before my parents missed me. So, we have to find a way to meet here in the city and outsmart our gaolers.'

'Very interesting Cath. If you've told me all of your passionate daring, at least you are not pregnant yet. Don't expect me to support any schemes for your sneaking out trying to achieve your ruin. Maybe that tingling was ants, they are plentiful in the bush.'

Mary easily dodged the thrown pillow. She relented.

'Thanks for telling me. Perhaps he's just right for you.'

Sister Benedict found Mary at tea, passing on news that her violin recital at the big school concert had caused outside interest. There was an offer for her to play in a concert at the Town Hall later in the year. It was up to Mary to take on the necessary work, if she thought it fitted her plans. Mother Cecilia was expected to give approval.

'I have clearance for you to come to the music room for half an hour tonight, and we will have a chat.'

The convent was drowsing down for the night when Mary joined Sister Benedict in the dimly lit, brooding, shadowed music room. A big black grand piano squatted, looking ready to pounce, like a large bloated black frog eying off his insect prey. Mary suspected the prey were unsuspecting students.

'How are you my dear? How did the holiday go?' Sister Benedict sat Mary beside her on the big chintz sofa.

They just chatted. Of the north coast news, of Pearl and Rose and Yan. Mary told her of Billy Montez and the story of her new violin, Arabella.

'Thank you, Mary. It's wonderful to have you back, I've missed you. Now how about you let me hear this new instrument of yours?'

The notes of her simple Mozart sonata danced in the shadows.

Even after Mary lifted the bow and lowered the instrument, it's melody tip-toed around the curtain-draped room. It brought a faraway time and place of men's powdered pomaded wigs, the tap of mincing, high-heeled, ornate buckled boots, swish of form hiding hooped skirts. It spun through the room. European elegance crossed the oceans, to a bolder, older land. Here the earth beat a harsh primitive percussion rhythm; that rhythm seemed part of and rocked off heat shocked shimmering landscapes. This land was old and dry when Europe emerged from the peat bog.

Sister Benedict, unspeaking, nodded her head slowly. She reached out, took the violin, balancing it gently in her long fingers. Mary added the bow to her teacher's right hand. Benedict placed the instrument body under her chin and, slowly starting at the G string, worked up the scale. At the top she stretched the purity, reach and volume from the E string to its potential. Lowering the instrument she carefully placed it and its bow on another padded sofa.

She pronounced slowly, 'That old violin is a treasure. Your Mr Montez has given you an instrument of rare quality. Perhaps the Lord has plans for you as a musician after all, else why place that instrument in your capable hands. I think we'll continue to practice with the other one.

Let that one live safe in its moisture proof home until time for the concert draws near, then we will fine tune it and you.'

Sister Benedict was confident of persuading Mother Cecilia to let Mary accept the offer of public participation. Before Mary went back to her room, the subject came back to Pearl. Sister Benedict was to be in charge of settling her in and wanted to find out as much of her background as possible. They knew little of Aboriginal people within the order and Mother Cecilia had needed much assurance that the experiment may work.

'It may be a start to my being given more contact with native people. It is the work I feel called to and is really why I came. I'll need your help, Mary.' Sister Benny confided.

New breezes blew at Rose Bay convent.

Music – Mary and Hope

Several months later, Mary received a summons from Mother Cecilia. She stood at attention behind the desk in the deep inner sanctum of Mothers private parlour. The interview started without preamble.

'I do not favour my students performing outside of school or church functions.' Mother Cecilia eyed Mary with careful perception.

She knew more about her students than they dreamed possible. There was maturity, strength of character in this girl that she recognised, liked. A stiff brocade chintz chair sat at the corner of her desk. It was for parents or visiting clergy only.

'Sit down, Mary.'

Mary sat, weak-kneed at such an unexpected concession.

'Now, this concert. Professor Neill has suggested you play. He thinks you have ability, and he is a well-known professional musician. Sister Benedict assures me you are capable and have been working well with her. I have always found you a sensible girl and you have always worked well in all ways with us. You are a better than average student. This is your last year here, perhaps you have plans. Do you want to play at this concert, and what about your future?'

'Yes Mother, I would like to play. I enjoy playing the violin, but I realise there are many good violinists. Perhaps, if I am good enough, I would like to continue on after school. It would be difficult for a girl to be considered in a professional orchestral career.'

'I'm pleased you have thought it out Mary. You have my permission to play. It is an honour for you and an honour for the school. We will have another chat one day. It seems your sister Jane and your friend Pearl are settling in well. Thank you, Mary.'

The interview was over and Mother Cecilia walked with her to the door. Unheard of!

As time for the concert at the Town Hall approached, Mary's workload increased. She was determined that if she failed it would not be because she had not given it her very best effort. A week before the Saturday night concert she and Sister Benedict decided to bring out Arabella and assure themselves all was well, and that there were no hidden problems with a different instrument. A new dimension crept into her fingers as the notes sang at her bidding from the age darkened instrument's anima soul. Her preparation was carefully planned. On the Thursday night they agreed she would play the whole recital and a backup piece as well. Friday night would just be light finger exercises allowing her fingers to taper down ready for the big event.

Sister Benedict played the piano introduction and accompanied her, giving the meticulous timing that would flow from a conductor and a trained orchestra. It went well. They both knew it was as right as they could make it. Now it was a case of could she deliver at that standard when a wall of people was out in the darkness and her concentration was focused on delivering without a slip. From the darkness of the corridor came three distinct hand claps, the door opened and Mother Cecilia entered.

'Wonderful,' was all she said. Sister Benedict looked as shocked as Mary. Mother was not given to big praise.

'I will be praying for you.' She left the room and closed the door.

'She said it,' Sister Benny smiled at her pupil. 'We are there Mary.'

The Big Night and Geoff Howe

Five tickets for the performance had arrived for the convent. Mary, Sister Benedict, Jane, Pearl, and Cath were those to go. The subject of dress had been discussed by Sister Benedict and Mary. They had decided that, while Mother would probably agree to street clothing for Mary, they would stay with her school dress uniform. The dark green was a perfect foil for her long auburn hair. She, Mary was adamant that it was not her appearance, but how she played that was important.

Cath worked hard on her hair and enjoyed the responsibility of producing her end work, well-groomed and striking.

'If I had your looks and figure, I wouldn't be hiding in a crummy old school uniform, but you probably look good enough to turn the heads of all those musicians anyway.'

'You talk rubbish. They may not be able to see so much of me, shaking in a uniform.'

The hansom cab arrived at 7 p.m. They bundled on board and it then trotted down through the gas lights of George Street. A line of cabs and private carriages dropped off their passengers. Many well-dressed citizens streamed into the huge building; here were many of the cultural elite of Sydney. Sister Benedict gave Cath strict instructions as to what the trio would do in the hall and assured her that she and Mary would join them in the two spare seats after Mary's recital. Mary, clutching Arabella, and Sister made the long trip around to the musician's entrance. Here, already pulsed a scene of organised chaos. If the sight of a nun and an attractive young woman in a convent uniform caused any surprise among the fellow performers, none was registered. A young man, who was also early on in the programme loosened his lips, playing scales on his flute, oblivious to the turmoil around him.

Inside from the stage area, sounds of a tuning orchestra fed back. A master of ceremonies for marshalling the performers into playing order and supplying any assistance necessary, hustled around verifying his list.

'And you are?' he bustled up, enquiring of Sister and Mary.

'Mary O'Reilly. Violin solo. Brahms Rhapsody,' Sister Benedict gave the necessary information.

They were slotted well forward in the programme chaos, two behind the young flautist.

Subdued excitement, nervous performers exuded a common bond of sweat, adrenalin, hope, no matter where in the music world a major concert happened to bring its persona. Sister Benedict, in her mind at this memory-raking procedure, departed from her physical, heavy, black habit. In memory recall she now wore a wonderful dress of frilled blue satin, back-tracking an ocean of space and time. She was a girl with violin clutched in hand, waiting at Dublin's big concert hall, her pulse quick and thumping with excitement. This scene in Sydney was turning back the clock enough to bring her a glow of anticipation. Back to reality of time and place. She breathed a constant prayer for Mary.

'Right, a quick check at the piano.'

Mary and she listened above the cacophony of tuning instruments to the four notes. They were still spot on from their tuning of today.

'That's it. It is up to you and God. You'll be fine.'

They settled ready in their slot of proceedings. Noise from the stage died, a ripple of applause for the conductor, and a short orchestral introductory number. Applause and the master of ceremonies ushered a mature soprano down the tunnel and into the hands of Professor Neill for introduction. Her powerful voice fed back to the waiting wings and she received generous applause from the audience.

They listened in a haze as each performer went and returned. The young flautist prepared to take the long walk. His eyes for an instant found Mary. She smiled, her lips mouthed, 'Good luck.'

He was swallowed into that tunnel from which the only reprieve and way back was to feed your life blood to that waiting ravenous audience that seemed too like a hungry dragon. The applause he received at completion was loud, enthusiastic.

The master of ceremonies was beside her, too late now for panic. She was walking to the tunnel. The stage lights flared, stunning bright. The orchestra looked immense. Out there across muted footlights, in the body of the hall, it was a dark void. Professor Neill smiled at her warmly.

'Take your time Mary, get used to the light. Remember the conductor will follow you, play it as you have practiced.'

He introduced her, she heard not a word. The orchestra led in. She turned off to everything except the conductor.

A last deep breath, and in that breath was her appeal to all that supported her. Then almost without knowing, she was playing. Her opening "C" note flowed strong, clear, right on key. The audience melted away. She played as they had practiced, the professional orchestra took over in the breaks, holding, carrying, and she led back ever stronger as the melody increased in tempo. They joined her in the closing momentum and then dropped her off. It was for her alone to carry the last climbing crescendo and its fall to a pure, simple long diminuendo A.

It was over. Perspiration sparkled on her forehead, her clothes from skin outward stuck to her body. She bowed to the orchestra, to the audience. Lights came up in the hall. Was it true? The applause was a building wave that lifted in momentum. Could that really be for her? Mary who never cried, knew tears were streaming from her eyes, obscuring her sight. She went to leave, but Professor Neill took her arm and stood her back on the rostrum. It was a blur of unreal fantasy. Applause swelled again.

'They are yours. Can you manage another number. The minuet you put down as alternative?'

She nodded through the tears. The professor announced it. Mozart's Minuet in C simple, melodic, light, vaporous.

It flew to every cranny of the huge hall, Arabella's voice lifted above the orchestra. Short. Soon it was over. She thanked the conductor. Again, applause long and enthusiastic carried her from the stage.

Professor Neill walked away into the tunnel with her.

'Mary, you were good. I'll be in touch.'

She was still shaking, when Sister Benedict, also shaking, folded her in and gave her a big squeeze. Sister Benedict was radiant.

'You made me so proud,' was all she said. They stowed Arabella in the strange custom-made case. Out at the back of the performers area there was a washroom.

'Wash your face dear.' When Mary came back, she was amazed to find Sister chatting to the flautist.

'This is Geoffery Howe. He wants to meet you and congratulate you.'

Sister made their introduction formal, chaperoned in correct propriety. Geoff Howe, probably a couple of years older, but a young man in music terms, congratulated her warmly.

'The ordinary, like me, can only listen in awe,' he said gallantly.

She fixed him with her uncomplicated Mary gaze, a smile hovered on her mouth, a mouth that some thought too large for fashionable beauty.

'Rubbish, Mr Howe,' was all she said. Then she smiled disarmingly, looking straight at him. 'But thank you so much for appreciating my effort.'

Down in the body of the hall, they found their vacant seats. Sister Benedict was probably relieved to find her pupils still in place. All three whispered their congratulations, during the brief lull before the next item.

'We led the applause in this section of the hall, but it seemed they were all determined for more of your playing,' Jane confided to her sister.

The long concert drew to its end and they joined the throng that flowed back out to George Street. There they were picked up by their cabby. Sister Benedict whisked the two younger girls off to bed once back at the convent. She left Cath and Mary in the privacy of their room for them to wind down after the big night.

Several days later, Mary received a summons from Mother Cecilia. On her desk sat a couple of open newspapers. In each there was a circled part of the column about a skilled young violinist who captured a big audience at the Town Hall with her "gifted violin playing."

'I have also heard from Professor Neill. He asks that he be allowed to come and see you. I assured him he had my permission to speak with you here in the parlour.

'Sister Benedict tells me you were even better than she expected, so my prayers must have been heard.'

There was hint of a smile on Mother Cecilia's face.

'I will see you have copies of the press clippings to send home to your mother. Well done, Mary, I know success will not turn your head.'

Martin and Politics

Martin Baillie and John Richards sat on a bench in the big shed, having a morning cup of coffee. Condensation moisture fuelled an occasional cold plop from the high, unlined galvanised iron roof ceiling as it fell on the concrete floor. However, the shed interior was fundamentally dry, even comparatively cheery, compared to the cold, misty, winter rain, persistent showers pock marking a dreary bleak outside world.

'What do you think John, if we pack the boxes in with tarpaulins over them, would they keep dry in the cart for you?'

'I think so. Provided the rain stays light and the wind keeps down. There's little weight in the load and Bonny can trot into Lismore in a couple of hours. I'm happy to go if you say so.'

'Right, we'll put them on.'

The six boxes had been wagoned up from Ballina two days ago, with their address stickers for a Lismore store marked *Urgent*. It had rained steadily ever since. O'Reilly's pledged prompt delivery service. Martin felt it was time for their good name's sake that they make a way to deliver. The light cart and Bonny were his only practical answer, if the good will of their pledge was to be maintained. They loaded the boxes and John Richards, muffled in oilskin and a seaman's sou'wester, headed for Lismore. Martin finished tidying and itemising undelivered content of the shed. He may as well head for home. There was plenty to deliver when the rain lifted.

It was a surprise for Martin when three of the areas prominent citizens arrived through the murk of the day and entered through the open door of the big shed. It was not a trio he expected to drop in for a casual chat. Rupert James, Duncan Brown, and Barney Shaw were not a group that Martin expected to find together, let alone with a common cause to visit him in the O'Reilly storage shed. He smiled at them.

'Good morning gentlemen, I only hope you haven't come as a deputation to complain about the service of O'Reilly Carriers. What can I do to help?'

He was soon in for a shock. It seemed Duncan Brown, the prominent sawmiller, was their elected spokesman. After they had thrown a comment on the misery of the weather, it was he who explained the purpose of their visit.

'We ha' talked together and we come to ask ye to consider a proposition we ha' for ye,' he said in his broad brogue. 'As ye well know from your time around the district as our clergyman, and for the past six months or so as part of O'Reilly Carriers, we are a fast, growing area with plenty of needs from our city-based government. We feel laddie, that city-based government be not doing much for this growing area. Now that we can elect a local representative to speak for our needs in the Legislative Assembly, we feel ye would be a good man to be our government member. We want ye to think about allowing us to nominate ye for the elections in three months' time.'

Martin motioned them to take a seat on the bags of grain stacked against the wall. He spread his hands with a wry smile at his visitors.

'I feel you have got it wrong. I know nothing of politics.' Martin shook his head. 'Your suggestion is a shock to me. There would be no chance of my being elected, but I don't think I would want to nominate. It's just not me. As you know, I was unwanted as a Minister of Religion when Bridget and I decided to marry. I am very happy with Bridget and happy as a carrier. There must be far better and keener potential politicians around than myself.'

Duncan Brown was not convinced.

'Perhaps, but we don't agree with your opinion. There would be plenty who think they have potential to be our political representative, but we like your background for the job. How about you just say you will talk to your wife and think about it. Everyone says you helped them as a man of the cloth. You would have opportunity to help people and the district as our representative. True you may not be elected but we think we could run a strong campaign for you.'

Rupert James added a voice.

'Who knows better than you, how much we need a safer entrance to the river? How much we need roads now that people are coming to farm this plateau. Many say sugar farming and modern sugar mills will bring money to the area. You know how much we need schools, how much we will need a hospital for the sick. We need someone capable of working and speaking up for us.'

The third member of the trio, Barney Shaw, by nature a man who said little, added his comment.

'There are others around here who think like us,' he said. 'We know you are capable of talking with educated men, but you also know how working men think. Please don't just say 'no'. Talk to Bridget, she may tell you our idea is not so daft.'

Martin looked worried; it seemed the deputation would not be put off their intention as easily as he had first thought possible. His reaction to dismiss them out of hand probably had been too hasty. It was not in his nature to make instant decisions, so he owed it to them to give something undreamt of half an hour ago, at least some consideration.

'Thank you for your confidence and offer of support. Could a man of God make a politician? I don't know. I will talk to Bridget; her opinion will guide me. Give me a couple of days. I think my answer will be 'no thanks', but perhaps I would like to know who other potential representatives could be.'

Duncan Brown held out his hand.

'Thank ye for listening to us, Martin, we will wait. I tell ye nar laddie, it will the big land holding squatters who will try to work in one of themselves. We dinna think that's good for this district. I've made enquiries, ye would scrape through the qualifications, as ye know there's no pay for a hard job, but hopefully this state may soon follow Victoria and start paying its politicians. That is how it must be for true representation.'

Rupert James offered.

'How about a small nip to warm you for the ride home? The bar's empty.'

Martin shook his head.

'Thanks, not today, but I appreciate the offer.'

The deputation left.

Martin closed the shed. He rode home in the cold, dreary rain not taking his unexpected visitors proposition all that seriously. Yet, he was not beyond imagination stirring thoughts; there could be aspects that interested him. He could see the growing district needed a voice, but was it his voice?

He used the stable entrance to save passing close to the house. There was a fair chance that Bridget had not seen him return. His horse rugged and fed, lunch for himself seemed attractive. Bridget probably was not expecting him so early. Maybe there would be something to warm his cold frame. His wet oilskin was hung up and left at the stable. He trotted over to the house, his damp boots left outside to dry.

He was in through the kitchen door and into the friendly warm atmosphere of Killarney kitchen, his sudden presence surprising Bridget.

'I'm home early, will you feed me?'

'Hmm, I'm not sure that shirkers should be fed,' she greeted him. 'Maybe I'll find you a crust, but only because I'm a Christian lady who wouldn't let a wet vagrant traveller go hungry.'

She kissed him lightly. She carried the wholesome scent and warmth of the kitchen. He breathed a basic baking aroma blending with her subtle warm body scent spreading from hair and woolly jumper. The old black cast iron stove burped an occasional combustion crackle through the open door. A couple of new pieces of solid bloodwood lifted new yellow and blue finger flames on the grate bed of coals.

'You'd better offer me something or I won't tell you my news,' he teased her as she wriggled out of his arms.

'Oh, all right, maybe just a little bread and water; if you behave yourself.'

The thick soup was heavy with well boiled mutton scraps, melted off its bones, greens from the garden and boiled barley added to the brew.

Martin broke big slices of bread into the bowl. They sat on opposite sides of the old table and ate.

'Well? Tell me, or that's your last meal, sneaking in here at midday with your bribery, disrupting my day.'

Martin told her of his visitors, and their completely unexpected request. He finished with the addition,

'I've told them virtually "no" but agreed that I'd talk to you. They seemed to think you were the boss, I told them I'd give an answer in a couple of days. Anyway, I'd be safe: there is no way they could get enough people to vote for me.'

Bridget looked at him, long, steadily, reading him. When she spoke, all she said was, 'Well, that was real news. Perhaps you earned your soup.'

There was a speculative tone in her voice. She packed their bowls and plates in the big washing up dish, ready for hot water. He wanted her comment.

'So, what do you think? The answer has to be "no" doesn't it?'

He tried to lead her hoped-for reply. Bridget looked at him speculatively.

'The answer does not necessarily have to be "no", Mr Baillie.'

She sat beside him, close, taking his hand in hers.

'You are still cold. Those clothes are damp, you'd best change before you catch pneumonia. The district can't lose a potential politician that way.'

'I know a way to get warm,' he whispered in her ear. She pushed him away in mock shock.

'And now it seems you be a tryin' to take advantage of a busy cookin' woman all on her own, doin' her house duties. You be a cunning schemer knowing that there be no one around for hours.'

He whispered in her ear, 'Yes I would.'

He kissed her, testing, tasting, revelling in the wonder of her presence.

Later, they lay side by side in their big bed, warm, spent, separated, but still very much one, savouring aftershock tremors of their lovemaking. They floated above it all; their chariot of perception drifted back toward reality from an outer universe of total sensation. Neither risked blunting that saga trip with mere words. Words could add nothing to the journey.

She looked at him.

'Martin Baillie, you could make a good politician.'

Bridget brought them back to the churn of reality.

'Why would I make a good politician?'

Martin content to humour her, wanted her wisdom and perception.

'You know how to talk to people; you know how to listen; you are aware of the needs of people; you could help the district and do good for ordinary people. I'd like to see who the other would-be starters are, but they are not as good as you.'

'Ah, your usually good judgement is clouded by personal sentiment.'

'Well, you will have to produce good reasons before we let you say no. The subject is to be discussed further. Now I have things to do, before Thomas arrives home from school and finds us here in bed.'

Sliding over him to find her clothes, she lay briefly on his wide chest, savouring the strong arms that momentarily grabbed her. She fought delicious, wild, tempting sensations that flooded what seconds before she had thought a spent satisfied lower body. A part of her wanted to stay there, daring him to renew their passion. No. She rolled free, out of the bed, face hotly flushed, grabbed a wrap to cover her nakedness.

'You sir, are dangerous, and I'll have you know it is a time of the month when those wild Scottish sperm of yours could bring results.'

'Good. I'm beginning to wonder whether I'm a failure,' was all he said.

Always News

The decision was made that Martin would run as a legislative candidate if his sponsors still wanted him. They took Major and the sulky to pay a visit to Duncan Brown. The little Scot sprouted a warm smile when told the news.

'Well, Laddie, we'll try really hard to ha' ye elected. Ah'm right pleased that ye ha' cum wi' him Mrs Baillie. We know he'd na think about it i' ye wer na behind him, an' that's how it should be.'

The Scots businessman showed a drip of dour humour

'And I'm a thinking, ye' ma'am may turn out to be our best election tool. You're a far better-lookin' sight than he.'

The word soon spread from foothills to coast. It was a warm topic of interest. Martin kept driving the wagon and organising O' Reilly's Transport, but there was a new breeze of interest in the air. Winter was drawing down and there was a hint of spring in the slightly lengthening days. Soon pink buds would swell on the now gaunt grey black speckled arms of the waiting plateau peach trees.

Bridget had wondered for several weeks. She felt a hint of spring in herself; it was past her period time. Since the high of their lovemaking that cold wet day when Martin arrived home unexpectedly, she carried a strange awareness. She had been wondering whether their bodies, although still very sexually active, were going to achieve a baby. After all, she was well in her thirties. It was 12 years since Thomas was born. Soon she'd know for sure and then time enough to tell Martin the momentous news.

The Brewsters had thrown themselves wholeheartedly into the election campaign.

'Why you are the very man for the job, we'll see it happens.'

Norah had volunteered to be campaign manager and was busily writing letters and making suggestions. Martin and Bridget tramped home from a meeting at the Brewsters. Norah's rallying call had brought about 20 interested people. It was 10 p.m. when the campaign plan ended and they headed home toward Killarney.

His arm encircled her and it was a pleasant walk. Martin aired his doubt.

'There is too much rubbish in this electioneering for my liking. I'm beginning to think my first thoughts were right,' he complained.

'It will be all right. Just be yourself, you know Norah gets carried away, but she will make sure people know you are a candidate.'

'Well, I think I may tell them not to vote for me.'

'You would not be game.' She tried to pinch him.

In bed, they snuggled close. The tempo of their interest grew. For a time, the political campaign was forgotten. Needs each from the other satisfied, they settled drowsily.

'Martin,'

'M'mm,'

'I haven't had a period this month. There may be three of us.'

His drowsiness disappeared.

'Are ye really so clever, Lassie? That would be great.'

'Well, I think so. Women usually know when they are pregnant.'

'And here's me making love to you in a delicate condition. Why didn't you stop me?'

'Don't you dare. There is no need for you to treat me as fragile. If there is a baby in there, it's perfectly safe, but you won't be if you turn your back on me. So, I hope we have that straight.'

They talked a while, and with her comfortably against his side, they drifted into sleep.

Selling the Candidate

A month from the election date, Martin hit the campaign trail with some vigour. Norah drew up a list of meetings and posted her hand bills wherever she felt they would be seen. O'Reilly vehicles all carried a poster "Vote for Baillie".

Of the other two contenders, one was a squatter grazier with plenty of resources from the Casino area, the other a cane growing, private mill owner from the Ballina area. It seemed the competition was strong, but Norah was confident they could pull a number of votes from all areas.

For Martin to win he would have to carry a significant vote from the coastal area. Jimmy Flaherty was given the task of putting up posters around Ballina advertising Martin's coming Saturday lunch time policy speech. It was to open their campaign. They would take down the wagon on the Saturday morning and set it up in River Street as the platform from which Martin would speak. Hopefully, Saturday morning shoppers would hang around to hear his message. Women could not vote but Norah and Bridget were confident that if his message was attractive to women they would work on their men folk to give him support.

The early morning coastal rain showers cleared. There was an occasional gust of southerly wind which fed in off the river, but not a bad morning. Martin took his place in the wagon from which the horses had been moved safely to the Australian Hotel stables. There was a sprinkling of people wandering toward his impromptu stand. Duncan Brown and Rupert James were the stand-up support on the wagon. At the tick of twelve, Duncan would say a few lines of introduction, then it would be up to Martin to hold his small audience and draw in more passers-by from a still active River Street.

When the introduction had been made, Martin cast a speculative, nervous eye over his assembled audience. There was a sprinkling of women and children, most men in working clothes and some in well-cut suits, a few obvious seamen, and an odd lean street dog hoping that a gathering meant food. One point of potential storm met his swift eye sweep over the audience. A large, sure to be seeking trouble, Bob Beames, comfortably draped against a street post. Martin took a deep breath and went into action:

'My friends, this growing area of ours is a place of huge potential. People came to harvest our timbers, but we have so much more. We have a wonderful healthy climate, rich soil for agriculture, bounteous ocean with sea foods, and a strong river that stretches far inland. Our future is unlimited if we work to develop the needs of these children here today, and those who will come after them.

'Now I am going to speak briefly about our river entrance, about our need for roads to open up country away from the river, about our need to have schools for our children, about our need to have places to look after the sick and injured.

'I will tell you my plans for those four subjects and I shall be happy to try and answer any questions that you ask of me.'

He set to work with a will. Once started, it came easily enough. He knew what was needed to make the area grow.

It was almost as if he were back speaking of the Bible and Jesus Christ, words formed and followed. His remarks on each subject he kept it simple, understandable, and brief. On several occasions, Bob Beames chimed in with bellowed comments, but the audience told Bob Beames in no uncertain manner to keep quiet until his time came to ask questions. Martin had learned from impromptu pulpits to quit while people were still listening.

'Right, I thank you for listening so courteously. If you elect me, I will do my best to work for all residents of this area. Now I am sure you have questions for me.'

There was a ripple of applause. It seemed to have gone over well enough, now how would he handle the questions.

He decided to go on the attack and throw the ball straight at Bob Beames as a starter.

'Now Mr Beames, you obviously have questions. I shall answer you to the best of my ability.'

The floor all his, and with people looking at him impatiently waiting his questions, this was off-putting to Bob. He was not expecting to be asked to fire the first question. He frantically clutched a straw of hope and tried to dredge something to disquiet Martin.

'Uh, yes, Mr Sky Pilot, what do you know about representing working men? You'd be in there for the men with the flash suits and big money.'

'Mr Beames, I take it your question is what do I know about representing working men?'

'Yeah, that's right.'

'As a sky pilot, the people I had most to do with were working people and their wives and children. Indeed Mr Beames, we are in this area all working people. I want to see working people make a fair living for their families. We have to supply opportunities for work. Sailors are working men and I was called on to bury many of those because there is no safe river entrance. I want to see our river much safer than it is now. It would help everyone. So do you have another question, Mr Beames?'

'No. I've heard enough of your wind. All talk, you know nothing of working men. I won't vote for you.'

Bob Beames stalked off muttering, hoping there would be like-minded detractors at the bar of his favourite hotel.

The ice was broken and many asked questions that Martin answered competently. His committee reckoned their first rally had gone well.

When the small crowd dispersed, he found Bridget. They went

across to Hilardts for a welcome cup of tea.

'Well. Was I bad enough to make sure I don't get elected?' he whispered when he found a space on their own.

'You did fine and you know it. Admit the truth, you really enjoyed it. Perhaps that worries me a little.' She looked at him speculatively.

The campaign stepped up. Martin was speaking a couple of times per week, wherever they could draw a crowd together. Bridget insisted on being at his side. Some mornings she ran outside the back porch, gripped with morning sickness but always she looked radiant by the time they reached the destinations they visited. Major and the sulky were travelling plenty of miles and O'Reilly Carriers was very much in the hands of Dan Riordan, which in turn threw more onto Nell. They knew if Martin was successful, then another driver would have to be found. It was decided to wait and see the outcome of the election. Rumour said the other candidates had strong support and were running strong campaigns. It was first past the post polling, logical that the winner would need a share of votes from all areas.

It was decided that Martin's important electioneering approach to the people of Casino would come at the end of his campaign. They knew, to have a real chance, he must take a good share of the Casino vote. He found the big heavy wagon lovingly designed by Pat O' Reilly, was also an excellent mobile platform, easier than speaking at ground level. This was to be the final campaign talk. It was arranged that Dan Riordan would arrive with a normal consignment of goods for the town and set up the wagon once deliveries were made.

Two canvas signs, slapped up with bright paint, draped around the wagon, depicted Martin Baillie's hopes for the district. Bridget the artist, helped in the ideas department by Norah, had brought together these meaningful murals. They showed a walled river entrance at Ballina. There were bridges across the rivers at Casino and Lismore. There were community halls. There were schools. All these topics showed a visual of future dreams. Norah's final gem of innovative thought that taxed Bridget's artistry was Martin in once clerical attire on his old grey horse Cardinal. They hoped voters would grab the message that these things would come for the area if Martin was elected. Their mural rolled down to hang from each side of the high wagon an hour or so before the talk. While it collected men who could vote, this was but a small proportion of those who looked. It was aimed to draw in mainly the women and children to look and work out the theme of the artwork.

Hopefully the relatively small number of voting men who looked at the murals would come under pressure from their families. Norah and Bridget knew women could not vote but most would be capable of straightening the thoughts of a mere male by one means or another.

At times over their journeys, when jogging around in the sulky with its "Vote Baillie" sign flapping behind, they were pulled up by a supporter or an enquirer. This meant travel time could vary considerably, but they knew a convinced voter could easily draw others to the fold. A small corner of Bridget's mural showed women lined up casting votes. They had discussed the pros and cons of this radical forward thought but Martin said, 'Leave it there.' It stayed.

Major, the tough Welsh pony, was called to stretch out in the final leg to Casino. They arrived with only three minutes to spare. A large crowd was gathered around and waiting for action. Dan had been helping Duncan field enquiries as to when the candidate should arrive. They heaved a sigh of relief; Dan took over the sulky and pony to unharness him and cool him down.

David Cameron came up.

'Ye can use my shed and trough should ye wish lad.'

Dan said a gracious, 'Thank you Mr Cameron,' and headed down to the Cameron shop.

Martin took his time, collected his thoughts and headed to the wagon platform. He was introduced by Duncan. Script in hand, it was still in hand, barely referred to when Martin finished speaking, he let the moment take over.

'People of Casino, and those from other places,' he started, 'it is great to see so many here. You realise this election is of great importance to the whole area, from the sea to the ranges. Now many here know me. Indeed, I lived here in Casino for 10 years. I hope that in that time as a Presbyterian minister, you found me an honest man. In my wanderings through a wide area, I learnt much of your problems and requirements. Now I will speak briefly of what I feel are issues that have to be addressed for this town to go forward. Some are issues where I feel I could plead a strong case.'

They listened. It was a talk of local issues, some related, similar, some different to what he had unrolled in other centres. In the break before he called for questions there was generous applause. He recognised plenty of the faces, many were of people he had preached to, but many were of persons who had passed on the other side of the street. Mrs Phipps his at times vitriolic, protective housekeeper, came up to the wagon. She exuded a pride of possession.

'Well done Mr Baillie. You can be assured I'll be telling the men of my family to vote for you.'

It gave him a lift, for he knew she had been one of his vocal critics when he announced his intention of marriage to Bridget.

The questions came. He answered them to the best of his ability. They felt it was a good meeting. Was it good enough? Now all that was left was the tiring task of travelling home and waiting for Saturday's polling day.

'You put the issues well. I hope they vote for you laddie. Be sure I'm telling any that asks me, you be our man.' David Cameron made a point of being seen with the Baillies and their supporters.

'Thank you for your support, Mr Cameron. Martin would work hard for the people of the district. You know that.' Bridget smiled at him, and added, 'We have done our best. It is now in the hands of the voters.'

'Well Mrs Baillie he'll ha' votes in Casino, but so will Irwin; he's a popular man.'

It was a long trip back to Killarney. They kept with Duncan and his stylish gig until they reached the Brown sawmill. It was well on the Duck Creek side of Lismore, but there was still a long journey home.

Duncan came up and shook Martin's hand.

'You have a great chance,' he said and he turned to Bridget, 'If we make it Saturday it will be because of you and Norah. Gu'nite and safe home.'

Polling booths were well scattered over the large area. Each with a booth manager in charge and a clerk designated to see fair play and supervise the count at the conclusion of available voting time. Results would not be announced until declaration of the poll in Casino at noon on the Monday. Logistics of having a Baillie supporter present at each booth taxed resources, but Norah was determined it could be done. Like a general marshalling her forces, she allocated people to areas. It would be another long 24 hours and a long trip home for many of Martin's workers after the definitive voting day, but a few votes turned Martin's way could be all important.

Norah's troops were away with the light on Saturday morning. They set up, displayed their banners and hoped for a good turnout of voters. Martin was allocated to Casino in the morning and back to Lismore in the afternoon, keeping him in the eye of the most populous areas.

'Surely they will have made up their minds by now,' he said to Jim Brewster.

'You know Norah, she's determined to sway a last few,' Jim said sympathetically.

The eventful day ground to its inevitable end. Darkness slid over the booths as kero. lights took over the impromptu counting tables at 6 p.m.

'Well, let's go home and forget all about it until Monday.' Martin gave Bridget's hand a squeeze. They bid farewell to those still around the Lismore booth and went to reclaim Major from his stall at the livery stable.

'You are the one who has suffered most.' Martin gave the pony an affectionate rub on the neck as he harnessed him. 'After Monday you'll be back to living a life of ease.'

They trotted home through the night. Major was very sure of his way. They sat close, tired, looking forward to a comfortable bed.

'You can be sure Norah will be assessing our chances from booth rumours in the morning,' Bridget said wearily.

'You should have said no three months ago and saved all this trouble,' was all Martin said.

It was a long time from Saturday 'til Monday. Duncan Brown, the James, the Shaws, the Brewsters all determined to be with them when the poll was declared. Rumours that filtered through from booths said they had done well but no one was prepared to call a result. They gathered outside the Casino Police Station, its veranda to be used as the designated platform by the government official to announce the poll.

It was a sizable crowd, something like a hundred interested

people, comprising supporters of all three candidates who gathered on the Monday.

The declaration officer, resplendent for the occasion in morning coat and top hat, called the candidates to the veranda. Addressing the large motley gathering in front of him, it was for him a moment of importance, and he was determined not to hurry the occasion. There was a fair sprinkling of women, adding some colour to the scene.

'Ladies and Gentlemen, it is my privilege to announce the results of the NSW Legislative Assembly poll for the seat of Richmond.'

He cleared his throat.

'Total number of votes recorded and verified as legitimate votes was 1547,' he said.

'It was a very close poll. The votes have been checked several times and retained in a locked box. Any candidate has the right to check the votes under strict supervision should he desire. The result is…'

He cleared his throat again, relishing the moment as he looked over at the waiting crowd. He played the moment. Then clearly and unhurried announced,

'Irwin: 502, Clement:518, Baillie: 527.' The results rang out across the expectant crowd. 'It is therefore my duty to declare Mr Baillie duly elected with a majority of nine votes as your member for Richmond.'

Close Call but Yes

A surprised Martin received a warm round of applause with cheers. Norah was jubilant. He shook hands with his opponents and held up his hands.

'Thank You. It was a result so close that any one of us could have been victor. I congratulate my opponents. As it is me, I pledge to do my best for all residents of this growing area. The hard work of my supporters carried me to this slender victory. I shall try to be worthy of the result. Thank you again.'

There were many who wished to shake his hand. Eventually he was free to be with his committee. He put an arm around Bridget and held her beside him. She just smiled at him, but he knew there were tears in her eyes. Mrs Phipps was one who arrived to offer her congratulations; Martin introduced her to Bridget. She smiled, a crisp, perhaps cynical smile at Mrs Baillie.

'I am pleased he has succeeded. Just see he doesn't spend all his time rushing around after those who will never leave him alone.'

It was not an unfriendly greeting she addressed to Bridget, who realised this severe lady had looked after him well for 10 years.

'It is good advice Mrs Phipps. I'll try to heed it. Martin has told me of your good care for him over many years.'

David Cameron came up to the group.

'Well done, would ye all like to come around for a cordial, afor' th' long trip home. Ther' be na strong drink at the Camerons, but Mrs Cameron would be happy to let ye taste her cooking.'

They accepted. Norah knew it was probably David Cameron and Casino who found them the slim few votes majority.

Martin's vote had been stable in the three main areas, with a better result than expected in Casino. By nine votes or 900, it mattered not, they had won!

Late that night back at Killarney, Bridget and Martin sat at the kitchen table, having cocoa. The clamour of the day gone, they wanted to leave it all behind and sleep.

'Well, Mrs Baillie, your husband is a member of the glorious state legislature, so now it is another mouth for you to feed. As a carrier I could earn my keep, as a politician I'll be a constant drain on our finances. I'll work when I can but how often will that be possible? Even a Minister of God received a pittance, but now it looks like I'm a kept man.'

'Don't worry. We will manage, as long as you don't develop a taste for expensive wine and expensive women. We'll even have to buy you some classy clothes. I noticed you didn't measure up well against the loosing candidates. I'll keep you, under certain conditions. Let's tidy up, thank God, and go to bed. We still have to appear at Norah's party tomorrow afternoon.'

There were plenty to slap Martin on the back at the Surreyville party and wish him well. The twenty who launched him onto the road to politics, grew with election success to probably double the score. Those original workers could cynically have held a thought that some present, not seen before the result, were there in case they had reason to seek help of their member. Martin asked that the speeches remain at a minimum. He kept it that way when it was his time to acknowledge thanks and victory.

'I did not want to disappoint those who made success possible, for me it was enough to do my best and lose graciously. Well, those few votes from somewhere brought victory, and for me a future course that some months ago had not been considered. My wife agreed to push and carry me along, that she may come to regret now that I am elected, but I will work for this district. I enjoyed working for God as his minister, it is my hope that our victory is also his victory.'

Not part of the election committee but supporters, the Johnsons came to the victory gathering. Johno Johnson sought his chance to talk with Martin. He came with an agenda. His subject was quickly that of sugar cane. He had Jim Brewster and a couple of others present listening attentively.

'This is our way forward,' he said. 'There is a good demand for sugar, it is easy to grow, the birds don't eat it. Once in the ground you get many crops from the one planting. All we need is enough growers to make efficient milling possible. We also need ships to take it to the markets. In time, who knows it may be trains. We know you will stress our need to the parliament for a safe river entrance.'

Martin Baillie realised he was now the one who would be expected to supply answers to many varied problems.

'I will do my best. This area has potential for many crops, sugar cane may seem the best at the moment. You will need to give me facts and figures.'

In the big kitchen, the women helped clean up the mess left after another good Surreyville party. Bridget found herself beside Flora Johnston.

'You have made Martin Baillie a happy man. I'm sure he knows now how much he needed a wife.'

She smiled warmly at Bridget who was pleased to see that she was accepted, by at least one of his old flock. Bridget answered her, 'Many didn't think it should be me. Thank you. We are happy. It is going to be difficult with him spending much time in Sydney. The business has to go on, we are not rich people and it will cost money for him to be a politician.'

'I'm sure you will manage. I congratulate you on the manners of your boy; he was with Martin the day they delivered the plough.'

'He's a good lad but I want him to have some education. Perhaps he'll want to work in the business later, but for now he must go to school.'

They finished washing their pile of dishes.

The party broke up; Martin, Bridget and Thomas walked home in the dusk. Thomas insisted on feeding the horses on his own, though it was an hour later than normal, and the feeding, watering of their stable took time.

Bridget said to Martin,

'I caught Nell eyeing me strangely, side view. She has probably guessed. My clothes are starting to shrink.'

Martin ran a speculative hand gently over her still trim stomach.

'I can't wait for you to look interesting.'

'Humph. All right for you. You are going to sail off to Sydney for the next few months.'

'I'll be back here long before this baby is due.'

'Well, its nearly six months away. Pregnant women can be grouchy as you probably do not know. You are lucky to be escaping.'

Bridget laid out a light cold tea, and they awaited Thomas returning from the stables. It was a chance to bring Martin's thoughts to their driver needs of the business.

'We will have to find a driver. Have you any ideas?'

'No, but you said yourself, Jimmy the Foster's stableboy could be handy. He would be good to train for the future.'

'We can't just ask him without talking to the Fosters first. We are looking for a replacement for you at the moment. I suppose we did not really think that you would come home a winner in the election race.'

Bridget knew she would sound out Dan as the first step. Perhaps he had met up with a horseman somewhere on the rounds of delivery that wouldn't need much training. One thing was certain, pregnancy ruled out any chance of her taking to the roads.

Thomas returned, washed, and they sat down for tea.

Change Brewing

Martin Baillie took up residency in Sydney. He found a small unpretentious flat down toward the harbour, within walking distance of the substantial Macquarie Street Parliament building. It was also within walking distance of his acquired daughters at Rose Bay convent. He knew Mary and Jane would be prepared to offer support in the big city. Already, he was beginning to wonder whether he should be thanking the Richmond River electors; three years of Parliamentary hot air seemed a long sentence. He hoped city life would become more acceptable; he had grave doubts.

The time came for Martin's first speech to the state legislature. He decided on two themes. One virtually spoke for itself: the danger of crossing the Richmond River bar. There had to be improvement or his constituency would always be a no man's land. Then there was the infant sugar industry. This could be a money winner for the state, if the Clarence, Richmond and Tweed Rivers had reliable river entrances. The Colonial Sugar Refining Company was spending big sums of money on modern sugar mills and the Sydney- based company was vocal in supporting his claim for government support. He felt he was on safe ground with those themes, though they may or may not interest many of his fellow members. He gave it his best shot, knowing protocol meant fellow members would not boo him from a maiden speech.

'Gentlemen, I arrived at the Richmond River on horseback, close to 15 years ago. My purpose as a Presbyterian minister was to provide spiritual backup to the few people already settled there. I constantly rode the tracks that linked Casino -Lismore and the port of the Richmond River. Now that place is well known as Ballina. The population growth has been rapid and while the area was settled for its timber trade, many crops are now grown. There is a variety of arable land that attracts would-be farmers.

'The latest and probably most promising crop is sugar cane. There is strong evidence that the Colonial Sugar Refining Company is to build a large modern central sugar mill on the Richmond River at Broadwater. That company already has modern central mills on the Clarence and Tweed. There is also rumoured planning for a large mill on the Big Scrub plateau near Duck Creek or Alstonville. There are many small sugar mills along the river. I emphasise to you that sugar will become an important crop on the Richmond River, for that area and for NSW.

'In order for that industry and all the other industries of the Far North Coast to succeed, there has to be better access for coastal shipping at the mouth of the river. The Richmond River is freely navigable from Ballina to Lismore slightly more than 70 miles, and on its other arm almost to Casino. It is a free flowing, deep water river but the entrance is shallow, shoaling, and often extremely dangerous. The many shipwrecks on the Ballina bar would be known to the members of this house. As a clergyman, I participated in too many sad funerals of many Ballina bar victims.

'For the area of the Richmond River I represent to progress, we must have a safer, more reliable entrance to the river. It is my intention to use any means at my disposal to keep this matter before the house so that a remedy for that entrance will be found. Thank you.'

He received polite applause and there were questions showing interest from some country members.

Martin's work and lobbying within the house continued through the session of Parliament. When he sought firm numbers to implement a plan for the Richmond, he found it was extremely difficult to line up a promised vote of support. It seemed all members had private agendas and winning votes required much trading. It was not the value of schemes that drew votes but often the attitude, 'I'll vote for you only after you have voted for me.' He wondered, could he gain support? The frustrations of being a politician soon became apparent to Martin Baillie.

He had promised to work for his electorate and work he would. At times he felt there was progress, at times he was completely frustrated by the politics of gaining support. All he could do was stick at his task. He wrote frequently to Bridget, at times threatening to resign and return home. He frequently visited the girls at the convent and they helped give him incentive to tolerate his life as a politician. He soon found that his electorate was unknown to most of the Sydney money holders and that his task was difficult.

Time slid by and he looked forward to a term break of the house and his booked passage back to Bridget.

Martin Baillie MLA- Bridget in Waiting

Several rain depressions swept across the plateau through a wet autumn. Small floods built in the plateau creeks, reddish capillary vein gullies bled into, and joined, bloated arteries of main watercourses. Eventually breaking free from the escarpment, swelling, red brown in colour, these joined the dun brown ponded waters working to the river. The Richmond on several occasions rose well above tidal level but did not cascade free over the river's low silt banks in major flood.

Perhaps this May downpour would follow the same pattern. Martin looked forward to home.

Now that the birth of their child was imminent, he had travelled by ship to Grafton, not risking being caught outside a closed Ballina bar.

By coach across to Casino, then a visit to the livery stable to hire a mount. He had changed at Cameron's barn into his oldest clothes. The ride, once familiar, common place, now seemed a long way. He chided himself for becoming soft. It gave him time to ponder his entry to this different, once familiar world. Two months since last home, he set out at four in the afternoon knowing it would be 10 or later, depending on his mount, before he made Killarney. O'Reilly Carriers would pick up his not extensive luggage from the Cameron shop on their next trip to Casino.

Fortunately, Parliament was now in recess and Martin intended staying firmly based at Killarney until after the birth of their baby. He was anxious to be home.

Heavy cloud scudded the night sky, blotting the intermittent stars. He was amazed, several times he felt lost, before picking up a familiar roadside landmark. Really, he chided himself again, it was not long since he had ridden the road, it should not be forgotten. He smiled wryly, *I'm no great bushman,* he thought.

The turn down to Killarney eventually came and it was a welcome sight. His mount did not know it but their trip was nearly over, none too soon. The cloud had thickened and light rain was now constant, falling steadily and making roadside streams trickle with saturated run off.

He avoided the front way into Killarney and entered quietly from the carting entrance. Inside the big stable, the air was warmer from the horses in their stalls. There was an empty box next to Captain. The old grey whinnied softly; Martin rubbed his friendly nose. He found feed for his hired mount, dried him down, gave him a bucket of water and a hessian rug to let him cool down slowly.

Once he was sure that all seemed well with the horse, he headed to the house. It was 10.45; he hoped Bridget was fast asleep. He slipped off his boots at the back step and unlocked the door. So far it seemed he was unannounced, but before he could throw off his outer damp garments, the bedroom door opened and a very bulky Bridget was in his arms.

'Why do you always come home wet?' she asked. 'Sit there.'

She stirred the embers in the firebox, placed in some kindling and a split block of bloodwood, that would soon smoulder and catch.

'Take off those outer damp clothes.'

'I'm not very wet.'

'Seems to me that story started all this.'

The fire caught. Bridget filled a saucepan with milk, came back with food, plate, knife and fork.

'When you eat you can tell me where you've come from.'

She sat beside him, awkward, ungainly, but happy he was home. He made their cocoa and they sat side by side watching the chatter of the flames. Always controlled, fire chatters its own welcoming story. He told her of his trip. There would be much to talk of tomorrow, but now it was bedtime. She lay close beside him on her back, a small mountain of child in her middle that lifted the bed clothes. A foot or arm beat a tattoo on her stomach. She steered Martin's large hand to the disturbance.

'Tell him to stop,' she said.

Eventually they slept.

Weather that week grew steadily worse. Even the normally well-drained deep soils of the plateau oozed water. Down on the river flats, big areas of water were ponded with no escape to the swollen river. Although the heavy rain delayed normal carrying functions, it was agreed that some goods must be brought up the cutting. Martin insisted he was available to work so Dan and Martin took two carts to Ballina, rather than the wagon. The roads on the cutting were a mess, parts of the gravelled inclines had washed down to bare slippery clay.

'We'll only try to bring up essentials,' they agreed before setting out.

Martin, while in Ballina, visited Doc Mason alerting him to Bridget's closing confinement.

'She says she's fine, but I want to know that you are available should we need you.'

'Of course, but as you know it takes a few hours, even in good weather. Tell her to wait until it fines up. You had better see if you can persuade your government to give us money for a hospital.'

Martin did not voice his growing parliamentary frustrations, simply saying,

'I am trying Doctor Mason, but government says we need more population.'

Their trip back up the cutting, even with their small loads was slow and difficult. At one wash away they used their shovels for half an hour, reclaimed enough washed gravel to fill a wheel track, enabling all four horses hooked together to edge a cart across the wash away without tipping. With both carts over on more solid ground, the rest of the trip was just wet, cold and unpleasant. They reached the shed and unloaded the goods ready for John Richards to commence distribution on an urgency basis. Rain still lashed in from the north. They drove together back to the stables at Killarney and spent another hour attending the horses.

'Dan, come over to the house and have something warm.'

'No, old Chief will have me home in no time. Nell will be sewing, waiting up for me.'

Martin found Bridget also waiting his arrival.

'Would your fellow members know you now?' She smiled at his forlorn appearance. 'Take yourself to the bathroom, there is plenty of hot water. That warm towel at the fire will work wonders. Make sure that you rub yourself dry. I've seen that your pyjamas are nice and warm.'

Bridget shuffled around and set out his tea. Later, she patched the many broken blisters on his soft hands. Use of a muddy, grimed shovel handle had worn weeping broken areas on both hands. He thanked her and added a whimsical comment, 'My hands would not be soft if you had allowed me to remain a carrier.'

She smiled at him.

'You are working for the common good down in Sydney. And you have done well today. The roads will probably be flood bound tomorrow. You did well to climb the cutting.'

When eventually in bed, his question was, 'How close is the baby?'

'I don't really know, but perhaps not far away. Norah was over this afternoon, her worthwhile suggestion that if the weather locks us in, Flora Johnson has delivered babies, and she has six of her own. It will be all right, now just go to sleep.'

Birth of Douglas Baillie

The next afternoon, the rain was easing but all the plateau creeks were running very high. It was more than likely that this time the main river had broken free and the lowlands would be flooded.

Bridget looked at him and said quietly, 'Martin I'm afraid it's time to find some help.'

'No urgency but go down to Brewsters, tell Norah I think it's happening. They will get Nell, and Rosie is staying overnight out in the flat, that may be all we can do. The creeks will be too high for Flora to cross today, maybe tomorrow, they go down fast. I don't think this baby is waiting until tomorrow. You do some praying on the way and come back here with me.'

Within half an hour he was back. Norah Brewster had sent Jim for Nell and said she would be over soon. Meanwhile, Rosie had arrived at the house to check. She had Bridget in bed with plenty of towels ready, a big supply of water heating. She was calm.

'She alright. We alright. We wait.'

Her comments did little to ease Martin's worry when he arrived back.

A large dish of warm water with a whiff of disinfectant lifting from its surface, sat on a small table near the bedroom door. Rosie's arms were scrubbed so clean they shone as polished ebony. She alone seemed completely relaxed.

He found Bridget propped up in bed.

'You can sit and talk to me. The contractions are still far apart. We'll wait and see what happens. If no one gets here, we'll manage.' She contorted in pain and remained silent. 'Check how long until the next.'

An hour later, Nell Riordan and Norah Brewster arrived. By that time the contractions were spacing down to about 10 minutes.

'This is terrible rain. There's no chance of Flora Johnson today; the creeks are way too high, maybe tomorrow morning.'

Norah sounded affronted by the weather spoiling her plans.

Bridget smiled at Nell, before she grabbed the sheet and winced as another contraction took over.

'Martin, you and Norah take over the kitchen.' She eyed Nell. 'Looks like you and Rosie have a job. Everything is there that you need. The baby feels like he's coming well down in position.'

Rosie, normally always in the background, took over. She washed her hands again and felt gently inside Bridget, her fingers could just make contact with the head.

'Good,' she smiled at Nell and Bridget. 'Not yet.'

There came a couple more contractions, of real pain. Perspiration dripped from Bridget's forehead. Rosie checked again.

'Close now.'

They lifted her slightly and when the next contraction shook over her, Rosie's strong, supple fingers came around the head that was momentarily held.

'Push now,' she said.

The head came free and a large boy baby greeted the world.

Rose held him up, slapped his back end and an indignant cry came from his mucous-filled mouth. Quickly she cleared throat, nose, ears and plonked him down on Bridget's chest.

Bridget whispered in a spent voice, 'Tell Martin to come in.'

The shy dark lady opened the door and beckoned with a bent

finger. Martin came fearfully through the door; then a smile of relief spread over his usually serious face.

Bridget greeted him.

'There, does he look like you? Have a look at your son and then out you go while they finish the job on me.'

Half an hour later, the chord tied, afterbirth removed, Bridget wearing her best nightdress and a frilly jacket, was a satisfied centre of attention. Norah, Nell and Martin sat around the bed. Rose, her job done, quickly went and busied herself back in the kitchen.

Norah was unusually quiet, then she said, 'What would we have done without Rose?'

Bridget spoke up from her pillows, 'We would have managed.'

Douglas Martin Baillie seemed strong and well. Dark-haired, dark-eyed, his small, strong mouth nuzzled around an enlarged, still unproductive breast, his smell instinct obviously delivering the right messages. Norah and Nell retreated to the kitchen. Martin sat in silence holding Bridget's free hand. She smiled at him, tired, drained. Words were not needed.

A new phase of their life had begun.